WOLF
TICKETS

ALSO BY EDWARD HOWER

The New Life Hotel

Edward Hower

WOLF TICKETS

VIKING

VIKING
Viking Penguin Inc., 40 West 23rd Street,
New York, New York 10010, U.S.A.
Penguin Books Ltd, Harmondsworth,
Middlesex, England
Penguin Books Australia Ltd, Ringwood,
Victoria, Australia
Penguin Books Canada Limited, 2801 John Street,
Markham, Ontario, Canada L3R 1B4
Penguin Books (N.Z.) Ltd, 182–190 Wairau Road,
Auckland 10, New Zealand

First published in 1986 by Viking Penguin Inc.
Published simultaneously in Canada

Grateful acknowledgment is made for permission to
quote an excerpt from *A Bright Spot in the Yard* by
Jerome Washington. Copyright 1981 Jerome Washington.
Published by The Crossing Press.

This is a work of fiction. Any relationship between actual persons, places, organizations, or events and the
ones in this book is coincidental and unintentional.

LIBRARY OF CONGRESS CATALOGING IN PUBLICATION DATA
Hower, Edward.
Wolf tickets.
I. Title.
PS3558.0914W65   1986   813'.54   85-41096
ISBN 0-670-81272-2

Printed in the United States of America by
The Book Press, Brattleboro, Vermont
Set in Linotron DeVinne
Book design by Kathie Parise

for Alison

Those . . . in prison have been convicted.
Everyone else is still on trial.

—Jerome Washington,
A Bright Spot in the Yard

The author acknowledges with gratitude support for the writing of this book from The New York State Council on the Arts, The Corporation of Yaddo, the Ossabaw Foundation of Savannah, Georgia, and the Fine Arts Work Center in Provincetown, Massachusetts.

WOLF
TICKETS

1 🍂

Steven hummed along with an aria soaring out of the car's tape deck as he navigated the old road from the highway. His tires found familiar grooves in the frozen mud and rolled through a tunnel of trees that opened onto the grounds of the state school. A light rain was washing snow from the railings of a wooden bridge that arched over the pond's inlet. Beside the main building, the lawn and frozen pond glowed white beneath the leaden sky as if stage-lit from some invisible source, Steven thought, like an opera set of a convent.

No nuns, though, could have made those swirling circles of footprints that fanned out from the building's back door, tested the limits of the grounds, then careened back toward the bridge. There, beyond a cluster of small pines, two figures dashed across the snow, free as gazelles and almost as graceful. Their bright red sweatshirts flickered behind the white-encrusted boughs; their faint cries leaped through the music like flute motifs. Steven smiled, shifting the engine into neutral to coast slowly by them. Then one of the figures tripped the other and fell on top of her. They started punching each other, their loud curses echoing against the building. These were not gazelles or grace notes, but two teenage girls—one here for auto theft, the other for multiple assaults—who should have been in class right now. Sighing, Steven switched off the music and gave the girls a blast on his horn that shot across the snow and knocked them apart in midscuffle. They jumped to their feet and ran off toward the building. Their whoops of laughter faded as they vanished into the back door.

Steven parked in a space designated FAIRBANKS SCHOOL, SENIOR STAFF by a varnished sign which, like dozens of others that filled several storage closets in the basement, had been made by kids in the wood shop during the previous administration. As he strode across the lot, his cowboy boots leaving deep treads in the snow, the institution rose up before him, a building without illusions: three stories of brick and stone, hard, formidable, fortresslike. Inside, the place was more cheerful. From the buzz of voices spilling down the stairs, Steven could tell that the girls were busy in classes and group therapy sessions. The pockmarked gray walls, always the dreariest feature of any reform school, were being transformed by murals and red flower patterns the girls themselves had painted. The foyer smelled of fresh paint; cans, brushes, and tangled drop cloths lay on the floor under the stairwell. Steven moved a spattered ladder against the wall.

Suddenly he turned around. Someone was watching him.

Nearly lost amid the clutter, a thin girl in a clear plastic raincoat stood beside her suitcase in an office doorway. Puddles had formed on the linoleum around her sneakers, and water was dripping from her snarled mop of hair. On her cheek was a dark bruise. She looked like a girl who needed a hug but would bite you if you tried to give her one.

"Hello," Steven said. "Did you just get here?"

"Yeah."

"What's your name?"

"Katrina Nelson."

"Katrina..." He didn't recall her name from the intake schedule. In fact, he hadn't scheduled any new arrivals for months and wasn't at all sure he should keep this one. She continued to stare up at him from behind the streaked lenses of her round, owlish glasses. He wondered why; then he noticed it, too—they both had the same kind of tight, curly hair, reddish-yellow steel wool that wouldn't lie down even when soaked. He smiled at her.

She took a step backward. "Who are you?" she asked.

"I'm Steven Fox. I'm a counselor here," he said. "What happened to your cheek?"

She turned the bruised side of her face away from him. "It got bashed into a floor by a matron."

"Ow," Steven said. He'd seen a lot worse wounds on kids' faces, but the way she'd said "bashed" made him hear the impact of flesh against cement as if for the first time.

"I don't care if you believe me or not," she said.

"Why shouldn't I?"

"Because it says in my record I was fighting and fell downstairs. At Maviskill, the dungeon I was in before."

"I haven't read your case record."

"Oh." Katrina looked down at her sneakers. "Just as well."

"Pretty bad, huh?" Smile lines appeared beside Steven's eyes again.

She shrugged. "No heavy felonies or nothing. I ain't killed nobody yet."

"I'm glad to hear it." He waited to see if she would say what *was* on her record, but she just stood still, dripping, leaning forward a little as if poised to bolt. A runner, Steven guessed. "Anyway," he said, "the staff here doesn't beat up on kids. The girls don't fight either."

Katrina ran her fingers along a painted-over dent in the wall that had been made, Steven knew, during a riot several years ago. "I never heard of a school without fights."

"Well, you're in one."

"I ain't ready for another place." She hunched her shoulders so that she looked even shorter and skinnier. "I really ain't."

"Do you want to walk around outside for a few minutes?" Steven asked, pointing to the door behind her. He needed more time to think about what to do with her. "See what the grounds look like?"

"Yeah." She turned around quickly.

On the front step, she balanced on the sides of her sneakers to survey the driveway's turnaround loop. The white lawn beyond ended at a tall barricade of trees whose bare branches were silhouetted against the sky like live black wires. Katrina walked along in a zigzag path several feet from Steven, keeping to the plow-scraped patches of frozen dirt.

"Did you come up from the city this morning?" he asked, guessing that her accent was Bronx or Westchester.

"Uh-huh. It was the longest bus ride I ever been on," she said. "I didn't know you could go so far and still be in New York State."

"We're about the end of the line here. You must have started early."

"The sun wasn't even up." She shut her mouth after each sentence, but she seemed to find silences intolerable and filled them fast. "My mother never got up so early in her whole damn life," she said. "But she really hated to see me go. She was crying and everything."

"You can call her tonight and let her know you got here okay," Steven said.

"Yeah, she's probably worried." Katrina turned her face away from him and walked faster. On the curve of the driveway, she began squinting around her, pausing to stand on tiptoe.

"What are you looking for?" Steven asked.

"The fence around this place. I must have missed it when I came in with that staff woman."

"You don't look like you miss much." Steven smiled. "There's no fence."

"How do you keep kids from running away?"

"Some of them actually like it here. Others stay because they think it might help them."

"Sure. And what about the rest of them?"

"I guess they stay because they've got nowhere better to be."

Katrina put her head down and walked on. Steven was pretty sure he knew which group she saw herself in. She stopped again, looking down at something at her feet—a bird's nest.

"They used to have those in the park when I was little," she said.

"You can keep it if you want. It doesn't look like anybody's living in it anymore."

"It'd just get busted inside." She scuffled her sneakers. "I don't hear no birds. I don't hear nothing at all."

Steven listened, too. The drizzle was still coming down but as a fog now, silently blending with the wet snow on the ground; across the parking lot near the bridge, it sealed the gray sky to the earth. "I hardly ever get a chance to notice how quiet it is," he said. "Nice, isn't it?"

"It's creepy." She frowned. "This one place I was at, it was on the river. I used to hear the sea gulls squawking all day. As long as you could hear them, you knew you weren't cut off from everything." She looked around wearily. "It's probably too far north here for birds in the winter, huh?" she asked. "Except penguins."

"Lots of penguins," Steven said. "Whole flocks of them sliding all over the ice on the pond—it makes quite a racket sometimes."

She started to turn in the direction of the pond, then dug her hands deep into her raincoat pockets. "Ha ha," she muttered. "The staff probably shoots them, and that's what we're having for dinner tonight, huh?"

Steven grinned. He'd never heard a kid talk like this before. "No, they're not in season yet." Seeing her lower lip jut out, he said, "I'm only kidding, Katrina. I couldn't shoot a penguin."

"Maybe." She glanced at him, her frown gone, and walked on along the icy outer border of the driveway. Steven picked up the bird's nest and walked beside her. He was aware now of the faint gurgling sound of the pond's inlet out in the fog. The damp, sweet smell of pines reached him from the woods. He breathed deeply, wishing Katrina would slow down; he was in no hurry to get back indoors. It had been a long time since he'd gone for a walk with a kid.

She packed a snowball in her hand, looking from right to left, and back at him, to see where she might throw it. Then, catching sight of a lone willow tree in a clearing between the drive and the woods, Katrina took a cautious step toward it through the snow, then another. The tree's branches, some of them hanging to the ground, were encrusted with ice; in the pale, silvery light, the tree became a filigreed glass umbrella. Katrina reached out to touch the glistening branches. From the driveway, Steven watched her mop of red-yellow hair vanish and reappear through the spangly curtain. She looked fragile and transparent herself, in her cellophane-like raincoat. He stood very still. When she turned her face up, her mouth partly open, he didn't even want to breathe.

Her arm swung at her side. Suddenly a snowball flew into the top branches. It struck one, and the whole tree shivered. In one long tinkling exhalation, bits of ice rained down on Katrina. She lifted both arms, palms up, and closed her eyes. When she looked around again, blinking, the ground was covered with glittering ice fragments; they rested on her shoulders and hair, and one in the palm of her hand. She raised it close to her face, examined it, then licked it with her tongue. A few last twig-shaped pieces of ice fell near her into the snow, then all was silent again.

On the driveway, Steven shifted his position, a small movement but enough to startle her. She glanced toward him, then noticed the stripped bare branches surrounding her. Her face clouded over.

"It would have all melted anyway," she said, her voice scratchy in her throat.

"I know." Steven smiled, and was glad to see her looking relieved. "It was pretty, falling down."

"Yeah, it was," she said, raising her eyes.

They walked back to the building slowly, without talking. Steven took the bird's nest inside with him. Back in the foyer, with its paint smell and the clatter of typewriters from nearby offices, Katrina's expression grew tense again. From inside his office, Steven heard the voice of Leah Gomes, a member of his staff, and opened the door as she hung up the phone.

"Good morning, Steven. You see what I brought us from the bus station." Leah was a tall, pretty woman with a big, gray-flecked Afro and a West Indian lilt to her voice. Walking out into the foyer, she flashed a smile at Katrina, who didn't return it. "I just told her probation officer that I don't know if we can keep her. We are full up already."

"That's all right," Katrina said. "I don't want to be here." She held her lower lip rigid to keep it from trembling; her eyes retreated behind narrowed lashes.

Steven and Leah exchanged glances. With Leah towering over her, elegant in a dark blue sweater and skirt, Katrina looked especially scruffy, Steven thought. "You know, this is a medium-security place," he told her. "We only take girls who want to be here."

"I heard that before." Katrina folded her arms across her chest. "Some probation officer tells you you'll get sent to a worser place if you don't 'volunteer' for the joint he wants to ship you to. So you say, okay, you want to go there."

Steven put the bird's nest down on an aluminum water fountain attached to the wall, and removed his trench coat. "You've been around, haven't you?" he asked.

"Around and around."

"You must be dizzy."

"I'm like one of those balls in a pinball machine," she said. "Somebody's always pushing the flipper buttons."

Steven smiled. "Did you ever push them yourself?"

"Sometimes." She shrugged. "Sometimes it's hard to tell."

"I know it is," Steven said.

"How d'you know?"

"I did some bouncing around myself, once."

"Yeah?" she asked. "When was that?"

"When I was your age. Maybe I'll tell you about it sometime," Steven said.

"Well, we don't have to decide anything about you right now," Leah said to Katrina. "There is no bus out of here until tomorrow."

Katrina frowned. "I got to stay here till then?"

"That's right," Steven said.

He watched her glance around at the half-painted walls, the closed office doors, the steel underside of the staircase, and then at him. She was trying to comprehend his maroon wool suit and his white-with-purple-dragons necktie, loose at the collar, one of the outfits he wore to infuse some color into the grayness of institution life and to keep the grayness from soaking into him. Now she was meeting his gaze directly, something that few people, Steven noted with mixed regret and satisfaction, could do. The steam pipes overhead rattled and went silent. Steven waited.

"I guess I'll check the place out till tomorrow," she said finally, as if she'd really had a choice.

"Good. We'll talk again, then," Steven said. "You'll be safe here for now."

Katrina said nothing.

Before moving into a room, she would have to have a physical examination, Leah told her, pointing the way. Katrina picked up her suitcase and walked toward the rec room. Misjudging the width of the doorway, she smashed the suitcase against the frame but kept going, tugging it along in a way that reminded Steven of his daughter carrying an oversized teddy bear by its foot. Katrina's sneakers made squishy sounds as she moved in an arc across the wide floor. She seemed to be trying to squint through the window curtains, which, dark and impassive like tangible shadows, merely absorbed her curiosity. Steven watched Leah catch up with her and steer her toward the Nurses' Station in the far corner of the room. There, Katrina slowed her pace and stopped short. Mrs. Evans, the nurse, white and solid as a refrigerator, was standing in her doorway.

Steven went into his office and put the bird's nest down carefully on a shelf beside a framed child's drawing. Twigs and flakes of mud were coming loose from the nest already, but he liked the way it looked here. His expression changed when he saw on his desk a thick dog-eared manila folder: Katrina's case record. He pulled out the cover letter.

Katrina, it said, was sixteen. She had been raised in a "decaying suburban neighborhood by a welfare mother and a senile grandfather. Father deceased. Subject reported poor relationships with mother's paramours," one of whom was investigated by police for allegedly molesting her. Finding Katrina "ungovernable," her mother had repeatedly petitioned Family Court to make her a ward of the state. Katrina had arrests for shoplifting, truancy, possession of marijuana, disorderly conduct, and—her only felonies, termed such because they constituted breaking probation—multiple absconsions. Steven's intuition had been right : in the past two years, she'd absconded from home eleven times and from six different institutions a total of twenty-two times. Her probation officer had found her on her last runaway and sent her directly from home to Fairbanks before the police could dump her back into the maximum-security institution she'd just escaped from. Her PO considered that place ''an unsuitable placement for this particular youngster in view of her previous failures to adjust satisfactorily to highly structured settings.'' Like so many kids Steven had known, Katrina ran away because she was locked up, and she was locked up because she ran away. And so it might go for the rest of her life, or until somebody threw away the key.

The kid runs away, Steven thought, so her PO sends her to a place that's easier to run away from. Did this make sense? About as much sense as the rest of her life in the juvenile justice system. But why the hell should he jeopardize the New Program he'd been struggling so hard to start by taking in a risky new girl he didn't have room for?

Then he pictured her standing in the foyer, touching the scar in the wall beside her and knowing what it meant. Suddenly he could remember just how he'd felt at her age on his first day in juvenile jail.

Was this a criterion for admission? Of course not. If he took in every scared, scruffy kid who needed a home, there'd be girls sleeping in the corridors and huddled around the furnace in the basement. He had to keep his program small for the time being if he wanted to be able to expand it later.

So why even think about keeping Katrina? No specific reason. Something about the way she'd stepped inside that willow tree's branches, and tilted her head back to gaze up at them, and shut her eyes to hear the ice clinking down around her. It wasn't an entirely reassuring picture, but it was an original one. Too much so for this place? Perhaps Katrina was too free a spirit to adjust to reformatory life. But if the Fairbanks School couldn't make a few adjustments

to do something for a kid like her, what right did it have to
stay in business?

For five years before coming here, Steven had worked in
schools where his main job had been to protect kids from each
other and from the staff. Counseling had consisted of stopping
fights, disciplining bullies, commiserating with victims, and
responding to continuous crises that were created as much by
the conditions of institution life itself as by the kids reacting
against them. But he'd survived, and now he had the authority—he'd recently been put in charge of half the school—
to create entirely different conditions, ones in which a girl
like Katrina ought to be able to thrive.

He thumbed through the reports in her file written by
psychologists, social workers, other expert labelers of state
kids, and then shut the folder. He preferred to get to know
Katrina on his own.

He didn't have to wait long.

"You're not shoving that fucking stick up me!" Katrina's
voice reached him all the way from the Nurses' Station.

Though he made it a policy never to run toward a crisis,
he left his office at top speed.

Mrs. Evans was gripping the girl by the arm and trying
to tug her back into the mouth of the examination room.
Katrina was losing ground. Her heels skidded on the linoleum.
Her suitcase dragged from her free hand. Suddenly she swung
it high off the floor.

"Let go of her!" Steven yelled at the nurse.

She did, and stumbled backward, squashing her behind
against the intake desk. The suitcase sailed through the air
in Katrina's hand, missing Mrs. Evans's head by about a foot.
Katrina lurched after the suitcase and fell beside it as it
struck the floor. She scrambled up quickly, her fingers still
curled around the handle.

"Are you all right?" Steven asked her.

She glared at the floor.

"Mrs. Evans?"

The nurse was gasping for breath, her face gone splotchy

red. "Don't . . . you shout at me, Mr. Fox!" she screamed.
"You're not my supervisor!"

"If you hadn't let go of her when I yelled, you would've
been clobbered."

"This girl was being totally uncooperative! I should be
getting . . . *support* from staff!"

Katrina walked over to a bulletin board with her suitcase
and pretended to read a NUTRITION FOR EVERYONE poster.
Steven could see that she was trembling all over.

He joined her, noticing for the first time the absurd grinning carrots that danced around the poster's border. "Have
you had anything to eat today?" he asked her.

She shook her head.

"Okay, go through that door"—he pointed—"and wait
there in the dining room. I'll send a staff to get you some
milk and a sandwich."

Seeing Katrina start toward the door, Mrs. Evans heaved
herself forward to block her path. "You think you're slick,
young lady, but you're not!" she said in a voice that would
have reached the neighboring farms if the windows hadn't
been tightly closed. "We used to have a lot more trouble with
new girls than I had with you. And we could handle them,
too, I can tell you!"

"Get out of her way, Mrs. Evans." Steven glared at her.

Her nostrils flared. "We used to get these big black girls
from the city in here. They wouldn't stand still for their
vaginal examinations either. Or their flu shots. One girl, me
and the assistant director, we had to rassle her to the floor.
Broke two needles in that kid's arm before we got it in. Blood
from one end of the floor to the other." Mrs. Evans stepped
aside, patting her ruffled gray hair and leaving the doorway
for Katrina. "After that, we didn't have no more trouble
from *her*!"

Katrina stood where she was, holding onto her suitcase.

"In those days," the nurse concluded, puffing her jowls
out at Steven, "we got support."

Steven knew he had just broken one of the cardinal rules
of social work: Never Back a Kid Against a Staff Member.

He'd stepped over the line. In Mrs. Evans's case, though, the step was necessary and long overdue.

"You can't treat girls the way you used to," he told her.

"What, this incident today? It was nothing—"

"It wasn't 'nothing' to me," he said, quietly at first. He glanced at Katrina, her glasses crooked and her cheeks tear-streaked, then back at the nurse. He hadn't been as enraged at a staff member in years. "It wasn't 'nothing' to this girl," he went on. "And it wasn't 'nothing' to you or you wouldn't be panting like that!"

"I beg your pardon, Mr. Fox—"

"Don't beg, Mrs. Evans. It's too late."

"Now you listen here! I've been doing this job for five years!"

"Yeah, and I've been watching you for six months!" he outshouted her. "You've been pouncing on new kids and scaring the shit out of them! You're not going to do it anymore!"

"You haven't the authority—" Mrs. Evans clutched her throat and gave off a volley of baritone coughs, a reminder to Steven that she was still suffering from a bad bronchial condition. She sat down hard in a chair and wiped her eyes. "I only came in today because we're understaffed," she choked. "This place is going to hell in a hand basket."

"Not if I can help it," Steven said.

"The assistant director's my supervisor, not you. He'll see about this!"

"You bully him around like you do the girls. He can't do anything for you."

Mrs. Evans began coughing again, her chin pressed down against her chest.

"Take a few days off, Mrs. Evans. You're in bad shape." He stepped back from her.

"I can take it."

"You're the only one who can."

She pushed herself out of the chair and clomped away down the corridor into the examination room. "You'll be sorry!'' she screamed, and slammed the door behind her.

"And you—" Steven turned to Katrina, his voice still somewhat fierce. "I don't want to see you swinging a suitcase or anything else at anyone, ever again! You understand?"

Katrina said nothing. She appeared to be smiling.

2

The woman called Leah took Katrina into the big dining room
and made her a thick baloney sandwich in the kitchen. Katrina gobbled it down and drank three glasses of milk. Then
she followed Leah down some back stairs to the basement,
which was an empty expanse of linoleum with faded shuffle-
board squares at one end near a stoolless soda fountain counter.
A poolroom was visible through an open doorway.

Leah unlocked a closet door and loaded Katrina's arms
with sheets, a towel, a pillowcase; eyeing her hair, she dropped
a glass bottle of shampoo onto the top of the pile. Then she
picked up Katrina's suitcase and led her up the back stairs
past the dining room. The second and third floors of the building were divided into two long corridors each, the woman
explained, with staff offices and girls' lounges at the front
of the building. The girls' bedrooms were on the east corridors
of each floor, the school classrooms on the west corridors.

Katrina's new room was the first one off the back stairwell
on the third-floor unit. Photographs of luscious peaches and,
also snipped from magazines, the words PEACHY, PEACH FUZZ,
PEACHES were taped to the door in so many places that the
blond wood was scarcely visible. Walking in, Katrina dumped
her linen on the bed. Then she headed straight for the window
and opened it as wide as she could.

A steel bar connecting the steel window frame to the sill
kept the window from opening more than about eight inches.
Katrina figured that that was too narrow a gap to squeeze

out of. She tested the steel bar. It could be pried loose from the sill with a butter knife, but the fall to the ground was too far. A girl at an institution where she'd been before had broken both legs sliding down a sheet rope from a third-story window. There had to be better ways out of this building. Even if she got outside, though, there wouldn't be anywhere to go. She squinted at the expanse of white fields bordered by a wall of trees, where a cloud of fog hung as if about to drop. The nearest sidewalk or subway station must be thousands of miles away, she figured. She focused on the steel squares of the window. Freezing drizzle clicked against the glass. She heard Leah put the suitcase on the bed and say something in her musical voice about lunch and then walk down the corridor, her footsteps fading into nothing. The trouble with having a pretty voice like that, Katrina thought, was that when the woman took it away with her, the silence sounded nastier.

Katrina looked up at the window's squares again and felt as if she'd been dropped onto the floor of a cage. She'd felt that way before, most recently at the bus station that morning. Her mother was red-eyed from a hangover and twitchy from being without cigarettes. As she sat on a plastic seat in the waiting room, she kept nodding off and then waking up with an expression like an insect had just flown into her face. Her blotchy gray sweatshirt was stuck in the zipper of her windbreaker on her chest; she just left it. She didn't care what she looked like now that her boyfriend was in jail. Katrina had hoped they might get along better without him around.

I ain't got enough money for cigarettes and the train home both, her mother said three or four times, as if it were Katrina's fault that she'd left her cigarettes behind. She yawned and pinched the bridge of her nose and yawned, until Katrina finally spoke.

Listen, Mom, you don't got to fucking wait here with me, you know.

You don't have to curse at me, her mother said, after everything you put me through.

Right then, Katrina knew that her mother was working up to a reason to leave before the bus came. She tuned out the excuses and didn't look up until her mother got to her feet. Her hand, level with Katrina's eyes, wiped slowly against her hip; the fingers were stained yellow, the nails bitten. Katrina tried not to watch.

Well, if you think you really'll get on that bus.

I'll get on it, Katrina muttered.

I hope to God that place changes you. If it don't ... Her mother pinched the bridge of her nose where she always got a sinus headache in the mornings.

You could call me up, Katrina said. My PO's probably got the number.

I hate talking to that man.

Katrina leaned forward as her mother took several steps backward. Hey, Mom, will you call Joey for me and tell him where I'm at? He'll be home tonight.

Her mother glanced across the room at the escalator. Soul music shrieked all over the waiting room as a boy carrying a suitcase-sized radio walked through. Somewhere nearby a hotdog was cooking, an obscene smell at 4:30 in the morning. When icy air blew through an opened door, hundreds of scraps of paper skidded along the floor and then lay down again in unison as if exhausted by the effort.

For God's sakes, behave yourself this time, her mother said.

I'm sorry I been so much trouble. Standing, Katrina held out her pack of cigarettes toward her mother.

Her mother eyed the escalator. You know I can't smoke menthols, she said. You know they give me a headache. She turned and shuffled away through the litter.

Katrina watched her rising on the escalator until she disappeared into the big square hole in the ceiling. I hope your goddamn toes get stuck in the top step, she thought—your legs and the rest of you, too, like in a meat grinder.

Katrina dropped down into a plastic chair and drew her knees up close to her chest and wiped her eyes. She hated this bus station. When she'd been twelve, she'd waited here three hours for her mother, who'd never shown up to meet her. But the boyfriend her mother had then did. Katrina had only seen him once before and couldn't be sure, sitting in the man's

car, if he might not be some creep who hung around bus
stations looking to kidnap little kids. He stared straight ahead
as he drove, not talking, scratching at a rash on his neck. The
house was dark when they got home. He went into the kitchen
and drank red wine, leaning against the counter; the light
from the hallway shone onto the side of his face and his neck.

When's my mother coming home? she asked him from the
next room.

Be home real late, he said, turning his face slowly. It's
just you and me.

And that's what it was, hours later when he woke her up
in her bedroom. He grabbed at her under the covers and
yanked her knees apart, holding his dick ready. But she kicked
and thrashed, and finally he just squirted like he was peeing
on her except it was sticky when she tried to wipe it off her
leg. He staggered around the room, zipping up his pants.

A scratching sound came from the bureau top like something trying to run in place. He was leaning over her hamster's cage, his hand moving inside it. He pulled out his fist
and held it in front of her face. The hamster's head stuck out
over the top of his thumb.

You tell anybody and this's what'll happen to you, he
said, and squeezed.

Blood dripped out of the hamster's open mouth. There
was a tiny snapping sound inside the fist. On his way out of
the room, he dropped the hamster onto the floor of the
cage.

Later, she got up and looked at it lying there among the
pellets and turds, unable to run anymore, its soft fur damp,
caved in. That's what she always felt like when she was dumped
into a new place.

Now she turned away from the window. The walls of her
new room had been freshly painted cream-white, but the low
ceiling was a tired gray. The room look less like a cage than
the inside of a fancy coffin with the lid open to a cloudy
sky.

She paced to the door and back, seven steps. On the wall
over a made-up bed was a movie poster of a woman roller-
derby skater careening at a precarious angle down a track.

The top of one bureau was crowded with greeting cards. Katrina inspected them: lambs and kittens, a black power fist, printed poems and handwritten messages inside, signed "R" or "Ronnie." Katrina read all the messages. Then, hearing footsteps in the corridor, she stepped back quickly. She didn't turn around to face the girl standing in the doorway.

"Hey," the girl said, "they putting you in here?" When Katrina just looked at her, she brushed the hair out of her eyes and shrugged. "I guess they are. I knew there was a new girl, but I didn't know where...." She bounced from one foot to another, her big breasts quivering in her tight halter top. Her figure was like the movie star's in the poster, and her hair was, too—thick and golden and spraying out over her shoulders as if she were about to break into a run. "It's funny to find somebody in my room."

"How come?" Katrina opened her suitcase and pretended to fold a crumpled shirt. "You don't have roommates around here?"

"Un-unh. There's only nine rooms on the hall."

"So?"

"You're the tenth kid." The girl lit a cigarette. "I'm Peaches."

"I'm Katrina."

"Is that what they call you—Katrina?"

"They call me lots of different things in different places. Katy, Trina, Kathy."

Peaches watched her. "So what're you going to be called here?"

"It depends on what I decide," she decided all of a sudden. "I'm sick of other people saying what my name is every place I go." She refolded the shirt and dropped it back into the suitcase. "But I might not stay. I probably'll just be here overnight."

"That's what my PO told me, too. 'Just see how you like it. Call me if there's any problem.' " Peaches shook her head, her hair splashing against her cheeks. "Once I was here, I was *here*!"

"Did you want to leave?"

"Sort of. But I done what I done to get away from home so it seemed stupid to go back, right into it again."

"What'd you do?"

Peaches took a long drag on her cigarette. "Borrowed a car off the street and drove it around." She laughed. "I didn't know the brake pedal from the clutch. The car went up on the sidewalk and into a store. Through the window. A whole bunch of people had to go to the hospital."

Katrina had been looking at Peaches' left arm. It was covered with homemade India-ink tattoos: crosses, stars, and initials, including a big *R;* there were also several scabs and raw places in the skin where she must have tried to sandpaper tattoos off. Until seeing Peaches' arm Katrina would have given anything to have looked like her.

Peaches stood up. "Hey, that's a badass shirt, girl," she said, picking up a red top from the suitcase.

Katrina noticed that she sometimes had a black accent, but then lots of white state kids did. When Peaches picked up her shirt, Katrina tensed, ready to swing—she wasn't about to let herself get ripped off first thing; nobody'd ever leave her stuff alone after that. But Peaches just put the shirt down again.

"So what's this place like?" Katrina asked.

"You know—shitty." Peaches tossed her cigarette into the sink in the corner. "They don't let you go off grounds hardly ever. All the girls are homesick as hell. Staff's always watching you all the time, trying to get you to talk about your 'problems' in group session." Peaches shrugged. "But in some ways, it ain't too bad."

"What ways?"

"I don't know. Some of the staff's okay."

"That one, Mr. Fox. He's the boss?"

"Yeah. Boss of the third floor. He's okay, I guess. Sometimes the girls all want to kill him, sometimes they all want to fuck him."

Katrina frowned. "Does he ever?"

"Nah. He don't letch after us. He got a girlfriend, nobody knows who. We used to think it was Princess—Sonia Porter,

her real name is—but it ain't 'cause she got a real cute husband picks her up after work sometimes. She's an okay staff.''

"I didn't see her yet.''

"So's Mrs. Gomes—Leah. She's black, from some country
in Africa—Trinidad or something.''

"She's the one that's Fox's girlfriend,'' Katrina said.

Peaches cocked her head. "Now why the fuck you think
that?''

Katrina hadn't, in fact, thought it at all until just that
second; she was just trying it out on Peaches. "I can always
tell with people,'' she said, narrowing her eyes, and noticed
that Peaches avoided her glance.

"You're something else.'' Peaches walked to the window,
then sat down on her bed. "Anyway, the rest of the staff
mostly sucks. The girls's okay. Before I got here, I used to
be thinking these places was full of murderers 'n' shit. But
it ain't like that.''

"We had three girls in for murder at Maviskill,'' Katrina
said. "One was my best friend.''

"Yeah? We got one, Heatwave, she's on the second floor.
She killed a girl in a gang fight, but she didn't mean to. Mostly
this place is for, like, medium-bad kids. Robbery, prostitution,
drugs. Some kids ain't done hardly anything—shoplifting,
runaway, chump change like that.'' She gave Katrina a ques-
tioning look.

Katrina glanced away. "You got to do a lot of work around
here?''

"Not that much. Like, you do your chores and work in
the kitchen. Some girls are painting walls. The Fox, he's
always running us around doing activities. That dude wears
our asses *out*.''

"What do you get paid?''

"Two fifty a week, more if you paint. But there's nothing
to spend it on except candy bars 'n' shit.''

Katrina took out her cigarettes. "It was the same deal at
other places I been in.''

"You don't get messed up here if you don't, like, give
people a hard time.'' Peaches walked to the sink and began

brushing her hair in the mirror. "I heard you got a big temper, though."

"Where'd you hear that?"

"I heard you conked the nurse over the head with your suitcase." Peaches turned to her, grinning. "That true?"

Katrina narrowed her eyes. "I almost did, the fucking bitch. I just missed her by an inch—" Hearing something, she turned around suddenly.

Another girl appeared in the doorway. Her dark face was hardly visible inside the hood of her red sweatshirt, which, like Peaches', was soaked as if she'd been rolling in the snow. "Who's a bitch?" she asked, striding in.

"You are, asshole," Peaches said, laughing.

"This the new kid?"

"Yeah. She's—what the hell's your name again?"

Katrina lit her cigarette and flicked the match on the floor. "Kat."

"Funny name. I'm Ronnie." Ronnie lay down on Peaches' bed and tucked her hands under the back of her head. "Where you from?"

"Brooklyn," Katrina said. Brooklyn was the only place she could think of that she wanted to be from. Her boyfriend Joey last lived in Brooklyn.

"At least she's not some damn hillbilly. We got enough of them already." Ronnie craned her neck to grin at Peaches. "You got a cigarette?" she asked Katrina.

Katrina watched Ronnie's arm flop out sideways on the bed, her hand opening as if to receive a whole pack. Katrina tossed one cigarette past the hand onto the pillow beside Ronnie's face.

"Close the door," Ronnie told Peaches. "You want some damn staff smelling the smoke?"

Peaches, swaying her hips, walked extra slowly to the door, shut it, and then returned to the mirror where she resumed brushing her hair.

Ronnie glanced at Katrina. "Did you know Mary DeMoto at the Annex? They called her Spider. Girls from Brooklyn talk about her."

"I heard of her."

"It's supposed to be hard time there. Lot of bull daggers, I hear."

"They don't mess with me," Katrina said. "I don't mess with them."

Ronnie watched her, lighting her cigarette. Then she strode over to the window so that Peaches had to squeeze up against the sink to get out of her way. The way Ronnie wore her sweatshirt hood made her look as if her face would explode if the drawstring across her forehead ever broke. She sat on the window ledge, resting her wet sneakers on the radiator below it. "What are you here for?" she asked Katrina.

"Runaway. Family problems. But they're all straightened out now," she said. "If I don't leave tomorrow, my mother'll see my PO and get me out."

"Everybody says that." She poked Peaches with her toe. "That's all you talked about when you first got here. Now that your mama's really coming to see you, you don't even want to change your shirt."

Peaches rubbed her arm with the tattoos. "I'm going to change it, shit!" she said, hanging her head. Her big almond-shaped eyes were almost hidden by her long lashes. "My moms wouldn't even be coming if my sister hadn't got on her case. She only lives twenty miles from here, and this's the first visit I had." Her lashes fluttered fast as she lifted her face. "My little sister's so *cute*!" she said to Katrina. "Wait'll you see her!"

"My mama'll come up here no matter how far it is, soon as they let her ass out of jail," Ronnie said. Then she turned back to Katrina. "How come you white bitches always be running away from home? I mean, y'all got families, nice houses some of you. Not starving or getting beat up by junkies or none of that shit. I don't be prejudice. I just don't get it."

Katrina shrugged.

"You probably going to try to split from this place, too, huh?"

"I might get shipped tomorrow," Katrina said.

Ronnie leaned forward, the whites of her eyes shining out

from beneath the hood. "Suppose you ain't? You going to take off?"

"If I want to."

Ronnie grinned. "Talking *bad*!"

Katrina stubbed her cigarette out on the bottom of her sneaker, then glanced up. "I ain't going to try and run away with Peaches, though."

Both girls stared at her.

"Just because I'm her roommate, I ain't going to be butch 'n' femme with her or nothing." Katrina stared back. Her suitcase lid fell, clunk. "All the places I been in, I never been in a family."

"Hey, nobody talking about no family here!" Ronnie said.

Katrina tossed her cigarette butt into the sink. "I just wanted you to know how things are."

Peaches laughed. "That's what we came in here to tell *you*. You're too much, man!"

"We ain't trying to sell you no wolf tickets," Ronnie said, her voice suddenly low. "Ain't making you no threats."

"That's good." Katrina glared at her.

"You're going to be the smallest kid on the floor, if you stay." Peaches tried to keep her tone light. "I mean—"

Ronnie cut her off. "It wouldn't be good for you to be running your mouth a lot. Me and Peaches, we keep it peaceful around here."

"Keep it any way you want." Katrina sat back down on the bed beside her suitcase. "Just keep it away from me."

3 ❧

Katrina stood in the dining-room doorway squinting around at the girls. They were dressed up for the visitors, and she felt scruffy wearing the same T-shirt, frayed jeans, and sneakers that she'd arrived in. When she touched her hair it felt like brittle wires that curled back itchily into her scalp. Her jaw ached from grinding her teeth. So did her mind from trying to decide whether to run or stay.

She wasn't sure if she dared try another runaway. She'd had to fight off a lot of drivers in a lot of states. But if she did get back home, maybe she could talk her mother into keeping her. Give me another chance, Mom, she'd whispered to herself on the bus upstate. She'd never actually gotten around to saying this at home. Her two days between institutions were hazy now, hidden behind a smeared gray mental window through which she viewed her past—and her future, too, the rare times she tried to imagine it. She remembered her mother's slurred voice constantly aimed at her, the feel of the catsup bottle flying out of her hand toward her mother's mouth, and the red explosion it made against the wall. But when she tried to picture her mother—maybe welcoming her in the doorway—all she could see was a blurry image of a TV rerun Mom who always wore a frilly apron and matching smile.

She tried to imagine Steven Fox and Sonia, the staff woman who'd brought her downstairs, as a TV Dad and Mom, but as they walked toward her across the room, the idea seemed

stupid. He was old enough but that mustache and crazy necktie somehow disqualified him; she was too beautiful, with her
long honey-blond hair and her flowered dress. Katrina looked
around at the girls in their clean slacks and blouses and makeup,
just standing around talking quietly to each other. Suddenly
she stepped up to Steven. "I already had a sandwich. I ain't
hungry," she said. "Can I go back upstairs?"

"Everybody's been looking forward to this visit all week,"
he said, smiling. "You wouldn't want to miss anything."

"The hell I wouldn't."

She tilted away from him, expecting him to yell. But he
did something confusing: he leaned over to speak to her; his
maroon suit jacket looked soft and woolly close up and smelled
like a just-lit cigarette when you're dying for a smoke. "You've
just come from home, Katrina," he said quietly. He spoke
her name as if he were about to share something confidential
with her, and she almost stepped nearer to hear him better.
"But most of these girls," he went on, "haven't seen anybody
from the outside world in a long time. The ones whose families can't visit them sort of share Peaches' mother and sister
today."

Katrina glared straight ahead. "What's that got to do
with me?"

"Well, if you don't join them, the girls'll think you don't
think the visit's important. It'll make them feel bad."

"Oh," Katrina mumbled. She had to look away from his
face; she couldn't remember any adult ever focusing on her
like that, as if he were sure she'd understand him because she
was just as smart as he was. In fact, though part of her did
understand him, another part of her thought he was completely off the wall. As soon as he'd turned toward Sonia,
too-late questions occurred to her: Why should these girls
care about what I think? Why should I give a shit about what
they think of me?

Sonia was looking at her. "How do you like the decorations?" she asked.

Katrina shrugged. "It supposed to be Christmas around
here?" she asked. Didn't the woman know it was February
outside? Red cloths with reindeer prancing on them covered

the tables; sprigs of plastic holly were taped around the serving window, framing a view of the huge black kitchen stove and a maze of ventilation pipes.

"I guess the waitresses wanted the place to look especially nice today, and this was all they could find," Sonia said. "It's the thought that counts, though, don't you think?"

"It still looks like a jail," Katrina said. The dining room had a fresh coat of paint—robin's egg blue—but Katrina, who wasn't fooled by paint jobs, could see the outlines of chips in the plaster, probably made by flying plates during a food riot. On the far wall, translucent plastic curtains revealed the steel squares in the windows.

Ronnie, dressed in a white waitress's uniform, strode up to Steven Fox. "How're we going to keep Mr. Paleno out of here today?" she asked in a quiet voice. "If he catch an attitude, it ain't going to look right."

Steven glanced at a door across the rec room with a big plastic ASSISTANT DIRECTOR nameplate on it. "Take a lunch tray into his office. Then he won't have any reason to come out here."

Ronnie nodded and hurried back to the kitchen.

"Thank you," Katrina heard Sonia whisper to Steven.

"I'm going to leave you in charge now," he told her. "But I'll be around."

When he had walked away, Sonia signaled the cook through the serving window and told the girls in the rec room that they could come in. She and Katrina stood in the doorway as they rushed past.

Behind the serving window, a kitchen girl was flipping cheese sandwiches from the grill onto heavy plates arranged in rows along the counter. Ronnie moved around the dining room pouring milk into plastic glasses and telling the girls at each table that if they played around with their food today she'd personally kick their asses. Everyone started eating quietly. The orderliness of the place made Katrina nervous.

She sat down at a table with Sonia and Peaches, who turned her head toward the doorway so often that she hardly ever got a spoonful of soup all the way to her mouth. She looked even more like the movie star in her poster than before, with so much pink and beige makeup on that her eyes looked as if they were peeking through almond-shaped holes in a magazine picture. Even though her tattoos were covered up by a long sleeve, she kept rubbing that arm as she waited. Maybe to distract herself from her nervousness, she began talking with Katrina about her little sister, as if she assumed Katrina would care. Katrina tried not to listen, not wanting to be sucked into anything the way she had been by Mr. Fox.

"... I always took Lurleen with me when I worked in the grape arbors after school, just to keep me company," Peaches said. "See, I had to pick grapes or there wouldn't've been no money in the house for food. My mother's so fucking lazy she don't even flush the toilet after herself."

Katrina wrinkled her nose. It was a good thing she wasn't hungry.

"And if I didn't get Lurleen out of the house, and my mother's boyfriend came over—you never knew what that creep'd get up to with us girls."

"My mother's boyfriend was a creep, too." Katrina turned away quickly, ending the conversation, she hoped, by pressing her lips together. She tried not to picture that man coming into her room—a dozen or so more times in two years, until she'd figured out that he probably couldn't kill her any more than he could finish raping her. When she finally got up the nerve to tell the Welfare woman, though, it was in some ways the beginning, not the end, of her troubles. She remembered the smacks she'd gotten in the face—but not her mother doing it—and being locked out on the front stoop all night. She almost got a mental glimpse of her mother slamming the door, but then she remembered the way the cold cement of the step felt under her behind—not too bad, because it reminded her of other places, like cement park benches in new towns, and the roadside curbs she'd sat on waiting to hitch rides. . . .

"How come your moms is so late, Peaches?" someone asked.

Katrina turned around fast. Now what? A Puerto Rican

waitress with flaming red hair was leaning over Peaches, who rolled her eyes and shrugged.

The waitress and another Puerto Rican girl lingered behind Katrina talking in Spanish. Katrina hated it when PRs talked in their secret language like that. They were probably talking about how they could rip her off. She heard the English words "new meat"—meaning her—followed by hushed laughter that made her squeeze her milk glass as if ready to use it for a weapon, which she'd once had to do in another institution. Then the smaller girl, who was called Lucia, said in English, "We wait and see," glancing right at Katrina.

Katrina narrowed her eyes, saying to herself, Don't hold your breath too long waiting. Every fucking new joint she arrived at, she had to prove herself all over again. She was goddamned if she was going to go through it all here—let these bitches think whatever the hell they wanted about her. She glanced around the room until her eyes came to rest on the back of a head of reddish-yellow curly hair—that counselor sitting in the corner in that sharp maroon wool suit. As if he'd overheard what she'd said to herself about the girls, he turned and gave her a wiseass grin. What'd he think, she didn't really mean it? She looked quickly back at Peaches, hoping for more chatter to distract her from feeling as if she were already cracking up in this place.

But then a huge black girl shouted, "Peaches, they're here!" The girls jumped up from their tables and, led by Peaches, made a noisy rush for the doorway. Several stood on chairs to get a better view. Katrina moved away from them to watch.

Peaches walked quickly across the rec room beyond the doorway, her arms outstretched toward her sister. The little girl wriggled out of her mother's grip and ran straight at Peaches. As she rose in the air in Peaches' embrace, she let out a high-pitched squeal that made several of the girls cheer. Even Katrina grinned as Peaches and Lurleen, hand in hand, walked toward the dining-room doorway.

Peaches said almost nothing to her mother, a gaunt woman in canvas shoes, dirty pink socks, and a too-big cotton dress.

She kept trying to catch Peaches' eye with a scowl, as if she blamed her daughter for surrounding her with noisy delinquents. Lurleen, though, was perpetually smiling. She had huge, trusting brown eyes, heavy-lidded; her lower lip hung slightly open. She must have been slightly retarded; despite being so small and giggly, she was in fact almost twelve, her age revealed by the tiny bulges—no tinier than mine, Katrina thought—in her pink T-shirt. A lock of whitish blond hair dangled over her forehead; her pale skin seemed to glow in the winter grayness of the room.

Peaches introduced her mother and sister to Sonia and Katrina at her table, and then to the rest of the girls. Her face was flushed from smiling. Katrina sat down gingerly between Sonia and Lurleen, keeping her distance from both.

Waitresses hurried over with bowls of soup and plates of fresh sandwiches. Voices were hushed. All eyes were on Lurleen, who leaned into the crook of Peaches' arm to chew on a sandwich crust.

"Look at that wavy hair!"

"Like a little doll!"

"She's so beautiful!"

Lurleen suddenly fixed her huge eyes on Katrina. Now the little girl was reaching for the leftover sandwich on her plate. For a moment, Katrina froze, going weak inside. She glanced wildly at Peaches, but Peaches was arguing with her mother and didn't hear. Smiling, Katrina slowly pushed the plate closer to Lurleen.

The girl leaned over, her elbow sliding the Christmas tablecloth with it. Katrina caught a glimpse of her bowl of tomato soup tilting off the table. Then she heard a crash. Pieces of heavy china skidded away; jagged red streaks of soup splashed out along the linoleum.

Sonia stood up fast. "It's all right! Please, get back—"

Too late. Several girls rushed toward the splattered soup with napkins. They crowded around, smearing red arcs across the floor—their eyes weren't on what they were doing but on Lurleen.

The streaks of red on the floor—slimy, spreading—made Katrina shudder so hard she had to lean away, doubling over with her hands pressed to her eyes, her fingers gripping the frames of her glasses. Now she could picture her mother—that morning after she'd broken a window to get back into the house from the front stoop and had flung the catsup bottle. Her mother stood in the kitchen in her old yellow bathrobe holding the door open for the cops and screaming, Get this kid out of here! She remembered her mother yanking her toward the tallest cop. She remembered digging her fingernails into her mother's wrist, dragging them across the back of her hand as her mother tried to pull free of her. She remembered the smeared blood on her mother's skin and on her own fingers. Then, as the cops yanked her hands behind her and clanked on the cuffs, she went numb, silent. . . .

Sitting very still at her table, she watched a mop sliding back and forth at her feet. Soon the linoleum was its usual worn, brown color. The room smelled the way dining rooms always smelled : mop water, steam table, sweat. The noises of silverware and girls' voices surrounded her again.

Was anyone blaming her for the spill? Or blaming Lurleen? Everything was just as before. The floor was clean. Maybe nothing had happened. But from the stricken look on Lurleen's face, Katrina could tell that it had. The girl's mother must have scolded her; now Peaches was arguing with the woman and Lurleen was left alone with her eyes full of tears. Katrina reached for the half sandwich to give her, but it looked so brown and dead on her plate she couldn't stand to touch it.

She leaned forward, then couldn't think of anything to say. "Don't cry," she finally whispered.

Lurleen just stared past her as if she hadn't understood. Katrina wiped her own eyes.

After lunch, the girls went into the empty rec room. A locked piano had been wedged into one corner ; a couch stood in front of a tall brick fireplace. Katrina leaned against a wall midway between the dining room and the couch where the girls were gathered around Lurleen and Peaches. Squatting down in front of the girl, they asked her questions and made funny faces that made her giggle. Katrina, watching, began to smile.

A girl with a huge Afro gave Lurleen a present wrapped in bright Christmas paper. Lurleen tore off the paper and held up a blue rubber ball. It was a superball, the kind that bounces very high and wildly. She threw it down and watched in wonder as it caromed off the floor, off the ceiling, and off a girl's forehead. The girls shrieked and ran after it. Katrina took several steps into the room, then returned to her vantage point by the wall. Following a scuffle near the fireplace, the girls came racing back with the ball.

"Throw it real hard this time!"

"Hey, not at me!"

"Really slam it, Lurleen!"

Lurleen did. It ricocheted like a tiny blue rocket around the room. Cheering, the girls dashed off in all directions.

Katrina saw an office door open a crack. Sonia was looking at it, too.

"Calm down!" she shouted suddenly. "It's time for classes!"

Nobody paid her any attention.

The door opened all the way. A man as tall as Steven Fox and much heavier stepped out into the room. His gray hair bristled and his swarthy face was dark red as if he were suffering from a bad headache. Sonia sucked in her breath.

"All right! That's IT!" the man bellowed, his deep voice rolling out into the room. "AT EASE, EVERYONE!"

The girls froze where they were. Katrina flattened herself against the wall. Lurleen ran to Peaches, kicking the Christmas wrapping accidentally so that it fluttered along the floor. The ball kept bouncing. It caromed off a wall and came dribbling across the linoleum toward Katrina. She grabbed it in both hands and held it behind her back.

"Sonia, I hear a lot around here about how the unit staff is supposed to be responsible for their girls," the man said, his voice quieter and resonant with importance. "But when things get out of hand, it's still me that's got to come and calm things down."

Sonia winced. "Nothing was out of control here, Mr. Paleno."

"No? What do you call 'out of control,' then? When they start breaking down the walls?"

"They were not breaking anything!" Sonia's voice cracked. "The girls were just playing. There're guests."

"I can see that. I haven't gone blind." He gave Peaches' mother a thin smile.

She had been sitting as far back as possible in the corner of the couch. Now she glared out the window across the room. Katrina had seen a look like that before, several times, in Family Court; it said to the judge: I did all I could for this kid—she's all yours now.

"It seems to me," Mr. Paleno continued, "that teaching responsible behavior is still part of our program. At least, I *think* it is." He scratched his head theatrically. "Unless it got thrown out with the rest of the old policies. Did it, Sonia?"

She glanced at the girls who had silently gathered around her. "We're . . . just about to go to classes now, Mr. Paleno. So we'll say good-bye."

"That's fine. But just a moment, please." Mr. Paleno turned slowly to Katrina and smiled down at her. "Now you think I don't know what you've got hidden behind your back, but I do."

"Me?"

"Yes, you." Mr. Paleno's smile vanished. His lips turned gray. "Give it to me. Right now."

Katrina edged along the wall. She started to tremble.

Mr. Paleno held out his hand. "Katrina—you see, I know your name—let's have it."

She squinted up at him. "It ain't your ball!"

Silence. Sonia bit her lip to keep back a smile. The girls jostled each other for good viewing positions.

Katrina glanced around. There was Peaches, who'd talked to her at lunch, and Lurleen huddled against her, her eyes glued to the ball in Katrina's hand. In the dining-room doorway, the tall man with the curly hair was watching her, probably waiting to kick her out if she didn't do what the other man said. Suddenly she didn't want to get kicked out of any more places. Her legs ached; she felt like sitting down in the middle of the floor, sobbing into her lap, letting the ball roll away. But her whole body stiffened against that idea. She took an unsteady step forward, then walked quickly up to Lurleen and held the ball out to her.

Lurleen took it and pressed it against her cheek.

"It's her ball," Katrina said to Mr. Paleno.

Several girls let out their breath. "*A*wright!" someone yelled. Two girls started to cheer but were silenced by a glare from Mr. Paleno.

"Now this," he said, "is pretty stupid."

"It sure is." Sonia stepped beside Katrina, who was staring ferociously up at Mr. Paleno. Several girls began a low muttering.

"Now listen, all of you—" Mr. Paleno was bellowing again, but the girls crowded forward, their voices rising.

"It ain't your ball!"

"Leave that little kid alone!"

Sonia held out her arm to block the girls, then dropped it and stepped out of their way, her eyes bright. The girls pushed past her. Mr. Paleno stepped back into his office, patting the air before him. His voice was drowned out amid the cries from the girls.

"Mean bastard!"

"Honky motherfucker!"

Eventually Sonia and Steven waded into the mob and herded the girls away. Steven and Mr. Paleno went into the office and shut the door.

"Lurleen still got her present!" someone yelled, and a cheer went up. Several girls lifted Katrina's hand and slapped her palm. She got some grins and bumps as Sonia pushed everyone along toward the far doorway.

"You coming with us?" a Puerto Rican girl asked.

Katrina shrugged and walked along with her, but then hung back. Sonia took Peaches' mother into another office to calm her down. Katrina watched the girls shuffle off toward the door, their voices echoing in the big room. She was still flushed from grinning, but the feeling faded quickly as the room emptied.

Seeing the red and green wrapping paper on the floor, she picked it up and began smoothing it out with her fingers. Peaches and Lurleen were still sitting together on the couch. Peaches' gold hair and Lurleen's white face glowed in the dim light. The fireplace behind the couch made a frame around them. They looked like a Christmas card.

Then they, too, got up and left. The room was empty like the inside of a box. Katrina squeezed the wrapping paper into a hard lump in her fist and wandered off toward the dining room. Angry men's voices rumbled behind Mr. Paleno's door. Then the door opened and she heard her name being called. She stopped but didn't turn around.

"Where are you going?"

It was Steven Fox's voice. She let out her breath. He was standing in front of her now, but all she saw of him was his fancy leather boots and the cuffs of his pants.

"You don't got to say nothing to me," she told him, raising her face. "I ain't even unpacked my suitcase." His smile made no sense so she ignored it as best she could. "I ain't sorry for what I did."

"Good," he said, his mustache jumping.

"What?"

"I'm not sorry for what you did either." That confidential tone was back in his voice.

Katrina's eyes rose to the little purple dragons on his necktie; she seemed to be watching a whole flock of them flying past a tie-shaped window. "How come you ain't sorry?" she asked. "You don't like that man?"

"Well...I was just glad to see Lurleen get her ball back."

"Yeah." Katrina squeezed the wrapping paper between her fingers.

"I think you ought to unpack," he said. "You can stay."

"I can?"

"If you want to."

She stared past him and the dragons at the wall, and stopped smiling. "It don't make me no never-mind," she said. "I ain't got noplace else to be."

Then, stuffing the bright wad of paper deep into her pocket, she walked toward the door where the other girls had gone.

4 ❧

Dear Joey
    Here I am in another school an I am real fucken bummed out. Their aint nothing to see out the window excep trees an snow an dark. 4 of the girls on my unit are nigers an 2 PRs an 1 indian an 3 of us whites. My room mate is gorjious youde creme if you saw her but you never will tuff luck ha ha! Her girl friend (lez) is black an she talks big an bad but I aint skaired of her
    They dont lock the doors in the day but I cant run away by my self no more. Joey I dont think I can make it here. I cant stand being shut away. I want to be free so bad all I can think about is being FREE! Please come up here and get me in your car!!! Just look on a map it is a place called Fairbanks an it is north of everything
    I hope I get a letter from you real soon saying your coming

love love love love love love love love
XXX XXXX XXXX XXXX XXX

KAT

ps you are all I got left out there Joey PLEASE dont let me down

ps if you go by the park where my grandfather always goes tell him Hi for me I miss him a hole lot

5

Steven counted every day that Katrina stayed as a victory for the New Program. After three weeks, he stopped searching for her name in the log first thing in the morning to find out if she had run away. She was getting along well with the other girls and saying exactly what she thought in group therapy sessions. Group sessions, he told them frequently, were the most important part of the New Program—kids could often help kids with their problems better than adults could. Since every girl had been through similar experiences with families, schools, the streets, the police, no one needed to be ashamed to bring her problems out in the open. Group sessions, Steven knew, also helped to keep the peace: the girls themselves and not just the staff were beginning to take responsibility for discipline. Anyone. who screwed up had to face a circle of peers who had a stake in seeing that she didn't do it again, since they faced a collective loss of privilege—a shopping trip, a late-night movie on TV—if she didn't straighten up. Arguments got settled in group sessions, and didn't turn into vendettas and gang wars like the ones that had gone on routinely at the institutions most of the girls had been in before. Steven sensed that Katrina had never lived in a place where she'd felt so safe.

She still didn't feel comfortable enough, though, to talk about the problems she'd had at home that had caused her to get in trouble. In his first individual conference with her, she'd answered his questions with grunts and monosyllables;

after a while, he felt like an interrogator, and wished he could find some other way of talking to her.

"Everything about me's in there," she said, jabbing her finger at the dog-eared file on Steven's desk.

"Social workers' reports all start to sound the same after a while." He stood up to take off his suit jacket. His office had gotten very stuffy; the gray ceiling seemed lower than usual. He loosened his tie and moved his chair to the side of his desk so that he was no longer facing Katrina across his blotter and in-out trays. "I'd rather hear your story from you," he said.

Katrina sat far back in her chair. "I don't feel like talking," she said. "I mean, it probably says in those reports that I was running away from my problems all the time. That ain't true. It was those damn institutions and the people in them I was running away from. They were my biggest problems." She picked at the frayed cuff of her jeans and scrutinized him from behind her raised knee. "You probably think that's a lot of shit, don't you?"

"No."

"You don't?"

Steven shook his head. "Sometimes you just have to get away from awful situations. You can't find out who you are until you're out on your own."

"Yeah...." Katrina's eyes looked very large in the round frames of her glasses. "Is that why you used to run away?"

"What makes you think that?"

"The day I got here, I asked you how come you knew so much about, you know, bouncing around. And you said you'd tell me about it sometime."

"Right, I did." Steven tugged a corner of his mustache, gazing past her. "Well, I think I ran away mostly to get in so much trouble that my father'd have to pay attention to me."

She rested her chin against her knee. "Did it work?"

"No. He was a lot better at running away than I was."

"My father, too."

"He left?"

"Mm-hmm." Katrina lit a cigarette and blew a stream of

smoke into the air between her face and Steven. "Who's that?", she asked, pointing to a picture on his desk.

Steven moved the frame slightly so that the overhead fluorescent light didn't reflect off its glass. "That's my daughter," he said.

"How old is she?"

"She's nine now."

"What's her name?"

"Sarah." It felt strange to say her name aloud; the only person he ever spoke about her with was Leah, and then he usually said "my daughter."

Katrina was leaning over to look more closely at the photo. "She's lucky she don't have to wear glasses."

"Some girls look very pretty in glasses."

Katrina shrugged. "Does your wife work for the state, too?"

"I haven't got a wife."

"Your daughter's illegitimate?"

"No." Steven smiled. "I was married before. My ex-wife's in Japan now, with her new husband and Sarah."

"Yeah? That's a long ways off."

"True." In time as well as space, Steven thought: the ringlets of curls beside the cheeks of the six-year-old girl in the photo had probably been cut back by her mother, who preferred short hair; the T-shirt with the cartoon bear had no doubt been replaced by a blouse or a school uniform.

"You miss her a lot?"

"Yes."

"I see." Katrina touched her fingertips together in her lap the way Steven often did when he led group sessions. He could see that she was enjoying switching roles with him. "You ever write to her?" she asked.

"Sure."

"Does she write you back?"

"Well, she sends me pictures she makes." Steven pointed to a green crayon drawing on the wall beside the shelf with the bird's nest on it. The drawing was the only patch of color in the office; the other walls were taken up with crowded bulletin boards and a huge grease-pencil events calendar.

Katrina stood up and walked over to inspect the picture, her face close to the paper. "It's pretty."

Steven smiled. "It's a Japanese temple."

"Are they really green?"

"I doubt it. Green was probably just Sarah's favorite crayon that day."

Katrina turned to face him. "Did you ever go to foreign places like that?"

"I was in the Caribbean. The Islands, like the one Leah Gomes comes from."

"What were you doing there?"

"At first I was in the Peace Corps. That's an organization of people who go to teach school and things like that in other countries. Then I just lived in the Islands for about five more years."

"Doing what?"

"I taught school, managed some hotels, traveled around."

Katrina rose slowly on the balls of her feet. "Did you ever go on any boats?" she asked, narrowing her eyes.

"Lots of them. Why?"

"No reason." She faced the window again.

"Do you like boats?" he asked finally, looking at the place on the back of her neck where her yellow curls splashed into the collar of her red blouse.

"Me? Nah. My father did, though. He took off from me and my mother when I was four—I don't even know what he looks like except from a photo I had. He joined the merchant marine. So I guess he liked boats, too."

Steven rocked forward in his chair. The front legs hit the floor hard and sent a thud up through him. "I was in the Islands before I even *had* a daughter," he said. "Not after."

"Okay, okay." Katrina stepped back closer to the wall. "Shit, you're always asking *me* stuff!"

Steven rubbed the side of his neck; his hand came back sweaty. Had he yelled at her? "No problem," he said.

"I got to get a drink of water." She was gone out the door before he could speak.

Steven slammed the desktop with his fist. What the hell was the matter with him? For the past hour, he'd been encouraging her to talk about herself, but when she finally did, he scared her away. He listened to her footsteps fading quickly in the corridor outside. She did seem to be headed for the water fountain in the foyer. Maybe she'd be back. He waited.

The office was bleak and empty; the wall calendar's grid looked like the steel squares in a smudged, gray window. Sighing, he stood up and paced over to the drawing of the Japanese temple, resting his elbow against the wall to study it. The drawing seemed brighter, clearer now that Katrina had noticed it.

For a moment, he felt he was looking at a map of a little girl's mind, of a world of bright color, bold lines, cheerful blank skies, where all distances were easily crossed with a few strokes of a green crayon. Then the map faded quickly, turning back into a small paper rectangle surrounded by larger black-and-white rectangles. As Katrina had said, Japan was a long ways away.

Remembering his last telephone call with his daughter, he tried again to imagine what her life was like. The phone call had been awkward. He'd asked her about the embassy school she went to.

What's your favorite class?
I don't know.
Do you still like science?
Krrrrkkkkk ... krrrrrkkk. ...
What?
Science ... in class. ...
I can't hear you, honey.
... a guinea pig in class.
That's nice. That's wonderful. Did it have a name?
I don't know. ...
Do you remember the rabbit we had?
Sort of. Was it at Mommy's?
No, it was at my place. You played with it when you came over Sundays.
I did? Was it white?
Well, white and brown.
Oh. Krrrkkkkk.

Its name was Fuzz.
Krrrkkkk . . . it die, Daddy?
Die? No, it didn't. Certainly not.
Krrrrrrrkkkkkkkk.
I can't hear you . . . Sarah?
Daddy, are you there?
I'm here, honey. I'm right here.
Krrrrrkkkkkk. . . .

It was hard to make conversation with a nine-year-old girl whose voice faded in and out on a staticky radio wave beamed at him from half the globe away, but he still loved talking to her. Also, it was good for her to know she still had a father, even if he was only a disembodied voice. Did she remember what he looked like? Maybe. Perhaps, like Katrina, she could only picture him by looking at an old photograph of him, if she had one.

The only way Steven could visualize his own father was by recalling a photo taken years after the old man had left the family. Steven could remember the hot leather seats and the smell of cigars in the old De Soto they'd driven on selling trips through Pennsylvania and upstate New York, but when he tried to remember what the man behind the steering wheel—who couldn't have been more than forty—looked like, he could picture only a white-haired old codger with a stubbly beard and a threadbare, stained jacket that he would never have worn to try to sell things in.

Riding in the car, Steven had listened to sales-pitch rehearsals for mile after mile. He'd waited long afternoons in motel rooms while his father went out to close sales. Once, to celebrate a big one, they'd gone out to a truck stop that looked like a magical silver railroad car and was full of the laughter of men in baseball caps and the smell of sizzling onions. They'd ordered roast beef dinners and had enormous butterscotch sundaes for dessert. But when they got home together, home to the trailer they were living in at the time, Steven's mother, sick and anxious, was waiting for them in her bathrobe at the kitchen table. Looking up from her overflowing ashtray, she asked, ''Well, boys, how'd it go?'' All the celebration drained out of the old man. He slouched into the bedroom; Steven's mother followed. From behind the closed door, his father's voice sounded like a whimper. At dinner, Steven could tell by the thin-lipped look on his mother's face that there hadn't been any big sale at all, and that the money spent on the celebration should have been used to pay bills. "We're in the doghouse now," his father whispered to him out of the side of his mouth, grinning. Steven grinned back, then turned away quickly, not only to avoid his mother's glare but to avoid feeling so close to this rumpled, lying man who messed everything up and made him share the blame.

Yet when his father took off on his next trip without him, Steven ached to go out on the road again, longed for the smell of cigars and the dusty little towns speeding past the car window. When his father didn't return, Steven, at sixteen, took off looking for him again and again. He hopped freights, walked, hitchhiked, forgetting after a while that he was looking for anyone and just moving to keep moving. The police always brought him back, sometimes in handcuffs, until he stole a car and wrecked it and spent three months in a juvenile jail in Kansas City, which cured him—until he'd finished college, at least—of running away.

Steven walked back to his desk. The bird's nest on the shelf was coming apart; he pushed a twig back into it but just dislodged other twigs and some flakes of dried mud. The office felt airless, sealed off from the muffled voices and footsteps in the corridor outside. He listened again for Katrina. Nothing. But when he turned to sit down behind the desk, she was standing in the doorway.

"Hi," he said, smiling.

Katrina swayed in place on the sides of her sneakers, her hands pushed down into the pockets of her jeans. "Hi," she said.

"Listen, I didn't mean to snap at you before." Steven spoke softly. "I do miss my daughter, and I guess it's hard for me to talk about her. Like it must be hard for you to talk about some things."

She looked at him over the top of her glasses. "No problem."

"Good," he said. "You know, you're the first new girl

WOLF TICKETS ▲ 44

who's ever said anything about that picture.'' He glanced at
the photo on his desk.

"I had a counselor once who said I was very observant.
Then she told me, 'Curiosity killed the cat.' ''

"You don't believe that, do you?''

"The only dead cats I ever seen got run over by cars,
'cause they were too stupid to get out of the way.''

Steven rested his chin in his hands. "You're original,
Katrina. And smart. Did you know that?''

"The teachers around here don't think so. They keep giving me Fs.''

"You must be a different kind of smart.''

Katrina pretended to scratch her cheek, hiding a smile
behind her hand. "Nobody ever said I was smart before.''
She headed around the side of the desk and picked up the
pack of cigarettes she'd left on the chair where she'd been
sitting. "That counselor told me the reason I ran away was
because my father did,'' she said.

"Do you think that's why?''

"It's not because of the last time he took off,'' she said.
"But maybe because of the times he ran away with me.''

Steven leaned back in his chair, giving her space. "He
ran away with you?''

"Sort of. We used to go on trips. I don't remember most
of them. He'd get drunk and say he was going to leave my
mother and take me. We never got very far. One time we
went out to Long Island, where they got farms. I never saw
a farm before. All those fields of potatoes, just wide open with
no buildings or streets or nothing. It was quiet there, like
outside here. But I didn't mind it.''

Steven watched her pick up a piece of volcanic rock from
Guadeloupe that he used as a paperweight on his desk. "Because you were with your father?''

She examined the rock. "Another time, we went on the
Staten Island ferry and just rode back and forth. It was like
a game—he kept saying, 'Do you think we ought to go to
Staten Island?' And we'd talk about it and decide no, the
boat was more fun, so we stayed on it. Then when we were
headed back, he'd say, 'Do you want to go to New York?'

And I'd say, 'Nah, let's not.' So we'd stay on the boat again.
I didn't ever want to get off it.'' She ran her fingers over the
rough, black surface of the rock, glanced at Steven, and then
took it to the window. ''We rode upstairs where the wind and
the sea gulls were, and we kept going by the Statue of Liberty.
It was all covered with people, the island at the bottom was,
like bugs crawling around a body or something. They had
their own fancy boat. When they finished crawling up inside
the statue, they had to go home again, but we didn't. Then
it got dark and you could see the little lights from all the
buildings. The water was black and the lights looked like they
was floating in it—that's what my father said. I kept asking
him, could we stay on the boat all night?'' She leaned back
against the windowsill.

Steven sat very still, watching her fingers moving slowly
on the rock. She gazed down at it in her hand as if it were a
reverse crystal ball. He remembered climbing the iron staircase inside the belly of the Statue of Liberty with his daughter
and his wife. At the top, he held Sarah up to look through
one of the tiny windows in the forehead, but he had to put
her down again after a few seconds because the crowd of
people pressed in on them. ''I couldn't *see*!'' his daughter
cried, but it was too late; his wife, getting claustrophobic,
was heading down the stairs. Why hadn't he taken Sarah on
the ferry instead, just the two of them? Too late.

''I explored that whole boat with him,'' Katrina said. ''It
began to feel like home after a while.''

Steven waited to speak until she glanced up. ''Sounds
nice.''

She shrugged. ''Like I said, I don't hardly remember him.
I didn't even know I remembered that much. I never told
nobody. . . .'' She walked to the desk and put the paperweight
down beside the blotter. ''My other counselor told me I didn't
remember things because I didn't want to. Because it was
painful. But it ain't painful.''

''No,'' Steven said.

''Until afterward, when you're stuck thinking about something. What are you supposed to do with it? That's the trouble
with remembering stuff—you can't forget it again.'' She lit

a cigarette, taking a deep drag. "I know what you're going to ask me now."

"You do?"

"Yeah—how come my father went back and forth on that boat for so long. Was he crazy?" She dropped her match into his ashtray. "No, he wasn't."

"I wouldn't have said so either. I think it'd be fun."

"I think maybe he couldn't make up his mind if he wanted to run away for good, you know?"

"Could be." All I have to do, Steven thought, is sit here and make uh-huh sounds, and she'll do her own counseling.

Katrina nodded slowly. "Just like me, you're going to say, right?"

"Okay, just like you. Why?"

"I don't know. I used to take off from those dungeons and hitch downstate to check things out at my house, find out if my mother had a boyfriend hanging around. I figured if she didn't, maybe things'd be okay with us. But it didn't seem to make much difference." She looked at the end of her cigarette when the ash fell off. "So I'd spend some time with my grandfather until she'd call the cops on me, and I'd fucking take off again."

It occurred to Steven that he hadn't heard her swear in almost five minutes. She looked weary. "Some life," he said.

"Yeah." She sighed. Then she leaned forward to squint at the watch on his wrist. Steven looked down, too. "Hey, I better go," she said.

"I forgot about supper," Steven said.

"I can smell it from here. Dead-cow loaf." Katrina held her stomach and made a face, one side of her mouth sinking.

"I know," Steven said. "I eat here, too."

"How come? You can go home anytime you want."

"I don't want to." He thought of his small, empty apartment. He never ate there. The only thing in the refrigerator was beer.

"You could go to a restaurant," Katrina said.

When he didn't have supper at school or at Leah's house, he was in the habit of stopping at the diner on the highway outside of town. He'd planned to go there tonight, but sud-

denly he couldn't face it : it seemed like a place for truckers
and salesmen with nowhere better to be. "I'd rather eat here,"
he said. "I like the company."
   She squinted at him. "Weird," she said, and moved toward the door. "Catch you later."
   "Catch you later." He gave her a wave, watching her
leave.
   Her footsteps blended into the noise of the girls stamped-
ing down the stairwell into the foyer. Staring at the open
doorway, Steven turned the volcanic rock, still warm, over
and over in his hand. Then, when the office started to close
in on him again, he headed for the dining room.

6 🌿

After supper, Steven opened several big boxes of photographic supplies that had arrived that week and took them into the basement, where he had been making over a storage closet into a darkroom. The equipment's manufacturer had donated them all free, as had companies that had given, among other free equipment at the school, two dozen tape recorders, seven new electric typewriters, hundreds of new books for the library, and thousands of dollars worth of videotape equipment whose exact purpose Steven had yet to determine. He'd traveled many miles in his car to make Fairbanks the best-equipped reform school in the state system. He'd written letters, visited home offices, written newspaper articles lauding Public Spirited Private Enterprises for Lending a Hand to Disadvantaged Youth. During his first years after his return from the Islands, Steven had worked in public relations and had developed a pitch that, even now, executives seemed unable to resist. If he'd been in business for himself, he'd have been rich by now. But he would never be in business again. He'd have to spend his time with the sorts of people he used to work with, whom he now fleeced for the sake of the girls. No amount of money could match the kick he got out of doing that.

He assembled the enlarger. He scrubbed a counter and pounded in some two-by-fours to reinforce it. Humming along, he set up the safelight, mixed the chemicals, and arranged the trays along the counter. When he was finished, the place was a darkroom. All it needed was some kids.

As he opened the door to the third-floor lounge, he walked into a hurricane of music : the blaring television, radios from the corridor rooms blasting a mix of soul and rock—an environment of perpetual sound that protected the girls from the threat of silence and paralyzing loneliness. The pale blue lounge walls, the thick curtains and carpet—all new in the last six months—made this room the coziest on the unit. The air was thick with smoke and the scent of shampoo.

Ronnie was sitting in the armchair with her red sweatshirt hood drawn up to cover her chin and forehead. Peaches, her hair flowing onto Ronnie's shoulder, sat on the armrest. A Puerto Rican girl named Inez sat on the floor in bathrobe and curlers, knitting a sweater for her daughter at home. Beside her, Yvonne, a beautiful tan-skinned girl with long silky hair and startling green eyes, was staring up at Steven.

She moved her shoulder in such a way that her quilted bathrobe opened slightly in front. He didn't register noticing it. Yvonne leaned toward him, and several girls turned their eyes away. They admired her looks but wished she wouldn't flaunt them ; sometimes they made fun of her for never being without thick dramatic makeup on her face and for bragging about her boyfriend, reputedly a pimp who drove a cream-colored Cadillac Eldorado.

"Hey, mister, you got saves?" Yvonne asked him, glancing from his face to the cigarette he was holding at his hip.

"In a minute." He took a drag on the cigarette. Ever since he'd given away saves—the last part of a cigarette— to Katrina last week, the other girls had been pouncing on him for them.

"Damn, man!" Yvonne pouted.

He handed her his cigarette without looking down. She put it to her lips in an exaggeratedly sensual way that made several spectators moan nervously. Yvonne collapsed forward, giggling. The girls laughed.

"Watch your TV show," Steven said, cuffing Yvonne on the shoulder but smiling.

Steven was aware of the girls' occasional seductiveness and could even enjoy it at a distance, but his reaction to it was always detached; at thirty-five, he had no wish to participate in adolescent sexuality, with its giggling and sulking and repressed hysteria. Besides, almost every kid in the school had been sexually wounded in the past; if he were to get involved with any of them, it would cause enormous emotional damage. It would also have felt to him like incest.

Yvonne smoked luxuriantly; the girls glanced from her to him and squirmed noisily. For a moment, there was a slightly hostile edge to their not-quite-stifled laughter: a chorus of *vaginae dentatae*. Soon, though, the television program became more interesting than the stony expression on Steven's face, and his presence was forgotten.

When a commercial came on, he walked to the front of the room and stood in front of the screen. "Remember those pictures I took of you last week?" he said. "I've got the negatives, and the new darkroom I told you about's all ready to go. You can make pictures of your beautiful selves, suitable for framing."

"Shit, I already been framed," Ronnie said, slouching in her chair. "That's how come I got sent here."

Peaches and Inez laughed; so did the girls who'd come out of their rooms to stand in the lounge doorway. Ronnie turned back to watch the gangster movie on the TV screen; several girls returned to their rooms. Ronnie's message was clear: don't cooperate with staff: stay away from the darkroom.

Steven walked along the corridor poking his head into open doorways, asking if anyone was interested in developing prints. Some girls had clothes to wash, others were too tired, others who had snatched up schoolbooks pleaded too much homework. A few said they might come down later; they looked interested, but Steven could tell that for now none of them quite dared to challenge Ronnie's authority. Ever since Katrina had arrived, Ronnie's and Peaches' efforts to control the girls had gotten heavy-handed. Through glares and intimidating comments, they'd prevented controversial topics from being brought up in group sessions. And they'd been able to discourage girls from joining in several activities initiated by the staff. But not, Steven was determined, in this one.

He rapped loudly on the last door on the left side of the corridor. Most doors were covered with handmade paper nameplates and magazine pictures of rock stars, puppies, seascape sunrises, and grassy open spaces. This door, partially open, was brown empty wood. Inside, though, the walls were covered with sixties psychedelic posters, wrinkled and torn. Sitting on the window ledge, her arms wrapped around her knees, sat a girl named Pam—small, chubby, bespectacled. She seemed not to hear Steven, but when she saw him, she burst into tears. Pam was hard of hearing, he remembered—the result of childhood beatings.

He put his arm around her shoulder. Her nose and glasses dug into his chest. "Okay, okay," he said finally, feeling her trembling subside a little. "I must have startled you."

"It's not just that...." Pam groped for a box of tissues. Steven, sitting beside her, took some too; his shirt was damp with mucus and tears. "I was reading my letters...." Pam gasped. "I was thinking about...my friends. We used to be...like a family...you know?"

"Take it easy. You're going to hyperventilate."

She sucked in her breath and let it out slowly. "Now we're all...split up. Like, Tommy took off for California, and Lew got busted. Mary Beth's pregnant. And Zed got killed on his motorcycle...."

"You told me. That's very sad," Steven said. On his second day at work here, Pam had read all her letters and then slit her wrists with a piece of glass. "But we agreed that it wasn't a good idea for you to wallow around in your loneliness, didn't we?"

Pam nodded, and pushed a wad of tissue against her swollen eyes. "But there's nothing else to do around this place."

"Sure there is. You can learn to develop photos in the darkroom. I took your picture last week."

"You took *my* picture?"

"Yes, I did."

Pam sighed. "I don't know. Do I have to come?"

Steven nodded.

"What if I don't?"

"Six years building restriction."

"I'm already on building restriction. For shoplifting from Rite Aid."

"Get off your ass, Pam."

She heaved a sigh, which caused her glasses to slide down her nose. Slowly she climbed off the window ledge. "I'm not going to develop any picture of me."

"You can develop any pictures you like," he said, and opened the door for her.

Now he had one girl, but one wasn't enough, especially since Pam was at the bottom of the pecking order and would not inspire others to follow her.

He crossed the corridor to a door that was still partially covered by cutout PEACHES nameplates. One side of it was now taken up by the letters K A T and a picture of two cats, one of them arching its back, the other rubbing against a child's leg. Rock music thundered out of the room from a radio, its bass notes causing the door to vibrate, Steven noticed, when he touched it. He knocked loudly, but the blast of rock didn't diminish. He and Pam walked in, and Pam turned down the volume.

Katrina was lying on her bed with her face buried in the pillow. The sight of her curls against the white pillowcase gave Steven a start. On the last day he'd seen his daughter, her face had been pushed into a pillow like that, her hair splashed like a child's drawing of ocean waves around her head. He continued across Katrina's room, beckoning Pam to follow.

"Leave me alone," Katrina said in a muffled voice.

"We ought to go," Pam said to Steven. "She's upset because her boyfriend hasn't written her."

"Damn you, Pam!" Katrina squirmed closer to the wall. "Mind your own business!"

"See?" Pam looked up at him.

He was still focused on Katrina. Over her head a single postcard was taped to the wall: a scene of Florida palm trees on a smooth white beach. "Yeah, okay, Pam," he said. "Avoid hassle at all costs. Just leave her stewing, right?"

"She's not crying, Mr. Fox."

"You really don't give a damn about people, do you?"

"Me? I care about people! I care about all the girls!"

"Well, you say that. But you let them get away with anything they want. You let them do things you know are bad for them, like pushing you around."

Pam gazed at the floor. "I know," she said finally.

"So are you going to do that again, with Katrina?"

"What can I do?" She waited but got no reply. "Talk to her?" Again hearing no answer, Pam pulled a wooden chair up beside Katrina's bed. "Hey, Katrina, I'm sorry you're upset, really."

"Mff."

"I get lonely, too, but it's no good wallowing around in your loneliness. I know how you feel—"

"Fuck off!"

Pam winced. "You could come develop pictures in the darkroom—"

"I want to listen to music!"

Pam got up and walked to the radiator, where she sat down. She glanced at Steven, then at Katrina. "You remember how you talked about the way you feel when the music's on—as if you were with your friends?" Pam asked. Katrina had said this in a recent group session. "But you're not really with them, Katrina. It's like Mr. Fox said about me—you're trying to disappear into the music, like you're trying to die."

Katrina rolled over and glared at her. "So what? I like music a lot better than this place. What's wrong with dying in it?"

Steven sat down in the chair Pam had vacated. "Katrina . . ." He folded his hands in his lap. "Do you think you'll get into Rock 'n' Roll Heaven?"

Katrina squinted at him. *"What?"*

He leaned forward. "Hey, this is serious. You might not get in, you know."

"Cut it out—" Katrina found her glasses and put them on to see him better. Her eyebrows still had a tragic tilt to them, but the corners of her mouth were twitching upward.

"We had a girl here once who OD'd on the Grateful Dead," he said. "But when she appeared before the pearly gates— with all those terrific klieg lights and strobes and everything—" He snapped his fingers and glanced at the ceiling, causing Katrina to turn her face away. "I mean, they were having a *party* in there that lit up the whole *sky*, and this girl could hear it going on right on the other side of the wall. They had billion-megaton amps and gold guitars and diamond-studded keyboards, and you could smell the clouds of dope smoke for, like, miles away. . . ." He sighed. "But they wouldn't let her in. You know what happened to her?"

Katrina covered her mouth and shook her head.

"She had to spend eternity in the studio of an easy-listening music station. In New Jersey." He prodded her in the shoulder. "Nothing but violins and clarinets, forever and ever."

Katrina stifled a giggle.

"Doesn't that make you want to *puke*?" Steven said.

Katrina glanced helplessly in Pam's direction.

"Listen, you know *why* she couldn't get into Rock 'n' Roll Heaven?"

"You're full of shit," Katrina said. "Why?"

He gripped her arm. "Because they asked her how many concerts she'd been to in the last year, and she said none. And they asked her how many albums she'd bought, and she said none. And how many dances and discos and clubs and everything. But she hadn't done any of that good stuff at all. So they sent her away. She wasn't cool, Katrina." He gazed at her and shook his head. "And it's because she was out of it for so long. She'd been hanging around places like Fairbanks, feeling sorry for herself and not doing anything that would help her get her act together, so she could get out of here and make the scene."

Katrina groaned over his archaic "make the scene." "Okay, okay," she said.

"Okay, what?"

"What do you want me to do?"

"You could take Pam's suggestion."

Katrina wrinkled her nose. "I already *know* how to develop pictures. I learned it at Connerton."

"You could teach me," Pam said.

"Do I have to go?" Katrina asked Steven.

"Not absolutely."

"He took a picture of you last week, remember?" Pam told her.

"Who cares?" Katrina drew a line slowly along her sheet with her fingernail. "All right, but listen, Pam—you owe me one."

Pam got down off the radiator. "He said you didn't have to—"

"Come *on*!" Standing, Katrina pushed her toward the door. "I know how to put different negatives of two people onto one print. You can make some really *disgusting* pictures. . . ."

In the darkroom, Katrina was meticulous in her explanations to Pam, who watched everything she did, moving her lips in concentration. The first print Pam did was one of Katrina. Pam dropped it twice while transferring it to the stop bath and fixer. Finally she fished it out with the tongs and held it up. Both girls made tiny squealing noises. Everything had worked the way it was supposed to! Katrina turned on the overhead light and the girls studied the wet picture in awed silence.

Katrina's first picture was one of herself, her head cocked to one side, grinning at the camera. Then she and Pam did one of Steven that Leah had taken, in which he was chewing on his mustache. They did another print, blowing up the teeth and mustache, and went into paroxysms of laughter. Soon they were rushing back and forth between the darkroom and the bathroom where they left the prints to wash under the tap. Steven sat on a counter in the dim yellow glow of a safelight, getting down to compliment the girls on their work now and then. Once, he showed them how to make a white moon by laying a penny on the developing paper.

"Hey, would stars work?" Katrina asked. "I got a whole box of them."

She ran upstairs to get them, and when she returned she had three other girls with her: Inez, an Indian girl named Mary, and Peaches. Steven was especially delighted to see Peaches venture off the third floor without Ronnie to watch over her.

"Since I got them, can I teach them?" Katrina asked.

"Sure." Steven grinned.

"All right, everybody, shut up and pay attention...." After Katrina had demonstrated the printing method and let each girl try it, she sprinkled a paper with tiny foil stars from her box. From then on, many of the girls in the portraits were surrounded by stars and moons like early Renaissance saints.

Katrina asked Steven to squeeze up to the counter with the girls to watch a group portrait developing. Ghostly forms appeared on the previously blank paper. The paper darkened and, on it, a group of girls clustered around Steven looked up out of the tray like a mirror image of the cluster of people staring down at it. But the paper continued to darken before their eyes. Suddenly the faces turned into black silhouettes which disappeared as if a dark shadow had fallen over them. Steven felt a rush of tension move through the bodies of the two girls pushing against him. He exposed a fresh paper, leaving the enlarger light on for fewer seconds. This time the print didn't overdarken. When it was done, the girls examined it, pointing out the people in it by name and laughing as if in relief that they'd survived.

Steven sat back on the counter behind the girls, watching them work, listening to the quiet murmur of their voices. Six bodies in the small room had made it very hot; he was drenched with perspiration, but had no desire to leave. The air smelled of sweat, cheap perfume, and the liquids in the trays. These chemical fumes were making him a little dizzy. Getting high was against the rules, he thought, grinning. Now he was aware of the institution outside the darkroom, and reluctantly looked at his watch.

It was past snacktime and almost time for showers. The

girls groaned when he turned on the overhead light. But they helped each other pour the chemicals back into the bottles and wipe up the splashings, which, despite Katrina's dire warnings, were all over the counter and floor. When the girls opened the door, cool fresh air rushed in. Suddenly aware that they were feeling queasy, they rushed out.

Steven went into the bathroom to see if the girls had left any prints in the sink, and found several floating facedown. He was washing them under the tap when the door opened. It was Katrina, dressed in a fuzzy state bathrobe several sizes too big for her. Her hands were swallowed by the sleeves. Her hair, sizzled by the heat and damp of the darkroom, hung in limp curls over her forehead. "It's a good thing I came back for these." She snatched the photos from the sink, dripping water onto her bare feet. "You probably would have thrown them out."

"No. I like them."

"Yeah?" She separated them, then stuck them wet onto the wall. Most were of her; one was of him. "Which one do you like?"

"That one's nice." Steven pointed to a close-up of her beside the mirror.

She stood back. "I look like a poodle with glasses on that's got left out in the rain."

"You don't either." Steven looked from her photo to her reflection in the mirror.

"You want it?" Katrina asked.

"Sure." He smiled.

She pulled the rest of the prints off the wall. "I might as well get these out of here," she said, and slipped the picture of him into the pile. She bumped her hip on the sink turning hurriedly toward the door.

"Thanks for your help tonight," he said.

"Anytime." She walked out of the bathroom, the hem of her robe dragging on the floor.

When she had gone upstairs, Steven turned out the bathroom and darkroom lights and, in the empty room outside, tossed empty soda cans like basketballs into the garbage can, making as much clatter as he liked. He did hook shots, long bombs, fadeaway jumpers, and seldom missed. Then he sat on the couch, out of breath. Things were still going right, he thought, despite—or maybe because of—the extra girl on the unit. Katrina didn't seem extra anymore; it was impossible to think of the unit without her.

He lay down, not ready to go home to his empty apartment, and began to nod off. Images from the evening wound pleasantly through his head, a succession of black and white faces.... He was trying to develop a girl's picture, but no matter how he twisted the enlarger's lens, the focus was always blurred; no matter how few seconds he left it under the light, it grew bright only for a moment in the developing tray and then darkened and darkened....

He stood up quickly and paced around the floor, shaking off the image. The basement, the whole building, was weirdly quiet. All the television and radio noises—and the voices—had been switched off for the night. The absence of sound seemed intolerable.

Driving home, he kept his tape deck on loud.

7 ❧

Before coming to work at Fairbanks, Steven had been a counselor at the Lakewood Center, a maximum-security state school
downstate. For a year, he had been in charge of a unit of
older boys. Leah had joined the staff for five months, working
with younger boys and doing research for a Ph.D. dissertation
in sociology from the University of Toronto. They had both
resigned following a riot on Steven's unit in which a boy was
killed. Steven had been ready to leave the Youth Service until
he and Leah had been offered jobs at Fairbanks, where he
could create his own program under a new director. In the
past months, the bad old days had nearly faded from his
memory, he'd immersed himself in his new work so intensely.
Recently, though, Leah had been summoned to testify at a
hearing in Albany which was called, after many delays, as a
result of reports she had made about the mistreatment of boys
at Lakewood. She and Steven had stayed up nearly the entire
night before she was to leave for Albany to testify. The next
afternoon, he drove her from the school back to his apartment,
where she'd left her car.

As he swung his old silver Buick off the rutted school
road into the highway, the glare from the snow on the fields
made him squint, and he put on his wraparound sunglasses.
Catching a glimpse of himself in the rearview mirror, his
curly hair still wild and his mustache bristly from the walk
through the wind across the parking lot, he liked that image
of himself: racing car driver, film actor—anything but the

harried counselor of the Lakewood Center senior boys' unit. He'd been thinking about the place all day.

Leah sat close to him on the front seat, warming up; the car's heater wasn't giving out anything but cool air yet. "Did you get Katrina to say anything in your conference the other day?" she asked.

"Some, yes."

"Then you're the first person to get her to talk about herself. How did you do it?"

"I let her play counselor and ask me questions about myself," he said. "Then she felt safe enough to talk. I didn't plan it that way, it just happened."

"What did you talk about?"

"Running away from home. My father."

"That broke the ice?"

"Mostly it was talking about my daughter." Steven glanced at Leah to see if the smile would leave her eyes; he knew it sometimes bothered her to talk about Sarah, since she had never been able to have children of her own. But she just continued to watch him, and Steven smiled back. Tall and graceful, her leonine Afro adding to her height, she was made, Steven thought, to lounge on the upholstered front seat of a big, slightly vintage luxury car, her lilting Caribbean voice pitched low to penetrate the loud purr of the engine. Leah's height and jet-black skin and assertive manner intimidated many of the school staff, black as well as white, but Steven was delighted with her. They were natural allies, the only two staff members who had lived outside the country—Leah had spent about half her life in Trinidad, half in Canada—and who had outsiders' perspectives on the school. They had been lovers for over a year, but since both had bad marriages behind them, they rarely spoke about any future commitments. The present was intense enough, professionally as well as personally.

"Katrina misunderstood something I said at one point," Steven said. "She thought I'd abandoned Sarah to go away to the Islands. I almost felt as if I had, for a moment."

"These kids are so sensitive about that subject. Can't blame them." Leah held the fur collar of her parka close to her face against the cold. "Sometimes I feel guilty just going home at night."

"I know. And here I am taking the afternoon off."

"You haven't taken a day off in weeks. How many weeks?"

Steven smiled. "The only reason I have to take days off is you, and you work as many hours as I do."

"We have very needy kids," she said. "Also, the school is the only place I feel warm in this Siberian tundra. Except your flat, of course." She gazed out the window at the hard white fields on either side of the road. The wind whipped up a gust of snow as fine as powdered glass; the black stripe of highway disappeared for an instant and then blew back into sight in front of the car's hood. "No wonder the girls never run away until summer," she said.

Steven jammed down the accelerator, barreling through a corrugation of small drifts, feeling their impact in the re-verberations of the steering wheel. The car passed a collapsed barn, its roof gone and its walls crushed inward, the beams leaning half-buried in the gray snow. The sky was the same shade of gray; it hung low over the land like the frozen underside of the surface of a lake in which most plant and animal life—stark bare trees, occasional ghost-eyed cows—existed in suspension until a thaw that might take aeons to arrive. "I do wonder," Steven said, "how I washed up in this place."

"A pair of refugees, we are," Leah said. "Is no accident we are in this line of work."

The highway narrowed and dropped like the end of a drainpipe into the town of Fairbanks. Its main street was deserted. No one had shoveled the sidewalks. The general store was open, displaying hunting boots and plaid jackets in its window; the other ten or so shops were boarded up with splintery plywood. Turning onto a side street, Steven passed a squat brick school building; outside, a swingless swing set stood on the snow like a giant petrified insect. Most of the farms in the area had gone under, and now the Youth Service, a few gas stations on the highway that led to the Canadian border ten miles away, and Welfare were all that were keeping the town alive. It was the sort of remote site chosen for the

storage of nuclear missiles—at an army depot near the highway junction—and juvenile delinquents. Steven often drove
miles out of his way to avoid the town on his way home.

Home was a four-dwelling apartment house inhabited only
by him, a cinder-block structure built like a bunker into the
side of a hill with a space around it that had been left pitted
by bulldozer treads the previous fall and was now windswept
down to its frozen, moonscape dirt. Steven drove into the
parking area past some enormous pipes pointed haphazardly
up the hill like abandoned spacecraft wreckage. Using the
grille of the Buick for a plow, he gouged away a snowdrift
until his car door was beside the outside metal staircase that
led up to his apartment. He and Leah climbed the steps holding the railing with both hands, heads down against the wind.

Inside, a jungle of color greeted them. Green plants hung
in all the corners. The walls of the one big room throbbed
with tropical foliage : photographs, calypso record covers, and
paintings of Caribbean scenes ; on a big picture window which
would have presented a bleak hillside were taped two identical
views : trompe l'oeil posters of windowsills, flowerpots, par-
rots, all looking out on a rippling purple lagoon. Hanging
flat along the ceiling a batik cloth—out of which some of
Steven's more brilliant neckties might have been made—hid
the light fixtures ; their glow through the cloth's patterns gave
the air the blue-green tint of sunlight filtering through palm
fronds. Or so Steven and Leah believed when they lay beneath
it sharing a bottle of rum.

Steven tossed his trench coat and suit jacket onto the sofa
bed, put on a quiet Haydn guitar quartet, and turned the
thermostat up to eighty. Leah, still in her parka, stepped past
him into the kitchen area.

"I need something to help me settle that state spaghetti
lunch," she said. "Do I have time for a cup of tea?"

"Sure. I'll make it while you're in the shower." Stepping
up behind her, he leaned his face into the soft fur of her
collar, inhaling its dampness along with the sweet scent of
her hair. She leaned back and slipped out of the parka, leaving
it in his hands as she moved off toward the bathroom.

"I didn't see these last night," she said, pausing in front

of some photographs taped to the wall beside the refrigerator. Fairbanks girls grinned and grimaced at her. "Look at those expressions." She clicked her tongue. "This is a good close-up of Katrina."

"Yeah, I like it."

"You're keeping a close eye on that one, aren't you?"

"I keep an eye on all my little lambies," Steven said.

"The good shepherd." Leah laughed.

Steven made a papal sign of the cross in the air, then dropped his hand to his side. "And I never turn my back on any of them."

He put the kettle on to boil, then changed into jeans and a flannel shirt, enjoying the waterfall sound of Leah's shower and the faint splashing notes of the guitar music. When the shower stopped, he made a pot of tea, strong and brown with milk and sugar boiled up in it, the way he'd learned to make it in the Islands. He hoped Leah would keep his orange bathrobe on—she looked like a Masai queen in it—but when he heard her opening his closet where she kept some outfits, he knew she was dressing.

They had their tea sitting on the couch. Leah's face beneath her towel turban was as somber as the heavy dark suit she wore. "This thing is too hot," she muttered, and ran her finger under the collar of her white blouse. Beads of sweat shone on her forehead. "Big women look so very awkward in suits, don't you think?"

"You look lovely in anything." Steven stood up and turned down the thermostat.

She smiled. "I had better look solid and respectable if I want that review board to think I am a believable person."

"I'm afraid you're right," he said. "But you could take the suit off now. You've got almost an hour."

She touched her forehead against his shoulder. "I don't know if I can get my mind off that bloody hearing." Lifting her face, she looked at him quizzically. "How can you be so insatiable, after last night?"

"You bring it out in me." Steven stroked her cheek with his fingers. "But I'm just as happy to be quiet here with you, too."

Pushing herself up off the couch, she slipped out of her skirt and jacket and sat down again, appearing thirty pounds lighter. "That's better," she said, smoothing her half-slip over her knees. "I looked in the mirror a few minutes ago and I saw a middle-aged lady prison guard."

"You probably just saw the person you felt like you were, back at Lakewood. It happens to me once in a while."

"What do you see?"

Steven rested the back of his head against the seat cushion, closing his eyes. An alarmingly vivid picture came back to him. "A cross between an ax murderer and a scared rabbit."

She furrowed her brow. "No!"

"You asked." Steven glanced away. "I used to get pretty angry in that place. Sometimes at the kids, mostly at the staff."

"And at yourself." Leah rested her hand on his leg. "But you are not a killer or a rabbit. You are a very gentle and brave man."

"Thank you." He touched the back of her hand. "But mirrors don't lie. They just give you another version—a reverse image. It's their nature."

"Treacherous things, them." Leah sighed. "You're in a pensive mood today, I can tell. It's your turn to talk if you want to, after I did keep you up talking last night." She moved sideways and patted her knees.

He lay down on his back, his head on her lap, his plaid shirt open on his chest. He and Leah always knew when the other one needed to let out the worries that got bottled up during the course of their jobs. "Well . . ." Steven stared up at the glowing tropical design in the ceiling cloth, and let out his breath. "Like I said, Katrina got me thinking about the past the other day. She's very direct, and I like that. But she pried open Pandora's box with just a flick of her voice."

"Everybody's got one child who gets to them," Leah said, leaning back. "With me, is Vonita."

"I feel like I have to make everything right for Katrina," Steven said quietly. "If I can't save her, I can't save anybody, including myself."

Leah glanced down at him. The guitar music on the stereo

rippled to the end of a piece and then clicked off. "Saving people. A dangerous way to think, my friend," she said.

"I know it."

"Is the occupational hazard of social workers, playing God," Leah said. "Do you remember how Ben Paleno used to strut around when he was acting director, threatening and bullying those girls?"

Steven felt his stomach muscles tense. "I'll never forget it."

"He is still dangerous, that man. Even more so, because he truly believes that his amiable imperialism is the only way to deal with kids. If Matt Steiner had not taken over, I might have left you to run the unit alone, Steven."

"I'm glad you didn't tell me that then."

"We must never let things get so bad again."

"That's what I said to myself after I'd finished talking with Katrina," Steven said. "I remember once she took her glasses off to clean them on her shirt, and her eyes looked so pale and vulnerable for a moment. I forget how crushable these kids are sometimes, they're so feisty and loud. But I looked at her, and I thought of all the vulnerable kids I've known. Including my daughter. Including that boy at Lakewood." He still couldn't bring himself to speak the name of the boy who had been killed in the riot. "Leah, I wonder if I'm ever going to stop feeling responsible."

"You know you're not responsible," she said softly.

"Rationally, I know it," he said. "But rationally is only one version."

"If you hadn't done what you did, more kids might have been hurt. You were cleared completely. They even promoted you."

"Whose benefit was that for, mine or the Youth Service's?" He glanced up at her. "Anyway, you didn't hear what I said—"

"Of course I did." She stared down at him with a pained expression on her face, as if trying to examine some internal injury through undamaged skin. "I just never know what to tell you."

Steven stood up and found some cigarettes in his suit

jacket. Lighting two, he sat down on the couch and handed one to Leah. They had talked about the riot at Lakewood so often they had only to mention it and millions of words passed between them in a single glance. On a winter morning about a year ago, Steven had come in to work to find that the boys had broken up the furniture and used pieces of it to smash all the windows of their sitting-room area. When he stepped inside, crunching glass underfoot, he'd smelled the acrid stink of sweat and violence. The boys fled, their catcalls echoing down the corridor. In one room, seven boys had taken turns raping a smaller boy on the metal frame of his bed; Steven found him whimpering on the floor, blood trickling from between his naked buttocks. In other rooms, fights were in progress, old scores being settled; the walls reverberated with the impact of bodies thudding against them. Steven had tried to wade into the midst of the noisiest fight, but several boys with stolen kitchen knives threatened to stab him and two boys they were holding hostage. The standoff lasted for hours, with the ringleaders holed up in a big barricaded storage closet they had somehow gotten a key to. Steven kept trying to talk to them, not wanting to call in more staff, most of whom he didn't trust. Finally, when he heard the boys breaking a window that would have allowed them to escape into the woods, he telephoned for help.

Police had already been called, he discovered. They had ringed the building, waiting for orders to move in. Now they and several guards stormed the doors. Tear gas canisters exploded; nightsticks cracked against flesh and bone. When the screams subsided and the air finally cleared, six boys were taken to the hospital; the others were hauled up the corridor in handcuffs and locked into individual detention cells. One boy was missing. Steven found him in a closet with his skull caved in. The boy never recovered.

"I should have known the administration would call the cops in," Steven said, sitting back on the couch. His hands felt trembly and unreliable as he lifted his cigarette to his mouth, and he was aware of the slightly too rapid rhythm of his heartbeat in his chest. "If I'd asked what the police positions were, I could have let the boys escape through the

window. The cops could have grabbed them one by one outside."

"It's not policy to let kids escape," Leah said.

"It's been done." Steven took a deep breath. "I knew
what my staff was like. I knew Bernardson was looking for
an excuse to unload on some black kids." At the hearing, a
guard named Bernardson had admitted helping one of the
police "subdue" the boy "in self-defense." The review board
had ruled that, since so many boys had had dangerous weapons, no excessive force had been used. Steven knew better;
he saw the smirk on Bernardson's face when the ruling was
read out in the courtroom.

Leah sat with her feet beneath her, facing him. "Sometimes I wish I hadn't written that report against those men
on my staff. Then there wouldn't be another hearing, and we
wouldn't be opening What'shername's box again."

Steven smiled and sat back slowly, feeling himself relax
a little. "It wasn't you who opened it. Besides, you couldn't
have lived with yourself if you hadn't written the report."

"Nor with you either." Leah sipped her tea, eyeing him
over the rim of her mug. "I only started working for this
Youth Service so I could do my research. I thought I would
be a detached observer. How did I get myself so involved in
everything?"

"I don't know," Steven said. "Maybe it was your insatiable passion for me."

"Don't puff yourself up so," she said, smiling. "It was
not just you."

"What do you mean, 'just'?"

Leah's tongue darted out at him, then she composed her
face. "This partnership of ours is not just you and me. Is
like taking on an endless family. Very complicated." She
pronounced it "com-plee-KEH-tod," an inflection Steven loved.
She put her tea mug down on the table. "Where are we all
going, my friend?"

"I hope," Steven said, "a better place than where we've
been." His gaze took on a blue intensity that was similar to
the theatrical look he sometimes assumed to quiet a roomful
of screaming kids; now, though, this look was involuntary,

and seemed to be directed within. "It damn well has to be better."

Leah watched him for several seconds, then sat back with her cigarette. "In my town in Trinidad, we had a traveling preacher would come who used to talk about a 'better place.' He had the same kind of quaver in his voice."

Steven frowned. "It's preachers like that who made me an atheist."

"I know. Me, too. But sometimes I worry that this job is some kind of personal quest for you. You're driven by something else than idealism."

"I don't feel idealistic anymore. I guess I like people better than ideals."

"Yes. But do you know what I mean?" She took hold of his arm.

"I know what you mean," he said. "Maybe I get so busy rolling my program along that I forget to think why I'm doing it." He rested his head against the black sofa cushion. "Maybe I'm in a hurry to get everything going right because I feel a case of social worker burnout creeping up on me."

"Another occupational hazard." Leah loosened her grip on his arm. "You do look tired."

"Do I?"

She nodded. "I suppose that if we thought about all these questions constantly, we would wear ourselves out and never do anything."

"Probably."

"Besides, is your afternoon off." She picked up her mug of tea, cold now, and stared into it. "Too much introspection can be constipating."

"That's what it is. I thought it was the state spaghetti." Steven saw Leah smile and felt better, then frustrated with himself. He'd shut the lid of Pandora's box without ever having caught and identified the things that were still flying around loose.

Leah stretched, her dark belly rising into view and vanishing again beneath the bottom of her blouse. "How much time have we got?" she asked.

Steven looked at his watch. "Twenty minutes."

She unraveled her towel turban and slowly lay down lengthwise on the couch behind him. He lay down beside her.

"Don't let me sleep long," she murmured.

"No."

They moved closer, their legs entangled. He gazed past the black blur of her hair to the window ledges and the still lagoons beyond, and closed his eyes. Holding her, he stroked her back under her blouse and felt himself relaxing as he had last night with her. Her thigh moved against him as if to push the elastic of her half-slip against his fingers so that he could slide them beneath it. He did, feeling her muscles begin to move; a happy warmth spread along their thighs.

Suddenly the jangling note of the telephone shot through him like an electric charge. He sat up immediately, his heels thudding against the floor. In the silence between rings, the wind wailed on the other side of the picture window; he could see white gusts of it swirling behind the paper lagoons.

Leah sat beside him, her hand on his wrist. "Steven, take it easy."

He gulped some air, and nodded. "I'm always like this when that fucking thing goes off." Leaning sideways, he snatched the phone from the end table and rested his hand on the receiver, taking a few long even breaths. Then he half-smiled at Leah. "Okay, let's see how clairvoyant I am. I think it's going to be Sonia. Some girl's giving her a hard time."

"Ronnie, or perhaps Whale," Leah guessed.

Steven picked up the receiver, stopping its ring. He was right: it was Sonia, the college trainee; she was bright and sensitive but not confident enough yet to handle crises on her own. A very large girl named Whale—Leah put out her palm and Steven slapped it—had barged into the staff office and, cursing and bellowing, was refusing to leave until Sonia called her probation officer in the Bronx for her. Steven asked Sonia to put Whale on.

"Didn't Sonia tell you you could call your PO after group session, Whale?"

"Yeah, Mr. Fox—"

"I just heard some disturbing news about you, Whale. I heard that you were giving my staff a hard time about leaving the office. That can't be true, can it?"

"Mr. Fox, I—"

"I'd hate for it to be true, because then I'd have to come back and throw your ass out that office window."

"Y'all ain't got no window in this place big enough for my black ass—"

Leah leaned over to speak into the receiver. "If *I* find you in that office, you're going to want to *jump* out, Baby Pie."

"Aw, shit! Y'all people just gang up—" The bluster in her voice turned to muffled laughter. There was a loud clunk as she dropped the phone, then heavy footsteps, then the slam of the office door.

"You all right, Sonia?" Steven asked.

"Oh, yes." She sounded breathless.

"What about Whale?"

"She was grinning on her way out. I think she got the attention she wanted."

"You're learning." He talked to Sonia for a few more minutes about how things were going at the school and then said good-bye.

Leah had stepped into her wool skirt. "The world intrudes," she said.

"Doesn't it, though?" Steven shook his head. "Never mind, we'll have other times."

Leah smiled, then turned toward the picture window. "How I don't want to go out into the weather!"

"I'll go with you if you like," Steven said.

"Thanks, Steven, but they might make me stay over until tomorrow, and you would be stuck in Albany two days."

"Right. . . ." Steven watched her step into the bathroom and reappear a few minutes later with her Afro tamed and her heavy suit bulging at her shoulders and hips. She put on the gold-rimmed glasses she wore for driving, and looked less like a woman prison guard than the president of a delegation of Baptist matrons. He helped her into her parka, pulling the hood up so that her dark face was framed with silvery fur.

"You'll freeze if you come outside with me," Leah said.

"It's all right. I'll see you off." Steven grabbed his trench coat.

They walked down the steps together to her car. It was partially buried in a drift, but with some pushes from Steven, she was able to get the screaming tires to catch the dirt and propel the car forward. As she revved up the engine, white fumes billowed out from the tailpipe in the frozen air. He leaned close to her window. "You'll do fine, Leah," he shouted, and she rolled it down. "If you need me to corroborate anything, just call me."

"I will, Steven. Thanks." She leaned toward him, her eyes shut from the blowing snow.

He kissed her and then stood watching her big Citroën drive off. Sweaty and shivering, he ran up the stairs again, his coat collar flapping in the wind. Inside, he leaned his forehead against the window between the two lagoon posters and watched Leah's car roll down the hill and vanish around a high-banked bend in the road.

The ticking of the snow blowing against the glass didn't prevent the room from feeling as silent as the inside of a drum. Now what? he thought, missing Leah, missing the Fairbanks girls and everyone he had ever cared about; their absences were packing the room tight. He put on a stack of opera records. Sitting in the middle of the couch with his clipboard and stationery, he began a letter to his daughter in Japan.

8 ❧

After two days of testimony, the hearing in Albany was de-layed indefinitely because of the sudden illness of one of the key witnesses. Steven and Leah again focused all their atten-tion on Fairbanks. When Steven didn't stay at the school in the evenings, he found out what had gone on there by reading the third-floor log the following mornings.

> *Venison hamburgers for supper again. Girls getting sick of them. Me, too. Maybe Mr. Fox with his charm and diplomacy can tell state troopers we appreciate their thinking of us but please don't deliver any more run-over deer here. Anybody ever wonder what they do with run-over people?*

Some of Leah's entries made Steven smile. Others worried him:

> *Helped second-floor staff get a fire extinguisher away from girls there. The floor is a mess, curtains in lounge white with foam, girls refusing to clean it up, Ben Paleno bellowing at them. Heatwave and Panda fighting, Julia (bystander) to Nurses' Station with cut lip. Second floor noisy past lights-out, thump, bam, screech, who knows what-all is going on down there.*

Steven put down the log, suppressing a sigh, when Ben Paleno walked uninvited into his office.

Ben handed him a thin newspaper, *The Youth Service News.* "Mind if I sit down?"

"Okay," Steven said. "But how about opening the window if you're going to smoke that thing?"

Ben took the cigar butt from his mouth, looked at it, and sat heavily in a wooden chair. "It's not lit."

Steven opened the *News*, a glossy public relations sheet designed to impress legislators who voted for the Youth Service's budget and to cheer up frazzled employees in various institutions. Its pages abounded with success stories ("Harlem Youth Wins Scholarship") and photos of kids receiving trophies at sports events.

Years ago, Ben had been good copy for the paper. He'd been photographed lecturing the school's entire population on Looking Before You Leap (Into Antisocial Behavior). At those meetings, he praised kids who acted responsibly—usually by snitching on each other to staff—and yelled at those who abused his faith in them. Many girls were reduced to tears every afternoon for weeks. But in those days, as Ben still told anyone who would listen, youngsters stayed in line out of respect for their staff.

Out of terror of the staff was closer to the truth. In old files and logbooks, Steven had found information—which had never, never left the institution—clearly showing that staff brutality had been a routine method of keeping order. In one instance, a girl had been hospitalized as a result of being thrown to the floor and kicked in the head. Unwilling to discipline loyal staff, Ben had knowingly signed a report stating that the girl's cracked ribs and concussion had been caused by a fall down some stairs. Steven had also found a letter sent to the acting director—Ben, at the time—written by a thirteen-year-old girl with a history of suicide attempts, complaining that a staff member had repeatedly forced her to have oral sex with him in his car. In the same girl's file was a memo written by Ben stating that, following a "constructive" counseling session in his office, she had decided to withdraw her "wild accusations" and accept a transfer to a minimum-security facility. In Ben's own file were several memos from Head Office praising him for running a tight ship.

The ship had only been tight because it had contained the violence it engendered. Steven had read numerous accounts of fights, stabbings, broomstick and bottle rapes, self-mutilations, and suicide attempts. He had counted 121 instances, over a three-year period, of girls being locked for days in solitary "security rooms," often for trying to run away. Any therapy or rehabilitation programs had been, like Ben's lectures, window dressing. Warehousing kids had been Ben's only real objective.

And it still was, as far as Steven could see from what Ben's girls occasionally told him. Though Ben had been repeatedly ordered to start the New Program on his floor, there was little evidence that he had done so. He held small group sessions perhaps once a week, in which he invited the girls to assign punishments for group members who broke rules. But when the kid got in trouble again, he imposed his own punishment, invalidating the girls' efforts to control her. He told girls that anything they said to their staff in counseling sessions would be strictly confidential; then he got reports from staff on what was said and sometimes announced it to the entire group in order to make an example of the girl. He told the girls that they should trust staff to protect them rather than defend themselves physically, but the staff, who made keep-the-peace deals with the stronger kids, looked the other way when these girls intimidated weaker ones into giving up money, cigarettes, sexual favors. Ben controlled his staff by holding their past mistakes over their heads, and the staff, afraid of losing their jobs—Fairbanks was about the only employer in this impoverished region—kept their mouths shut about what went on on the second floor. But of course the news got out, as in Leah's log entries.

In his research, Steven had also discovered that Ben had once been considered for the school's directorship, until an incident occurred which had probably cost him the promotion. He had tried to take a stolen kitchen knife away from a girl and had been slashed with it. In fact, all the girl had slashed was the front of his slacks, but Ben screamed out, holding his crotch in both hands, and fell onto a couch where he remained immobile while other staff members wrestled the knife away from the girl. No one accused him of anything more serious than failing to call for help to disarm the girl, but for months afterward, he had been loud and combative, hoping, some said, to force another confrontation in order to get a second chance to prove his courage. Eventually he resumed his usual avuncular approach to the girls and staff. But when the directorship came open again, the Youth Service brought in Matt Steiner, a black-bearded former law professor from Louisiana. One of his first acts as director was to start stripping Ben of most of his functions as assistant director in order to get him to resign. Ben, remaining stoical, made a show of supporting the New Program on the second floor while at the same time cultivating his contacts in Head Office who approved of his old methods of dealing with kids.

Steven leaned back in his chair, holding up the *Youth Service News* between himself and Ben.

FAIRBANKS SCHOOL TRIES NEW APPROACH TO RESIDENTIAL TREATMENT PROGRAMMING

On the third floor of the Fairbanks School for Girls, an interesting experiment in rehabilitative social interaction is under way. Its treatment philosophy is called Guided Group Responsibility.

"The girls are being helped to take charge of their own lives," explained Steven Fox, Unit Administrator. "In the New Program, major decisions are made in group therapy sessions by the residents. For instance, if a girl feels she is ready for a privilege, a trial visit, or a discharge, she asks the group to evaluate her readiness. One of the criteria is her willingness to take responsibility not only for her own behavior but for the behavior of other group members as well. Thus she is encouraged to help her peers control their destructive impulses and gain insight into their problems. Eventually, the girls themselves will bear full responsibility for rewarding and disciplining group members."

Fox believes that many institutions socialize residents

into functioning only in institutional settings and not in the outside world. "There's no point in merely teaching them to obey the staff and rules, since there's no staff and few rules in the streets," he stated.

"The treatment group becomes like a small family," Fox went on, "but unlike gang subcultural families that often develop in institutions, the group is supposed to reinforce the positive norms of the program rather than attempting to resist them."

"The staff is no longer just watching over the girls," Matthew Steiner, the school's Director, stated. "They share in all aspects of a girl's treatment. They make decisions as teams, rather than merely taking orders from above. They feel a commitment to projects they have developed themselves. This, at least, is our goal."

So far, both residents and staff report that they are enthusiastic about this radical new approach to rehabilitation. Good luck with your exciting social experiment, Fairbanks!

"What do you think of the article?" Ben asked, watching Steven's face. He ran his hand over his stubbly crew cut.

"It's okay," Steven said. Apart from reducing everything he'd said to social worker jargon, the article was accurate enough. That the paper described what he was doing as "radical" told Steven that the Head Office bureaucrats—like Ben and his old-guard allies on the staff here—were viewing his program with a lot of skepticism.

"I feel bad about the article, myself," Ben said as Steven folded the paper. "It makes it look as if only your part of the facility's behind the New Program, not mine."

"Yeah, it does," Steven said.

"You know I'm behind it, don't you?" Ben fiddled with his cigar. "I'm doing small group sessions and everything, have been for weeks."

"Have you?"

"Absolutely." Ben's eyes glistened with sincerity. "But the paper makes it look as if we're not all working together as a team."

"What can I do, Ben?"

Ben looked down into the palm of his hand. "If you'd ask

Matt to write a short letter—just a correction, like newspapers have—it'd probably get printed. They'd print a letter from him.''

Steven clacked the edges of several folders against the desktop and lay them down slowly. ''Ben, I can't say that I know what you're doing on your unit. If you want to write a letter, I don't give a damn. But I'm not going to speak to Matt for you.'' He raised his eyes to meet Ben's watery stare.

''Never mind. It probably doesn't make that much difference.'' Ben stood up, his hands rising from his knees. ''I'm probably just making a mountain out of a molehill, aren't I?''

''Probably.''

''Okay. We'll just forget it.'' Ben smiled, taking a matchbook from his pocket. ''What's important is what we really do for these girls, not how it looks in the papers.''

''Right.''

''How are things on your unit, anyway?''

''Fine. We're doing okay.''

''That's great. My girls seem to like the changes, too. We'll see how it goes.''

''Yeah.'' Steven smelled something, and sniffed.

''Okay.'' Ben shuffled his feet in place, then headed toward the door. ''Well, good luck,'' he said, leaving a cloud of cigar smoke behind him.

When Steven walked into the director's office for his meeting, Matt was talking on the phone. Steven sat down in an armchair that wasn't as comfortable as it looked. For something to do with his hands, he shelled and ate some peanuts from the bowl on the desk. There were no trophies or framed newspaper photos here, just a neat desk and three sketches of New Orleans street scenes on the walls. Small and wiry, Matt was a man who, despite a slow Southern drawl, did not waste words. Smiles and other nonverbal small talk were not returned. Most of the staff were unnerved by his intensity; they joked uneasily that, though he rarely left his office, he had telepathic powers that allowed him to know what everyone was doing (or not doing) in every corner of the institution.

Despite Steven's inability to relax with Matt, he trusted him. After working for a succession of beer-guzzling, back-slapping directors in downstate institutions, Matt Steiner was a breath of fresh—albeit cold—air.

The director put down the phone and swiveled his chair toward Steven. "Where the hell's Ben?"

"He was poking around here a few minutes ago." Steven glanced out the office door. "I didn't know he was going to meet with us. I thought we were going to talk about the canteen project again."

"That's the pretext."

"For what?"

The director didn't explain. He picked up a copy of Steven's proposal and, stroking his beard, leafed through it. Steven had proposed that his girls run the soda fountain in the basement, serving staff, visitors, and other girls several days a week.

"Looks good," Matt said, putting the papers down. "Do it."

Steven smiled. "That's all?"

Matt nodded. "As far as I'm concerned. But you haven't got enough staff to cover the project."

"I know. I'll have to take some from Maintenance. Ben isn't going to like that." The Maintenance Department and Nurses' Station were the only areas Ben still had jurisdiction over as assistant director.

"I hope he doesn't like it. I hope he puffs up and explodes from apoplexy. That might be the only way we'll ever get the sonofabitch out of here, unless they change some civil service regulations about firing folks."

"You hate him, don't you?"

"I surely do. Hell, you read those old logs. You saw what he allowed to go on before we got here."

"It made me sick," Steven said.

"Be interesting to see how you handle him." When the director turned his head, sunlight glinted on his rimless glasses. "Speaking of the devil..."

Steven hadn't heard any footsteps, but now he did. There was a soft knock on the doorframe. Ben forced a grin as he

ambled in and settled his bulk in a chair far from the director's desk. "Better late than never," he said.

"Not necessarily," Matt said.

"What?" Ben glanced from Matt to Steven.

"We were talking about my canteen project," Steven said.
"You missed a lot."

"Well, I got a copy of the proposal. Since my departments
aren't in on it, it's not my problem." Ben smiled. "But I'm
glad to be consulted around here for a change, don't get me
wrong."

"I won't." Steven turned toward him. "I need more staff
for the project," he said. "I've asked Spike and Bobby to
help cover it. They agreed. I thought you ought to know."

Silence. Matt sat back, watching Steven.

Ben's smile had disappeared. "Hell, yes, I ought to know!
I can't spare any Maintenance staff right now."

"There's no grass to cut with snow on the ground, and
there's only so many times a day the men can adjust the
furnace," Steven said. "They're tired of hanging around
waiting for you to call them to break up fights. They jumped
at the idea of working in the canteen."

"Listen, Steven, you had no business going behind my
back talking to my staff."

"Your back wasn't anywhere in the area at the time."

"Come on. You could have talked to me first."

"No. If I had, you'd have found some way to discourage
Spike and Billy."

Ben shook his head slowly. He glanced around, taking in
Matt's steely gaze. He sighed. "Well, I guess I got no choice
except to cooperate. Staff's got to cooperate with the New
Program. I realize that."

"Good," Steven said.

"So I guess we're going to supervise Spike and Bobby
jointly."

"No."

"Now wait—"

"I want Spike and Bobby transferred to my staff. If
they're working on my project, I want them accountable to
me and nobody else."

"You can't just requisition somebody else's staff!"

"You should have been here when Matt and I discussed it. You're a little late now."

"It's true." The director narrowed his eyes. "I've approved Steven's staffing proposal."

Ben slid down a half-inch in his chair. His hand went to his forehead, then to his shirt pocket where he found the stub of a cigar. "I walked into a setup, didn't I?"

"Did you?" the director said.

"Hell, yes!" Ben lurched forward out of his chair and stood up, swaying in place. His cheeks and jowls were dark red. "You think I can't see that? How stupid do you think I am?"

"How stupid?" The director stroked his beard. "Let's put it this way, Ben," he said. "If your brains was cotton, there wouldn't be enough of it to make a Tampax for a red-eyed beetle."

Ben stared at the director. The room was silent except for the sound of a peanut being cracked open in the director's hand.

"You don't like the way I talked to you, do you?" the director asked. The expression on his face was as close to a smile as Steven had ever seen.

Ben wiped his mouth.

"Nothing much you can do about it. Except get your behind out of here," Matt said.

Ben shook his head slowly.

"You can apply for a transfer if you don't want to resign. I'll recommend you for a transfer."

"I still care about this place."

"This place doesn't care about you," the director said. "This place has demonstrated that to you over and over again. Haven't you got the message yet?"

Ben's spine seemed to slip in such a way that his shoulders were suddenly rounded. "You're a bastard," he said.

"No doubt about it," Matt said.

The room was silent again. Ben gazed down at the cigar in his hand. It was squashed, staining his fingers brown like insect juice. He clamped his fingers over it and turned away.

Slowly, he walked out of the office. Steven listened to his footsteps go through the anteroom and fade into the sound of murmuring in the foyer.

"Whew," Steven said.

"You didn't care for the way I treated him?" The director watched his face.

"I don't know. I doubt if he'll quit."

The director nodded. "What do you reckon he'll do?"

"Ben doesn't mind being a martyr...." Steven stared into the bowl of peanuts. "He'll probably get on the phone and plead his case to his pals in Albany."

"And plead and plead."

Steven looked up suddenly. "And maybe they'll finally see what a mess he is."

"You got it. That's what I'm hoping." The director nodded again. It occurred to Steven that this was his way of smiling. "I may as well tell you something now," Matt said. "I'm being considered for a promotion. A regional directorship downstate."

"I didn't know that."

"Nobody does. Nobody but you and Leah Gomes ought to know a thing about it for now. I won't have a decision till May or June."

"Why Leah?"

"We need women administrators here. This is a place for girls, with three men in the top positions. We've got about sixty percent black and Puerto Rican kids. And only three black staff out of forty-six. None of them anywhere near the top. Affirmative Action's breathing down my neck about this, and they're damn right."

"What do you have in mind for Leah?" Steven asked.

"Unit administrator. Your job. You better talk to her about it. See what she thinks of the idea," Matt said. "Maybe have a promotion for you, too."

"To what?"

"Assistant director. But in fact, you'd be senior man here for a long time before anybody'd get appointed over you. You'd be acting director."

Steven swallowed hard. He'd expected some sort of promotion in the next year or so, but not such a big one, or so soon.

Matt dumped his ashtray into the wastebasket beside his desk. Peanut shells landed noisily on paper; a small cloud of cigarette ashes rose from the basket and disappeared. "Head Office likes your energy, though they've got a wait-and-see attitude about your—the New Program's—ideas. Make them work and get this promotion, you could go up fast in the Youth Service. You started late and you're a little older than most people at your level, but that won't necessarily hurt you. Of course it might, too—personally."

"What do you mean?"

"You know too much about the system. You've got a broader overview and sometimes you hate what you see."

"Go on," Steven said.

"You'll have to pay more attention to the whole place, spend less time with your girls. Manage the staff, not them. Spend more time with Head Office folks so that they'll back you. You'll have a hard time with that."

"Why do you want me for the job, then?"

"You're honest and committed. Rare qualities. You could make things happen. . . ." The director sat back in his chair, watching Steven's face. "One way or the other."

"I could," Steven said. "I'd like to run this place the way I'm starting to run the third floor. I want to be sure that's possible."

"Think about it."

Steven cleared his throat. "I will."

The director nodded.

Steven stood up. He wondered if he, too, would one day develop a nod.

9 ❧

The sudden change in the temperature on the last day of February had Katrina confused, melancholy, restless. She sweated in her winter clothes, trying to ignore the freakish warm weather which, like everything else the state provided her, seemed to offer an unreliable promise of things she'd never asked for. Alone in her room, she opened the window as far as it would go and pulled off her sweater.

She tried to feel the sun's warmth through her T-shirt, but couldn't. Lifting it up, she felt a little warm air against the skin of her belly. Then she pulled it higher and glanced down at her breasts. They hadn't grown any since the last time she'd checked. They probably wouldn't in this place. They were probably one reason Joey might be leaving her to rot up here. Who wanted a girl with a chest like a boy's? She yanked down the shirt angrily, then pinched her nipples hard to make them show through the cloth. Maybe there'd be a letter today.

She sat on her window ledge and stared out at the fields. For a moment, the expanse of white space reminded her of the beaches in Florida where she and Joey had slept out, and she had another impulse to run away. But here, the open countryside looked frozen and nasty, and she understood why the other city girls said they'd be scared to run away. There were no flat surfaces to walk on, only bumpy ground with holes in it and thornbushes to get stabbed by and other dangers like ... cows, maybe, with sharp horns to chase you, or

farmers with pitchforks and shotguns—mountain men, the
black girls called them—who'd blow you away just for target
practice.

Still, she wasn't as scared of the outdoors as, say, Vonita,
who believed that frogs had teeth and werewolves lived in
the woods. She'd rather be out there than shut up in here,
wouldn't she? Maybe. If she weren't alone. Damn Joey. Damn
the mail, late again. She wasn't going to wait any longer.

Katrina slipped out of her room and down the back stairs.
She tiptoed through the empty dining room and rec room,
moving fast in her silent sneakers, ducking under the windows
of the Nurses' Station and assistant director's office. She
hurried past the soda machine, the candy machine—OUT OF
ORDER—past the bulletin board—HELPING TROUBLED YOUTHS
HELP THEMSELVES (Right, she thought, I'm only going to
help myself)—and around the corner into the secretaries'
office. She made it just in time; Leah passed the doorway on
her way to the front stairs, but didn't see her. In the office,
two secretaries were typing at desks along the wall. Along
the other wall were three doors to smaller, empty offices.
Katrina headed for the farthest one.

"Hello?" Mrs. Williams, the second secretary, looked up
at her.

"I'm doing Pam's chore today," Katrina said, taking a
broom from the corner.

The secretary smiled at her and resumed typing. Katrina
went into an office and began sweeping noisily back and forth
in the same place. Behind Mrs. Williams' cabinet was the
day's mail, waiting to be checked for contraband. In a few
minutes, the secretary walked over to a coffee machine by
the door. Katrina darted out, grabbed the stack of envelopes,
and ducked back out of sight. Her hand trembled as she went
through the letters, sorting more slowly as she got toward the
bottom of the stack. The last letter . . . it was for her! Finally!

She ripped open the envelope and yanked out the stationery. The paper was bright yellow with pink flowers in the
corner—it was from a girlfriend of hers in Brooklyn. She
skimmed it, looking for Joey's name. When she found it, she
froze.

The other letters fell out of her hands, sailed in various directions to the floor. A faint, sharp cry scraped up Katrina's throat. Her eyes flooded with tears. She squeezed the letter in her fist and flung it onto the floor.

Slamming the door behind her, she walked unsteadily out of the office, not hearing what the secretary was asking her. Then she dashed up the stairs to the third floor and shoved open the staff office door.

"Damn, Katrina!" Leah looked up from the desk. She and Steven had been leaning over some papers spread out on it. "You ever hear of knocking on doors?"

Katrina ignored her, and glared wide-eyed at Steven. "I got to go outside! You got to sign me out!"

Steven stood up straight, his pencil still on the papers. "Not now, Katrina. It's almost time for classes."

"You got to let me go outside!" She bounced hard on her heels. "Steven, I just got to!"

"What's the trouble?"

"If I don't get out of this building—" She stared at the two faces staring back at her—one black, one white, both faces saying No, Katrina, no! Whatever it is you want, you can't do it—can't—can't—

"You fucking people!" she screamed. *"All you care about is keeping us locked up in this place! You don't care—"* She fled out into the corridor, swinging the office door behind her with all her strength. It cracked against the doorframe like a pistol shot. The sound reverberated down the hall, bringing girls out of the lounge and the rooms. She rushed past them and ran into her own room. Wailing, she collapsed onto her bed. The door opened a few inches behind her.

"Leave me alone!" she screamed.

"What happened?" Pam stuck her face cautiously inside.

"He was the only one who could help me!"

"Who? Joey? Did he ditch you?"

"No!"

"What, then?"

"He . . ." Katrina choked. She rolled her head sideways. *"He's dead!"*

"Oh, my God—" Pam's eyes filled with tears.

Katrina leaped off the bed. Clutching her blanket, she ran out of the room past Pam and through the mob of spectators. She sailed down the corridor, the blanket flying high, and plunged down the back stairs. At the bottom, she dashed across the basement rec room and into the poolroom where she fell onto the couch, gasping for breath.

When she heard the girls' voices around her, she sobbed even louder. Then they retreated, and she heard Leah.

"He's dead!" she screamed, covering her head with the blanket. As Leah started to sit down on the couch, Katrina kicked her.

Silence. The next voice was Steven's. "Calm down, Katrina," he said, resting his hand on her arm. "What's the matter?"

"I got . . . a letter." She sniffled. "From my . . . boyfriend. He got . . . shot. In Florida. . . ."

"Katrina—"

"I'll never see him again!" Her voice broke into sobs.

"I'm sorry," Steven said quietly.

"I want to be dead!"

Steven held her arm. "I know you must feel that way but—" He stared down at her. "I'd hate for you to be dead. We all would."

"It's so unfair!" Her face appeared from under the blanket, streaked and blotchy red. Her glasses had slipped off; her eyes were watery and unfocused. *"I can't stand it!"*

"I know it doesn't feel like it, but you're going to survive this, you really are," he said.

She pressed a handful of blanket against her face. Biting into it hard, she only succeeded in choking herself. "Can I— can I stay in my room this afternoon?" she asked finally. "I couldn't just . . . go to class."

"Yes, of course."

"Maybe after group, I could . . . I could sort of go outside? And walk around?"

"We'll see."

He helped her to her feet and walked slowly upstairs with her. "I'll be just down the corridor, if you want to talk or use the phone or anything," he said, leaving her in her room.

"There're a lot of people here who care about you, Katrina."

She paused in her doorway. "Thanks ... Steven," she said, and shuffled to her bed, the blanket trailing on the floor behind her.

He watched her lie down. Then he went to the staff office, leaving the door ajar so that he could hear her. He called the Westchester County office to find out what he could about Joey, but Katrina's probation officer was on vacation.

News of Katrina's grief spread throughout the school. Within twenty minutes, every girl had heard one version or another of it, even though they were separated into various classrooms. Whispers spread up and down rows; girls met in corridors and bathrooms to discuss the tragedy, which cut across the normal boundaries of hostility between units, and united black, Puerto Rican, and white girls in an upsurge of sympathy and solidarity.

"Those cracker cops sure is cold!"

"What, Joey was black?"

"Why you think they shot that poor boy like that?"

"Shot him in the back, too!"

"Katrina talking about killing her own self."

"You watch, staff going to wolf her into going to group and everything."

"Staff just as bad as cops, anyway."

"They worse. They *mind* cops!"

"If that girl off herself, it'll be they fault."

"Damn straight!"

"Katrina be better off dead than in this place."

"How you talk, girl?"

"At least maybe she'd get to see Joey that way!"

In the classrooms, no one concentrated on lessons. In English, the girls reading about an Olympic figure skater's wedding choked up and had to leave the room. In history class, no one volunteered to read aloud: the chapter on "Opening the American Frontier," with its descriptions of settlers massacring Indians, paralleled too closely the recent massacre in Florida, and the teacher had to occupy the class time talking into a wall of damp, burning eyes.

Leah patrolled the hallways and bathrooms, chased the girls back to class, sat in the classrooms with them until her presence forced them to at least keep quiet. Then she checked to see if Katrina was all right. She was lying on her bed staring at the Florida postcard on her wall.

"What I wonder," Leah said to Steven, "is how she got this news before mailtime."

"That's a thought." Steven looked up from his desk.

"Start group session without me." Leah headed down the front stairs to talk with the secretaries. When she bore straight down on Mrs. Williams in the front office with a narrow-eyed, determined look on her face, Mrs. Williams' fingers froze in the air above her typewriter keys.

"Why that girl Katrina got her mail early today?" Leah asked her. "Was she in here trying to sweet-talk you again?"

"No. She came in to clean." The secretary looked around quickly, as if expecting to see Katrina somewhere. "She said she was doing another girl's chore."

"And you believed her?"

"The mail's gone!" Mrs. Williams gaped at the filing cabinet behind her.

Leah surprised her with a smile. "That child's going to make us all look like monkeys before she is through with us."

"But she was just in there." Mrs. Williams pointed to the last office.

Leah walked in, then leaned over and picked up some envelopes from the floor. "Right. We're on the track. . . . I think I have got it." She picked up a crumpled ball of paper from the corner.

Unfolding it, she held it close to her face to read the scrawled lines. "Hunh!" she said, and clicked her tongue loudly—a particularly ominous sound she sometimes made. Whenever the girls heard it, they held their breath; it meant that somebody's number was up.

Group session in the lounge was nearly over when Leah walked in. The girls were sitting in a circle in folding chairs, not moving except to light cigarettes and pass half-smoked saves to each other. To bring everyone's anxieties out in the open, and thus try to prevent hysteria from breaking out later, Steven had been encouraging the girls to discuss their own experiences with death. This would also give Katrina comfort in knowing that others were familiar with grief, too.

Leah, who had been standing behind the chair left empty for her, crossed the circle and handed Steven a crumpled letter. She saw Katrina's face suddenly go pale, and calculated how fast she would have to move if the girl tried to make a dash for the exit.

Steven smoothed out the letter. Inez began to tell the group about her uncle who'd been knifed in the hallway of his building. Steven frowned as he read. His jaw tightened. He pulled a cigarette out and clamped it between his teeth as if to prevent them from grinding together.

The letter read:

> ... and so when I seen Joey at the Super Sub with Franny I gave him your letter and axed him what are you going to do about Kat? He went, what the fuck am I supposed to do, she is locked up aint she? An the next day him and Franny split for deleware. I always toll you you hadnt ought to of trusted that dude

Steven stared at the sprig of pink flowers above the scrawled handwriting. The stationery was dime-store imitation rag paper, thick and yellow and dumb—a prop in a soap opera too tacky even for the afternoon TV shows these kids watched. Not too tacky, though, for him to have played a supporting role in.

Across the circle, the story continued about the uncle who got knifed, the aunt who was too grief-stricken to eat for weeks, the cousin who swore revenge but just got drunk and smashed up his best friend's car. This, too, was bad drama. But like Katrina's grief at her abandonment, it was real.

He glared at her, then dropped the letter into his lap and took a deep breath. ''That's a sad story about your uncle,'' he told Inez. ''When you get a knife in the back, it makes you want to retaliate, doesn't it?''

Silence. The girls stared at him. Cigarettes being passed were pulled in.

"And there're different ways of getting stabbed," he continued, picking up the letter. "You can get stabbed with words, can't you?" He had what the girls called his crazy look in his eyes. "But what happens when you stab somebody back?" He pointed at Lucia, a girl who had been arrested for, among other things, stabbing another girl in a school bathroom.

"Me?" Lucia's face went red. "You get in trouble. You feel real bad, man." She shook her head. "Payback ain't worth it."

"Thank you." Steven lit his cigarette and blew a long stream of smoke out of his nostrils. He turned slowly toward Katrina. "That's the best I can do for you, kid."

Katrina covered her face with her hands.

Out of the corner of his eye, Steven saw Leah leaning forward in her chair, watching the girls' reactions. He glanced at his watch. "We've only got a few minutes left," he told Katrina. "Is there anything you'd like to say?"

Her hands fell slowly. She stared at the cigarette in Steven's hand.

"Can I get saves?" she asked.

"Hunh!" Leah said. She clicked her tongue like the crack of doom.

10 ✍

The instant group session was over, Katrina hurried downstairs, avoiding the glares of the other girls, and slipped out
the front door. She ran in a crouch between the cars in the
parking lot, and then dashed onto the wooden footbridge that
arched over the narrow end of the pond. Halfway across, she
stopped suddenly. The melting snow on the other side looked
very cold. It would soak through her sneakers right away. As
soon as she got into the dark woods beyond the field, her jeans
and T-shirt wouldn't be warm enough. She'd have to run
faster to keep up her body heat, but eventually she'd collapse,
exhausted, onto the snow. The wind would howl through the
trees; night would fall. Steven and Leah and the girls would
go looking for her, worrying, feeling awful. It would take
them days to find her frozen body, if they ever found it at
all. . . .

Feeling the bridge reverberate beneath her feet, she gripped
the railing. She half-turned around. Steven was approaching
her slowly.

"You don't have to run." His voice was calm. "I won't
hurt you or lock you up."

She didn't move. The planks trembled. She didn't want
to look at him. Those crazy blue eyes of his would look right
through her. "I ain't going back in there," she said, facing
away from the building.

He rested his elbow on the railing, saying nothing. His

suit jacket was unbuttoned; his bright red tie shone in the weak sunlight.

"You can't make me go back," she said.

"Okay, I won't try and make you," he said. "I'm sorry about Joey."

Katrina frowned. She hadn't expected to hear that from him. Joey. She tried to bring back a picture of him, so that she could feel sad and deserve the sympathetic tone of Steven's voice, but Joey was hard to picture. She preferred to remember him behind the wheel of his car. The way he leaned forward as he drove, the way his arms flexed as he swung the car into a turn—he'd seemed to be mysteriously propelling her along the road with just the energy of his body.

And now Franny—that asshole, why *her*?—was driving someplace with him. She ought to have felt jealous of Franny, but all she envied was that somebody else was speeding off someplace, with the trees swishing by, leaving everything behind. Leaving her behind. She wasn't going anyplace. And she wouldn't be. She'd lost her what?—not her boyfriend, so much. Her ticket. He'd been her ticket. Like the old Beatles song, "She's Got a Ticket to Ride"—it was as if that music had been playing in her mind for as long as she could remember. It was her theme song. And suddenly somebody'd switched it off and pulled out the plug. All that was left was silence.

She squinted down at the pond. Some of the ice had melted and the surface of the water was ripply, reflecting a darkening blue sky. Clouds drifted across it, still white and fluffy. They seemed to be in a hurry because of the way the breeze blew the ripples, but they never reached the pond's bank. The bridge swayed whenever she or Steven shifted their weight. She felt as if she were standing on something that was floating in place rather than being attached to the land.

"Joey ain't the only friend I got," she said, her voice loud and scratchy. "I got lots of friends at home. They won't snitch on me when I get there."

"You're thinking of heading for home?" Steven asked.

"You don't think I'll make it, do you? You think my

mother'd turn me in. But my grandfather won't let her! Me
and him are real close.''

''I see.''

''Even if I had to go back to court,'' she insisted, ''the
judge probably wouldn't send me back here.''

''No?''

''I heard of lots of kids who split from joints and the
judge figured if they couldn't make it in a bunch of institutions, they might as well have another chance at home.''

''Maybe.''

''I been in Family Court lots of times,'' she said, almost
yelling at the pond. ''I know every judge in Westchester
County!''

He leaned over the railing to look sideways at her. ''Who
are you trying to convince?''

''Nobody.'' She turned her face away. Something inside
her had just collapsed. Her voice was barely audible. ''Would
you call the cops if I split?''

''I'd have to.''

''I don't care.''

''I hope you wear something warmer than what you've
got on. This weather won't last long. It's supposed to snow
tonight.''

Katrina squinted up at him. He was looking at the place
where the pond turned into a brook. She didn't like the look
of that little river. There was ice on the rocks; they shone
like silver teeth. Katrina shivered. The breeze seemed to be
blowing faster over the water. Her nipples were hard inside
her T-shirt, which was sort of embarrassing, but not so much
that she turned all the way away from Steven.

''You don't give a damn if I leave, do you?'' she said.
''You must be pissed off at me for lying about—about what
the letter said.''

''I was plenty pissed off. But I don't stay mad very long.
Not for something like that.''

''Like what?'' Katrina's lower lip stuck out.

''Well, the way I figure it, you were hurt, and mad as hell
at Joey. So you killed him off—in your imagination.''

"You think you're real smart, don't you?"

"You bet." He grinned. "But you know, it wasn't so hard to figure out. I've killed off a bunch of people, myself."

"You have?"

"Sure. People who've hurt me, or cut out on me, or whatever. Sometimes they get accidentally run over by a truck, or they get some kind of awful disease—syphilis, leprosy, something that wastes them away slowly, you know what I mean?"

Katrina pretended to scratch her cheek to cover a smile.

"Sometimes I even have them shot, like you did. There's a recurring fantasy I have about my ex-wife. A Japanese bandit breaks into her house, right? When she gets home and opens the door, he panics and—bang!—right between the eyes." Steven slammed his fist into the palm of his hand. "Afterward, I'm very sad, of course. I put on my best suit and go to the funeral. I tell all my friends what a good woman she was, despite the way she treated me. They're impressed with my sincerity. But as I walk away from the church, I'm inwardly all aglow." He watched her face. "So even though what you did was sort of a lie, I can understand where you were coming from."

She squeezed against the railing, the wooden crossbar against her stomach. The sun had dropped beneath the tops of the trees. The lawn beyond the pond was not as green as it had been, and she could make out big patches of snow along the edge of the field. She hugged her arms across her chest to keep from shivering.

"Those girls in there, they won't understand where I was coming from," she said.

"Not without you around to explain it to them," he said.

"I ain't got nothing to explain to them."

"You must be pretty scared about facing them. I don't blame you."

"I don't give a damn what they think. I ain't scared!"

He leaned toward her so that she had to turn her face away. "Maybe just a little bit chicken?" he asked.

"Fuck you!" Katrina ground her teeth together until they hurt. "Damn, anybody'd be nervous. The girls've got to be really pissed at me. They probably think I was trying to get over on them or something.''

''Yeah, they might think that.''

''They'll fucking kill me! My ass won't be worth two cents!''

''Oh, I don't know,'' he said. ''Maybe a nickel.''

''Ha ha.''

''I don't think the girls will stay mad at you all that long. Not if you're straight with them.''

''You don't know that group. They got their little cliques—Ronnie and Peaches and the family 'n' shit.''

''I can see you're in a tough spot.''

She squinted up at him. ''You going to help me explain?''

''Hell, no. It's your responsibility.'' He flicked a leaf off the railing.

Katrina watched it float under the bridge. ''How come you want me to stay so much? I must be nothing but a big pain for you.''

''Sometimes you are,'' he said. ''But I kind of like you.''

She turned away. ''How come? I remind you of your daughter or something?'' The way he jerked his head around toward her made her wish she hadn't asked that.

''Well . . . I guess all you girls do in some ways. But my daughter's only nine, so there's not a close resemblance or anything.'' He leaned over the railing. ''I know you girls better than I do her—that's funny, isn't it?''

Katrina watched his face. The smile lines beside his eyes were still there, though he wasn't smiling anymore. ''You see us all the time,'' she said. ''We're all you got.''

''Yeah. . . .'' He stared into the pond, where Katrina's and his reflections were floating like a wrinkled picture on the water. ''I'm not fond of you because you remind me of some-one else, though,'' he said. ''It's because of who you are, Katrina.''

She didn't move. The bridge trembled under her feet again when he shifted his weight beside her. No one had ever spoken to her this way.

The breeze was blowing right at her, making her nipples so hard they almost hurt, but she didn't care. Steven looked

as if he didn't mind staying here with her—not talking, just
being here. Had he noticed how skinny she looked with just
her T-shirt? Maybe he thought she was retarded the way
Vonita was, no cunt hair or anything, like she was just a little
kid. If he knew she wasn't like that, he might roughhouse
with her and hug her in play, the way he sometimes did other
girls. The thought made something catch in her throat.

She'd felt like this yesterday after a dream. Not a dream,
more a daydream, a picture story she'd gotten in her head
several times since she'd been at the school. In it, she and
Steven were driving to the hospital because she had sprained
her arm. It was real snowy on the road, and the car skidded
into a ditch and they were stuck there. He said, Katrina, we'll
just have to stay here until another car comes along. But no
car did come because the roads were so slippery, so they just
sat there and talked a little and looked out the window at the
snow falling all soft and white. Then the car's heater broke
and he said, Katrina, you can move up close and keep warm
if you want. So she did, because it really got cold and she
was shivering, and after a while she was sort of sitting on his
lap because that was the only way she could sit comfortably
with her sprained arm. He said, Katrina, I'm sorry about
your arm, you're being an even braver little kid than my
daughter was when she hurt her wrist once. She told him that
she was brave because she really wasn't a little kid. But she
wasn't sure he believed her. Then she said she had to get out
and take a piss. No, she didn't say it like that, she just did
it. And her underpants got wet in the snow, so she took them
off before she got back into the car and hid them under the
seat. She wasn't wearing jeans; she had on a state dress so
she could go to the hospital looking like a lady. But it wasn't
an old faded one like Mary wore, it was pretty and new-
looking, light blue like her eyes with stitching on the pockets
It was nice, except it was too short, it hardly covered her
knees. And because she and Steven were sitting so close on
the seat, his hand sort of fell down between her legs and he
felt that she had hair down there. And he said, Katrina, you're
really not a little kid at all. And she said, Hell no, I'm a

woman. And he said, I know, I can tell that now. And he just kind of stroked her down there. At first he did it in the kidding way he ruffled the girls' heads sometimes. But after a while he was stroking her more seriously, harder, like he meant it for a woman. He didn't stick his finger up her like Joey with his damn broken fingernail, he just stroked the hair and the bump inside it and she leaned her face against his shoulder as he stroked and nuzzled her cheek with his mustache, and suddenly she got her climax. She kept holding onto him. His arms went around her. And they just stayed sitting together like that without saying anything, and that was all they did, he didn't tell her to play with his dick or anything, he just liked to be there in the car with her, with the snow falling outside and his arms around her. . . .

Damn!

What the hell was she thinking about? Man, if he dared lay a finger on her now, she'd scream like hell and everybody'd come running out of the building. Maybe she wouldn't scream *that* loud, just loud enough so that he'd know he couldn't push her around. . . . She slid along the railing away from him.

"Katrina," he said finally, and smiled at her—just an ordinary smile but it made her turn away with burning cheeks. "I think we ought to go back inside now."

"I don't want to go back in there. That place ain't helping me," she said. "You can't help me!" she added wretchedly.

He sighed. "All I can do is try. But mostly, you've got to help yourself. You know that."

"Okay, *okay*!" Katrina had heard his rap about learning to be straight with the group, learning to be responsible for her actions and so forth. She could tell from the tone of his voice that he didn't want to talk about that stuff any more than she wanted to hear about it. The way they'd been talking to each other before was much better.

"How do I know I won't get stomped in there?" Katrina asked.

"You won't have to fight anybody."

"How do you know? You're not around all the time."

"We haven't had a fight on the unit since before you came here. The girls are talking about problems in group session instead."

"I ain't afraid to talk up in group."

"I know you're not. But I think you can do even more." He took out a cigarette, then offered Katrina one. "Lots of times you get mad and say what you think, and that's great. But then you give up quickly and just say the hell with it. You let people get away with stuff after you've called them on it."

"What, like Ronnie and Peaches?"

"Well . . . like Ronnie and Peaches, for instance."

She took a cigarette from the pack. "You want me to break up the way they run things, is that it?"

He shook his head. "I didn't say that," he told her.

"You meant it, though. I can tell."

"What I meant is, if you see girls messing up, hurting themselves or others, you don't have to just let it drop as if you couldn't do anything about it. You've got as much power as any girl in the group. That's all." He waited for a match from Katrina, but she held onto her matchbook after she'd lit her cigarette.

"Sure, okay." Katrina turned the matchbook over in her palm. "But you got to be straight with me. If I do this—if I take on Ronnie and Peaches—what are you going to do for me?"

"I'm not asking you to take on anybody, dammit."

Katrina raised her cigarette to her lips and inhaled deeply, eyeing him carefully as if he were a loan shark. "What if some girls, say for instance Ronnie and Peaches or somebody, try to kick my ass?"

"We're not having any violence on our unit."

"Just suppose?"

"Well, I'd back you, of course."

"Deal!" She handed him the matchbook.

He frowned at it. "I don't make special deals. I don't want you to think that."

"Whatever you want to call it." Katrina glanced away, her cigarette poking out between her lips. "Anyway, what about my coming out here today? How long do I have to stay locked up?''

''There're no more detention cells or anything like that here.''

''Not even for runaways? When they're brought back?''

''No.'' Steven lit his cigarette. ''Besides, you're not a runaway. You never left school property.''

She grinned. ''Hey, yeah!''

''You were out of the building without permission, though. You'll have to take a discipline for that from the group. They're going to get on you for it, and I'm not going to stop them either.''

''Deal.'' Katrina snatched the matchbook out of his hand and started to walk past him across the bridge.

He held out his arm, blocking her path. ''It's not—''

''It's an agreement, okay?'' She walked into his arm. She stopped, turning so that her cheek rested against his cuff. ''I'm glad I didn't take off when I saw you coming,'' she said. ''I almost did.''

''I'm glad we talked, too. You're not so nervous anymore, are you?''

She took a step forward. The bridge trembled underfoot. The way she was pushing against him, his arm almost had to go around her shoulders. But when he pulled her close for a moment, she knew he'd done that on purpose. ''Who was nervous?'' she said as he started to walk beside her. ''You're nuts if you think I was going to run away. I just wanted some fresh air.''

So that he wouldn't let go of her, as he would have had to do in a moment, Katrina squirmed free and ran across the parking lot toward the building.

11 ❧

As soon as the midnight-to-eight lady was asleep in her armchair at the end of the corridor, Ronnie knocked lightly on Peaches' door. Katrina, half asleep, rolled over in her bed to face the wall with a snorting sound.

Peaches sat up. "Damn, you took long enough," she whispered to Ronnie, pulling on her pink state bathrobe. "I almost started without you." The two girls tiptoed along the corridor and scampered down the back stairs, Peaches' slippers flop-flopping against her heels.

They ran across the basement rec room to the door of the large closet which, in former times, had been used to lock up violent girls or returned runaways. Now it was used for storage. Ronnie and Peaches called it their "nest." Ronnie opened the door with a key that she'd bought for three cartons of cigarettes from a second-floor girl; she and Peaches made the place their own in a series of ritualized movements. Ronnie climbed on a stack of tires and screwed into the fixture a safelight bulb stolen from the darkroom. Peaches handed her up a tasseled lampshade, also brought out from its hiding place beneath a tangle of jumper cables. Then they made a pallet on the floor out of some heavy overcoats. The gold light looked warm like a muted sun but the air in the room was freezing. The two girls lay down and hugged each other tight, oblivious to the audience of silhouetted gas cans, rubber boots, and snow shovels surrounding them.

Ronnie kissed Peaches slowly, fiercely, her tongue sliding

along the inside of her lips. Peaches began to gasp and squirm against her, making high-pitched squeaking sounds. Then, with a sudden "Ow!" she pushed away from Ronnie.

Ronnie sat up. "What?"

"You hurt my mouth with your teeth," Peaches muttered. "Some kinda Dracula."

"I didn't mean to, girl." Ronnie pressed her hand against her stomach.

Peaches looked at her hand, then up at her face. "Your ulcer bothering you again?"

"Yeah. I got to get more pills, but I hate to go to the Nurses' Station when Evans is on." She leaned forward, her fingers digging into her bathrobe. "It started in group session today. Did you see how that fucking Kat tried to take the whole thing over? Whenever she around the Fox, she be coming out her mouth any damn way she want to."

"*I* talked up, Ronnie," Peaches said.

"I know. It didn't do no good."

Peaches took Ronnie's free hand and pressed it over her breast. "You said a lot of good stuff. I couldn't have thought of the stuff you said."

"I couldn't talk as much as I needed to. It was Whale's radio Pam stole. One black girl backing another one—they would've been all over my ass." Ronnie frowned. "You see how Yvonne went along with Kat today? Yvonne ready to jump into my place ever since that girl come here."

"Everybody knows you're the boss, Ronnie. Nobody wants to fuck with you."

"Not yet." Ronnie shook her head. "But I just know the Fox put Kat in your room to bust us up."

"I ain't getting off with Kat." Peaches turned on her side, propped up on her elbow.

"Better not be."

"I ain't. Damn, Ronnie, she ain't even into butch 'n' femme stuff."

"Yeah, okay. But she still going to mess up the family if she keep running her mouth in group."

"Our family's real together compared with the second floor," Peaches said. "You know Panda, suppose to be the big butch down there? She can't control her girls for shit. Heatwave and Sheba left her last week; now she's trying to wolf Julia's girls. That's how come Julia jumped her."

"I heard." Ronnie held her stomach again, sucking in her breath sharply. "You're not messing with any of those second-floor bitches, are you?"

"Hey, not me!" Peaches sat up. "If I listened to any of those girls, my head'd be *all* fucked up. Ever since I started going with you, I been more together than I ever been." She wiped a tear from her eye. "I don't understand why you get uptight with me. You're my man, Ronnie. I love you. I don't want to be scared of you."

Ronnie reached out and stroked Peaches' hair. "I ain't trying to scare you."

"Before I come here, if some dude said they liked me, it meant they'd always be pushing me around, grabbing at me, slapping my face if I ever looked sideways at anybody else." Peaches shivered and pulled her bathrobe around her. "They'd be holding me till I felt like I couldn't breathe and I had to explode or something to get away. You never done that, Ronnie."

"It ain't you. It's just that when somebody think they bad enough to try and take my woman, I get down to kill like a motherfucker. I know Kat probably ain't trying nothing but sometimes when I look at her, I feel crazy."

"As long as you're here, I ain't going with nobody else." Peaches moved closer to Ronnie and pressed her lips against her cheek.

"That's good. 'Cause if I wasn't here—"

"Well, if you wasn't *here*—"

Ronnie turned her face, pushing Peaches' nose with hers. "Yeah, you be fucking everybody in sight, like you was before."

Peaches grinned. "Maybe."

"You *would,* too!" Ronnie punched her lightly in the arm. "You be fucking the squirrels out of the trees and the roaches under the sink."

"I don't know about no roaches, but some of them squirrels is kinda cute." Peaches punched Ronnie back.

Ronnie's arm went around her neck and together they slid sideways onto the coats. Peaches opened up her bathrobe, her big breasts rolling apart on her chest. Ronnie ran her tongue over them, feeling the nipples hardening between her lips. Peaches began to moan softly. Her legs parted immediately when Ronnie's fingers burrowed into the soft hair beneath her panties. Peaches squirmed, thighs rising and falling, her head thrown back so that her hair swirled out onto the floor.

"Lift up!" Ronnie whispered, struggling to pull Peaches' panties down over her hips. "Damn, you got a fat ass!"

"*You* like it." Laughing, Peaches arched her back, then went "Oof!" as Ronnie lay on top of her.

With one arm beneath her belly, Ronnie wedged the back of her hand into her own crotch, her fingers moving into place between Peaches' legs. She ground slowly against her knuckles and Peaches' thighs. She wanted to rest her face on Peaches' soft breasts and let herself go, but she didn't dare—if she relaxed completely she might come, but then the agony in her stomach would start up afterward sharper than ever. Ronnie was excited enough just to feel Peaches squirming helplessly beneath her, every moan and cry directed totally by the slightest movement of her fingers.

"You my woman forever?" Ronnie whispered, leaning close to Peaches' ear.

"Yes—"

"Say it!"

"I'm your woman, Ronnie!" Peaches gasped. "More— *inside*—"

As Ronnie slid two fingers into the moist opening, Peaches cried out, her head rolling back. Ronnie concentrated on the thrusting movements of her hand, and for a moment, without even touching herself, she felt a warmth creeping up inside her. But then Peaches cried *"Harder!"* in a voice loud enough for the night watchman to hear, and Ronnie had to cover her mouth.

Whimpering, Peaches rolled her head; her free arm flailed out and clanged against a gas can. Finally she arched her hips, made a long sobbing sound, and collapsed back down.

She lay still, groaning. Ronnie lay beside her, her knees drawn up tight against her stomach.

"Ronnie?—"

"Mm."

"What about you? Don't you want me to—"

"I'm all right."

"You sure?"

"I'm all *right*." Ronnie straightened her legs and held Peaches in her arms.

"Ronnie, you're so strong. You love me so good."

Ronnie touched her finger to Peaches' lips. "Shhh." Shutting her eyes, she stroked Peaches' hair.

Peaches snuggled in tighter, but no matter now close Ronnie held her, Peaches couldn't stay still. Finally she rolled over onto her back, her bathrobe open, her bare legs and thighs glowing in the yellow-tinted light. "Cold," she whispered, groping for an overcoat.

Ronnie covered her and tucked the coat around her. Peaches' beautiful hair was spread out in a swirling pattern on the cement floor behind her head. Lying close to her again, Ronnie pressed a handful of hair against her cheek, inhaling its scent of sweet shampoo and the smell of Peaches' sex on her own fingers, letting the softness of the hair make her feel nothing but soft inside.

Much too soon, she heard the night watchman's footsteps upstairs. Reverberating down the walls, the sound tramped in spiked boots along the lining of her stomach.

Steven and Leah took a weekend off in New York. When Steven returned, the first thing he saw was a wad of bloody sheets overflowing the garbage can beside the back door. He ran up the steps two at a time. Katrina, who had spotted his car through the window, was waiting for him just inside.

"What the hell's going on?" He pointed at the sheets. "Did one of our girls get hurt?"

"No, it was Panda." Katrina pulled him by the cuff of his overcoat. "Come on, you got to look at her!"

He walked quickly with her through the Nurses' Station to the two rooms behind it that served as an infirmary. Peering through the window of one of the doors, he saw a plump white girl huddled on the floor in the corner of the room. Her dark hair with its peroxide streak hung shaggy over her face. Both her arms were wrapped in bandages. Except for a blood-stained bra and panties, she was naked. All the room's furniture had been removed; around her the wallpaper was in tatters, as if an explosion had ripped through the place. Patches of smudged white plaster showed through like flayed skin.

"Hadn't you ought to get her out of there?" Katrina's voice was scratchy. "I mean, you said there weren't any lockup rooms here anymore."

"I know, I know." Steven leaned his forehead against the door.

"Are you just going to leave her in there?" Katrina shot out her arm to point at the window.

"No. I'm going to find out what happened—"

"If you'd been here, you'd know what happened!" Katrina dropped her arm and sighed through her teeth. "All right, I'll tell you what fucking happened. Panda stabbed a second-floor staff and then Mrs. Evans beat her up. And now Paleno's going to ship her."

"Thank you, Katrina." Steven pulled off his trench coat and wanted to remove his suit jacket as well, he was so hot and sweaty. "Now I'm going to get on the phone and see if I can't get her out of this room, so—"

"It's about time!"

"So if you'll get back to class—"

"Okay, okay. Fuck!" Katrina walked away, her head down.

From what he could find out, Panda had been trying to bring new girls into her family—Peaches' and Katrina's names were mentioned—and had been attacked by two girls from a rival second-floor family, one of whom swore afterward that Ronnie had put her up to the attack. When a staff member intervened, Panda stabbed her in the thigh with a sharpened butter knife stolen from the kitchen. It took four adults to drag Panda upstairs from the basement. Mrs. Evans had called Ben Paleno, who had given her permission to lock the girl in the infirmary. Though she was strip-searched, Panda somehow managed to bring into the room a pop-top from an aluminum soda can. Left alone, she slashed the wallpaper, cut the bed sheets to ribbons, tore open the mattress, and emptied the stuffing all over the floor. When no one came to confront her screams, she sliced the pop-top up and down both arms until they were dripping with blood. There was some question about whether Mrs. Evans had used excessive force in taking the pop-top from Panda. A girl who said she'd witnessed a beating retracted her story shortly after talking with Mr. Paleno.

When Steven finally reached Matt Steiner at a conference in Albany, he got permission to release Panda from the infirmary room for the afternoon. There was no reason, though, to countermand Ben Paleno's decision to send her to another institution; with her extensive record of previous violence, she should never have been admitted in the first place.

Steven had the maintenance men strip and paint the infirmary room, and by late afternoon the place looked as if nothing had happened there. But the damage had been done— the staff were discouraged; the girls were scared and edgy. As in the days before the New Program, violence was out in the open, not just as an expression of one girl's anger against the staff, but of the institution's power over the kids.

After Panda left, Steven went into his office to get ready for group session. He made himself a cup of tea, stirred sugar into it until it spilled over, and then didn't drink any. Footsteps clumped around upstairs; girls screamed down corridors, slammed doors. Every sound made invisible blood vessels jump like insects trapped just under his skin. It was a sensation he'd first had as a kid in a juvenile jail, one which had come back at other institutions where he'd worked whenever there were vibrations of impending violence in the air. If he didn't find some way around the civil service regulations that protected Ben Paleno's job on the second floor, those days would be back again. Meanwhile, he had to at least keep the violence from spreading to his own floor.

Katrina arrived in the lounge early and set up her folding chair not in its usual position near Steven but directly across the circle from him. Being angry with him, she wanted to sit as far from him as possible; being scared that he was mad at her for her bad temper earlier, she wanted to be directly in his line of vision so that she could check his facial expressions for signs of forgiveness. The other girls shuffled in. Inez, who was making another sweater for her daughter, took out her knitting. Ronnie assumed her usual position in the armchair no one else dared sit in during group sessions. Peaches tilted her chair toward Ronnie. When Steven sat down, everyone stopped talking. Matches flared as cigarettes were lit.

"So, who's got something to bring up?" Peaches opened, as she usually did. After a few seconds of silence, Katrina saw Ronnie give Peaches an eye signal. Peaches leaned forward, a worried look on her face, and said, "Somebody's ripped off my hairbrush. It don't look like we've helped Pam get over her stealing problem yet."

Pam, her forefinger pressed to the bridge of her nose to keep her glasses in place, tearfully denied stealing the hairbrush. Immediately she was in an argument with two girls sitting across from her. Smiling faintly, Peaches and Ronnie sat back in their chairs. Katrina turned away from the group, grinding her teeth. Only when she heard Steven's voice did she turn back.

"I think this is bullshit," he said, his voice cutting off the argument like a falling ax. "There're a lot more important things to talk about than Peaches' hairbrush, and you're all avoiding them."

No one spoke. The only sound in the room was the clicking of Inez's knitting needles.

"Isn't anybody upset about what happened to Panda?" Steven asked.

The girls glanced at Ronnie and Peaches. Ronnie sat far back in her chair, her sweatshirt hood low on her forehead, her jaw set tight. Peaches, with a spacey expression, gave off the same message: Keep Quiet. Katrina saw it, but she also saw the look on Steven's face: his lips taut, his eyes slits of ice-blue anger. She couldn't stand to see him looking like that. "I'm upset," she said to him, her voice husky. "You told me you didn't have no lockup rooms here, and no fights. So how come you couldn't keep all that shit from happening to Panda?"

Suddenly everyone seemed to be talking at once, fears and

anxieties flapping in the air like birds released from cages.
The black girls, it turned out, feared retaliation from white
staff because the two girls who had originally attacked Panda
were black. The white girls had similar fears: Panda had
stabbed a black staff member. Katrina forgot that her question hadn't been answered. The loud talking and nervous
laughter were exciting, but scary. She was grateful when
Steven finally interrupted it.

"So this is a race issue?" he asked.

"No!" Katrina said, and was amazed when everyone agreed
with her.

"So what kind of an issue is it?" Steven asked.

Silence again. Nearly everyone looked at Ronnie.

"I don't see what all the uproar's about," she said. "Hell,
I'm sorry Panda got violent and had to get shipped. But
everybody knows those second-floor bitches always be fighting
and carrying on. It don't got nothing to do with us."

"Everything's cool up here," Peaches said. "Square business, man."

"Amen," said Whale, a huge black girl in a tentlike dress,
and Vonita, a skinny black girl with a child's voice, repeated
"Amen." Girls passed cigarettes back and forth, took deep
drags, blew smoke into the air.

"If it's so damn peaceful around here," Steven said, looking around at everyone, "why do I still feel so much tension?"

"It must be coming upstairs from the second floor," Ronnie said, getting some brief laughs.

"I'm worried," Steven said, not smiling. "I think girls
from our floor were involved in the violence downstairs. If
we don't talk about that, then we're going to have our own
troubles."

More silence. Inez's knitting needles clicked faster. Steven's gaze passed from girl to girl. Katrina tensed when he
got to her. She could tell he was still angry. When he got to
Ronnie, Ronnie turned her face away.

"Aw, don't be looking at me like that, man! I ain't done
no violence." She pushed herself farther back in her chair.
"Shit, you people always be thinking I love to fight. That's
a damn lie! You don't know how much I hate it!" Katrina

was amazed to hear Ronnie's voice, always so controlled, cracking. "Don't you remember how I told the group how I hated living up to my rep in my old neighborhood?" she went on. "One of the things I don't mind about this place is I don't have to worry all the time about whose ass I got to kick before she kicks mine."

"I do remember you saying that, Ronnie." Steven stood up and walked slowly around behind his chair. He pushed the window open on its hinges as far as it would go; the heavy cloud of smoke that had been hovering over the circle of girls began swirling slow motion toward it. Steven sat down again. "I'll tell you what I heard about Panda," he said, and everyone froze. "I heard that there're two families on the second floor, and the reason Panda got jumped was that she was trying to recruit some third-floor girls for her family."

"I never heard nothing like that." Ronnie glanced around.

Steven didn't reply. Katrina kept facing Steven, wondering what he would say next. Families had never been discussed in group sessions. Katrina had assumed that the same deal worked here as elsewhere: the staff left the families alone, and in return, the families made the staffs' jobs easier by keeping a certain amount of peace. Katrina—and from the looks of them, several other girls as well—hoped that Steven would break the subject wide open. She was sick of having to pretend that family life didn't exist—it was like having a wild elephant in a small room with you that was stomping on your toes and drooling into your food, but you couldn't get rid of it because nobody, including you, dared let on it was there.

Steven leaned forward, his elbows on his knees, his muscles under his rolled-up sleeves tense. "I know, and I know you know, that there's never been a girls' institution where girls didn't get involved with each other. Sometimes as friends, sometimes as lovers." No one looked at him except Katrina. No one moved. "In some places the staff try to keep girls from having emotional or sexual relationships. We don't do that here. Everybody needs affection, and there wouldn't be any point in trying to keep girls from having it." He paused.

Katrina rested her ankle on her knee and tugged at the

frayed threads of her cuff. Sounds that had never been part of group sessions—a car engine outside starting up, a dog barking far away—got into the room through the open window.

"I also know," Steven said, "that a lot of girls miss their families at home, or the ones they wish they'd had at home, and they make up families here. So on the second floor, there're fathers and mothers, brothers and sisters, husbands and wives. This arrangement gives some girls a lot of emotional support. The trouble is, it leads to jealousies and rivalries. And eventually you get the kind of violence Panda was involved in." Steven sat up. His mustache looked bristlier than Katrina had ever seen it.

"I never heard about any of that family shit on the second floor," Ronnie said finally.

"I never did either, Mr. Fox," Peaches said, and gazed around at the girls. No one disagreed with her. Several girls shivered from the cold air.

The longer the silence went on, the angrier Steven looked. Katrina couldn't take it any longer. "We had a family setup at Maviskill," she said. "They called it the racket."

"That's what they called it at Belton," Whale said.

"At Harlem Annex it was just 'butch 'n' femme business,'" Lucia said.

Suddenly it was safe to talk, and everyone wanted to; the subject was other places, not here. Katrina cleared her throat loudly. "Anyway, I was always scared at Maviskill," she said. "The families had weapons and they were dealing drugs 'n' shit. If you was in one, you always had to defend it from other families. If you wasn't, like me, you didn't have nobody to protect you. Anybody could rip you off or slam you up against a wall anytime they felt like it."

Vonita, who was so excitable she never could sit still in group sessions, had been rocking in her chair ever since Katrina began. "Hey, dig it—" she said. "At this juvey hall I was in, there was these two big bull daggers, right? And one time they asked me, 'Don't you want to finger-pop with us, honey?' I didn't even know what it mean, I was so dumb. I was only twelve, shit!" She leaned forward, her face dropping into her hands. Katrina thought she was through, but she spoke through her fingers, gradually raising her voice. "They got me in this closet and they held my legs wide open—"

"Damn, Vonita!" Peaches said, making a face. "Will you stop—"

"Naw! It's true! Don't tell me it ain't true!" Vonita was almost screaming, her high voice making everyone squint as if she were dragging fingernails across their eyeballs. "That's why I ain't a virgin no more! That's why I can't get no periods or no climaxes neither!" She doubled over again, covering her face.

Katrina gripped her cuff tight, waiting. Vonita often started screaming or weeping or both; she could stop as quickly as she began. She leaned sideways against Whale, and Whale put her huge arm around her shoulder. Sniffling back a loop of mucus, Vonita looked at the group again. "I'm sorry," she whispered.

"It sounds like a lot of you've got memories of what it's like living with families," Steven said, filling the silence. "Sounds like you've had some scary experiences."

No one looked at him, but nobody disagreed or shook her head. Katrina noticed that the third-floor family was sitting in about the same pattern as the way it was organized: Ronnie and Peaches were together, Ronnie, the father, in the highest chair; Whale was being Vonita's mother as usual; Yvonne, Peaches' sister, was trying to edge up close to her; Lucia and Inez, daughters-in-law, were together on the couch. The girls not in the family—Pam, Mary, and her—were all on the opposite side of the circle together.

"I remember what it was like," Katrina said. "That's why the families on the second floor got me worried."

Everyone stared at her. Another taboo violated—no girl had ever talked about Fairbanks families in front of the staff. Katrina felt a trembly sensation in her legs; she kept her eyes fastened to Steven's face, and saw the tightness of his mouth relaxing. For a moment, everyone else disappeared, and she spoke just to him. "I don't want those girls coming after me again."

"Again?" Steven asked.

Katrina took a breath of cold, fresh air. "Yeah, Panda was trying to wolf me in the basement bathroom last week. She was saying third-floor girls weren't shit, I better join up with her now or I wouldn't have no choice about it later."

Ronnie turned her head slowly toward her. "Snitch," she said.

"I didn't snitch—Panda's not *here* anymore." Katrina glanced at her, then at Steven. "Hell, I wasn't the only one she was after."

When she said it to Steven, it sounded just right, and she felt her whole body relaxing. But when she looked around, the trembling inside her started up again fast; possibly this was the worst thing that she could have said. If he didn't know it already, Steven now knew that Peaches had been the other girl Panda had come after—otherwise, why would Ronnie be trying so hard to shut everybody up? And if he knew that, he could guess that Ronnie had put those two girls up to jumping Panda. Everybody knew they'd owed Ronnie favors. What everybody—the girls—knew was getting dangerously close to what Steven knew. Katrina didn't care any longer.

"I knew Panda was after third-floor girls," Steven said. "The second-floor staff told me Katrina wasn't the only one." He looked around.

Katrina sat back in her chair, feeling better: Steven was backing her. And he didn't expect her to say anything more now. Voices and footsteps echoed up the stairwell beyond the lounge door; the second-floor girls were coming upstairs from their supper shift. Their door slammed; the silence in the lounge swelled and swelled.

Finally, Peaches couldn't keep still any longer. "All right, it was me Panda was after," she said, and several girls let out their breath. "Damn, Mr. Fox, why didn't you just say it?"

"Thank you for speaking up, Peaches." Steven ran his fist along his mustache; it looked more like its usual shaggy self when he dropped his hand back to his lap. But his voice was still angry. "The reason I didn't say it was that I wanted you girls to bring this thing out in the open yourselves," he said. "If you won't, then there's going to be more people getting beat up and stabbed around here. We'll have the same kind of family hell-raising you've seen other places. Do you want that?" He glared at girl after girl until some of them shook their heads and mumbled "No." "Maybe you want the staff to lock everybody in their rooms and patrol the halls with shotguns. That's the only way it'll be safe around here if you don't take some responsibility and speak up."

"Talking don't solve everything," Ronnie muttered.

"It's the only way we've got to solve problems here," he said, his voice low and resonant, "and I'm going to make goddamn sure we use it."

The girls still looked uneasy, Katrina noted, but a lot less so than at the beginning of the session. It seemed easier to breathe. Inez's needles clicked along slowly. Along with everyone else, Katrina watched Steven look at his watch.

"Okay, we'll have to knock off now if we're going to get any supper. Just hold it—" He held out his hand as Ronnie began to push her armchair back against the wall. "I was going to put the group on a week's restriction for being so quiet. But Katrina's made a start, and Peaches, too. I'm still not satisfied, though." He stood up. "I'm putting the group on building restriction until we meet tomorrow." He strode out of the room, his boot heels reverberating down the corridor.

Muttering, the girls left the lounge quickly. Katrina, taking her time, folded her chair and then stood by the open window looking out. Tire tracks wound like white ribbons along the snowy driveway leading away from the school into a gap in the woods. The footbridge beside the parking lot was covered with snow. She remembered the afternoon she and Steven had talked there, and felt the cold air through her T-shirt. She turned away from the window, smiling. Then she stopped; Inez was watching her.

"Yo." Inez gave her a wave as she picked up a pack of cigarettes she'd left on top of the television. "You saved us all a week restriction. That's what the Fox wants us to think, anyway."

"I don't get you."

"Yeah, you do." Inez smiled, one hand on her hip. She was a chunky sixteen-year-old girl with big needle-scarred arms and a broad brown face. Everyone respected her, not just because she had served a year in jail for armed robbery, but because she never took sides in group politics. "I feel sorry for you, though, girl," she said, opening the lounge door. "Now you started, you ain't going to be able to stop."

"Stop what?" Katrina asked, but Inez was already on her way downstairs.

At supper, Steven sat by himself at a table in the corner of the dining room. He didn't feel like making small talk with the girls; besides, he needed to be a stern, angry parental figure for them right now.

He watched to see if the girls were giving Katrina a hard time for talking about family matters in front of staff. Though extra restless, they all seemed in a good enough mood, relieved, perhaps, that the worst had happened and no thunderbolt had exploded in their midst. They visited between tables, made loud jokes, yelled through the serving window at the kitchen girls until Sonia quieted them. Katrina, sitting at a table with Inez, Yvonne, and Mary, was yelling with the rest. At one point, Yvonne followed her to the food counter. Steven leaned forward to watch, his fork stopped in midair in front of his face. But Yvonne was grinning; whatever she said made Katrina nod and smile as she picked up a bowl to take back to her table.

Steven wondered if she had spoken up because she really believed that group sessions could prevent violence, or because she needed his approval more than the other girls did, or perhaps just because she enjoyed being original. Whatever her reasons were, she seemed to be all right for the time being.

But what about the rest of them? He knew perfectly well that no matter how many restrictions he put on them, they wouldn't challenge Ronnie and Peaches' authority until they saw the danger to themselves of *not* challenging it. Right now, they were probably glad that Ronnie had set things up so that Panda had gotten shipped. Never mind that Panda might have killed somebody. Never mind that Panda's family might seek retaliation on the third floor.

Fighting violence with violence was, to these girls, a more familiar survival technique than the one he was proposing, and he couldn't change their attitudes overnight. In other institutions where they'd been, the staff had ruled with an iron hand and they'd learned to band together for protection. Now, in times of crisis, they reverted to old instincts.

Steven pushed chunks of greasy venisonburger around on his plate, not hungry, brooding again. Wasn't he encouraging those instincts by dictatorially imposing a group punishment? No. Soon he'd start giving the girls back their decision-making freedom. He'd have to, or group session would become a meaningless ritual, like the meeting of a phony parliament in an absolute monarchy. What, though, would they use this freedom for? Could he—could anyone—give kids freedom while at the same time confining them in an institution?

"Hey, Steven—it's chocolate pudding tonight. Don't you want some?" He heard Katrina's voice nearby, but by the time he looked up, she was gone. He smiled. Then, as he headed for the food counter, Sonia called him away to the telephone.

Matt was calling from Albany. The second-floor staff, unable to reach Ben Paleno at home, had called Matt to say that the two girls who had attacked Panda had just run away. What do you want to do? Matt asked Steven, a question Steven knew was part of his training as future acting director. Let's tell the troopers, when they pick up the girls, to send them back to their hometowns for new court dates, Steven said; he would contact the judges himself to recommend the two girls be sent to more secure places—not Fairbanks. Sounds good, Matt said; do it.

By the time Steven returned to the dining room, only a few girls, mopping the floor, were left. Steven's plate of half-eaten food had been removed. In its place was a bowl of chocolate pudding. For a moment, Steven had a notion to take a picture of it.

That evening, Steven stayed at school with Sonia and watched a Jacques Cousteau TV documentary assigned as homework by the girls' science teacher. The program was called "Strange Creatures of the Deep." The girls were still very restless and didn't want to watch the show. Throughout the evening they kept getting up and leaving the lounge to fetch hairbrushes and skin cream and candy bars and cigarettes. Steven and Sonia kept bringing the girls back from their rooms to the lounge, only to find others gone. Tempers flared until finally the girls were put to bed.

That night, Steven dreamed that he was pushing a heavy wheelbarrow up a steep incline which ran alongside a precipice above a sea. The wheelbarrow was loaded up to his nostrils with live creatures of some kind—they looked like octopi and gave off loud wordlike noises. Writhing and kicking, they were all trying to squirm out of the wheelbarrow. As he pushed it, he simultaneously had to reach out every few moments to prod an octopus back in or pick up one that had slithered out. The wheelbarrow tilted on its single wobbly wheel. He couldn't stop pushing it for a moment; its forward motion was all that was keeping it upright. Suddenly it rolled backward onto him, pitching sideways. Creatures spilled out, crawling every which way, tumbling over the cliff. He lay half over the edge, trying to grab them as they fell, but they slipped through his fingers and disappeared forever among the waves. . . .

12 🙝

Katrina stood beside the open classroom doorway, waiting for the English teacher to turn the other way so that she could slip in unnoticed. Miss Freeman, the teacher, was a young woman in jeans, checkered blouse, and ponytail. She walked around the clusters of desks handing out the day's materials: workbooks, *Scholastic* magazine, high school equivalency examination study books. Also some comic books—"*After* you've done the homework pages!" The girls worked quietly in groups. An egg-shaped white girl with a STEVIE WONDER T-shirt walked around with a plastic bag of doughnuts, setting them down on girls' desks. Miss Freeman moved from group to group, looking over shoulders, helping girls with problems. As soon as she left them, the girls read the comic books on their laps.

Katrina, ducking low, scurried across the room to her desk by the wall beneath a poster of a cartoon rhinoceros in red basketball sneakers, captioned BOOKS ARE FOR EVERYONE. She opened her workbook in front of her face. Seeing her staring off into space, Miss Freeman sat at the empty desk beside her with a Spill 'n' Spell game. The object of the game, she explained, was to make as many words with the letter dice as possible within the time allotted by a plastic, two-minute, hour-glass-shaped timer. Points were given for each word. Katrina rolled the dice. She made RAT, BAT, BIG, GIG, then for bonus points, BRAT, DRAG, BRAG. . . .

"Hey, is this a word?" Katrina asked.

"Pronounce it."

"B . . . BRI . . . BRIN."

"Did you ever hear of it?"

"I don't know. There's lots of words I never heard of."

"Better look it up in the dictionary."

"Shit, all the sand's going to run out of the timer."

"It doesn't matter."

"The hell it doesn't. I won't get hardly any points."

"I'll turn it over."

"I don't got to cheat to get points. I ain't stupid." Katrina stood up wearily and got a dictionary from the Resources Shelf. It took her several minutes to find the BRI page. Miss Freeman sat beside her, a faint smile of encouragement nailed to her face.

"That word ain't in the dictionary," Katrina reported finally. "You knew that all along, didn't you?"

"I wanted you to have the experience of finding it out for yourself."

"Shit."

"I bet you can find another word with BRI in it."

Katrina slammed the dictionary shut. "You must think I'm a real dummy."

"Of course I don't, Katrina. . . ." Miss Freeman wiped her forehead. She pushed the letter dice around on the desk. "Look, here's a word."

Katrina glared at the dice. "That game's all fucked up," she said, meaning that Miss Freeman was. She snatched a Wonder Woman comic from the next desk and opened it on her lap.

"Those comics are for *after*—"

"Leave me alone. I'm reading."

"Well, all right. But I want you to write down three new words you find. Is that a deal?"

Katrina sat sideways in her chair, her shoulder to Miss Freeman. "I only make deals with people I trust," she said.

Miss Freeman sighed and looked at her watch. "Time to go to history," she said.

In a matter of seconds, the girls emptied the room, cigarettes already in their mouths as they raced toward the bathroom. Katrina led the pack.

▲   ▲   ▲

Mr. Swigart, short and powerfully built, with close-cropped hair and glasses, stood outside his classroom, his eyes narrowed against the loud voices of the girls crowding the corridor. Several of them tried to punch him in the stomach as they shuffled into his room. He pushed them away, smiling wearily. Yvonne slunk past him, tossing her long shiny hair so that it brushed his face. "What's happening, Swiggy baby?" she said over her shoulder. Whale waddled slowly through the door, aiming straight for him; he stepped deftly sideways. Katrina was the last to arrive; she stepped on his toe and darted away when he tried to cuff her.

Several girls were poring over a big *Picture History of Soul Music* book on a shelf. Mr. Swigart waded into their midst and closed the book. "You can look at it after we read." He stood at the front of the room, tapping his foot, his arms folded across his chest. Eventually the class was quiet.

Mr. Swigart had remodeled the room to make it look homey and as nontraditional as possible. All the school desks had been replaced with armchairs and huge pillows on the carpeted floor. There was a worktable in the back of the room. Whale and Ronnie, who were ahead of the other girls, often sat there doing their homework. No one else did homework.

"Today, I want to start part two of *Bury My Heart at Wounded Knee*. Who can recap what part one was about?"

"It's about a bunch of redneck Indians," a girl named Heatwave said from her armchair, yawning.

"Native Americans," Ronnie corrected her from the back of the room.

"Mary calls herself Indian," the girl said, "so kiss my ass!"

"Your momma can kiss your ass."

"Hey, Ronnie, your momma blows winos!"

"Yo' momma suck dog dick!"

"Yo' momma—"

"Cut it out!" Mr. Swigart yelled.

"I'm a native American," Ronnie said. "My people was here before yours were, Mr. Swigart."

"Right on," Whale said. "We ought to be the ones teaching *you*."

"You are, you are." Mr. Swigart shook his head. He started passing out paperback books. "Now who wants to read today?" he asked.

"Not me."

"I got a sore throat, man."

"That book's too hard."

"You know I don't like this class. Don't look at me."

Mr. Swigart looked at Katrina. "How about you?"

"I read too slow," Katrina said, glancing away.

"I'll read, Mr. Swigart," Inez said.

"Thank you, Inez." Mr. Swigart sat down hard on a pillow.

Inez read very slowly. The girls settled back onto their pillows, following the words in the book with their fingers. One by one, most of them closed their eyes and dozed.

In the back of the room, Whale finished her part of a joint book report and passed it to Ronnie, who was to write the conclusion. The book they had read was about life on a Sioux reservation; the massacres Ronnie read about in the report grated together in her mind with the descriptions of the Indian wars Inez was reading aloud. Meanwhile the pain in her gut throbbed as if it were rhythmically trying to gouge open a hole in her stomach. Pressing one hand against it, Ronnie snatched up a pen and began writing.

Reservations are not anything new to me. I always lived on one. The ghetto is just like one. We even got US Cavalry (cops) to patrol it, spies (social workers), and people selling fire-water (drugs). Everybody know its Mafia people selling all the heroin that the junkies always be shooting up. The reason the Mafia don't all get busted is because the US Calvalry want them around so they can kill off all the young braves real slow with drugs. If they didn't, the braves would be raising all kinds of hell like they done in Watts and Newark in the 1960s.

Now I am on a New York State Youth Service Reser-

*vation called the Fairbanks School. I am getting filled up
with history which is just one big heap of skeletons and
corpses. What am I supposed to DO with all this history
inside me?*

*You think I be smart enough to stop swallowing it.
Just sit around smiling at the TV set and listening to
disco records and practicing my typing to keep me from
getting mad. But I am not going to, I am going to just
KEEP RIGHT ON reading, keep RIGHT ON swallowing
every book I can get my black hands on. You think you
slick, Swigart and Fox and the rest of you folks, you
think you can always mow us down if we start acting up.
But you don't know what you got going here, it is bigger
than you think. You think we finished raising hell when
you moved your tanks into our ghetto reservations in the
1960s and shot our braves down on the street, you DUMB
people because you FUCK with my mind you going to
have to DEAL with the rest of me, ME and my SISTERS,
I got 13 counts of assault and Whale is almost up to 300
pounds and for a place like this that's a damn tank, she
already knock down one door, next time it be some WALLS
and they going to come crashing down on your heads and
THEN what you going to do motherfuckers?*

Ronnie stopped writing and stared out the window beside
the worktable. When Whale asked her if she were finished,
she turned her face away and rubbed her eyes with her forefinger. Whale pulled the three pages of paper toward her and
read them.

"Damn," she whispered. "You can't hand this in to him."

Ronnie gazed at Mr. Swigart at the front of the room and
nodded slowly. She took the papers from Whale's hands. Inez's
singsong voice had stopped. Mr. Swigart was talking to the
class. Katrina's pillow was empty.

Clamping the papers under her arm, Ronnie strode quietly
toward the open door. She didn't answer when the teacher
called after her but moved fast up the corridor and into the
bathroom. There, she separated the pages of the report into
crumpled balls and dropped them, one by one, into a toilet.
She had to flush several times to make them all disappear.

Katrina stepped out of the first stall, almost bumping into Ronnie. "What's the matter, it's clogged?" Katrina asked.

Ronnie glared at her.

One look at Ronnie and Katrina's institution-conditioned reflexes took over. She headed for the sinks, glancing around for something to use as a weapon.

"Class must be over by now, huh?" she said to Ronnie. "They'll all be crowding in here in a second." Katrina found some soap and made lather with it—for Ronnie's eyes. It would be better than nothing.

Ronnie continued to glare at her. The overhead light bulbs reflected weakly in the three dirty mirrors over the sinks. The toilet stopped gurgling.

Then the door burst open and three girls walked in noisily, pulling out their cigarettes. As they passed Ronnie on their way to the window, Katrina slipped by them and out the door.

Standing in the corridor, Yvonne watched Katrina walking quickly out of the bathroom, and noted the feisty expression on her face. Next to come out was Ronnie, looking tired and even more irritable than usual. Yvonne watched her walk over to Peaches at the top of the stairwell. Peaches had one foot up on a metal rung of the railing, the tight round curve of her behind on view in pink jeans. Her golden hair swept back and forth across her shoulders as she moved her head. When Peaches, noticing Yvonne's stare, gave her a grin, Yvonne grinned back.

In her next class, secretarial skills, Yvonne sat in a carrel with partitions on both sides of one of the huge new electric typewriters Mr. Fox had gotten for the school. She took a brush from her handbag and slowly ran it through her silky black hair. In sunlight, it had a dark reddish tint to it that matched her wine-colored blouse and set off her smoky tan skin nicely. She propped her compact mirror on the type-writer, but saw only a washed-out reflection with fluorescent ceiling lights in the background. The bright green of her eyes didn't show up, but the bruise beneath her eye did.

Both the bruise and the new blouse were gifts from her man Sugar, who had visited her last night along with one of his wives. Thinking of the visit made Yvonne squirm in her seat. She had felt like fainting with admiration, listening to the way Sugar talked to the staff in his deep smooth voice, introducing himself as her brother and the white broad as her sister-in-law. Mrs. Healey, the four-to-midnight staff, drooled at his three-piece suit and attaché case. She tripped all over herself finding them a nice quiet room to have a family talk.

As soon as she left, the white broad blocked the little window in the door and Sugar started slapping Yvonne's face.

"I sent you up here to take care of business—" Slap! "—but you ain't taking care of nothing, far as I can see!" His voice stayed soft, velvety, as he slapped her harder. "Yvonne—bitch—" Slap! "Listen to me—bitch—" With a closed fist, he caught her under the eye and sent her sprawling to the carpet.

Kneeling, crying, she hugged his leg. "I'll do right for you!" she sobbed. "Please—" Sugar lifted her into the big state armchair and pulled her knees apart. "That's good, honey child. I'll do right for you, long as you take care of business," he said, pinning back her arms. "Carlotta, show Yvonne what business we in. Show her what we drive all the way up here for." Sugar twisted Yvonne's head toward the white woman who, as Sugar snapped his fingers, pulled down her slacks and panties. "Blonde pussy," Sugar said. "You dig?"

Yvonne squeezed back tears. "Carlotta your first wife now, Sugar?"

"Naw, babe. It's still you. Carlotta *like* to see me treat my first wife real fine." His dark eyes slid sideways, causing the zombie-faced woman to snap to attention.

"Yeah, Sugar." And Carlotta began stroking her yellow pubic hair. Her thighs rolled like a go-go dancer's; her purple eyelids half-closed in a sudden expression of ecstasy.

Then Sugar turned Yvonne's face back to him and yanked up her skirt.

By the time he was finished, Yvonne was sobbing again but now from joy and relief. Sugar wasn't mad at her anymore. She was so grateful she wanted to kiss him all over his smooth beautiful face. But he pulled back to protect his suit jacket from her damp makeup.

The three of them then sat around a coffee table to discuss business. Sugar opened his attaché case and took out some bracelets and a ring. They were for the girl Yvonne had written him about—Peaches—and any others she could bring along with her back to Sugar's stable.

Then, for her, he pulled out the wine-red blouse, wrapped in soft tissue paper that whispered elegantly when he folded it back. It hung silky and sheer from Sugar's fingers, the light shining through it like the sun through a colored church window. The way the silk caressed her when she held it against her cheek made Yvonne want to cry, it was so beautiful.

"That's a seventy-dollar blouse." Sugar grinned at her. "Make you feel fine all over, doesn't it?"

Yvonne closed her eyes.

Now in the classroom she ran her fingers along the blouse's silky collar and remembered feeling like a million dollars. Right at the moment, she felt like about five hundred thou, which still wasn't bad—a whole lot better than she had felt in the days before she'd met Sugar.

She remembered herself with terror and disgust—a skinny little runt in grade school getting laughed at for her strange pale tan skin and straight hair. And being shamed by her mother at home—*Be* somebody in your life, girl, you going to *be* somebody!

But did Yvonne want to *be* somebody like her mother, with a high-school diploma and two jobs scrubbing out office buildings sixteen hours a day just to put food on the table? Hell, no! Every day she watched her mother join the crowd of women with swollen ankles and shapeless dresses and old head rags shuffling off to the bus stop to go do their scrubbing jobs. She saw the garbage rotting on the sidewalk, and smelled the junkies ogling her from the alley.

But then she saw the dude in the big hat and gold chains just sliding that cream El D through the neighborhood, stereo speakers built into that fine cushioned interior and thudding out the beat for all the street to hear. The beat bounced off the windows of the discount stores and gypsy parlors and soul food shacks, and it made folks—especially the girls who were hip to the message—move along with a diddy bop in their walk. You could walk all hunched over and slow like her mother going off to work. Or you could follow the diddy bop.

For a while, she tried working on her own, but one night a tourist with a funny mind tied her up and crushed cigarette butts out on her stomach. Sugar took her to the hospital. She joined his stable.

The men he sent her to meet were all important types who wore eight-hundred-dollar suits and never used her stomach for an ashtray. And they paid. When she brought those rolls of bills back to Sugar, he made her feel like a star. She was worth a fortune.

But then she and another girl beat up a foreign diplomat outside a midtown hotel; she got thrown in jail and wasn't worth any more than a dime for a phone call. Sugar and his lawyer got her off with ten months at Fairbanks. Sugar told her that if she came out alone, she could count on getting her throat cut as soon as she tried to show her ass on any street corner in New York. But if she brought out a girl or two for his stable, then—"Like the song says," Sugar said, stroking her cheek, " 'We Are Family'!"

It was the only family she had now, Yvonne reminded herself, running her fingers along the collar of her blouse. She had to get moving. Katrina was a possibility, but the first project was getting Peaches away from Ronnie. She stared down at the typewriter keys, thinking.

Writing a fake kite to Peaches from some white bitch, getting Ronnie crazy with jealousy, getting her to hate whites even worse than she did and making Peaches uptight—that could get things going around here. A message from a mystery lover, maybe.

Yvonne, grinning and chewing a strand of hair, attacked the typewriter.

TO:	*PEACHES*	*FROM:*	*????????????*
REASON:	*Watching and Waiting*	*TIME:*	*What the Future Holds*

HOPE:	*You Feel the Same*	*DAY:*	*Or night*
WISH:	*You will Understand*	*PLACE: In My Heart*	
DESIRE:	*Your Every Happiness*		
SONGS:	*Touch A Hand, Make A Friend*		

Looking For A Love
(To Call My Own)

Some Day, Some Way

(I'm a) Boss Lover

Dear Peaches,
*   While sitting here with time on my side and you on my mind, i thot i would rite you this to let you kno that some body is notising you and how fine you look and how you send him (me). i kno you are another dudes woman rite now but you see i am so bad i do not even care. If I thot your group had there shit together i would stay out but i can see that it does not have it together any more. So i just want to tell you that someone (me) cares alot and if you ever need a helping hand you are going to find one coming out of the blue from a true blue admirer.*

T.L.A.   *555 - Soon*
S.W.A.T.K.   *62 - Always*
                  376 - You never kno

Yvonne sat back grinning. She'd never typed so fast before—Mr. Fox and the teacher would be proud of her. The letter had to be left . . . yes, under Vonita's door. Vonita would run with it straight to Ronnie. . . . But not yet. Yvonne would save it for just the right moment.

Then she got another idea. Biting her lip to keep from squealing with excitement, she retyped the letter, deleting the question marks at the beginning. Instead of leaving the signature space blank, she typed in

K A T

Then she folded the letter carefully and slipped it into her blouse.

13 ❧

UNIT THREE	READING SCORES	
RESIDENT	READING LEVEL	CHANGE SINCE PREVIOUS TEST
Marie Dexter (Whale)	11th grade	+ .4 grade
Veronica Jones (Ronnie)	9th grade	+ .2 grade
Inez Ribeiro	7th grade	− .2 grade
Pamela Devereaux (Pam)	6th grade	0 grade
Katrina Nelson*	6th grade	+1.5 grade
Lucia Vasquez	5th grade	− .3 grade
Gail McNulty (Yvonne)	5th grade	− .1 grade
Aliceanne Scaggs (Peaches)	4th grade	+ .2 grade
Vonita Thomas	1st grade	− .5 grade
Mary Dogflower	1st grade	0 grade
AVERAGE	5.5 grade	+ .1 grade

* Previously tested 12/7 at Maviskill Training School.

Steven read over the girls' reading scores and groaned. How could the scores be so abysmal? If it hadn't been for Katrina's jump in reading level, the group as a whole would have made no improvement at all during the past three months. It would have even had a minus score. How was it possible for people to read *worse* than they had before?

What were those teachers doing in the classrooms? If he became acting director, would he have to fire them? *Could* he fire them, with their jobs protected by civil service regulations? If he could, who would come all the way up to frozen Fairbanks, New York, to replace them?

He shoved the scores into his desk drawer and read over the log from the previous day. As soon as he saw Mrs. Healey's entry about Yvonne's "brother" and "sister-in-law," he called her probation officer and found that Yvonne's only brother was ten years old and unmarried. Yvonne admitted in group session that she'd lied. Her visitor, she said, had really been an old family friend who'd always been like a big brother to her. Knowing the rules about nonrelatives being prohibited from visiting, she had simply called him her brother and his wife her sister-in-law. The girls in the group to whom she'd bragged about Sugar kept their mouths shut. Yvonne was given a week's building restriction by the group, which she accepted as fair. Steven didn't believe her story about the family friend, but when he'd suggested that her visitor might have been her old pimp, she had burst into tears and sworn on her mother's grave that she had given up the street life forever.

The other problem concerned Mary. Last evening, during a rehearsal for a musical show that the girls wanted to put on sometime in the spring, Mary had disappeared. She sat down cross-legged on the floor beside the water fountain in the foyer and refused to move. Steven had found her there this morning when he arrived at work.

Various staff members tried to talk to her. She held her long straight hair in both fists against her cheeks and said nothing. When the girls gathered around her, she was silent with them, too. She sat absolutely motionless, her gaze never wandering from a fixed spot on the floor. Inez and Pam tried to get her interested in watching the dance rehearsal. Peaches told her how sad the group was going to feel if she didn't join them. Ronnie and Whale told her that if anybody had been calling her a dumb Indian again she ought to tell them and they'd take care of it. Katrina told her she'd share a candy bar with her if she'd come upstairs. Mary pulled the frayed hem of her dress over her ankles. Her round face remained impassive. Finally she raised her eyes and stared at Katrina.

"My father's going to come and take me back to the reservation where I belong," she said.

Steven dispersed the girls. Dance rehearsal went on without Mary, as did the evening extra-credit classes in Spanish and shorthand. At 9:30, when it was time for evening chores, Mary was still refusing to move. She had settled into the corner between the water fountain and the wall, her head resting against the chrome edge of the box. She looked as if she were asleep with her eyes open.

Steven told the girls to do their chores and get into their bathrobes. There would be an emergency group session at 10:15 in the foyer by the water fountain. He got Mary's case record out and looked through it in the staff office.

"You trying to find out if she's crazy?" Katrina, looking very skinny in her jeans and purple T-shirt, stood watching him in the doorway.

Steven tugged at his mustache, frowning. He had just found an observation report from a state hospital: "Subject manifests occasional mild schizophrenic behavior, catatonic type." He tossed the file onto the desk and straightened his tie. "Let's go try and talk to her, Katrina," he said.

The emergency group session was not a success. The girls sat on the floor in their fuzzy bathrobes and slippers and tried to talk to Mary. She wouldn't say a word. Everyone smoked cigarettes and looked at her. She looked at the tile next to her ankle. Her silence hung over the circle of girls like a drone. The girls couldn't take the pressure; they sighed loudly and made joking remarks. Mary looked quite peaceful, almost radiant, like the guest of honor at a party. At 11:30, Steven announced that she would be allowed to stay downstairs until morning, or until she wanted to come up to bed. He asked a group member to volunteer to take mattresses downstairs and stay with her.

The next morning, Mary was still sitting beside the water fountain. She had her dirty blanket covering all of her except her face, and didn't take it off all day. Girls volunteered to take watches sitting with her. Several staff visited with her, and eventually walked away shaking their heads. Matt Steiner, the director, sat with her for fifteen minutes.

"Did she say anything to you?" Steven asked him, when he had returned to his office.

"Yes." Matt frowned over the top of his glasses. "She said that her father was going to come and take her back to the reservation where she belonged."

Another emergency group was held after dinner until bedtime. Mary did not speak. At one point, there was a moment of hope; the girls cheered and clapped; Mary stood up. She lumbered off with everyone watching. But she was merely taking one of her trips to the bathroom down the hall. She returned, had a long drink of water from the fountain, and resumed her silent sitting position.

After two nights and two days, Steven decided that if she was still there the next morning, he would have to have her picked up bodily and taken to the mental hospital for observation. As a last resort, he mentioned this to Katrina, who had volunteered to spend the night with Mary.

"What do I get if she comes upstairs?" Katrina asked.

Steven tilted back in his chair. The usual smile-lines beside his eyes were all but gone. His damp white shirt stuck to his chest, and his necktie lay on it like a long tongue. "A lot of gratitude," he said.

"Fuck that. I want a one-way bus ticket out of this dump." Katrina sat on the edge of his desk and tucked one ragged sneaker under her.

"If you want to help Mary, then do it because you care about her. Otherwise, forget it."

"I care about her," Katrina said. "I don't want her to get shipped."

"Me neither."

Katrina jumped down off the desk, landing on the balls of her feet, already in motion toward the door. "Okay, I'm going to bring her back alive."

Downstairs, she set up her mattress, sheets, pillow, and blankets in front of the water fountain, and sat down. "They're going to ship your ass off to the nuthouse tomorrow if you don't go upstairs," she said, glancing at Mary.

Mary shrugged.

"That's what you want, isn't it?"

Mary just stared at her.

Katrina stared back. "The way I got it figured, you're doing this to get out of here." She lit a cigarette. "You got a real original way of expressing yourself. You and me, we're both original."

Mary was looking at Katrina's cigarette pack. Katrina slid it and a matchbook across the floor to her.

"I got to admire you, Mary. The way you just tune out the whole place. I try to do that sometimes, but it only lasts for a few minutes."

Mary smiled. "I like it here," she said, lighting a cigarette.

"Hey, you're talking!" Katrina said, then saw Mary frowning. "Sorry. But let me ask you—you don't have to say nothing, you can just nod or shake your head, okay? What do you mean, you like it here? You mean Fairbanks?"

Mary nodded slowly.

"Or by the water cooler here?"

Mary nodded again.

Katrina lay back on her mattress. "You really got me confused now."

"I like it here." Mary tapped the side of the water fountain.

"Oh. Okay." Katrina touched the shiny aluminum box. "Well, they probably got water fountains at the nuthouse, too."

Mary sat forward. "They don't let you sit next to them. They lock you in your room."

"Yeah?"

"The way Mr. Fox lets me stay by the water here, they wouldn't do that at the crazy hospital. And the girls come and sit with me, and even stay here at night." She smiled faintly.

"It sounds like you're sorry to be leaving."

Mary shrugged. "My father will come for me wherever I am. It don't matter."

"Yeah, I guess."

Mary leaned back and rested her head against the side of the water fountain again.

Katrina stubbed out her cigarette. "You look like you're listening to something."

Mary nodded slowly.

"You are?" Katrina sat up, holding her blanket around her. "Could I hear it, too?" When she didn't get an answer, she shifted her position until her ear was pressed against the cold metal. After a few minutes, she sat back on the mattress, rubbing her ear. "Well, I'm glad *you* can hear something, anyway."

Mary watched her readjust her blanket around her.

"I listen like that sometimes," Katrina said. "I stand at my window when there's a breeze and I try to feel it on my face. Then if I can, I try to, like, hear it. It's hard. I have to listen real close in between all the other noises we got all over this joint. But sometimes I can close my eyes and think about quiet places that are open and free. And I think about my grandfather. He used to take me for walks on Sunday morning when the park was empty. Sometimes it's like I can hear his voice if I listen hard enough." Katrina felt strange. She hadn't known she would say so much. "You know what I mean?" she asked.

Mary nodded. "That's why I like the water."

"Water?"

Mary pointed to the water fountain. "My people," she said.

"I don't understand."

"My people can help me." Mary wiped a tear that suddenly rolled down her cheek. "When I get thinking bad thoughts too much, my people can help me."

Katrina handed her her sheet, and Mary wiped her face on it. "I think too much sometimes, too. What do you think about?" Katrina asked.

"Nightmares," Mary said. "I dream I'm inside a burning building and I'm looking for some way to get out."

Mary told of setting fire to her father's store. The social workers and psychiatrists thought she had done it to hurt her father, or maybe her mother, or maybe because she was jealous of her sister. The real reason she'd done it was because she was ashamed of being poor. When she'd heard her father talking about how fire insurance worked, she knew right away how she could help the family. But she didn't know her little sister was inside the store, and barely got her out of the fire in time. Afterward, Mary wandered around the reservation whimpering and soaking herself with water constantly, the way the tribal doctors had soaked her sister. "The burning feeling under my skin never went away, though," Mary said. She ran her fingernails along one arm, where Katrina could see she'd been scratching a lot. "In my nightmares, the feeling turns into real flames. I can't put them out."

"Whew." Katrina touched her own arm. "Is that why you want to stay near the water fountain?"

Mary nodded, gazing far away. After a while, she looked at Katrina again, almost smiling. "You think about your grandfather. I like to think about my uncle. He tells me and my sisters stories. My favorite one's about the people who live in the water."

She leaned back against the wall. Katrina lay down to listen.

Once there was a boy named Dirty Clothes, Uncle said, who was always being teased because his clothes were ragged and old. Then one day he was nice to some tiny little people he met in the forest, and they took him on a canoe journey with them across a long pond. Uncle pointed to some leaves floating on the water—their canoes were just that size, he said. The blurred weeds under the pond's surface were the crops of the little people. At night, they would come and harvest them, but sometimes, during the day, if you looked closely, you could see them hoeing. Mary and her sisters lay down on the bank and stared at the plants and reeds and fishes. "I see one!" a sister would shout, and everyone would crowd over to her and look. Mary loved the little people, and always left pieces of bread floating on the pond for them before she left for home.

The little people made Dirty Clothes tiny like them, and gave him a suit of beautiful new clothes made out of white buckskin. When Dirty Clothes returned to his village, full grown again, he still had on the new clothes. He taught the people of his village the songs and dances that the little people had taught him. After that, Dirty Clothes was very popular in his village. If he ever felt sad or scared, he would go to the pond and talk to the little people.

Perhaps, Mary said, they would tell her how to find her way out of the fire in her nightmares. The water fountain was the place with the most water in the entire school building. "If the water in the box was spread out, it would make a small pond," she said, her dark eyes solemn as she studied it. "It feels good to be here."

Katrina, lying back on her mattress, folded her hands under her head. "Yeah...."

"You ain't going to tell nobody, are you?" Mary asked suddenly.

"No, I won't tell." Katrina half-shut her eyes and imagined little people in tiny canoes sailing through the water like goldfishes. Above the ceiling, the TV was murmuring and footsteps thumped, but by concentrating on the little people, Katrina could tune out the noise. After a while, she squinted at the water fountain, hoping to see it changed in some way, maybe glowing. But it looked the same.

"There's only one thing I don't get," she said. "That fountain's not full of water."

Mary frowned. "Yes, it is."

"No, I saw the maintenance guy repairing it one time. It's just a lot of pipes inside."

"It's water."

"In the pipes, yeah. But not unless you push the button."

"I don't believe you."

"Hey, how do you think the water gets in here? In *pipes*! It's no different from your own house, Mary."

Mary shook her head. "We ain't got no pipes."

"Huh? Where do you get your water from, then?"

"From the creek."

Katrina narrowed her eyes. "Okay, right. But how does it get from the creek to your house?"

"In buckets."

"What, you *carry* it?"

"Me and my mother. Sometimes we use bottles, when we find the big plastic kind."

"Yeah, and how do you flush the damn toilet?"

Mary shook her head again. "It don't use water. It's just a hole. An outhouse."

"Damn...." Katrina stared at Mary's round face. "Okay. Well ... anyway—" She reached into the pocket of her bathrobe and pulled out a dime. "The guy unscrewed the thing down here," she said, lying down to find the screw near the floor. She removed it by turning the dime in the groove. The metal side of the box opened. "Lie down. You can see the pipes under here."

Mary did. Then she scrambled to her feet. She pounded on the top of the water fountain with both fists, spraying water, making a sound like a drum. "I thought it was full of water!" she cried, and hugged her arms across her chest. Her blanket fell to the floor. She began to make a low moaning sound that made Katrina shiver and scramble to her feet.

"I'm not saying there's no water in the pipes!" she said.

Mary turned her face to her. Her eyes were wild and damp, her cheeks puffed out. Katrina grabbed her by the lapels of her bathrobe. "I mean it! Look!" Katrina jammed her fist down onto the button and water squirted out of the aluminum hole. "It doesn't have to be full of water all the time. I mean, you probably did hear those little people anyway because— I don't know—because this is where the water comes from!"

Mary looked sideways at the water fountain, choking back tears.

"Hey, yeah," Katrina said, still holding Mary's lapels. "If you can hear them here, where there's just pipes, then you can hear them anyplace where there's pipes. Like, in the sink in your room."

Mary picked up her blanket and wrapped it around her, covering herself completely except for her face.

"You want to go up and try it in your room?" Katrina asked.

Mary looked dubiously at the staircase.

"You won't have to go to the nuthouse." Katrina squeezed Mary's arm.

Mary took a deep breath. Then she nodded. "I ain't going to tell them about what I told you."

"I won't either."

Mary stared at her for a long time. "I trust you," she said finally. Trailing her blanket, she headed for the stairs.

In the third-floor lounge, only the flickering glow of the television screen illuminated the faces of the girls. Wearing their bathrobes and slippers, curlers and headcloths, they sat huddled in small mounds as if facing a campfire. The air was thick with the scents of shampoo and hot-ironed hair. Occasionally, a match flared, a cigarette end glowed red, a note of quiet laughter interrupted the murmur of the television. No one noticed Mary and Katrina walk in, so Katrina slammed the door hard behind her.

Several girls turned around. "Mary!" they screamed, and everyone rushed her.

She greeted them with a scared scowl, but no one saw it in the darkness. The girls wrapped their arms around her, punched her, shoved each other to get closer to her. Mary had to sit down on the couch and cover her face with her hands.

Seeing Steven in the doorway, the girls pushed him forward. He looked stern at first, but then said, "Welcome back," and, grinning, ruffled Mary's hair. He turned to Katrina. "How'd you do it?"

Katrina shrugged.

When he had gone back into the office, the girls made room for Katrina to sit beside Mary on the couch. Getting no answers from Mary, they asked Katrina, Why was Mary sitting down there? Was she temporarily insane? How'd you talk her into coming back?

Mary smiled up at the girls' faces. Finally, Katrina waved her hands in the air, shushing everyone. "I can't say why she was downstairs and everything," she said, her voice suddenly quieter than anyone had ever heard it before. "She's got religious reasons for what she done."

The girls crowded in closer, insisting that Katrina explain. But she shook her head slowly. Her curls were loose and damp on her forehead, her face was calm. The girls backed off again, but not in anger. They looked as if they were encountering some mysterious force that was coming not only from Mary, but now from Katrina as well.

14

In the third-floor staff office, Steven sat on the recessed window shelf with his back to the snowy night outside and his feet on the radiator, reading a draft chapter of Leah's doctoral dissertation. Sonia was at the desk; her long blond hair swept the blotter as she leaned over to write in the logbook. The radiator gave out a soft garbled whisper; heat rose through the soles of Steven's boots and made him drowsy. The office had a tropical feeling to it tonight. Surrounded by the girls' colorful paper door decorations in the corridor, the room might have been a ramshackle colonial outpost in the midst of jungle flora. It was furnished much like the teachers' lounge in the school where Steven had taught in Jamaica: several wooden chairs, a big steel government-issue desk, and a print of a European painting—Sonia's Degas dance poster—bravely trying to relieve the bleakness of the off-white walls. A tattered armchair was wedged into a corner as if cringing from the door—as well it might, since every time a girl rushed in, the door whacked it hard. With the door shut now, the sounds of girls' voices, radios, television, music throbbed faintly and persistently like wild bird screams, cicadas, footsteps thumping through the underbrush.

When Steven thought of the tropics, he remembered not so much the places where he had lived toward the end of his seven years in the Islands but the way Jamaica had felt to him during his first weeks there. The sparkling green dawns, the brilliant afternoons, the new scents of impossibly bright flowers, the sounds of children's play rushing at him across fields and along footpaths, and especially the kindness of the people—all had gently pried open the depression he realized he'd been carrying around since childhood like a lead box fastened tightly around his head. Free of it, he could be whoever he wanted to be. Living among people who had no notions about what a normal, successful American was supposed to be like, he'd been able to adopt a relaxed, accepting attitude toward himself. As a teacher, he was immediately an important person in his village, and never lacked for friends, girlfriends, and colleagues. He found he could return the people's welcome: he loved teaching their children and discovered he could do it extremely well. Because of his work, their lives changed: instead of remaining peasants scratching the earth for survival, they could become shopkeepers, teachers, civil servants. Steven had never had an impact on anyone before, not even himself.

Staring out windows at frozen upstate New York, as he was doing tonight, he sometimes asked himself why he had ever come back. He remembered breaking up with a woman he'd hoped to marry. Her daughter had spat at him. He continued to pay the child's medical bills and school fees for years afterward, but never forgot the bitter, despairing look on her face as she spat. After that, the pristine simplicity of village life began to look more like stagnancy and poverty. He moved to Belize, then Dominica, but the schools remained shabby, sad little places: textbooks were obsolete, teachers were discouraged, students were frustrated by lack of learning materials. Steven got in trouble for some overambitious schemes to supply his school. Often his paychecks arrived months late and were too small to live on; he began to manage a hotel to make ends meet, a job which he feared turned him into a tinpot imperialist commanding brigades of busboys whose servility he was in business to perpetuate. His idealistic Quaker ancestors spun in their graves. He returned to teaching, but began to wonder if he wasn't ready for more challenging work, even if this meant moving back to the States.

Then he met a pretty young tourist who reminded him of the stable, pert, upper-middle-class girls he had always wanted to date in college. She found him, with his curly blond beard and his "native" friends, irresistibly exotic. After a brief courtship, they were married on a moonlit beach. Now he had a definite reason to go back to the States. In New York, suddenly broke and bewildered, he took a job with his father-in-law's public relations company. For the first time in his life, he wasn't poor. After a few months living on his fat salary, he was surprised to realize that the money didn't have much effect on him. His earning power was useful, however, in making his new in-laws think that he might one day adjust to what they called "the real world" and master the role of husband to their daughter.

He had blamed his own parents for depriving him of a normal family life. Now his life was relentlessly normal. His wife's family seemed just like the ones who'd watched over him as a child from flickering TV screens in motels and rented houses from coast to coast. Except now he was locked in the box with them. They always knew their parts, never muffed their lines, always smiled on cue. During his Sunday dinners with them he felt as if the determined cheerfulness with which they filled the apartment was about to squash him flat against the wall with his fingernails dug into the velvety wallpaper. They pretended not to notice his awkwardness, optimistic that he would learn his role by being exposed to their energy and patience. the way a foreigner will learn English if you speak it to him loudly enough.

He felt like a stranger in New York, and wondered if anyone ever recovered from reverse culture shock. None of the other former Peace Corps volunteers he met seemed to have done so either. After years as a big fish in the small ponds of village life, he was a tiny, floundering minnow in a sea of crustaceans. But for a while, his job kept him feeling purposeful : he wrote publications that convinced the government to fund community self-help projects in ghettos and barrios. Then the company began turning out materials asking the government to allow drug companies to sell to Third World countries products that had been banned in the United States. The more research he did, the more clearly he came to understand the dangers of these drugs. He remembered how sick one of his girlfriends had become trying out various American birth-control pills; he recalled neighbors spending small fortunes on worming tablets that had, he now learned, caused cancer in laboratory rats. When he sent a copy of the report he wrote to the Food and Drug Administration, he was fired; the company assigned an armed security guard to watch him clear out his desk.

His wife said she understood his actions perfectly. She was also perfectly, tearfully certain that her father would never work for a company that hurt people. He stopped trying to convince her, remembering how he had felt when his father had been arrested for talking Puerto Rican women into putting up their life savings for bogus job-training courses. He was no longer invited to Sunday dinners with her parents. His wife began to go alone. He began to notice that various of his attributes which during their courtship she had found original and adventurous she now considered merely peculiar and irresponsible. He tried not to hate her for this, but the only way to avoid doing so was to think about himself as she did. To keep from hating her, he had to hate himself.

As months of unemployment went by, his wife's patience grew thin. "I know you've got to find what you feel is best for you," she said, but she said it with a sigh, and soon the apartment was full of sighs. The laundry sighed when he folded it. The icebox door sighed as it opened. The toilet chortled prophetically down its subterranean passages and gave off a long hissing sigh that followed him from room to room. They were like emissions of poison vapors, those sighs; he didn't dare take a deep breath in that apartment. One day, gasping, he left it.

Seven months later, his wife gave birth to a daughter without ever having told him she had been pregnant. She had moved back with her parents; he had to get a court order to visit the baby. Sarah grew into a child with soft curly hair and bright eyes, and teeth as tiny and white as lily buds. She giggled when he hugged her and never sighed.

Steven sued for custody and, to show the judge he could support a child, took the first job he found—his Peace Corps work qualified him, more or less, to counsel juvenile delinquents for the state Youth Service. But the job paid half of what his former position had, and the judge was not impressed. Steven lost his daughter.

But he kept his job. He found that he loved the work. He had to struggle to win the kids' respect, but the struggle was always worth it. Sometimes he felt as if his father had miraculously come back as himself and was discovering the enormous satisfaction to be gained in helping kids like him to feel better about themselves. By concentrating on caring for individual kids, Steven was able for several years to remain oblivious to the workings of the overall system of which he was a minor part. But as he grew more and more competent, he was put in charge of larger groups of kids in more violent institutions. Then he could no longer ignore the neglect, indifference, and brutality that he had first encountered as a kid in juvenile jail and that he had, he realized, been terrified of rediscovering at his job.

Now, perched on the window shelf at the top of the Fairbanks School with the snow falling through the darkness outside, Steven was reading a paper that made the job of helping kids seem even more difficult than he had imagined. He wasn't completely shocked by Leah's revolutionary ideas themselves; that they were applied to his school, however, and by someone he thought he knew so well, was unsettling. Finishing the chapter, he stared at the office door; the tropical sounds on the other side of it evoked less nostalgia than they had before.

Sonia had gone out; now she returned with Leah and made three mugs of tea at the electric kettle on the corner table. When she had handed Leah and Steven theirs, she took her own and sat down in the armchair so that Leah could read the log at the desk.

"Vonita peed in her sheets last night? Damn!" Leah looked up from the book. "What are we going to do with that child?"

Sonia shook her head. "She had another nightmare, too. Woke up half the floor."

"I don't like to see the group punishing her for it, though," Leah said. "Who was it led that movement—Katrina? She is getting to be a little crusader in group sessions."

"No, it was Ronnie." Sonia tucked her feet under her and

smoothed her long flowered skirt over her knees, making herself comfortable in the old chair. Her wide-eyed expression reminded Steven of his ex-wife when he'd first known her; strangely, it endeared Sonia to him, as if she were a younger relative, now grown, whom he vaguely remembered as a childhood playmate. From the way her gaze stuck to Leah's face, he could tell that she was thrilled that this wise, beautiful, older woman was accepting her as a colleague. Like Sonia, Steven loved the camaraderie the three of them enjoyed in the office on all-too-infrequent slow nights like this one. It was the closest thing to family life he had.

"The punishment wasn't for the bed-wetting or the nightmare," Sonia said. "Vonita put her wet sheets in the dryer without washing them, and then she started doing the dozens on the girls when they told her to take them out."

Leah clicked her tongue. "Who got the abuse this time?"

"Well, she called Whale a fat whore about twenty times in that shrieky voice of hers. She told Lucia—" Sonia bit her lip. "She told her to kiss her ass, lick the crack, and call it heaven." Sonia's face reddened. "Then she called Ronnie a cocksucker."

"Lord! Wrong thing to say to that one." Leah pressed her palm to her forehead. "Did Ronnie deck her?"

"No, but Peaches nearly did. Then Whale wanted to sit on her till she apologized. Ronnie was fairly cool about it. She dragged Whale away."

"Vonita, Vonita." Leah sighed. "Going to get herself killed for sure, that girl. Is no joke."

Sonia composed her face. "We shouldn't laugh."

"Got to laugh to keep from crying." Leah stood up and took a more comfortable seat on top of the desk, leaning back against the wall and stretching her legs out so that her feet, the shoes kicked off, were free to wriggle their toes. She turned to Steven. "What do you make of all that?" she asked, pointing to the dissertation chapter he was holding.

"Not many laughs in it." He handed it to her. "But fascinating, anyway."

"What is it?" Sonia leaned forward in the armchair.

"A paper I am writing. Some of my theories."

"Could we hear them?" Sonia asked. "You and Steven used to talk about the Islands. I haven't heard one of your stories in a long time."

"There never was an author who could resist a request like that." Leah smiled. "Do you mind, Steven?"

He was sitting sideways on the window shelf, his head resting against the window; the glass felt cool against his scalp through his flattened hair. "Why should I?" he said.

Leah straightened the stack of paper on her lap.

The Fairbanks School, she explained in her lilting voice, could be considered a Colony. The Colony was given limited self-government by the Mother Country—the state. And it was run by people she called the Settlers—the staff. However humane the Settlers might be, their function was mainly to Keep the Place in Business. Why? Because the Colony was a tremendously profitable enterprise. What if it did cost the taxpayers $43,000 a year to maintain one girl in the place? It still did well. First of all, think of all the middle-class folks the system kept employed and able to consume the products of the nation's industries. Then think of all the companies that supplied food, clothing, heating oil, construction materials, office and medical and educational supplies; the state-wide contract for, say, floor wax must be in six figures. Each Colony lost money for the taxpayers but made a fortune for private enterprise. The juvenile justice system, if you looked at it this way, was a billion-dollar industry.

Leah turned a page. To keep the Colony running smoothly, she said, the Settlers, who were vastly outnumbered, got the help of those elite Natives who were best at imitating Settler (middle-class American) values. Strong, clever girls became leaders, and a classic Deal was struck between the Settlers and the Elites: keep the niggers down for us and we'll keep you in gravy. "Gravy" meant permission for the Elites to exploit weaker kids—the Masses—for maid service, sex, contraband, and other favors.

Fairbanks, Leah allowed, was a little different from most Colonies: it took official policy—which said that the rights and welfare of the Natives were more important than those of the Settlers—at its word. (Official policy had to sound humanitarian to woo taxpayer support and attract idealistic employees.) If Normal Conditions could be kept going, there was a chance that the New Program experiment could work.

Normal Conditions? They existed, Leah explained, when the Natives were kept busy with tribal (racial and interfamily) feuding, thus taking out their hostility on each other instead of on the Settler authorities. Or when the Natives were preoccupied with sexual intrigues—you can't rush the barricades very fast with your drawers down around your ankles. Or when they were satisfied with token participation in the system: in the Native Courts (group sessions), in the Marketplace (the commissary and the new canteen where they spent their two-fifty-a-week "wages"), and in Apprenticeships (academic and vocational training that was supposed to help them leave behind their backward Native way of life and assume the civilized one of the Settlers). When, in general, the program was keeping the kids perpetually distracted from their real grievances about being trapped in the system.

In order to know whether the Natives were distracted enough, the Settlers had to learn as much as possible about their moods by listening to the drum....

"What drum?" Sonia asked. She was sitting with her knees tight against her chest in the armchair, frowning.

On the window shelf, Steven took a sip from his mug, watching Sonia's face. He didn't like to see her so upset. But as annoyed as he was with Leah for disturbing the cozy atmosphere of the room, for disturbing also his own cozy notions about how Fairbanks was run, he didn't want her to stop talking.

"The *drum,* honey," she said, and, leaning forward from her desktop throne, she turned Sonia's head in her big hand so that Sonia was facing the corridor. "Listen!"

"You can hear the drum in the crash of a dinner plate getting knocked off a table," she said, "or a mop splattering against the wall. Listen to the clothes dryer grumbling with too heavy a load of clothes. Listen to whether the girls drop or slam their coins into the soda machine. Listen to their footsteps—how quickly they retreat behind a corner of the hallway as you approach. Listen to the jagged edges of their voices when they yell jive challenges at each other. And you had better listen, too, to how quick or slow the just-kidding laugh comes after one of them's threatened to whup you up-side yo' head, Princess....

"But don't just listen to the girls. Pay attention to the staff, too. Hear how hard someone taps a cigarette against her thumbnail before lighting up. Listen to how many curse words she uses without meaning to. See if she jumps when a dish tray comes cracking against the end of the dishwasher chute. Listen to the squeal of tires in the parking lot when the staff heads out the driveway."

Sonia sighed, staring down into her mug. "So what's going to happen if all this keeps up?"

"Maybe nothing. If we make the New Program work."

"And if we don't?" Steven asked, frowning.

"Trouble," Leah said.

In times of crisis, she explained, repressed rages exploded among the Natives like old oil-soaked rags in a hot, dark basement. The Settlers panicked and called in military help from the Mother Country. Then, faced with equal opportuni-ties to get their skulls cracked open by the police, who con-sidered them all niggers, the Natives, white and brown as well as black, banded together for protection. The Elites got their hands dirty making weapons alongside the Masses. The most "cooperative" kids "reverted" to "delinquent" behavior. Everyone went Native.

Steven shook his head slowly. "That's the way it was at Lakewood," he said, his voice hushed.

Sonia turned in her chair to gaze at Leah. "If I thought this place was a penal colony, I wouldn't go on working here," she said. "I've never oppressed anybody and I don't ever want to."

"Of course not. That's not your job," Leah said. "We're the Missionaries. It's our job to soften up the Natives with useful Christian ethics—Turn the Other Cheek, Render unto Caesar, and so forth. This keeps down the resistance."

"I get plenty of resistance," Sonia said. "I'll be the one softened up if I'm not careful."

"Sure." Leah smiled. "We absorb the shocks of the Natives' resentment so that they don't disturb"—she pointed a finger in Steven's direction—"the administration."

"Thanks," Steven said, forcing a smile.

Leah leaned back against the wall, sighing, as if suddenly weary of her theories. She turned toward the door, behind which TV rock music was rhythmically thudding. Only half her face was visible to Steven in the harsh light of the overhead fixture; he wanted to touch her ankle on the desktop near him as to make sure he still knew who she was. She'd looked queenly, in her purple cardigan and long silky dress; he was almost sorry to see the ironic glint gone from her eyes.

"That is all I have in chapter one," she said, her voice sounding more familiar. "But I have thought of more. What about the personal relationships we are developing with these kids?"

"I hope they're reducing tensions," Steven said. "Keeping the crises away."

"I hope so, too." Leah turned to him. "But suppose they can't deliver what we've led the kids to expect from them?"

"A revolution of rising expectations?" Steven asked. "Would you prefer lower expectations, more distant relationships?"

Leah shook her head. "No. Is a dilemma, though."

"Well . . ." Sonia stood up and stretched. "I like personal relationships. They're what keep me working here. Maybe that's selfish. Do you think so, Leah?"

"If I knew that," Leah smiled, "my dissertation would be finished."

Sonia was looking admiringly at her again. "It's going to be a terrific dissertation, Leah."

"Not too good, I hope." Leah stood down from the desk and felt under it with her stockinged feet for her shoes. "Meanwhile, there are chores for me to inspect. And you were going to leave an hour ago."

Sonia went to the window to check the progress of the snowfall, and decided that she could make it home if she left right away. Steven watched her chatting with Leah, her face still faintly flushed but relaxing as Leah's smile brought the havenlike warmth back to the bare little office. He felt a rush of sadness: the moment seemed so fragile. He looked around him as if taking photographs, recording in his mind the way Sonia and Leah were standing beside the armchair, the position of their tea mugs on the desk, the whisper of the radiator, the smell of cigarette smoke, the glow of the overhead light reflected in the deep black marble of the window glass.

15 ❧

Later, after the girls had gone to bed, Steven came back up from his downstairs office where he had been wrestling with the weekly staffing schedule. Outside, the snow angled in on the noisy wind, splattering against the window. Through a cone-shaped hole in the darkness made by a searchlight beam, the flakes careened down into the parking lot like swarms of moths. Steven's and Leah's cars were turned into fuzzy white mounds. Steven called the highway department, asking the men to bring Mrs. Lert in their truck for the midnight shift. By then, the roads would be impassable for ordinary cars. He and Leah planned to spend the night in the infirmary. He had taken some calypso tapes and a half bottle of rum from his car, knowing that as exhausted as they would be after twelve-hour shifts, they would be too wound up to get to sleep without some drinking and dancing.

He sat at the desk writing in the log, resting one elbow against Leah's leg—she was sitting on the desk again, her head against the wall, her eyes half closed.

He felt the muscles tense under the silky material of her dress. "Bloody hell. Somebody is up," she said.

Steven cocked his head to listen. He could usually tell which girl was outside in the corridor just by the sound of her footsteps. "Vonita," he said.

"Vonita." Sighing, Leah pushed herself off the desk.

Opening the office door, Steven heard the flurry of a bathrobe and turned down the hall just in time to see Vonita's door closing. He and Leah went into her room.

"Now what the hell were you doing out again?" Leah whispered loudly.

"I just left something in the bathroom." Vonita rolled into bed and covered herself. The only part of her visible in the glow from the corridor was her dark knuckles gripping the white sheet.

"Don't you lie to me, child! You smell like cigarettes."

The skinny form tightened into a ball. "I couldn't sleep, Mrs. Gomes!" she screamed.

"Shhhhhh!" Leah sat at the edge of the bed and held her shoulder.

Steven stood in the doorway, his chest suddenly filling with a sharp ache. He remembered trying to coax his daughter to go to sleep many years ago, in another, faraway life. Then the sensation passed.

"All the fucking places I been in, I couldn't never sleep!" Vonita, spotting Steven, squirmed onto her side to yell past Leah at him in her shrill, child's voice. "It's true, Mr. Fox!"

"We believe you," he said.

Steven did. Vonita, an orphan, had spent her entire life in institutions, and had many scars to prove it. She had no idea how to function among people who had lived in the outside world; when she'd arrived at Fairbanks three months ago, she had immediately antagonized everyone with her foul mouth, her scab-scratching habit, and her refusal to take a shower. She was terrified, it turned out, that someone would notice that, at seventeen, she hadn't reached puberty. Believing that if she could achieve an orgasm she would start growing pubic hair and breasts, she paid Lucia fifty cents a week for masturbation lessons, but so far had achieved nothing more than a trip to the hospital for the removal of a plastic bottle top.

"It's scary, going to sleep, isn't it?" Steven said.

Vonita's eyes squeezed shut. "Lucia say when you go to sleep, you go to where dead folks at. And they doesn't have to let you come back, 'less they want to."

"You don't truly believe that, do you?" Leah asked. "I don't."

Vonita studied her face. "Naw, I don't believe that shit."

"Good."

Vonita propped herself up on her elbow. Her eyebrows were arched clownlike into her forehead. "Hey, why can't I come into the office with you two? I'll empty the ashtrays for you—y'all be smoking so much you need that office cleaned—" She glanced from Leah's face to Steven's, her tongue squeezed between her lips. "Why can't I? Aw fuck, you damn people—" She flopped down again.

Leah picked up Vonita's blanket from the floor, shook the dust from it, and spread it over her.

"What you doing?" Vonita asked.

"I'm tucking you in."

"What's that?"

"Nobody ever tucked you in before?"

"Naw."

Leah walked around the bed, smoothing down the blanket and tucking it under the mattress. "You have to hold still or it won't work."

Vonita heaved a sigh but lay very still, her eyes following Leah's hands.

Leah smoothed the sheet over Vonita's neck. "Turn on your belly. Go on." She sat down on the side of the bed and began massaging Vonita's back. Even through the blanket, Steven could see the shape of Vonita's thin shoulder blades rising and falling.

"What you *doing*?" Vonita covered her head with the sheet.

"Pull that sheet down, child, so you can breathe. Come on, let's see that pretty face."

"My face ain't pretty. I'm ugly."

"Pretty is as pretty does. Look at the coconut I had to start with—" Leah leaned close to Vonita's nose and scowled hard, making lines shoot up her forehead and down from her wide nostrils—"and nobody is calling *me* ugly."

Vonita giggled.

Leah began to hum.

"What you singing?" Vonita narrowed her eyes.

"Just a song. My mommy used to sing it to me, in the Islands."

Vonita turned her face away.

"You want to hear it?"

"Don't care."

Leah rocked back, her hands still kneading Vonita's back.

"Sleep, sleep, Mama's own little one,
Sleep, sleep, sleep, Mama's own little dove ..."

Steven hoped she wouldn't sing the next lines: "If you do not sleep, lobsters will eat you"; how any child ever went to sleep to those lyrics, he never knew. But Leah just hummed the rest of the song in her deep quiet voice. The light from the doorway shone on her bare arms and on her face; her big dark eyes were downturned and smiling. She'd never looked so beautiful; watching her, Steven forgot to breathe.

"Mrs. Gomes?" Vonita turned her face on the pillow. "You and Mr. Fox going to be on duty tomorrow night?"

Leah squatted down beside the bed. A tear, or perhaps it was hair-straightening cream, was trickling down Vonita's face. Leah wiped it away with her finger. "We'll be here, child," she whispered, and kissed the clean spot on Vonita's cheek.

She tiptoed to the doorway and leaned against Steven, feeling to him as if she had just taken on all the weight of Vonita's sadness. Steven put his arm around her; he shut his eyes for a moment as her hair and warm forehead pressed against his cheek. They stood together, motionless, until they saw Vonita's shoulders begin to rise and fall in the slow, even rhythm of sleep.

At midnight, Mrs. Lert still had not arrived in the snowplow truck. Steven and Leah waited in the TV lounge. They weren't entirely comfortable there, since it was the girls' territory, but there was a long couch Leah wanted to stretch out on. The heavy orange curtains had been pulled over the picture window, the floor vacuumed, the armchair and metal folding chairs arranged neatly in front of the television set. The one table lamp Steven left on made highlights on the freshly painted blue wall above it. Steven was pleased that the girls were keeping up the room since they'd painted it and chosen its furnishings a month ago; he could tell a lot about the girls' morale by the way they cared for their surroundings.

He sat down on one end of the couch, feeling very heavy himself, as if he too had absorbed the kids' sorrow and rage all day long. His legs seemed made of stressed concrete; he would have liked to run around the building ten times at top speed.

Leah lay with her head in his lap and breathed deeply through her mouth for several minutes. Then, turning her head, she sighed up at him. "It's your turn, my friend."

Steven opened his eyes. "For what?"

"A story," she said. "One of your tales of amazing true adventure."

Steven smiled wearily. He focused on the dark doorway leading to the corridor and gradually his mind began to function again. "Okay, I'll tell you about something I was remembering while you were doing your colonial analogy."

"Good." Leah turned on her side, facing the room, her cheek resting close to Steven's knee.

"I was thinking about the colonies I'd been in, and excolonies. Like Jamaica."

"Crazy place," Leah said.

"I never told anyone about this before." He rested his hand on Leah's waist. "I was teaching in a secondary school way out in the country. A real bush outpost. Even the flies were undernourished. And bored. When you went to slap them, they just sort of looked at you and shrugged. I was going off my head in that place."

"I can imagine."

"Yeah. But boredom is the mother of invention. So I started getting new classrooms built at the school, hustling up new equipment for the kids."

Leah smiled. "It does sound familiar."

"Sure." Steven cleared his throat. "Anyway, I was seeing

a woman who was the wife of the district governor, and she was very enthusiastic about educational development. Or actually, about having her picture taken for the newspapers while she cut the ribbon for some new educational development. What she especially liked was language training centers. So that's what I specialized in getting built.''

''Lust is the mother of idealism.''

''It was even more fun than lust. I was busy and productive all the time. I got six of those language training centers built. Mostly . . .'' He glanced down at Leah.

''How did you do that?''

''American foreign aid. There wasn't much cash but there was lots of American surplus grain. Tons of it lying around the warehouses. So I arranged for it to be used to pay for labor and materials. The workers loved it. The American embassy loved it. The district governor and his wife loved it, because they were the ones officially distributing the grain and getting votes.''

''I daresay they owned the transport company that delivered it,'' Leah said.

''Of course. Everybody was getting what they wanted. And all over the district, bricks and mortar were arriving at work sites, men were digging foundations, villagers were crowding around and watching. Man, it was something, what I was getting done.'' Steven waved his arm in the air like an orchestra conductor. Then he dropped it, sighing.

''What happened? The governor catch you with his wife?''

''No, no. My school got its language training center completed—all but the roof. Then one day, the district governor was arrested. It turned out that he and his wife hadn't just been distributing the surplus grain, they'd been selling it to merchants at a profit.''

''You didn't know?''

''What did I know? I was too busy rampaging around in my Land-Rover.'' Steven's voice fell. ''So, suddenly I was invited to leave the island by the permanent secretary of the Ministry of Education—the same man, as fortune would have it, who'd campaigned against the governor in an election several months before.''

"Politics." Leah clicked her tongue. "What happened to the governor and his wife?"

"Nothing much. Nobody went to jail. The scandal got buried in the courts. But I did hear about all the projects. The kids at my school tried to thatch the new building. But it was too high or too rectangular or something, and every time it rained, the thatch roof collapsed. Eventually the language training center became just a place where the local farmers tethered their goats."

"Did the other centers get finished?"

"Two of them did eventually. But at my school, where I'd started everything, all I had to show for a year of hustling was a goat pen—nothing but a hole in the ground, really. A hole lined with concrete. With a cornerstone inscribed with the date, the name of the governor's wife—the ex-governor's ex-wife now—and a bronze plaque proclaiming the friendship between the people of the United States of America and the people of the Republic of Jamaica."

"You are so damn hard on yourself, Steven," Leah said. "You got two buildings built."

"I know." He ran his fingers along Leah's arm. "But it drove me crazy leaving that empty hole behind."

"It must have done." Leah turned on her back, smiling.

"I used to dream about it a lot." Steven stared across the room at the darkened corridor doorway. It looked like an empty hole. "Sometimes I think I've seen too much to be working in a place like Fairbanks. That's what Matt said once, when he told me about our promotions."

"Is my problem, too." Leah stopped smiling. "I want to think only about taking care of our kids, but sometimes I can't. I look at Fairbanks as if I were looking at the way America works. Then I do wonder whether I should be here."

"I know." Steven leaned his head back. Neither of them spoke for several minutes. Then they heard the door clunk shut on the landing downstairs and Mrs. Lert's footsteps approaching the stairwell. She was a gaunt, white-haired farmer's widow who wheezed when she walked and whom Steven had been trying to coax into an early retirement for months. He and Leah went into the staff office to drag out the armchair into the corridor so that Mrs. Lert could supervise it sitting with her portable radio on one armrest, her Western novel, cigarettes, and ashtray on the other. When she was settled, Steven signed out in the log and went downstairs with Leah.

The infirmary room was cold when they arrived, but the electric heater and the rum warmed them quickly. Leah blocked the little window in the door with a clipboard. Steven brought in a mattress from the other room to use as a backrest on the bed, and covered it with a blanket. He sat beside Leah with a mug of rum in his lap, his bare feet touching Leah's. The tape deck on the floor played soft calypso music, the thumping guitar of The Mighty Sparrow drowning out the wail of the storm outside. The little room felt to Steven even more intimate than the staff office upstairs had earlier; all the rooms high at the top of the building were far away now; he imagined himself in a secret chamber deep below a massive castle. In the semidarkness, the walls disappeared; the red wires of the heater glowed at him like a fire from the far end of a cave.

He got up to dance, feeling dizzy from the rum, the exhaustion, the closeness of Leah's breath and warm flesh. Sweating, he stopped to pull off his clothes and fling them into a dark corner. Leah danced in her gold slip, which, against her deep black skin, made her glow all on her own. Her body was supple and lithe; Steven moved his eyes along her hips as she swayed to the music, feeling her gaze on him, as well. Laughing, they bumped into the invisible walls as they danced. He began dancing close to her again, his head on her shoulder, hers on his, eyes closed.

"Let's turn up the music," Leah whispered, tossing back her head, her white teeth flashing in the darkness. "So we can scream if we want to."

Steven knelt unsteadily beside the tape deck. "Yes," he said, finding the dial. "I want to scream."

Calypso guitars and wailing saxophone notes filled the room. Steven lay down on the bed and watched Leah, standing in the rays of the heater, as she raised her slip over her head.

The red light splashed up her long bare legs, sparkled in the beads of sweat in the hair below her belly. She hurried across the room, her heavy breasts in motion, and rolled onto the bed beside him. He held her close for a long time. Her mouth was hot against his; their tongues slid over each other's as if talking in a preliterate silent language. Stroking her belly, he heard deep moans bubbling up from within her. He caressed her between her thighs; her flesh became moist beneath his fingers, and as he felt the tension flowing rhythmically from her body, something inside him became unclenched and let go as well.

Now she was pushing her thighs against him, squeezing his fingers into her; every time he moved them, she sighed with pleasure. How good it felt to be able to make her happy so simply, so easily. A strength welled up in him; it came from giving himself permission to express all the tenderness he had in him, directing it into one tiny, intense caress. A sobbing edge came into her breathing and he rested his hand still on her, cupping her gently as if to calm the mound moving slightly against his palm. He ran his tongue between her thighs, licking her as if the salty, vulnerable flesh were a pink wound that he could soothe, as if doing so would moisten and heal some deep, stinging emptiness within him. Now her breathing had notes of laughter in it; he hugged her tight, pressing his cheek to her strong flat belly, delighting in the solidity of her. He lay with his face to her breasts; he was gently sucking her nipple, feeling it swell between his lips. Shutting his eyes tight, he was dizzy for a moment, carried away and almost frightened that he was doing something forbidden, asking for more comforting than he had a right to. But then he heard her voice: "So lovely, that..." and felt her lift her breast so that he could rest, utterly happy, upon it.

He slipped his arm beneath her shoulders and, rolling onto her, entered her easily. Her body was firm beneath him, as big and as strong as his own; as she wrapped her long legs around his waist and ground herself hard against him, he could thrust himself deeper and harder into her with no fear of hurting her. Leah's face tilted far back; he heard her cry out as he did, until their screams made one sound that sank into breathy laughter and then into long, mirthful sighings. Steven lay still, his face resting in the warm hollow between her neck and shoulder, his eyes damp with her sweat.

Lying beside her now, he slowly kissed her nose, her cheek, her lips. Her hand moved up his neck, fingers burrowing into the tangled mass of his hair. A strange sensation came over him: he knew just the way his hair felt to her, wiry and soft almost like her own hair; he knew she knew how her skin felt to his hand, too. It seemed that they had begun the evening as partners and friends and then had become, in stages, comforting parents to each other, then passionate adult lovers; and now they were happy, fond brother and sister hiding out together in the dark.

Smiling, Steven wiped the sweat from her chest and belly with the soft edge of the blanket. "I love you so many ways," he said.

"You surely do," she chuckled, her lips and tongue wet against his ear.

He knew she didn't understand what he'd meant but he didn't care. He snuggled down beside her again. Lying on his side, he felt the warmth of her skin against him even though only their toes were touching now. He wanted the sensation never to end.

"I love you, too," she whispered. The sound of her voice had changed—no more sobs or mirth; the spontaneity was gone, and he knew she was telling him she loved him because he had said it and she didn't want him to feel neglected. Not that she didn't love him—she always loved him in the present; whether she would in the future, when their lives might separate, she could not tell any more than he could. "How you do scream!" she whispered in his ear.

"You, too." Steven shut his eyes. What were they now— still brother and sister? Lovers?

"Our kiddies've probably got their little ears pressed to the floor upstairs," she said.

We're parents, Steven thought; not each other's, but the girls'. They were partners again. "It's educational for them," he said.

"I don't really think they know about us, do you?" Leah asked.

"No." Steven lay on his back; she rested her head on his chest, and they did not speak for a long time. The tape deck on the floor clicked and the music stopped. Now he was aware of the silence, and the movement of her body as she breathed.

"Are you asleep?" he whispered.

"Not even close."

"I can't seem to turn my brain off, as tired as I am," he said.

"I know. . . ." Leah pushed herself up, leaning on her elbow. "I think I upset myself with that lecture this evening, not just Sonia and you. I never spoke of those things before. I was thinking about them just now. Were you?"

"Yes. I was trying to figure out what they could mean for us." Steven sat up. He found the bottle of rum on the floor and half-filled the mug with it.

"All the while I was talking," Leah said, "Sonia's look seemed to be asking me, 'Well, which are you—Settler or Native?' "

Steven took a drink of rum; it sent a shiver through him. "And you . . ." He sat on the bed beside her, gripping the edge of the mattress against a dizzy sensation. "And you kept staying in the middle, the detached observer."

"You were onto me."

"Yeah."

"Is hard. I am a staff member, but the closer I get to the girls, the more I feel for them."

"Me, too." Steven wiped the sweat from his neck, staring into the darkness.

Leah rested her hand on his leg. "With me, I sometimes worry it is racial. How can I, a black woman, side with the Colonials against the Natives? You know, those kids get so frustrated with me about that. 'Can't you just be *real*?' the black girls ask. I think to myself, dammit, I *am* being real—I am being an educated West Indian/Canadian, forty-year-old professional woman. But when Vonita asks me, 'Why don't you just be a nigger like us?' I know what she is saying, and I ask myself the same question."

"It's harder on you," Steven said.

"Not necessarily. But I do feel cut off from everyone sometimes. I don't know anybody like me."

"Yes...." Steven had felt that way in the Islands at times. He and Leah didn't talk much about race anymore, usually assuming it was something they had worked out when they'd first become lovers. But now and then they were reminded that the subject was one that nobody in this country ever finished working out. So many things that never get settled, Steven thought. He took a sip of rum and passed the mug to Leah. Lovemaking had loosened him up to an alarming extent; now he couldn't get his mind back together, and the rum, which he was willfully swilling, wasn't helping at all. "If I take the director job ..." he said, turning slowly toward Leah, and then forgetting what he had planned to say next because he was startled to have heard himself say "*if...*"

"I feel like I'm on the verge," he said, "the verge of really being able to do something big in this place. But then sometimes I feel as if I haven't even started to make any difference in these kids' lives—as if there's no way in hell I ever could because ..." He stared past the glowing wires of the heater at the darkness beyond it. The walls no longer seemed invisible, they were close around him. "I don't know why," he said finally, taking the mug of rum back from Leah.

Leah gazed off in the same direction, as if she, too, could see the walls of the building just beyond the darkness. "Perhaps," she said, "because of the place itself. Perhaps it is just the nature of the beast."

"The nature of the beast," Steven repeated, and took a sip of rum. "No, listen—if the two of us ran this school, we could do something good with it."

Leah leaned against him for a moment, then straightened up; though the air was hot, he felt a chill along his skin where hers had left it. "I don't know if that is true, Steven," she said. "We are not the whole system. You are not going to pressure me to stay here because we are involved together, are you?"

"No. No, I wouldn't. But..." The mug was empty. He started to get down from the bed to refill it, but didn't feel steady enough and gripped the edge of the mattress with his free hand. He'd forgotten again what he'd meant to say. "We ... I have to take over the director's job, Leah," he said, his voice swerving out of his mouth. "We're all these kids've got."

She frowned. "They've got homes."

"No. Nobody wants them there."

"They still want to go home. They talk about it constantly."

"Perhaps. Perhaps they do. But you've seen, seen what those homes are like." Steven transferred his grip from the mattress to Leah's arm. "They can't survive there."

"We can't keep them forever, Steven." She lay her hand over his.

Steven shut his eyes. The room spun. "But we can keep them till we've taught them something, how to be stronger and smarter and, and how not to be victims anymore." He leaned close to her face. "Nobody else gives a damn. If we don't, they're ... alone. We can't abandon them!"

"I know...."

"Leah?" A sob caught in his throat.

He felt her fingers on his cheek, softly wiping away tears. She was speaking to him in her low, lilting Caribbean voice. When he tried to blink open his eyes, they continued to leak; the moisture was all over his face, salty in the corners of his mouth. He couldn't remember the last time he'd cried, even as a child. Sitting up suddenly to keep from tilting off the bed, he lost touch with Leah—as if she'd vanished—and felt that chill again along his skin. "Nature of the beast," he mumbled, not what he'd had in mind to say; it was such a terrifying thought it sobered him up a little. He managed to get his eyes open and wipe them with the back of his hand. "Music," he said.

"All right, Steven." Leah started to move from beside him.

"No, stay here—" He lurched down off the mattress, swayed in place like a man on the edge of a cliff, and miraculously straightened himself. "Mighty Sparrow!" he said, and gave out a laugh. Kneeling beside the tape deck, he started the music again. Then he somehow climbed back onto the bed.

Leah was lying down; he lay with his face against her shoulder. Where was the beast now? he thought. Just beyond her, all around him. He was part of it, or would be soon. Would it be part of him? The question seemed to be hovering in the darkness, perhaps inches from his head, whirring against his eardrums like an enormous moth with razor-blade wings. Listen to the Mighty Sparrow, he told himself, and shut his eyes cautiously. The room spun slowly. He concentrated on the music, the warm softness of Leah's skin, the even rising and falling of her chest. Behind the music he could hear the howl of the chill wind, almost feel it against his ear. He hoped he could go to sleep before it blew all the music out of the room.

16 🌿

Katrina had volunteered to mop the kitchen after meals not only because she could take small amounts of food that wouldn't be missed from the lockers to sell upstairs, but because the job gave her a chance to be alone. At Fairbanks, as at the other institutions where she'd been, it was a lot more difficult to steal time alone than it was to swipe some hotdog rolls or apples from the kitchen, but the time was worth infinitely more to her than any money her contraband might earn her. So when she heard the unmistakable Steven-sound of cowboy boots clock-clocking toward her across the dining-room floor, she felt at first that her territory was being invaded and turned her back to the door, pushing the mop faster along the linoleum.

But then it occurred to her, as she heard him taking a mug from the shelf behind her, that he might just get some coffee and leave without even saying hello, like other staff sometimes did after meals. She tossed the mop into the sink and turned around, hooking her thumb in the side pocket of her jeans. "You want me to get you some coffee?" she demanded.

He was standing only a few paces from the coffee machine, but he stopped and smiled at her, holding out the empty mug. "Sure," he said. "Thanks, Katrina."

It was hard to keep her frown on when he said her name with that personal, confidential tone in his voice, as if they had been in the habit of getting things for each other for a long time. She liked his outfit today: new slacks, a corduroy sports jacket as black as leather, a dark shirt, and a pale yellow linen tie that looked like a strip of sunny weather suddenly appearing in a stormy sky. He was so in charge of things that he could afford to look unbosslike and original if he felt like it.

"You want milk?" she asked. "Yeah, you do." She held the mug under the plastic milk dispenser, making it squirt; she'd seen him drink coffee before. "And two spoons of sugar, right?"

"Right." Steven leaned against the metal counter, watching her. "Take some coffee for yourself, if you want."

"Me?" Katrina filled his mug and handed it to him. Only staff were allowed to get coffee in the kitchen—what was going on? She filled a mug for herself quickly before he might change his mind. "Hey, did you see my report card?" she asked.

"I did, yes," he said. "Congratulations on your reading."

"I only got a C minus, but it's passing. First time."

"I know. It looks like you're getting close to passing math and history, too. Those D pluses were an improvement."

She grinned. "Do you, like, memorize all the girls' grades?"

"Not all of them. I couldn't."

She watched him sip his coffee. Why did his mustache look so droopy? "In reading, I'm going to finish a book this week. I never read a whole book before."

"Is it hard?"

"Well, it's a hundred and forty-seven pages." She made a groaning face. "But nah, it's not so hard. It's about this Indian girl from some big city in Texas. She goes out to this reservation and discovers all kinds of stuff about herself she didn't know before." Katrina sipped her coffee; she'd forgotten to put sugar into it but didn't want to stop talking to get some. "Mary gave me the book. She's still saying her father's going to come take her back to the reservation. You think he really will? I think it's sort of like a dream with her, you know what I mean?" She set her mug down.

"Perhaps," Steven said, his voice very quiet. "Katrina, I've got some news for you."

"Yeah?"

"I've had a letter from your mother."

"That's more than I've had." Katrina scowled. "What the hell's she want?"

"It's not good news, I'm afraid." Steven put his mug down on the counter.

The hard sound it made against the metal made her start. The room went still. She waited for him to speak.

"It's about your grandfather. You know, he was a very old man—"

"Oh, no!" Katrina gripped the edge of the sink beside her. She heard only the word "...died." The huge black stove, the food lockers, the maze of pipes overhead that filled the air with metallic-smelling heat all crowded in on her. She leaned over the sink as if she were going to cry, but the mop strings at the bottom seemed to squirm like a nest of gray worms. She couldn't cry here. Where, then? No place.

"I'm sorry, Katrina." Steven laid his hand on her shoulder.

It calmed the thudding sensation in her chest a little. She turned toward him. "My grandfather was so nice to me," she said finally, her voice whispery and strange. "He didn't understand things too good—his mind was kind of senile. But he never blamed me for nothing even when I fucked up. He didn't care. I mean, he did, he cared about *me*, not what I done—" Katrina hugged her arms tight across her chest, staring at a food locker whose chrome door was reflecting an eerie picture, like a melted Halloween mask. Lucia said that faces in the mirror were spirits that lived behind it. She shuddered. "I want to go to the funeral," she said finally.

"I wish you could," Steven said. "But they've already had it."

"Christ! My damn mother!" Katrina shook her head slowly. "A funeral would have been, I don't know—I could have said good-bye. There's all these things I never got a chance to say to him."

"He knew how you felt about him, though," Steven said. "I'm sure he did."

"You are?" She turned slowly toward him. His hand was warm on her shoulder. The light bulb behind him glared through his curly hair. He was realer than anyone still alive in that blurry place that had long ago been home to her. You're all I've got left, she thought, the words rushing at her like sand blown into her eyes on a hot wind, making her want to cling tight to him but at the same time want to push herself far away from him. "I'm going to go find out where my grandfather's grave's at," she choked, rubbing her eyes with her fist.

"You will one day," he said.

"Why can't I go now?" She stepped back from him.

He sighed, lines appearing beside his eyes. "I don't know where you'd stay."

"I'd stay with my mother." Katrina jutted her chin forward. "We fight a lot, I know, but this is an emergency, ain't it?"

"I doubt if she'd think so. Maybe after she's gotten over her father—"

"It wasn't her father. He was my father's father. She didn't give a shit about him. She put him in the old folks' home once. She couldn't afford it so they made her take him back. That's when his brain got messed up." She glared at him. "Listen, I want to go—"

"Katrina—"

"Why the fuck can't I?" she screamed, and kicked the leg of the sink, hurting her toe.

Steven reached into the inside pocket of his jacket. "I guess I'll have to show you the letter," he said.

She snatched it from his hand and began to read.

Dear Sir,

I am writing you about my daughter Katrina who is a student in your school. Her grandfather has passed away. I would tell her myself but I and Her do not get along good because of all the trouble she has caused the

Family. Tell her it is No good coming here because we already buried him and I have rented her room so there is No place for her here. Thank you for helping my Daughter.

Yours truly

Mrs. Patricia B. Nelson

Katrina dropped her hand to her side, crumpling the letter in her fist. No place. The heat of the room bore down on her. No place except this one, which was worse than no place.

"I think she'll eventually change the way she feels," Steven said. The personal tone in his voice made Katrina wince and turn away. "But for the time being—"

"It don't matter," she said, glaring across the room at the outside door. "I'm still going to find my grandfather's grave."

Katrina waited to leave until Steven went to a conference in Albany two days later. Going on instructions from Pam, who had run away eight months earlier, she headed across some fields behind the school toward a dirt road which connected to a paved highway that led south and—so the Fairbanks girls believed—right into the heart of downtown Manhattan.

Exhausted from running, she tripped over a cornstalk and fell hard onto the frozen ground. Her glasses fell off. When she crawled over to where they lay in a patch of hard snow she found that one and a half lenses were smashed. She hurried on anyway, seeing almost nothing but a blur before her; two fields farther, she fell again, landing on her stomach. Weeping loudly, she flailed her arms against the dirt. It was the first time she'd been able to cry since she'd heard about her grandfather's death, and for a while she thought she'd never stop. Finally, shivering all over, she stood up, grabbed her plastic shopping bag, and scrambled on across the furrows toward the trellises of an old grape arbor.

Once there, she stopped and brushed herself off furiously. A blur of weird skeleton shapes leaned close to her at crazy angles; wisps of stringy stuff hung off them like hair and dried flesh in a late-night horror movie. She hurried away up the hill behind the arbor.

Halfway up, she rested on a large flat rock. Yanking a red state sweatshirt out of her plastic bag, she spilled the rest of its contents onto the coarse brown grass: some clothes, a stuffed kitten, some candy bars and cigarettes, a packet of letters, and a big jackknife that Pam had sold her, probably stolen from a second-floor girl. She put on the sweatshirt and sat back, squinting around her.

The field beyond the arbor no longer looked like the mucky, half-frozen place she had stumbled over; her blurry vision made it look almost smooth, like faintly rippling water. Like a wide river.

She remembered walking with her grandfather along the Hudson River when she was little. They always went for walks, even in the rain, when her mother's boyfriend, who got drunk and yelled, was in the house. She and her grandfather pretended that the park benches were islands in their own river system of paths. They moved from island to island; leaning against her grandfather's bony arm, she lifted her feet high to keep them from getting ''wet.'' As they sat on a bench his white beard blew against her cheek and tickled her. She laughed and stared up at his face. One bright blue eye focused on her, the other eye wandered off sideways—''Out to sea,'' he said, ''watching for storms.''

He told her about his days at sea—about storms, sunsets, schools of whales, about a first mate who'd been beaten to death by Indians in Brazil and a woman in a bar in France who had only one leg and one eye—and as she remembered his stories now, Katrina could picture the skin of his face wrinkling as he smiled, rippling the way the river had, the way the field did now so that she could almost see tugboats and barges floating by. She remembered leaning back against his chest, listening to his scratchy, whispery voice so close to her ear. . . .

There was a cat on his ship that was named Katrina and had curly hair, he said. She always giggled and told him there was no such thing as a cat with curly hair, but he insisted there was. What did the cat do? Katrina always asked. Well, she liked to walk along the riggings, even when the sea was rough—*especially* when the sea was rough—and she never fell off. She lay on top of the fo'c'sle, right on the very edge, with her curly tail hanging over the water. She could jump six feet up and catch sea gulls out of the air; sometimes she jumped on their backs and rode them as they soared over the waves. Katrina laughed; but she always looked carefully at any sea gulls she saw flying above the river.

Katrina lay back on the rock, staring at the sky.

''Do you remember last Christmas?'' she said—not quite aloud, but moving her lips. Her mother had put up a tree and even bought a box of ornaments and a wreath—it was going to be a big-deal day. But it wan't. Her mother's boyfriend had stormed out after a fight and her mother followed him and didn't come back for a week. On Christmas morning there was nothing to eat in the empty house but some cornflakes and margarine. So Katrina had gone to the old folks' home and told the people she was taking her grandfather out for the day. ''Do you remember how I broke the window of that fancy butcher shop, where they'd never take our food stamps? And those three huge steaks we got, and all the sausages and lamb chops? I loved the way you just carried them all under your coat and laughed to yourself in the bus. That was the best Christmas dinner I ever had. . . . ''

Katrina sat with her head down beneath her raised knees. Tears rolled down her cheeks, dripped slowly from her chin. Finally she picked up the packet of letters from the grass and opened it. Most were from friends she'd never see again. She tore them into tiny bits and watched the wind blow them away. The one remaining letter, written in scrawled pencil on lined paper, was from her grandfather.

WHEN ARE YOU COMING HOME KATRINA
YOU ARE THE ONLY ONE WHO LIKES ME HERE
I WD LIKE TO TALK TO YOU AGAIN KATRINA
I MISS YOU   LOVE   GRANDPA

She stared at the letter. Her lips moved as she read the words over and over. Finally, she folded the paper neatly into a small square. With her jackknife, she gouged out a hole in the earth beside the rock and laid the folded letter in the bottom. Then she filled the hole again and made a small mound of dirt over it with her cupped hands.

She walked around the meadow until she found a small tree branch. With the knife, she cut most of the twigs off it until it was roughly cross-shaped. Then she pushed it into the mound of earth, the three prongs pointing up at an angle. When she sat back, it looked like a real grave, only miniature. She wanted to say something, but she'd only seen a funeral once on a TV show and couldn't remember any prayers. Still, she said, "Please God, keep my grandfather safe and let there be lots of people around to talk to where he is, and maybe some cats and a ship to sail on...."

The wind took her voice away as soon as the words were out of her mouth. She moved her lips silently now. I'm sorry I wasn't home more with you, Grandpa, but I couldn't stand it there. But you always knew how much I loved you, didn't you? Steven said you must have. He's my counselor, I trust him, he backed me up in group session when I talked about the family and some of the girls got mad.... She stopped, feeling confused and choked up mentioning Steven, whom she'd never see again. Talking about him to her grandfather was strange, but then she'd always been able to tell her grandfather all about people she knew; he'd always been interested, even though he'd never met them. She sat very still, staring out at the rippling field.

After a long time, she stood up and walked slowly backward away from the grave, her shopping bag knocking softly against her leg. I don't know where I'm going now, Grandpa. Maybe I'll just hitchhike around like I used to till I find a place. If you're a spirit now maybe I can talk to you again, like Lucia can, and Mary. I wish you could talk to me.... A gust of wind blew against the back of her hair. She shivered, not from the cold, but because she remembered a voice just behind her ear. She watched the wind blowing down waves of grass along the hillside and jiggling the twig-armed cross on the mound beside the rock. When the wind was silent and the air went still like a held breath, she started walking on up the hill.

Suddenly she stopped, her mouth stuck open. The shopping bag dropped from her hand.

Those trees—they'd been watching her! White, white trees standing in a white row along the crest of the hill. The trunks were edged in silver light. Their branches, leafless and taut, were flung up against the sky as if in surprise—as if, the very second she'd looked up, they'd leaped right out of the ground with a shriek that echoed the voiceless cry leaping in her throat.

She clapped her hand over her mouth. Swaying in place, she turned her eyes away from the trees, but still sensed them watching her. She'd never seen white trees before. When she glanced up the hill again, she expected them to have turned an ordinary tree color. No, they were exactly as pale as they'd been before. What *were* they? She thought of spirits rising from the earth into the sky, and shivered.

But now she was fascinated by them. She approached them slowly. They didn't move or make any sound. At the top of the hill, they looked pretty much like regular trees except their bark was mottled white and peeling. She reached out and touched a strip of bark. It felt like paper. Underneath was pale raw wood, like skinned flesh. She dropped her hand. The trees were scary, but she liked them. She'd never felt anything so smooth as that bark, or seen anything so white as the wood.

Her shopping bag was lying on the grass where she'd dropped it but she didn't want to fetch it. Her jackknife and frames were in her pocket. There was nothing in the bag that she really needed that much. Except maybe the stuffed kitten. No, let it stay there with her grandfather.

She walked over the top of the hill. It was so easy going downhill that she started to run, letting gravity pull her along. Then, hearing the sound of a car engine, she stopped and ducked down behind some bushes. The noise grew louder. Something black glided out of the trees along the road below her—the state station wagon. After its engine sound had faded completely, she began walking along the road.

Soon she passed a farm and rested in an empty stall in a barn. Lying on the hay, she saw sunbeams slanting into the open doorway through the hay dust, turning it gold; outside, invisible birds were singing. She closed her eyes, thinking about the grave on the hillside and the beautiful white trees watching over it. Then something moved in the next stall, bumping against the wooden partition.

Katrina leaped to her feet and squinted over. It was a cow—not more than a foot from her. It stared at her. She stared back blurrily. The cow's stall smelled, but she had gotten used to the odor by now; it was almost sweet. Cautiously she leaned over and touched the cow's neck. Its coat was silky and incredibly warm. It was actually giving off warmth. She wished she could get into the stall with the cow, but the animal was bigger than she was and had horns. After resting her hand on its neck for a while, she felt the day's chill leaving her. Suddenly she thought: if only I could live here, on this farm! She could hardly believe she'd ever been scared of the country.

"Moooo," she said to the cow.

It turned its head to gaze at her. It seemed to be smiling. Katrina hated to leave.

Mrs. Healey, the third-floor staff member who had been on duty when Katrina left, rode with Alice Evans, the nurse, in the state car, peering out the window through her steel-rimmed glasses into the woods, hoping to spot Katrina. She was a tall, wiry farmer's wife dressed today as always in khaki slacks, a flannel shirt, and her son's old blue baseball windbreaker. She had raised five children on Christian faith and hard work, and was trying to do the same for the Fairbanks girls, although they often mystified her. "These girls got nothing to run away *to*," she said to Mrs. Evans. "The school gives them free clothes, free medical, all the food they can eat. I'd like to been able to feed my own on what they get, I can tell you."

"I think about my Marcie," Mrs. Evans said, her red cheeks puffing out as she exhaled cigarette smoke. "Such a pretty little thing. We had money saved for her college. She could've been anything she wanted." Mrs. Evans's fifteen-year-old daughter, an only child, had died several years ago following a long, painful illness. "What gets me is how these kids don't give a damn about their lives. Fighting, filling up their bodies with drugs, running away like this Katrina. And every one of them healthy as a horse!" She shook her head, pressing her heavy lips together. "It's just not fair, that's all."

Mrs. Healey nodded and resumed watching out the window, though she couldn't completely agree about the girls' health. She remembered the case of hookworm Vonita had when she'd arrived, and Pam's deafness, and Lucia's gonorrhea, and the cigarette burns that some man had put onto Yvonne's stomach that kept getting infected. But she never contradicted Alice Evans, who was a professional, with a college education. Besides, she owed Alice a lot; Alice and Ben Paleno had gotten her this job just when her family's farm had been about to go under.

"Check and see if the handcuffs are there," Mrs. Evans said, pointing to the glove compartment.

"We won't need them," Mrs. Healey said. "Katrina's so small."

"She's not too small to chuck a rock or swing a fence post." Mrs. Evans turned sharply toward her. "Get them ready, Jean."

"Well . . ." Mrs. Healey sighed. She took a pair of handcuffs out and laid them on the dashboard.

When they reached the highway intersection, the sheriff and a deputy were waiting for them. After a short conference, the two cars fanned out in opposite directions. Mrs. Evans drove in a full circle on the roads around the institution. When she approached the intersection again, there was a car parked along the shoulder beside a drainage ditch.

It was a dented sedan, paintless, scoured to the color of slate. The sloping front end seemed to be rooting in the grass; its back was jacked up high over wide drag-racing tires. Beside the car, three boys in dungarees, T-shirts, and denim jackets were looking down into the ditch laughing. When they heard the station wagon skid to a halt behind them, two boys whirled around, the third hastily zipped up his fly.

Mrs. Healey stepped out and immediately saw Katrina standing in the ditch, her red sweatshirt bright as a flame against the backdrop of dark earth. She was filthy, her face and clothes streaked with dirt, her hair matted. Squinting fiercely up at the roadside, she held one arm up between her face and the boys. The blade of a jackknife in her hand glinted palely. When she saw Mrs. Healey and the state car, she lowered the knife and took several steps along the bottom of the ditch toward them. Then, as Mrs. Evans moved heavily around the front of the station wagon, she froze.

"What are you doing with that girl?" Mrs. Evans shouted at the boys.

They glanced at each other. No one spoke. The sight of Mrs. Evans's fat red face and nurse's uniform seemed to paralyze them for a moment.

"She was hitchhiking," a boy with acne-pitted cheeks said. "We stop to give her a ride and she starts giving us a hard time."

Suddenly he took a step backward as Mrs. Healey stepped forward, the lines in her weathered face taut.

"I know you! You're Bob Kroker's boy." She glared at him through her steel-rimmed glasses. "You get on home, before I tell your father what you're up to!"

"We wasn't doing nothing!" The boy scuffled his boots in place.

"The sheriff's meeting us right here." Mrs. Evans stepped in front of Mrs. Healey. "If you don't clear off, we'll tell him what you had sticking out of your pants a minute ago."

One boy snorted, a laugh that was erased by the long look the others gave him. The boys straightened their shoulders, moved slowly away, their eyes harder and meaner than before now that they were retreating. They slipped into the front seat of the sedan and yanked the doors shut behind them. The car skidded off the shoulder, spraying gravel, and screeched away, leaving a black strip of rubber on the asphalt.

The air slowly cleared of engine noise and fumes. The roadside was still. No one moved. A bird squawked nearby.

Katrina glanced behind her up the steep slope of the ditch.

"Come on, Katrina," Mrs. Healey said. "Nobody's going to hurt you now."

Katrina breathed slowly through her mouth. She rubbed her bare eyes.

"I'll go talk to her." Mrs. Evans started sideways down the slope, and pointed toward a drainage pipe that crossed the ditch several yards away. Mrs. Healey took the signal— she was to walk around behind Katrina to block her escape.

Mrs. Evans lurched down into the trench, pushing herself upright at the bottom. "You see what running away got you?" she screamed at Katrina, puffing to a halt about six feet from her. "You almost got it from those boys, didn't you? Maybe we should have drove on and let you learn your lesson!"

Katrina took a step backward. She raised her arm. The knife blade, dull edge out, pointed at Mrs. Evans' face.

"Just you try to stab me with that thing!" Mrs. Evans rocked forward on the balls of her feet. "I've taken lots bigger weapons off lots bigger girls. You think you scared me with that suitcase when you first came in. Don't kid yourself...." She suddenly looked behind Katrina and jabbed her finger in the air. "Get her, Mrs. Healey!" she screamed.

Katrina whirled around. No one was there. Mrs. Healey was still edging across the pipe. Before Katrina could turn around again, Mrs. Evans had lunged forward and grabbed her wrist. She yanked it high in the air and, turning sharply sideways, slammed her elbow into Katrina's neck.

The knife flew out of her hand. Choking, she staggered backward. Mrs. Healey, who had run up behind her, jumped into the trench, and grabbed her around the neck.

"I got her, Alice! Let go of her!" Mrs. Healey shouted, but Mrs. Evans seemed not to hear. "Leave her, Alice!"

Katrina saw the nurse's hand coming, but was choking too hard to dodge. Her face was knocked sideways by the blow, then swung hard in the opposite direction by a second explosion against her cheek.

"Alice, *don't*!" Mrs. Healey shouted, loosening her grip.

"Little slut has to learn!" Mrs. Evans, panting, drew her arm back and smacked Katrina's face again.

The force of the blow sent Katrina spinning off balance, making her scream, a sudden piercing sound that took Mrs. Healey's breath away. Hugging her from behind, she tried to lift Katrina out of the way of Mrs. Evans's fist. "Stop it! Christ almighty, Alice!" she pleaded.

Mrs. Evans rested one foot against the slope of the ditch and caught her breath. Her skirt was hiked up; the underside of her leg flashed pink where the elastic top of her stocking had slipped down. "Stop what?" she asked, her voice raspy. "The girl came at us with a knife. We took it off her. She had to be subdued. 'Clear and present danger to herself and others.'" Mrs. Evans smiled. "We didn't leave any bruises on her, did we?"

Mrs. Healey shuddered at the meaning of "we." "No, but—" She stared at her friend incredulously.

Mrs. Evans wiped her mouth with the back of her hand. "Listen, Jean, I've been on a lot more runaways than you have. If you don't teach them a lesson when you catch them, they raise all kinds of hell on the ride back. Believe me, I know."

Mrs. Healey shifted her grip on Katrina, holding her under the arms. "Let's go, Alice. Okay?"

Mrs. Evans leaned forward, her face an inch from Katrina's. "If you open your yap about this at school, I'll bring assault with a deadly weapon charges against you for that knife. You'll be doing time till you're fifty." She patted Katrina's cheek. "Nod, if you understand, young lady."

Katrina shut her eyes. The pats on her cheek started to get harder. She nodded.

Mrs. Evans stepped back and picked up the knife. "You keep her there," she said to Mrs. Healey. "I'll get the handcuffs."

Mrs. Healey tightened her grip on Katrina. "No cuffs," she said.

"What?" Mrs. Evans turned her face sharply toward her.

"She don't need no cuffs."

"Listen, she's been struggling. Don't be stupid, Jean."

"I ain't stupid." Mrs. Healey spoke through clenched

teeth. She shook her head hard. "I don't want no cuffs on her. I mean it."

"You've got to sit in back with her." Mrs. Evans glared at Mrs. Healey. "If she tries anything, you'll have to be the one to rassle with her."

"I know that, Alice." Mrs. Healey squeezed her cheek against Katrina's damp hair. "You won't try nothing, will you, honey?" she whispered.

Katrina moaned.

Mrs. Healey picked her up and carried her in her arms toward the car.

Katrina lay on her side on the seat, her arms pressed against her chest. The pain in her head throbbed every time the car ran over a bump. She thought she would never be able to move again, but the weight of Mrs. Healey's arm on her hip— the woman was holding her by the belt—got so heavy that she had to push herself up into a sitting position. Something shiny lay on the seat beside her—her glasses. They must have fallen out of her pocket. Slowly she put them on. Staring out the window, she tried to see through the one half-lens. Bushes were rushing by, green flashes that made quick whooshing sounds. Then they were all gone; she could see fields and, in the distance, a hillside and a stretch of open sky. Between the hill and the sky was a patch of bright white. It looked like a row of feathery white fountains leaping out of the ground. The trees.

She was grateful now for those trees that showed her where her grandfather's grave was. Seeing them again made her feel that he was nearby and that she could be with him again. No matter what happens to me, she thought, I'm glad I found his grave.

Katrina rested her head against the back of the seat. She shut her eyes and saw the white trees shining against a black sky.

17 ❧

When Katrina arrived back at Fairbanks, she was told to go to her room and stay there until supper. Her runaway would be discussed and a punishment handed out in group session the next day. The girls had to appear disapproving of Katrina—she'd let down the group by deserting it. They partially felt this, but they were also envious that Katrina had gotten off grounds on her own all day, and disappointed for her that she hadn't made it home. Pam was the first to visit her as she lay in bed; for a few minutes, Katrina talked to her about her grandfather, then turned her face to the wall and tried to sleep.

Lucia and several other girls had been listening from the doorway; some of them hadn't quite believed that Katrina's grandfather was dead any more than Joey had been, but now they believed it. Lucia said it was a shame Katrina hadn't been able to go to the old man's funeral; his spirit must be restless. She said she was going to do something about this tonight, after lights-out. Anyone who wanted to help out ought to be ready.

At half-past midnight on the third-floor corridor, the dim bulbs overhead reflected dully off the walls, making the paint look darker than it was, giving the hallway the appearance of a tunnel where patches of light were starving for oxygen. Protuberances that looked like breasts severed from bronze statues stared down from the ceiling: they were smoke detectors, looking dead but occasionally giving off low whines as if dreaming of subterranean bonfires.

Katrina, wearing a gray blanket over her bathrobe and nightgown, stood rubbing her eyes in her doorway. She could hear Lucia's faint tapping signal being relayed along the radiator pipes from room to room. The girls tiptoed out into the corridor, some of them looking at Katrina as if expecting her to explain what was going to happen. Dazed with exhaustion from her runaway, she had no more idea than they did, though she didn't say so. Watching Lucia step into the hall, it occurred to her that Lucia could just as well have knocked on the girls' doors; the coded signal, she figured, added mystery to the coming events.

Certainly there had been no danger of waking Mrs. Lert, the midnight-to-eight staff. Wearing a faded cotton smock and canvas shoes, she sat sprawled in an armchair dragged out of the staff office at the lounge end of the corridor. Her paperback Western lay pages down on her belly, her glasses were tilted sideways on her nose, and her mouth was open, filling the corridor with long whiney snores.

In their bathrobes and fuzzy slippers, curlers and kerchiefs, the girls moved silently along the dim hallway and down the back stairs to the basement. Missing were Ronnie and Peaches, who were together in Ronnie's room. Yvonne opened the door to the poolroom with the key she and Lucia had rented from Ronnie, and told the girls to bring folding chairs in with them. The only light came from two small windows near the ceiling. A faint silver-white haze outside was illuminated by the searchlight beam in the parking lot. At times, ragged patches of heavy fog drifted by, darkening the room almost entirely.

Several girls made ghostly noises and were told to shut the fuck up by Yvonne as she walked around collecting a six-cigarette fee from each girl except Katrina. When someone grabbed the back of another girl's neck with her fingertips, the victim gave out with a muffled yelp and everyone had to clutch their mouths to keep from laughing or screaming.

Lucia entered the room, taking her time, knowing that a nervous, impatient audience was a receptive audience. She had learned a sense of theater from her mother, whose private ceremonies she had observed since she had been a little girl. She and her mother were mediums in the *santería* cult of the Water Spirits, which flourished in the Puerto Rican areas of the South Bronx.

As soon as all the whispering had stopped, Lucia picked up a cardboard carton and placed it on the table. The girls watched in rapt silence as she set out an aerosol can called "Lady Luck Room Spray," an institution-sized mayonnaise jar half full of cloudy homemade wine, a dining-room pitcher, a feathered Indian doll, a framed print of Christ's crossed hands with a spike through them, and a candle. She set the candle on a tinfoil ashtray and, after striking three matches and blowing them out, lit the wick and stepped back.

The flame burned straight up toward the ceiling, quivering now and then as if suspended by its thin string of smoke. The girls' cheeks and lips glowed in the light; their eyes were deep hollow shadows. Katrina, with her face nearly invisible inside her hooded blanket, looked especially spooky.

"Take that damn thing off," Vonita whispered. "You look like something dead."

"Shhh," Pam whispered. "It's her grandfather we're going to contact, she can wear what she likes."

The girls quieted down, watching Lucia. She walked slowly around the table, her arms raised. In the glow from the candle, the shadows of her bathrobe sleeves fluttered along the walls like giant wings.

Vonita gripped Katrina's arm. "I want to get out of here!" she whispered, staring wide-eyed at the shadows.

Lucia slowly set the framed print of Christ's hands on a windowsill, then returned to the table and picked up the pitcher in both hands. Speaking softly in Spanish, she lifted the pitcher three times in front of the print. She moved slowly, with a soundless rhythm to her gait that was like that of someone else wearing Lucia's bathrobe and kerchief.

Through her broken glasses, Katrina watched a blurry Lucia dip her fingers into the pitcher and flick water into each girl's face. The water felt warm, yet Katrina shivered. Lucia clinked her ring against the side of the pitcher, making a sound like a tiny bell. Her head tilted back so that only the whites of her eyes were visible. A low moan came out of her mouth. Her head swayed back and forth as if she were delirious. Pam's head began to sway, too.

Suddenly Lucia stood up straight, her head snapping forward. Nobody moved.

"*Buenas noches,*" she said in a voice somewhat like Lucia's but a lot hoarser.

"*Buenas noches,*" Pam said. She was sitting forward, her glasses balanced on the end of her pudgy nose.

Vonita, shaking her head slowly, made a low moaning sound.

Katrina said nothing, but she mouthed the word "Hello," feeling a little the way she had on the hillside earlier. Her eyes filled with tears.

Lucia glided away from the table holding the aerosol can high in the air in both hands. She gave the can three long squirts in each corner of the room. The air now had a heavy, bitter-sweet odor. Several girls coughed. Katrina stared into the candle flame, feeling dizzy.

"Now the room is pure," Lucia said slowly in the strange hoarse voice. "The spirit can come." She filled a plastic cup with wine from the jar and placed it carefully in Katrina's hands. "Drink it," she said.

Katrina did. The wine seemed to clear her mind, leaving her with a sweet taste in her mouth and a sleepy half-smile. Time slowed down. Pam was gazing around as if looking for spirits. Vonita let go of Katrina's arm, giving Katrina the sensation of rising slightly in her chair like a released balloon. Thick clouds of smoke from the girls' dropped cigarettes swirled slowly in the cool breeze from the window. The candle flame shrank, darkening the room; then it shot up, sharp and brilliant, as if trying to writhe free of the wick, and the rapt faces around the table were visible again.

Lucia stepped behind Katrina and placed both hands on the blanket that was covering her head. "A shroud," she said, pulling back the blanket so that it lay over Katrina's shoulders. "You are missing somebody."

"Her grandfather..." Pam whispered, gazing around her. Vonita nodded.

"Grandfather," Katrina whispered. She felt the fingers moving in her hair, pressing gently against her skin, as if they were stroking her exhausted brain, untangling knots of rage, smoothing out swollen lumps of grief. As the candle flame rose again into the darkness, she felt as if she were sinking softly.

She could picture the grave she had made on the hillside, and the trees leaping to the sky like a row of white candle-flames. She could see herself sitting beside the grave, the moist dirt sticking to her fingers, the cool wind blowing against her face....

"Greet your grandfather," Lucia whispered.

Katrina's lips moved. Closing her eyes, she smiled. The white trees shone at her, flickered, and shot high into the air. She turned her face up as if following their flight. Now she could see her grandfather's face clearly in her mind, even when she let her eyes half-open. Wisps of smoke drifted past her face.

"Greet your grandfather." Lucia's voice was close to her ear.

"When..." Katrina cleared her throat. She wanted to explain that she had already spoken to him before. "When I saw him..."

"She saw him!" Vonita gasped.

"I see him, too!" Pam screamed suddenly. "He's got a white beard, just like Kat said! He's *here!*"

"Oh, God!" Vonita slapped her hands to her face, her fingers apart over her eyes. "I see him, too!"

"No—" Lucia moved to calm her. "Shhh!"

Pam leaned forward, her arm stretched out. *"He's by the window. His face! Look—it's all white!"*

"He's here!" Vonita moaned, pointing out the window, where white patches of fog were drifting. The girls stared at them.

Katrina gazed at Pam and Vonita, thinking in a blurry way that she ought to explain that if her grandfather was anywhere, he was on the hillside. But how could she be sure where he was? Perhaps they *had* seen him, and her saying he wasn't here might make him go away.

Suddenly there was a crash as Pam, jumping to her feet, knocked her chair over backward onto the floor. *"He's here!"* she screamed.

Everyone scrambled up. Another chair collapsed. The girls bumped into each other as they squeezed past the pool table. The candle flickered wildly. The pitcher, set rocking on the edge of the table, clanged to the floor, spraying water onto several girls who shrieked as if they had been scalded.

The girls dashed for the door. Whale and Yvonne reached it at the same time, knocking into each other. Vonita was flung sideways. Her wrist cracked against the doorframe; she collapsed to the floor, her face contorted. The girls stumbled past her, shoving, screaming, and dashed across the basement toward the stairs. Katrina, holding her blanket around her, strolled after them.

In the poolroom, Lucia paced around the table, striking matches and flinging them against the walls, cursing in Spanish. The flames died as they fell to the floor, adding a bitter sulfurous scent to the smoky room. She switched on the light by the door.

Vonita was lying on the floor. "My wrist's broken!" she moaned, holding it up.

Lucia began gathering up her paraphernalia. She dragged the folding chairs out into the basement rec room and hid her carton behind the soda fountain.

"I need a doctor!" Vonita wailed.

"Okay, okay." Lucia, spotting a smoke detector overhead, pulled a folding chair beneath it and climbed up. She held a burning match under the bronze nipple of the device. It began to whine.

Upstairs, footsteps were thundering every which way. High-pitched screams trailed off and started up again at either end of the building.

"Come on, come *on*!" Lucia muttered, setting the match-book aflame and holding it up by the corner. Suddenly a loud ringing filled the entire building—an electric staccato din that made Vonita, despite her injury, press her hands over her ears. Lucia jumped down from her chair, grinning.

"Now we really got some spirits in this place!" she shouted over the noise, and crossed herself.

The girls from both floors were evacuated into the parking lot where they waited with their staff for the alarm to stop. But the alarm didn't stop. The building kept clanging and clanging and clanging from every window as if it had been stabbed in some secret nerve and was shrieking out its agony to the woods and dark empty fields. The girls milled around nervously, draped in bathrobes or blankets that dragged behind them across the asphalt. In the mist-swimming searchlight beams they were turned to a restless chorus of Furies, clouds of silver breath-fog clinging to their shadowy faces.

"Hey, Ronnie!" one of the second-floor girls shouted across the asphalt. "Your girls think it's funny or something, setting off that damn noise?"

"Fuck you!" Ronnie shouted back. "It must've been y'all done it! It wasn't us!"

Vonita suddenly grabbed Pam's arm. *"Kat's grandfather set it off!"* she screamed. *"He still in there!"*

Lucia walked beside Mrs. Lert, who was scuttling over to quiet Vonita. "It ain't none of us," Lucia explained, "so it must be him."

Mrs. Lert wrung her hands. "If that noise doesn't stop soon, we're going to have to call the state troopers!"

"Better call a priest," Lucia suggested.

A scuffle flared up between Ronnie and three second-floor girls. Peaches moved in and threw a punch and got her bathrobe ripped down one shoulder, drawing whistles and catcalls from some spectators. Squashing her exposed breast against her chest, Peaches kicked the nearest girl in the knee. The girl, shrieking in pain, tumbled hard into Mrs. Lert. Mrs. Lert went down, landing hard on her stomach. The girls backed away. Mrs. Lert pushed herself up into a sitting position, but could move no farther. Wide-eyed, her cheeks trembling, she stared around her. The clanging continued.

The night watchman, a retired village policeman looking official in dark khaki work pants and shirt, waded into the mob with a shovel held before him like a riot baton. He pushed Peaches and Ronnie back. A second-floor staff woman got a charging girl in a full nelson and lifted her, legs flailing, back into the crowd.

Suddenly the clanging ceased, leaving behind an amazing stillness.

Everyone gaped at the building. Nobody moved. Then cheers went up.

Once back inside, the third-floor girls stayed in their lounge. Nobody wanted to go into a bedroom alone, especially since there was no staff on duty—Mrs. Lert had stayed down in the rec room recovering from her fall. In groups of two or three on the couch and on the carpet, the girls huddled together and argued in loud strained voices about whether Katrina's grandfather could have set off the fire alarm.

Katrina sat in a corner by herself, feeling invigorated by the trip into the fesh air. Gradually the voices in the room began to get to her: Vonita's whining about her wrist, Pam's and Vonita's sobbing insistence that they'd seen a white-bearded face outside the basement window. Suddenly Katrina got to her feet.

"Shut up!" she shouted.

The girls went silent. Everybody stared at her.

"My grandfather wasn't trying to scare nobody." She pulled her blanket tighter around her, surprised that she was saying this, since she still wasn't convinced that she'd seen anything outside the basement window. It didn't seem to matter now. Everybody was listening to her. "He wouldn't do that."

"He wouldn't?" Pam asked, her voice choked.

"No. He was a good man." Katrina didn't sound quite like herself. Her voice had a resonance and authority that made the girls settle back in their sitting positions around her. "Maybe he's just watching over us to make sure we're okay."

The girls looked at each other and then back up at Katrina. She smiled in the direction of the lounge window, where the

fog was still visible over the parking lot outside. Lucia pulled
a pack of cigarettes and matches from the pocket of her bathrobe and passed them around.

"I told you the spirits wouldn't hurt nobody," she said.

Ronnie, who'd been standing in the corridor doorway,
stepped into the room. "Hey, don't everybody be smoking,"
she said, trying to snatch the matches from Lucia's hand.
"You want that damn smoke alarm going off again?"

Lucia pulled her hand from Ronnie's grip. She lit a match.
"It was not smoke that made that alarm go off," she said.
Several girls nodded.

"You weren't there, Ronnie," Katrina said, her voice calmer
than ever.

"Aw, who asked you?" Ronnie stomped away to lean
against the television beside Peaches.

"You *should* have been there, Ronnie!" Vonita spoke up,
her voice choked. She held her wrist in her lap like a wounded
bird. "I *asked* you to come. Why didn't you come?"

Several girls glanced at Ronnie and Peaches and made
snickering sounds.

"I needs a doctor," Vonita moaned. "Where the staff
at?"

Katrina stood up and walked toward the door to the front
stairs. Her bathrobe flapped quietly against her legs. "I'm
going to look for the staff," she said.

"Hey, Kat, thanks," Vonita said.

The girls watched in silence as Katrina pulled open the
lounge door. "I'll be right back," she said over her shoulder,
as if to reassure them.

18 &

Yvonne

*I got your letter, about time. OK I will wait for your
girl peaches discharge in June cause I can not hide no
fugative white fox here, but you I can so you better get
your ass down here in June, discharge or AWOL, with
or without that curly head other girl. I mean it, Bitch, I
did not invest good bread in no damn lawyer to get you
sent to that farm just so you could lay back and play with
yourself. Do not cross me. In my stable you are gold. On
your own you are cold meat in the street.*

SUGAR

Yvonne stood before her mirror holding Sugar's letter in
one hand. In the other was the love letter she'd written to
Peaches weeks ago and ended with the typed signature
"K A T." What she had to do was to leave it for Ronnie to
find. Then all hell would break loose. Ronnie would explode
at Katrina, and her explosion might get her shipped and out
of the way for good. At the very least, the letter would make
Ronnie so desperate that she'd scare Peaches off. Either way,
Peaches would be in Yvonne's bag.

Still, she wished she could have postponed using the letter
a little longer. She'd almost begun to believe she really did
care as much about the girls as she'd been saying she did in
order to take over group sessions. Yvonne had never had any
real friends at Fairbanks until recently. She wasn't like other

girls, who were all either white or black or Spanish. With her pale tan skin and straight hair and green eyes, she was something else: either a freak, or unique, as Sugar said. And whether she ended up cold meat in the street or in the front seat of a Mercedes depended entirely on her playing up the beautiful unique.

She slunk tigerlike toward her mirror, raising her eyebrows and puffing out her lips like Lola Washington on the jacket of her *Live at the Persian Room* album. She ran her fingers down her wine-colored blouse over the points of her breasts, across her pelvis to the inside of her thighs. Half-closing her eyes, she saw not the reflected plaster walls and ceiling, but a nightclub landscape of black vinyl and chrome, of silver spotlights and sparkling diamond prisms spraying rainbows all over her. She danced in place, grinding against her long beautiful fingers, waiting for a hot shivery feeling to wash over her like applause ... but it didn't.

She was too worried about the damn letter.

The sooner she got rid of it, the better. She snatched it off her bureau and strode off into the corridor.

Ronnie smelled the letter. She ran her finger over the typed words. She held the paper up to the light to search for telltale marks. She read it so many times she could almost recite it to herself. In fact, she couldn't stop various phrases from hissing repeatedly into her mind as if someone had jumped up behind her when she wasn't looking to whisper them into her ear.

At supper, she sat with her chin in her hand, her face motionless except for her eyes that swept slowly around the dining room from girl to girl. The letter could have been a forgery—anyone could have typed it. None of these girls had been backing her in group session recently. Katrina wasn't the only suspect, though she was, irrationally, a prime one. Ronnie pressed her hand against her stomach beneath her sweatshirt, terrified that she'd lose control of herself or that her ulcer would explode instead.

When she had arrived at Fairbanks, she had hoped that being away from her mother might help her get rid of the ulcer. Here, she had been able to establish the kind of peaceful family life she'd never known at home, and had learned some nonviolent ways of safeguarding it. But when something like this letter came up, she remembered that she was her mama's girl, like it or not. She was a fighter. All her life, she'd lived in a racial battle zone. She'd heard about white devils at her mother's knee, and had nightmares about mobs marching in hoods into her room carrying flaming crosses like in her mother's picture books. Her mother had formed organizations to take on the landlord, the city government, the Welfare, even the cops. Ronnie remembered the night the cops had dragged her mother kicking and screaming down the stairs, blood dripping from the gash their nightsticks had put in her hairline. Ronnie had dreamed of breaking into the jail, guns blazing, and bringing her mother out while pink-faced guards dropped like dead roaches from the cellblock tiers.

At school, she'd joined in the annual spring race riots and gotten her own head busted by cops many times. But something funny had begun to happen afterward: when the kids had bragged about their adventures in the riots, she'd found herself swapping tales with white kids as well as black. She'd discovered that it was sometimes possible—as in a basketball rivalry—to respect an opponent if she put up a good fight. She still hated whites, but more impersonally, the way you might hate a lethal epidemic that was going around or a tidal wave that was looming over your neighborhood poised to crash. At the same time, she'd gotten curious about how, when you talked with whites one at a time, they could behave almost like regular people.

Right now, though, she couldn't stand the sight of any of them. She shoved her chair back from the table and started across the dining room toward the door.

"What's wrong with *you*?" Peaches looked up, her eyelashes in motion.

Ronnie opened her mouth, but then didn't dare speak.

Katrina lay on her bed holding her new Snoopy wristwatch up over her face so that the red glow from the EXIT sign in the hallway could shine on it. The little dog held both its paws straight up : midnight.

The watch was a gift from Yvonne, who got things in the mail from her man and gave some of them away, mostly to Peaches. Though Katrina usually refused Yvonne's presents, she hadn't been able to resist the watch. She'd always wanted one. Nobody else was going to give her things. Why not take it ?

She watched Snoopy's paw move to five past twelve, ten past, fifteen past. Other people had pets, why shouldn't she ? On the TV last night—a "Brady Bunch" rerun—the teenage daughter found a kitten that nobody wanted and her father finally let her keep it. That kitten was so cute ! When the girls saw it licking the daughter's face at the end, they'd cried.

She lay on her side with the watch against her cheek, listening to it tick. Poor Snoopy, he had to spend all his life behind that round plastic window waiting for time to go by. That's what she'd been doing this morning, checking every few minutes to see how close it was to when Steven was supposed to start his shift. After the séance, he'd had a long talk with her in his office about her grandfather. He showed her more drawings his daughter had sent him, and even talked about when he'd lived in Jamaica, which she was amazed to discover was a lot like Florida. By the time the conference was over, she'd managed to convince herself that she wasn't mad at him because of what Mrs. Evans had done to her. During the week's restriction the group had given her, he'd kept an eye on her, but in the past few weeks he'd seen her only in group sessions. When he'd arrived today, he'd gone directly into the director's office, where he was spending a lot of time lately. Well, never mind. Katrina lay on her stomach, squirming under the covers.

She remembered Peaches telling her on her first day that sometimes the girls wanted to kill Steven, sometimes they wanted to fuck him. She squirmed harder against the mattress but then stopped, feeling funny. She remembered a night when she and Peaches had listened to Pam talking about the things her father had done in bed with her ; Peaches had said,

Stop, you're getting me turned on, and then Pam had suddenly looked sick. "Me, too," she whispered, and started to cry. Katrina felt sort of like that. She had to get up and walk around. Pulling her bathrobe on over her cotton nightdress, she glanced at herself in the mirror. She liked the blue-framed "designer" glasses the school had bought her to replace the broken ones. The two big plastic circles on her face made her mop of curly hair seem styled that way, like the models on the back of magazines in the "You've come a long way, baby" ads. Those women looked as if they really *liked* having bad eyesight and no tits.

Katrina walked down the corridor. Several bulbs were out along the ceiling, making it look darker and narrower than usual. The EXIT sign reflected red on the glass door of the fire hose's wall cabinet; the hose seemed coiled too tight inside.

Ronnie's door was ajar. Peaches couldn't be in there with the door ajar, but she wasn't in her bed. Where was she? Yvonne's room, probably: Katrina tiptoed past Ronnie's open door. No sound came from inside.

Mrs. Lert was snoring in an armchair outside the staff office, her legs with their varicose veins stretched out in front of her. Katrina stepped over them and padded quietly into the staff office. She sat cross-legged on top of the desk, smoking a cigarette and looking through the logbook. Inside it was a letter marked PRIVATE AND CONFIDENTIAL, Katrina's favorite kind. But it was only from Whale's probation officer, telling Steven that he didn't want Whale coming home for an emergency visit to look for her baby, since Welfare had no record of her having one and her relatives all denied any baby existed—a child was a figment of Whale's imagination: "not an uncommon longing among overweight black teenage girls, who often view motherhood as the only worthwhile profession open to them," said the probation officer. Poor Whale, Katrina thought; she's going to have a fit when she finds out.

Katrina flipped through the log, looking to see if Steven had written anything about her. She found an entry written by Mrs. Healey:

Katrina, Yvonne, and Peaches are working nicely on their own rehearsing for the show. They have made up their own skit but won't tell anybody about it.

Katrina covered her mouth to keep from laughing—"working nicely"! Wait till the staff saw that skit! It got funkier and filthier every time they rehearsed it. She wondered if they'd ever have the guts to put it on.

She shut the log and went over to the window ledge where she picked up the BIG CHEEZE coffee mug that the girls had bought Steven last week for his thirty-sixth birthday. She curled up in the armchair with it, sipping what was left of some cold sweet coffee. The chair sank unevenly under her weight, the worn material soft against the skin of her legs. She inhaled the scent of yesterday's cigarette butts, of shredded-rubber pencil erasures, and mimeograph-inked forms— the smell of authority, all enclosed by the official off-white walls and shut black windows. The office felt like the safest place on earth. She turned the mug in both hands in front of her face, humming quietly, reading THE BIG CHEEZE in blue letters every time it came around. Her watch ticked contentedly close to her ear.

Finally, when Snoopy's shorter arm pointed to the two, Katrina stood up, yawning. She decided to wash out Steven's mug.

She stepped over Mrs. Lert's legs again and padded quietly down the corridor toward the bathroom. Just as she was about to go into the bathroom, she thought she heard a noise inside, and stepped back. The hallway was dim and quiet. The faint murmur of radios and the sound of people breathing in their rooms like curtains flapping slowly in a breeze were all that she could hear. Holding the mug tight against her chest, she pushed open the door.

The bathroom was so brightly lit she had to squint. The white plaster walls glared; the fluorescent tubing overhead made an intense buzzing Katrina could almost feel against the skin of her face. The room smelled of soapy underwear that had been left soaking in one of the sinks; a glass shampoo bottle stood not quite straight on the edge of another sink.

Suddenly Katrina heard the noise again; someone was throwing up. Then the stall door at the end of the row opened. Ronnie stepped out. When she saw Katrina, she dropped the wad of toilet paper in her hand.

"What you want?" Ronnie's voice was scratchy.

"Nothing." Katrina looked at her curiously.

"What you squinting at like that?"

"Nothing." Ronnie's hair looked strange—low on her forehead like a tight stocking cap; no wonder she usually kept it covered with her sweatshirt hood. What looked even stranger were Ronnie's eyes: they were red-rimmed from crying. Suddenly they swelled with rage. Katrina knew she never should have noticed them.

"What you *want*, bitch?" Ronnie's voice broke.

Katrina slipped into the nearest stall just as Ronnie took a step toward her. She latched the door shut and sat down on the toilet cover, keeping her bathrobe wrapped tight around her legs. All she had to use for a weapon was the BIG CHEEZE mug. She could smash it against the latch, threaten to cut Ronnie with a sharp piece of it... she should break it now, while Ronnie, breathing loudly outside, padded back and forth on the linoleum. But she didn't break it, even when she saw Ronnie's fingers grip the bottom of the stall door.

With a loud grunt, Ronnie jerked the door up. The crosspiece popped out of the latch. Bright light flooded the stall. Katrina held the mug up in front of her face.

Ronnie's arm shot out. She grabbed Katrina by the hair. The mug fell and rolled away. Katrina stumbled forward, dragged by the hair. Ronnie's knee rose up fast and cracked her on the chin. Katrina collapsed. Her glasses were gone. She saw—too late—a blur coming at her out of the blinding light: Ronnie's foot caught her on the cheek, sent her spinning over sideways. Her head slammed into the floor.

The next sensation she felt was Ronnie yanking her back onto her knees with an arm under her stomach. Katrina gasped for breath, then pitched forward as Ronnie's fist thudded into the back of her neck. She felt cold air rush up her legs.

Then something colder, something hard, was sliding along

her skin. She let out a scream as it jabbed her up between her legs. Suddenly she was thrashing on the floor; Ronnie held her down by the back of the neck with one hand and with the other rammed the shampoo bottle into her crotch. Katrina squirmed sideways; the bottle shattered against the floor. A point of glass sliced into the inside of her leg.

Then Ronnie was gone, her footsteps fading quickly down the corridor outside the bathroom door. Katrina lay collapsed on her stomach, her bare buttocks in the air. As soon as she could stop gasping, she pushed herself to a kneeling position, and gingerly felt her wounds. Her fingers came back bright red with blood.

"I've been raped!" she cried out. Silence. No one had heard her. After a few minutes of swaying on her knees, she pulled herself up and shuffled over to the nearest sink. She found her glasses, unbroken, beneath it, and put them on. Behind her on the linoleum she saw a mess of shattered glass and smeared blood. She had to hold onto the sink with both hands to keep from collapsing.

Eventually her heart stopped thumping so hard and she turned on the tap. Very slowly, she pulled some paper toweling down from the dispenser and washed herself between her legs. The cool water took some of the pain away. Leaning over to try to look at herself, she discovered that she had not quite been raped after all—the blood was from a gash in her leg that was still bleeding. A few inches away, the outside of her vagina hurt worse than the cut, but she had no internal injuries.

She gave up trying to stop the blood and made no effort to wipe off her leg. Still dazed, she moved toward the door. Her foot struck something that skidded away. She leaned over and picked it up: the BIG CHEEZE mug. She shuffled slowly with it out the door and up the corridor. A thin wavy line of red marked her unsteady progress toward the office.

Mrs. Lert was still sprawled in her chair, lips slightly open as she snored. The office looked bleak and shabby and ugly. The bulb overhead was dimmer than Katrina remembered it. She leaned against the desk, the mug in one hand clunking against the blotter, and pulled the telephone toward her.

The staff numbers were posted on the wall behind the desk. She dialed Steven's number carefully, her fingers trembling. The phone rang and rang and rang, and with every ring, she heard a scream inside her head—her own voice trapped behind her teeth, waiting for the opening of the phone line to release it. But the line never opened. Finally she put the receiver down. Leaning over the desk again, she looked at the staff numbers.

Sonia? No. She dialed Leah's number, pressing the mug, its handle between her fingers, against the side of her head along with the receiver. Leah's phone rang and rang, too. Katrina suddenly looked at her watch. She'd forgotten about it. It ticked, the hands moved—it had no internal injuries. Snoopy's hands pointed out the time—2:25.

"Hello? Who is this?" It was Leah's voice, but sounding different—foreign.

Katrina tried to speak, but no sound came out of her mouth. The task of saying in words what had just happened to her seemed beyond possibility—suddenly she was so ashamed and confused it seemed she'd never be able to speak again. Then she heard another voice on the phone.

"Who is it?" That was Steven. Steven. He must have been standing close behind Leah. He sounded different, too. Annoyed. Katrina heard music playing: thumping guitar chords.

"Leah, hang up." Steven again: there with Leah. Katrina jammed the receiver tight against her ear. Her mouth opened. "Steven?—"

Too late. Click. The receiver buzzed. She put it down, ramming it every which way between the prongs of its cradle until finally the buzzing noises stopped. The office was silent. Shivering, Katrina pushed herself back from the desk.

Her grip on the mug loosened. She watched it slip from her fingers.

Then she was sitting in the armchair, feeling dizzy with pain, crying. She wiped her eyes and squinted at the place on the floor where the mug had exploded. Nothing was there but some bloody smears her footprints had made. By the corner of the desk, she spotted a piece of china.

The big blue letters on it didn't spell anything. She began to cry again.

To move her leg hurt terribly, but she pushed herself sideways in the chair and kicked the piece of the mug far out of sight beneath the desk.

When Ronnie, lying wide awake in her bed across the corridor, heard the mug shatter against the office floor, she sat up suddenly and slapped her hands across her ears. Too late—she'd heard Katrina's gasping voice. Mrs. Lert hadn't, though. Ronnie stood in her doorway, waiting for the woman to wake up and go take care of Katrina. Finally, as Katrina's faint weeping seemed to fill the corridor like sirens, Ronnie snatched an empty soda can from her bureau and flung it sidearm along the floor. It clattered against the wall near Mrs. Lert and rolled noisily against the leg of her chair. She woke up with a loud snort.

Ronnie slipped back into her room. She took out her stationary, but it took her several hours of pacing before she could sit down to write.

TO: *PEACHES*   *DAY: EVERY*

FROM: RONNIE   *TIME: DARK*

Songs: *TRYING TO HOLD ONTO MY WOMAN*

          FOREVER CAME TODAY

          GOING UP IN SMOKE

Dedication: *(So you will know where I am at)*

             That's the sound that lonely makes
             Oh that's the sound my heart can't take
             Streets deserted, only emptiness in me

             Time for dreamin'
             'Cause reality makes me cry

Dearest Peaches

It is 4:40 in the morning and I still don't know where you are at, but I got to write you this. I think I am going to get shipped. If Kat snitches. She came snooping around and I fucked her up with a bottle. I just went crazy. I was going to ram it up her but then I stopped, I hated myself more than her. Now I hardly hate her at all, I feel sick, even worse than I did after we got Panda beat up.

All the meanness of this place got inside me and made me crazy. When Kat talked up in group about families that day I knew I couldn't keep it in much longer. Then this letter (it is in the envelope for you to see). I'm sure it is a forgery but it has her name at the bottom anyway. Maybe one of those 2nd floor bitches wrote it, but maybe it is one of OUR girls! It is terrible to think you can't even trust your own family!

Do you remember how it was before Kat came here? When we were always together and in each others arms we were FREE of this hell, FREE, of all the hate and meanness in the world. I was never free like this even at home. I was scared of you at the beginning, did you know that? But then I saw how beautiful you are, right down to your soul.

And I get to thinking, if there is one beautiful white femme like you in this world, then maybe the world is not like I thought. Maybe it is not a mountain of hate and meanness I always got to be banging my fists against.

Maybe we can build a tunnel through this mountain with our love. On the other side there is grass and trees and sun and clouds and blue sky. And birds, lots of birds, Peaches, all flying around the place. And they are all different colors like blue and green and red and golden like your hair and black like me. In this place the crow is as beautiful as the eagle.

And we are lying on the grass watching those birds. They are just singing and making nests. It is all at peace there. It is warm there like Africa.

This is a clear place in the jungle. And we are just holding hands and laughing and getting it on any time we feel like it right out there in the open.

Peaches, it can be like this again. I don't care where you were tonight. But now we got to make plans. If Kat snitches maybe we have to run away together. No black girl ever run away from this place, we are all scared of these mountain men and their mad dogs and shotguns, but I am willing to take a chance. I am willing to risk a lynching to keep us together and free.

Meet me in the nest downstairs, during Miss Rhode's sewing, 4th period.

Now that I have wrote this I don't feel so hateful and crazy, I just feel like I want you up against me.

PEACE	*RONNIE*	*LOVE*
&	*&*	*&*
LOVE	*PEACHES*	*PEACE*
	FOR	
	E	
	V	*
	E	* *R* *
	R	*

19 ❧

The next morning, after Leah had left for an early shift, Steven drove to work from her house around noon. The day was pale and clear; a whitish sun shone high above the unplowed fields with their edges of hard, muddy snow that refused to melt though the grass beside the highway was trying to turn from brown to green. Steven veered off onto a dirt road where he saw a schoolbus turn. What was it doing out at this time of day? Perhaps returning kids from an overnight trip. Or perhaps it was a phantom schoolbus. Intrigued, Steven followed it. The road wound through hilly pastureland where occasional shotgun houses stood in patches of dirt surrounded by matted grass. Many of the house fronts had been repaired with strips of metal from advertising signs which rust had made illegible. Steven drove slowly behind the bus, an old orange one that spouted black fumes, bounced and rattled over every pothole.

Each time it stopped, red lights flashing, children stepped down onto the road and ran across it down dirt driveways. Once a solitary girl with pale cheeks and straight brown hair paused in the road before walking in front of his car. She was about nine but wore a dress that looked too old for her: long and faded, with a hem brown with dust. Pam and Peaches and other rural girls had arrived at Fairbanks in dresses like that.

She stood beside the bus facing Steven. He motioned for her to cross. She stood still, staring back at him, her heavy black lunchbox held up in front of her chest as if to keep his car at bay. Finally, with an inaudible laugh that lit up her face, she fled across the road and down an incline into a littered yard. The bus ground its gears and rolled away. Steven watched the girl jump up onto a cinder-block stoop and disappear into the doorway of a ramshackle house with opaque, plastic-insulated windows.

He sat in the front seat, idling his motor, remembering the look on the girl's face as she'd stood hesitating in the middle of the road. She'd looked sullen and tense—a future Fairbanks kid, perhaps. But beautiful in the same way they sometimes were, when she'd laughed. Even the plainest, angriest, most foul-mouthed girl had certain facial expressions, certain postures and movements which, for an instant, could communicate pure loveliness. He thought of Katrina's smile behind her round glasses as she'd handed him a cup of coffee in the kitchen. Such moments kept him cheerful; sometimes they were all that kept him going. But they could not be prolonged. To watch too intently—as he'd stared at this girl in the road—could be dangerous. When a girl stared back with that bristly what-you-looking-at-man? expression on her face, her eyes filled with an explosive mixture of pleasure, embarrassment, desire, fear, and rage, all swirling chaotically together at him, he felt as if he were holding a match over a narrow dark dungeon in which a pale figure, naked and emaciated, suddenly glanced up at him . . . and screamed, and he would have to hurry away, pretending not to have seen, not to have heard, never to have felt the trembling in his own scorched fingers.

The car engine died. Sitting in the midst of the sudden silence, Steven didn't want to drive on, to cause his picture of the girl to begin fading slowly into a harmless, unevocative memory, the way a phantomlike presence beneath the murky liquid in a developing tray turned into a mere photographic image on a piece of paper. Had he driven on, she might not have reminded him of his daughter, but now she did, and he could imagine what his life would have been like if Sarah had lived with him. She'd have probably been in that girl's grade. She'd get off a schoolbus every day. Some days he'd arrange his schedule so that he could meet her as she ran across the yard with her lunchbox. But not a yard like the one of this house. Never.

Steven's father had once left him and his mother in a shotgun house in a backwoods area like this one. It had flaking plaster walls and a rusty wood stove, but what Steven remembered most were the fleas: fleas in the armchairs, in the mattresses, in the pillows, and little red fleabites on his scalp, showing on the back of his neck no matter how he tried to keep his shirt collar up. When he arrived home from school, his mother scolded him about the spots of blood on his collar that he'd made by scratching the bites. The spots turned light brown in the wash but never faded away.

Perhaps Sarah was better off where she was. The kids around here would bring fleas and lice to school with them; the teachers would be ignorant and overworked; the bus rides would be interminable. In Japan a limousine drove her home from school; sometimes, he knew, her stepfather, whom she called Henry, waited for her beside the driver. But she still missed America, he was pretty sure: many of the drawings she sent were of rural American scenes: barnyards, cows, and lots of horses.

He'd tried to talk to her about that when he'd last spoken to her on the telephone.

Henry says I can start ballet lessons next month.
Oh, yeah?
I'm going to get tights like Mommy's.
That'll be nice.
Uh-huh. Henry says Krrrrrk . . . . krrrrrk . . .
What, honey?
Krrrrkkkkk.
Never mind. Sarah? Okay. Do you still like horses, Sarah?
I can't hear you, Daddy.
HORSES. DO YOU STILL LIKE HORSES?
Oh. I don't know.
Did you get the horse book I sent you?
Uh-huh. It was nice. But, Daddy, I caught a butterfly, it was all orange and spots and everything but I didn't keep it.

No?

No, Henry said krrrrrkkkkk ...

What?

Steven, I'm going to get on the extension here—

Dammit, Anna, I'm talking—

No, I'm sorry, but I won't have you criticizing to Sarah things that go on in this house. It's none of your concern whatsoever—

I wasn't criticizing anything—

I heard you—

You were listening in?

This time I was. Every time you call, Sarah's upset, so this time krrrrkkkkk ...

Will you get the hell off the line!

Krrrrrkkkkkk and as soon as Sarah mentions ballet, you bring up horses, because horses are your thing—

I don't give a damn about horses! Sarah used to like them—

Daddy?

Sarah, dear, get off the phone—

Let her talk, Anna—

Daddy, I still like horses—

Sarah, dear, I told you—

No, she can talk to me—

Daddy?

Sarah?

Krrrrrkkkkkk.

Sarah?

... click.

How could he love someone so much with only fragile threads of wire and invisible radio waves to connect his feelings to her? Had she heard them? Yes: *Daddy, I still like horses.* And her feelings had flown back to him, aerated and compressed through the phone receiver—a welcome ghost of a voice....

Steven looked around. The house was silent, dark. The yard was empty, strewn with rusted tin cans, broken toys, scraps of cardboard. Who was he waiting for?

Sarah wasn't there. He twisted the key in the ignition,

rammed the accelerator to the floor. A two-hundred-horse-power roar blasted through heavy pipes to drown out the silence. He shifted into gear, and the car lurched off toward the school, tires skidding in the loose dirt.

Buried under bedclothes, Katrina had lain awake all night. In the morning, when the staff found her, she'd agreed to go to the infirmary only after the nurse promised that Mrs. Evans wouldn't be in today. She dozed and woke up with her bandaged cut throbbing like a scream inside her skin. Once, thrashing and kicking, she dreamed that a black wolf was standing over her with its long teeth tearing into her cunt. A year ago she'd talked about dreams with an institution psychologist; she had no trouble figuring out who this wolf stood for.

But when she saw Ronnie in the dining room at lunch, Ronnie didn't come off big and bad at all—just the opposite. She kept her face lowered; instead of looking as if she could sell Katrina all the wolf tickets she wanted now, she seemed even more scared of Katrina than Katrina was of her. She moved hesitantly, without her usual stride, almost as if she were thinking of coming over to Katrina's table and apologizing. Katrina pictured what might happen: she'd throw a bowl of scalding soup in Ronnie's face; she'd thrust the serrated edge of her butter knife into Ronnie's throat; or she'd tip the table over onto Ronnie—this was more likely—and run like hell.

Katrina managed to eat a few bites, determined not to show how upset she was because she'd told everybody she'd tripped and fallen while carrying the shampoo bottle. Not a very believable story, she knew, but she stuck with it when the woman doctor from the hospital came to spray her leg with liquid ice and sew four stitches into her skin. The doctor, who'd worked in a women's prison, talked as if she thought Katrina had gotten stoned on something and tried to masturbate with the bottle. Well, letting people think that wasn't as bad as what would happen to her if she told the truth. A snitch she'd known at Maviskill had had her face dunked over and over again into a toilet bowl full of diarrhea until she'd passed out with her lungs full of liquid. A snitch's life wasn't worth living.

She had another reason to keep silent, too : Ronnie might not dare touch her again out of fear Katrina would drop a dime and get her shipped, never to see Peaches again. Hell, Katrina might be able to wolf Ronnie now—for cigarettes, stolen food, support in group session, all kinds of favors. But she didn't feel like trying to. The less she had to do with Ronnie, the better. There was no telling when Ronnie might explode again. She was like Dr. Jekyll and Mr. Hyde on the late movie; last night in the bathroom she'd been like some crazy red-eyed animal wearing Ronnie's clothes.

Katrina had once overheard Sonia telling Steven how amazed she was that the girls' moods could change so quickly. The whole place's mood seemed to Katrina to have changed today. The ceilings were lower, the walls closer, the light dimmer, the food smellier; the girls were younger, the staff bigger and more distant, as if older. Leah, despite her warm, musical voice, had lost all her qualities except her foreignness and blackness. Turning her face to the infirmary wall, Katrina had refused to speak to her; all she could think about was this woman spreading her long black legs last night so that Steven could ram his dick in and out of her. *Damn Steven!* Katrina remembered a country girl saying he walked around the place like a fox in a chicken yard. Was he the wolf, fox, whatever it was, in her dream ? Wondering this made Katrina so confused and scared she had to press her fists against her eyes to keep from trembling all over. *Damn Steven*—he'd probably look different today, too.

The person who seemed the most different today was herself. You were supposed to feel changed after you'd lost your virginity, but she hadn't felt as weird after the first time with Joey as she did now. Maybe she'd lost her actual virginity before Joey, when her mother's boyfriend had managed to get his finger into her when she'd been twelve. A dick, now that she thought about it, was comparatively harmless—you evidently had to give it permission to get into your cunt or it got soft and couldn't, whereas with a finger or a bottle, a person could fuck you over as much as he—or she, it didn't matter—wanted to. No wonder ''fuck'' was a curse word.

That fucking had anything to do with getting turned on was bullshit, as far as she could see. The few times she ever got turned on, all she wanted was stroking and hugs—but that was probably bullshit, too, since she'd never had any.

Even thinking about it seemed dangerous today. *So stop thinking!* she thought, *stop thinking!*

After her mother's boyfriend had messed with her, she'd thought maybe she'd hate guys and turn into a lez, expecially after getting locked up in so many girls' jails. Now it was pretty certain she wouldn't like girls in that way either. Who the hell was left? It seemed bullshit and really weird now that anyone ever got turned on by anybody, but she knew most people did; even the girls who weren't into family life here went around giggling and talking about finger popping. It must be her that was weird. But so what? She'd rather be weird than raped. Still, it made her want to burst out crying to think that at sixteen she might be finished with getting turned on.

Thinking was so confusing! Everything was so fucked up!

She rolled over on the infirmary mattress, staring at the shiny white walls around her. Leah had told her that if she stayed here and rested, she'd feel better. *Bullshit!* As scared as she was of facing Ronnie, or Steven, or the girls, she had to get out of this damn room or she'd think herself into going crazy.

On the third floor, she made herself somewhat comfortable on the window ledge in her room, despite the way her cut stung. The other girls from her unit were in group session with Sonia. Below her in the parking lot, some second-floor girls were washing Mr. Paleno's new car, a long, cream-colored sedan with a landau roof that the girls called a pimp-mobile. The smell of the soapsuds reached her along with the scent of hose water on asphalt. She was glad for the chance to be by herself. To be alone was the only way to clear her mind, to separate what was real from what was bullshit. She wasn't exactly sure what was real, but she did know that one way of finding out was to see what, if anything, was left over after she'd decided what was bullshit.

Bullshit was the sticky-sweet way the building always smelled of new paint on old walls. It was the bitter smell of Vonita's pissy sheets going round and round in the dryer without being washed first. It was the way the toilets stank some mornigs after absolutely nobody at all had ever dreamed of clogging them up with Tampax.

The smell was everywhere. It was the stink of grilled ass-hole-and-armpit-of-run-over-deer that the kitchen staff called "venisonburgers." It was Mr. Paleno's whiskey-and-dead-cigar breath. It was the way Mrs. Lert's breath smelled of indigestion when she snored. It was the smell of a secretary's nail polish when she looked up from her little bottle to tell you she was too busy to check the mail right now, it'd be ready in a couple of hours. It was the smell of the stale doughnuts that Miss Freeman gave out in English when you read something right that any third-grader could read and that bored you so much you'd start throwing pencils or chairs or Miss Freeman out the window if you weren't busy stuffing your mouth with sweet, dry dough.

And sometimes, like now—Katrina started, gripping the edge of the window frame—it was the stink of exhaust fumes from Steven's huge, shiny old car when he revved up his engine, practically making it explode before he switched it off in the parking lot.

Katrina shut her eyes and saw all the smells mingling outside the building, floating along the corridors, trailing into the rooms. They hovered over her bed at night, swirled slowly up her nostrils and out her lips as she breathed. No matter how many windows she opened, the stench of bullshit lingered in the air.

The staff, though, said it was perfume. They said it smelled as sweet as, say, those pink plastic roses that grew magically out of toilet bowls in the TV commercials. Some staff had been breathing the smell of bullshit in and out for so long they really believed what they said about it. If a girl learned to go around saying that she, too, smelled the roses, then they said she was rehabilitated and gave her a discharge from the place.

Well, when it came time for her to get her discharge papers, Katrina might learn to smell roses in the toilet bowls—

in the ashtrays, in the mashed potatoes, in the mop-water buckets, what the hell—but meanwhile she could have used a gas mask.

She looked at her wristwatch, the only thing about her that was unchanged from last night. How long would it take for Steven to telephone upstairs to have her sent down to his office—five minutes? After seven minutes, she began to fidget. She didn't want to talk to him, but the bastard could at least call. He was probably talking with the director, like he usually was nowadays. After nine minutes, she suddenly sat back with her eyes shut and was completely sure he wasn't going to call. She hated the way feelings were splashing over her today like crazy waves. When the phone did ring in the corridor, it sounded like a fire alarm right next to her ear; she nearly fell off the window ledge.

Holding tight to the railing, she made her way downstairs. The sight of Steven's office made her heart start banging in her chest. It looked as if it had been trashed. His green temple drawing was leaning at an angle against the empty wall; his desk and armchair were covered with splattered cloths like pointy ghosts; old newspapers and rollers and paintbrushes lay strewn on the floor. The air smelled sticky.

"I'm in here."

She heard his voice behind the door and froze for a moment, then slowly turned around. He was standing by the big desk in the director's office across the hall. Behind him, windows taller than she was blazed with sunlight. He was wearing a new tan suit and a white shirt, and on his face was the tense, narrow-eyed look that the director, Mr. Steiner, always wore. His hair looked frizzled, his mustache droopy—like he was tired of playing director already. Most people wouldn't have noticed this—he still had on one of his swirly ties, light blue with silver highlights—but Katrina was used to checking out his face and today it didn't look right. *It's his and not his,* she thought.

"Come on in." He put out a cigarette in a glass ashtray on the desk. "We can use this office."

She stayed in the doorway. The walls here had been freshly

painted, a porcelain white whose sweet stink scoured her nostrils. The pictures on the wall were of that foreign city Mr. Steiner came from. The desk was too big and there was no framed photo of Steven's daughter on it. She was used to looking at the photo during their conferences. There was no black rock on the desk to hold in her hand either.

"I got nothing to talk about," she said.

He gazed at her until the silence he gave off swelled like a balloon taking up all the air in the room. *Was he mad at her?* For a moment she felt as if she'd done something bad last night in the bathroom. She clenched her fists at her sides and put the idea out of her mind with the first sentence that flew into her head.

"What're you, going to take over being director now?"

"Not yet...."

His eyebrows were trying not to frown. She realized she'd asked an important question, not just something to burst the unbearable balloon of silence. "So you really are," she said. "When?"

"I don't know." He smiled too quickly. "June, maybe. Or in the fall, or maybe never. Nothing's official." He took a peanut out of the fancy china bowl on the desk and pushed the bowl toward her. "I'll be talking to you girls as soon as I hear something definite. How'd you hear about it?"

"The grapevine." Katrina turned away from him and the bowl. When Vonita had first told the girls that she'd overheard the secretaries saying Steven might "move up" in the summer, some girls had panicked, but then they'd forgotten about it—the summer was much too far ahead to think about. Katrina had tried to forget hearing about it, too. She'd tried not to notice that he was staying away from the third floor sometimes, letting Leah or Sonia run group sessions, and that she'd seen him from the foyer sitting in the director's office with Mr. Steiner and men in suits from Youth Service headquarters. *The bastard's been taking lessons on how to be a director,* she thought, as if for the very first time.

"I wish you'd come in," Steven said, his voice straining to sound calm.

Pushing her toe against the floor made the cut in her leg hurt. "I got things to do upstairs."

"We need to talk."

"Not me." She glanced around, avoiding his steady gaze. "All right, all right," she muttered, and limped across the carpet to slouch into a hardback chair.

"How'd your talk with Leah go?" Steven sat on the edge of the desk, facing her.

How'd your all-night nigger-fucking fuck with Leah go? Katrina glared at the carpet. "Her and me didn't have nothing to talk about," she said.

"I thought it might be easier for you to talk to a woman."

Katrina sighed loudly. "Nobody raped me with a bottle." *It's true! Nothing got into my cunt—ask that doctor!*

"You want me to believe you just tripped and fell on a shampoo bottle?"

"Yeah." Katrina shut her eyes tight, trying not to look at the picture that had just popped into her head—the trashed, bloody bathroom floor, the broken glass, the fluorescent light vibrating against the tiles.

"I'm sorry, I can't believe that," Steven said.

She ground her teeth. *Sorry's what you are, man.*

"Katrina?"

"I fell."

Steven's boots swung once against the side of the desk and went still. "I want to help you, but I can't if you won't be straight with me."

Help—bullshit! Leah, hang up! Hang up on her! Katrina turned her face farther from him.

"I can't allow this kind of violence to go on here." He stood down from the desk. His mustache bristled.

Trying to look big 'n' bad, mean and hard like a prison warden, but look at your crazy tie, your sad crazy blue eyes— director, my ass! She pushed her toes into the carpet to stop the waves from splashing over her, but just made her cut sting fiercely. *Maybe the stitches are coming out and I'll start bleeding all over the floor. Maybe then you'll see . . .* Shutting her eyes again, she saw a trickle of blood dripping down her leg, soaking into the rug, spreading in a big stain toward his boots. She shook her head hard, chasing away the picture; it was too much like the one of the bathroom.

"If you'll tell me who did this, Katrina, I'll see that they're gone this afternoon," he said.

Katrina rested her ankle on her knee, winding the frayed threads of her jeans cuff tight around her fingers. *What if I did tell you and you shipped Ronnie—what do you think the black girls would do to me then?* She glared up at him.

"I mean it. . . ."

Suddenly her fingers went awkward and rubbery. He was leaning over her.

"I know this is hard to talk about. . . ."

He was so close that she could smell his breath: tobacco and peanuts, sort of toasty, almost nice. She felt a shiver pass along her skin.

"I'm very sorry you were hurt. . . ."

His gaze, sad and crazy, brushed across her face, and he did look hurt. He looked as hurt as she felt. She squeezed the cuff of her jeans tight. She couldn't stand the way he looked at her—*you're trying to make me feel the hurt all over again!*

"I don't want anything like this to ever happen to you again. . . ."

She stared at the blazing window until her eyes stung with tears. He wasn't the wolf in her dream; he had no sharp teeth or fingers. He had other ways of getting into her: that smell that flew up her nostrils like breath, that gentle, worried voice that slid into her ears, and that look of his, trying to stroke open her eyelids, to make her see that trashed bathroom—

"NOTHING HAPPENED TO ME!" she screamed. "LEAVE ME ALONE!"

Her foot dropped off her knee, leaving her with frayed cuff threads tangled between her fingers. Squeezing her legs together, she turned as far sideways in the chair as she could. The cut throbbed as if it had just been made; it really must be bleeding now. She wiped her eyes. "If you're so goddamn sure about everything, whyn't you bring this up in group session?" she demanded. "Group's for solving everybody's problems, right? It's the most important part of the program, right?"

"Yeah." Steven sighed. "But I'm aware that it could be dangerous for you. That's why I'm not ready to bring it up yet."

Katrina sniffed hard, inhaling the heavy sick-awful bullshit smell of white paint, the smell of the director's office, of the color Steven's old office would become. They painted over everything around here, like the foyer and dining room walls, like the infirmary room after Panda had ripped all the wallpaper off. But maybe the bullshit painting-over was better than having to look at all the craziness and mess underneath. It might be, if it really hid anything. But it didn't.

"What's the matter, don't you believe in group sessions anymore?" She squinted at him.

"Katrina. . . ."

Hearing his hesitation, she plunged into the silence. "Don't you believe in this place anymore?" she asked, her voice coming out loud and raspy.

"Of course I do," he said, frowning. "But—"

"I WANT TO GET OUT OF HERE!" she blurted. "I want to go back to court! I'll take my chances with the judge!"

"Sit still." Steven held out his palm level with her face so that she had to rock back in her chair. "If you left here now, Katrina, you'd just get locked up someplace else."

"How can I stay here if it's so fucking dangerous? Damn, man, you said if I talked in group, you'd back me up. So I did. I talked about families 'n' shit, and look what—" She covered her mouth with her hand and cleared her throat. "Anyway, you can't protect me if you're down in this office being director. Especially if you don't believe in it anymore—"

"Listen," he said, his voice louder, strained with the effort of sounding calm. "I believe in everything I've done here. As for seeing to it that you're all right, I can't see any reason why I shouldn't be able to. I'll probably be your counselor for quite a long time. And then Leah—"

"You're putting *her* in charge? Fuck!" Katrina lurched to her feet, gripping the back of the chair for support. "I won't have a chance then. The place'll be Nigger Heaven!"

"I've never heard you talk like that before!" Steven scowled at her so hard she had to hold the chair with both hands. "What's the matter with you?"

"I been here too long!" *My leg hurts, you bastard. I hurt all over and you can't help me!* "I want to get sent back to court!"

"I know you're upset now. But do you remember how we talked about plans for you, about court and so forth?"

"No." She did remember talking about something like this, but it seemed like a long-ago conference between two other people. Steven leaned back against the desk. The peanut bowl rocked noisily, stopped. The room was silent. The air stank of whiteness.

"I explained to you then, you haven't been here long enough to leave. No judge in the state will give you a new placement hearing after you've only been in the program three months."

"Why not?"

Steven wiped his forehead with his sleeve. "There's no change in your legal situation now," he said. "I'd have no reason to send you back to court."

Katrina pushed herself off the chair and limped toward the door. "I'll give you a reason, then!" She narrowed her eyes at him. "I'll give you more damn reasons than you'll fucking know what to do with!"

20 🎗

At suppertime, Steven was still brooding about the look that Katrina had shot him as she'd limped out the office. He remembered the dire stare of the schoolgirl on the road, before she'd laughed, and almost believed she had been there to warn him of something unspeakably awful he was about to find at the school. If so, what had the laugh been for? He didn't want to think about that too much.

He wasn't thinking very clearly about anything; all the circuits in his mind seemed jammed with the awareness that Katrina was hurting, that he couldn't take the pain away, and that he was responsible for it.

When he'd been Katrina's age in the juvenile jail in Kansas City, what had terrified him the most was that if some kids should decide to pound his head into the floor or ram their cocks up his ass, there would be no way he could escape: he was locked in with any violence anyone might decide to direct at him. And now Katrina was feeling the same way he had. . . . Steven paced around his office, smacking his fist into his palm. She was going to have to continue living with the girl or girls who'd done this sickening thing to her. He knew— and had always known, despite hopes to the contrary—that girls could be just as violent as boys, just as capable of directing their rage at each other's most vulnerable body parts, even if their weapons didn't grow conveniently out of their loins. He'd promised Katrina a life without violence here, and he'd let her down.

He hated violence, not just in the abstract, but personally. When violence got into an institution, he could always hear it panting just around the corner. He could smell a trace of its stink after it had slunk out of a room. Violence was contaminating; he could never quite scrub off the clamminess it left on his skin, or pour enough liquor down his throat to wash away the taste of rottenness it coated his tongue with. Violence was a street thug, ugly and scornful and capricious, with filthy hair and drug-reddened eyes and tattooed knuckles. Children, flowers, music; shit, pus, puke—all were the same to it. When it got a restless impulse, it just reached out and gutted the next passerby with a knife, or knocked her down and stomped the life out of her, and then leaned back against the wall picking its teeth, staring up the corridor while the victim's body was dragged away. . . .

Steven sat down at his desk, his elbows on the blotter, his chin in his hands. Strange, that he should be picturing violence as a white male, when the perpetrator in this case was female and probably—from the way Katrina had said the word "nigger"–was black. The white male specter had probably surfaced from his memories of the riot at Lakewood. He shuddered. That riot, he remembered, had started with a rape. That Katrina had not quite been raped was some consolation—the girl could have rammed the bottle all the way into her but must have chosen not to at the last minute—but it wasn't enough. He knew that he had to be more vigilant than ever about keeping situations from developing that encouraged violence; he'd have to be utterly ruthless about subduing it if it appeared again. How much of this necessary ruthlessness was he capable of?

He listened to the girls clamoring along the corridor on their way down to supper. They sounded like their usual raucous selves but, to Steven, they weren't the same anymore. They were suspect. He knew he'd get over thinking this way, but right now he didn't want to sit in the dining room with them, watching to see which girl seemed especially nervous or mean-tempered.

Skipping supper gave Steven a headache and a growling stomach. He finally left his office and wandered out toward the rec room, where he'd heard the sound of piano music. Second- and third-floor girls were rehearsing the musical show together, an experiment in détente that occurred once a week. Sonia had taken a dozen girls downstairs to the poolroom; the rest were being supervised by Johnny, a part-time recreation director. Steven had planned to make himself a sandwich in the kitchen, but seeing Katrina among the girls, he sat down on a couch at the far end of the room to watch her and the rehearsal.

She was sitting with Yvonne and Peaches in a corner of the room away from the portable wooden stage. A gray blanket was wrapped around her like a poncho; otherwise, she looked normal to Steven, her face animated as she spoke in a low voice.

The other girls sang and danced onstage, but a pervading tension put a sharp, cackly edge to their voices. Johnny, a slim young man in an open shirt and tight red slacks, banged on the keys to get their attention. He was attractive, black, and male—qualities in short supply here; the girls, gripping their music sheets, sang at the top of their lungs for him, and soon obliterated the melody. He shouted for them to be quiet again. They giggled and made faces at him.

What a scruffy crew, Steven thought. Shorts that accentuated fat thighs or skinny legs. Dresses stretched too tight or hanging too loose. Hair fluffed out into huge, lopsided Afros; heads dripping with yellow ringlets. Arms scarred with needle tracks or tattooed with homemade crosses, swastikas, initials. Steven saw the girls every day, but had never seen them quite like this before: en masse . . . bizarre.

Their makeup was bizarre, especially: burning pink cheeks— even the black girls—and scarlet vinyl lips, spiked lashes and recessed, shadow-bruised eyes. They'd turned themselves into a mob of painted phantoms at a masked ball. But they thought they looked like the TV stars whose perfect complexions glowed down at them from the magazine pictures taped to their walls. Tonight the girls were, they were sure, at their most spectacular.

But Steven could see that Johnny, frustrated and bad-tempered now, wasn't treating them like stars. He was treating them like a bunch of damn kids. He was undercutting their painstaking efforts to please him with their glamour. Naturally they were confused and hurt and angry. They milled around, poked each other in the ribs, and demanded cigarettes from each other in the middle of a song. He'd sabotaged their act; they'd sabotage his.

Finally, he gave up trying to teach them to read music and let them just become stars. A girl put on a record and they all danced on the stage. They swayed like sea anemones pulled by invisible currents. They began singing, in perfect unison suddenly, along with the record. Johnny sat in a folding chair, smoking a cigarette and nodding. In the back of the room, Steven smiled, beginning to relax a little.

Ronnie stepped to the front of the stage. With a swaying chorus line of Ronnettes lip-synching the song lyrics behind her, she belted out a slow soul ballad. Her voice was sweeter than the recorded one; its resonance reached the back of the room where Steven was sitting. The girls on the floor stopped chattering.

For a few moments, Ronnie's jeans and sweatshirt were transformed into a spangled gown; her face, no longer tense and tough, expressed all the tenderness, joy, desire that the lyrics described. Her arms rose, stretched out; her fingers curled upward.

She smiled into the eyes of her admirers. Even Johnny, standing now, moved his lithe hips to the slow rhythm of her song. Just at the end, she caught his eye. Her lips parted. Johnny smiled back. Suddenly she hunched forward, her hands covering her face. The recorded voice finished the last few bars without her. Ronnie jumped down from the stage, strode toward an armchair, shoulders rolling, and lunged into it. She drew her knees up against her chest and wouldn't speak to any of the girls who crowded around her. Peaches pushed her way through them. Ronnie took hold of her hand and pulled her down onto the arm of the chair. Peaches snuggled in close with her head resting on Ronnie's shoulder. Finally, Johnny came over and herded most of the girls back to the stage. The music started up again.

Steven watched Whale lumber away from the stage; then

he leaned forward, ready to spring to his feet as she sat down next to Katrina. He sat back again; Katrina was leaning close to her to whisper something. Whale wiped her face with the sleeve of her tentlike dress; drops of sweat remained like glass beads in the rolls of fat under her chin. With her huge arms and angry close-set eyes, Whale looked dangerous, but Steven knew she had been in serious trouble only once. Her aunt, with whom she lived, had tried to prevent her from trying to call her mother, whom Whale insisted had taken her little girl down South to place with relatives. Whale had beaten her aunt so badly that the woman was partially paralyzed afterward.

Whale looked angry enough to paralyze someone tonight, Steven thought. But then she often did. She'd learned to channel her frustrations into a thick, hardbound journal which she often carried around to write in. Sometimes she calmed herself down by grabbing her fist in one hand and cradling it against her breast as if rocking a baby, as she was doing now. Leaving the journal on the couch, Whale pushed herself to her feet and walked off slowly toward the basement stairs. Steven decided to stay and keep an eye on Katrina; he wanted to see how she reacted if Ronnie came near her.

In the basement poolroom, Sonia, supervising the girls, sat in an armchair leafing through one of the art magazines she'd brought in. Her college degree was in art therapy, but so far she had only been able to interest half a dozen girls in her two one-hour classes. They weren't sure how to deal with her as both a staff member and a teacher. Taking her cues from Steven and Leah, she dressed with a colorful originality that made her at least look different from the authority figures the girls were used to seeing in institutions. But since she was so young and small and blond, she had to spend a lot of time being strict enough that the girls wouldn't take advantage of her; it was difficult for her to switch roles then and get them to relax with paint and clay in a studio. The girls sometimes teased her about her clothes, telling her that she'd never be able to move fast enough to fight in the long flowered skirts she wore, like the one she had on tonight; her high-heeled white sandals would be no good at all for kicking anyone. Sonia, who came from an elegant suburb of San Diego and had never in her life dreamed of getting into a physical confrontation with anyone, laughed off their warnings. She hoped that her refusal to change her style would be taken as a sign of her confidence in her ability to solve problems without fighting.

Tonight she had played eight games of team pool with the girls and, though exhausted at the end of her shift, had managed to sink several balls. Now she watched the girls over the top of her magazine as they wandered around the table in curlers and bulky bathrobes, sharing one broken-tipped cue stick. They no longer took aim with it, they just slammed the cue ball into the midst of the other balls to make them ricochet wildly around the table. A record player in the corner blared urgent amplified whispers—HHHHEY BAYBHHEEE DISCO CRA-ZHHHEEE—out of one stereo speaker until the needle got stuck. A girl snapped it with her fingers; it skidded along the record's grooves shrieking like a cat landing on a buzz saw. Sonia sat back with her knees tucked up tight against her and her hands covering her ears.

But even her hands and the music couldn't block out Whale's voice from the stairwell. *"Where's is the damn staff at?"*

Sonia got up quickly and walked out into the basement rec room. Whale charged down the stairs at her and would have knocked her flat if she hadn't ducked sideways.

"Where's my suitcase?" Whale shouted. "I know you got it in one of these storerooms!"

"What do you want with your suitcase?" Sonia backtracked as Whale bore down on her.

Whale lumbered to a halt. "I heard what that damn probation officer said about my baby—'figment of my imagination,' the man says!" Her words came out in bursts. "Well, I'm going to go find my little girl! Going to AWOL this fucking place! Don't think you going to stop me, neither!"

Sonia stepped beside the couch, pressing against the armrest as Whale glared at her, her massive shoulders at the level of Sonia's forehead. Sonia swallowed hard. "I'm sorry. I can't let you have your suitcase."

Several girls came out of the poolroom and stood watching. Whale strode past Sonia toward the nearest door, the fat of her hips and arms quivering under her dress. There were five storage closets off the big room, all of them locked. Sonia caught up with Whale but not before she had given the first door a savage kick with her wooden-toed clog.

"Come on, Whale. Let's talk about this—" Sonia, looking pale, walked quickly beside her, trying to get between her and the next door. Her yellow hair bounced chaotically on her shoulders.

Several girls appeared on the back stairs, including Pam, who whirled around and raced away looking for Steven. The others crowded in closer, grinning.

"You better move, Princess! I ain't afraid to kick you!" Whale's round cheeks were puffed out with her heavy breathing; her eyes were molten. "Kick those fine little titties of yours right through your back!" Crash! She kicked the door inches from Sonia. Splinters flew.

The girls moved in closer.

"*Get* it, Whale!"

"Whoo, she gonna kick this place *down*!"

"It sure needs it, honey!"

"Get it, *Whale*!"

Their fuzzy bedroom slippers made squeaking noises as they rushed along beside Whale and Sonia. Sonia glanced at the girls around her; they grinned back. Several began to clap rhythmically. Sonia looked ill.

"Stop this, Whale! Stop it!" she yelled, her voice cracking.

"Y'all people gonna keep me from my suitcase, I'm going to break down every fucking door you got!" Whale turned and strode toward the closet at the far end of the room. Sonia hurried past her and stood in front of the door. She saw the mob of girls pushing their way into place for a good view, saw the gleeful look in their eyes as Whale came closer.

Whale leaned over, her face inches from Sonia's. *"Get out of my way! You hear me, Princess?"*

Sonia sucked in her breath. Her forehead gleamed with

sweat. "I hear you," she said in a wobbly voice. "But my name's Sonia, not Princess. And I'm not moving."

"*Whoo!*" Several girls laughed nervously. Then they turned toward the stairs.

Steven walked quickly across the room toward Whale and Sonia, his boot heels clunking against the cement. The girls parted to let him through.

Suddenly Whale lurched around Sonia and made a lunge for the door. Panting, she slugged it with her fist: CRACK! The girls winced at the sound. Katrina, who also had come down and was standing behind the others, retreated to stand in the bathroom door, where she could duck out of the way if there was a stampede for the stairs.

Steven grabbed Whale's arm, but she broke free and made one final lunge at the door, plowing into it head and shoulder first.

The lock ripped loudly through the wooden frame; the door gave way to Whale's three hundred pounds. She stumbled through, carried by her momentum. Her legs buckled under her. She hit the far wall of the closet with a heavy grunting sound.

Rubber boots skidded across the cement floor as she collapsed. Empty gas cans clanked like cymbals. She lay still, sprawled on her side. Her dress was torn up her leg to the roll of fat above her knee.

She opened her eyes. One eye filled immediately with blood from a gash in her forehead. She blinked hard, staring around her at the dim walls. The closet was a jumble of tires and snow shovels and overcoats. But no suitcases. Incongruously, a blue tasseled lampshade leaned against Whale's ankle, a hole in its side revealing its wire skeleton. Ronnie and Peaches, at the back of the mob of girls, glanced at each other and made for the stairs.

It took Steven, Sonia, and two nurses to pull Whale out of the closet. Once on her feet, Whale offered no resistance; she allowed herself to be led to the couch, and sat down silently. Sonia dabbed at her cut forehead with a gauze pad while the nurse got her to hold her fist in a pot of cold water. Eventually the nurse drove her to the hospital in the state car.

Steven shooed the girls upstairs to the dining room and told them to wait there for their evening snacks. Then he returned to the basement and sat on the couch with Sonia while she caught her breath and stopped trembling.

"How're you doing?" he asked.

"I'm okay." She turned to him, vertical lines appearing above the bridge of her nose. "God, I was so scared!"

"I don't blame you," he said. "But you stood up to her. You were brave."

"I guess I was." A smile appeared on her lips, then faded. "But I hope I never have to go through anything like that again."

"So do I," Steven said. "So do I."

They went into the closet to put the scattered equipment back against the walls. Steven found some wrinkled overcoats that were gray with ground-in cement dust, as if they'd been lain on. When he picked up a broken wristwatch from a corner, his heart sank. "This is Ronnie's, isn't it?" he asked.

"Yes." Sonia knelt down beside the tasseled lampshade. "And this used to be in Peaches' room."

"Shit." Steven squeezed the watch in his fist. "They've got the keys to this closet, and maybe to a bunch of other rooms, too. I'm going to have to be the one to get them back."

Sonia was smoothing the torn blue paper over the hole in the lampshade. "I wish we'd never found all this," she said. "I hate it that people have to make love on the floor of a closet. It gets to me sometimes, this school. Katrina getting hurt, then Whale, this closet..." She pushed some damp strands of hair away from her face. Her blouse had come loose from her skirt and was dark with sweat under her arms. "Most of the time I keep too busy to see it. All day I'm pushing the girls from one activity to another, bouncing them off walls and up corridors and down staricases. But sometimes I look around this building and I wonder, is it really helping them?"

"We can't let them stagnate," Steven said. Sonia kept staring at him; he could see how badly she needed reassurance. He looked disheveled himself, he noticed: a long dirt streak in his jacket and a rip in the knee of his slacks had been made when he'd fallen against the wall helping to pull Whale out of the closet. He tried to button his jacket but the button had been torn away. This storage closet seemed to be a place that altered people who entered it; but not permanently, he hoped. "We're the only ones in these kids' lives who've cared enough to give them something worthwhile to keep busy at," he said. "So what if they make love in a closet? At least they still can. The only place I had for that when I was their age was the seat of a broken-down car. But that's not the point." What was the point? Whom was he trying to convince? "If they weren't busy here," he went on, "they'd be doing stuff in the streets that'd get them sent to prison, or get them killed. We're not just keeping them busy, Sonia. We're keeping them safe."

She rested her head against the back of the couch. "I hope so."

"If we're not, then we've got no business keeping them at all," he said, his voice suddenly shrunk almost to a whisper. The glaring fluorescent light overhead buzzed faintly in the big room; it seemed to make his skin prickle.

"Well, we're doing the best we can for them," Sonia said, letting out a long breath. "That's got to be good enough, doesn't it?"

"Right." Steven managed a smile.

"Okay." She stood up. "I guess it's time to go up. Will you wait for me a second?"

"Sure." Steven watched her walk across the floor toward the bathroom, her hair hanging limply to her shoulders.

He brushed as much dirt as he could from his jacket. Then he leaned the closet door against its broken hinges, trying to wedge it into the frame. As soon as he let go of it, the door collapsed inward, making a booming sound against the floor that made him clamp his teeth together. Never mind—the maintenance men could fix it tomorrow, put a new lock on it, make it look as if nothing had happened. Sonia returned, her face washed, her blouse neatly tucked into her skirt. He walked with her up the stairs.

When they reached the dining room, the girls were still

waiting for their evening snacks. They leaned in a row against the serving counter, glaring like movie cowboys in a hushed saloon. All grumbling stopped. Soul music thudded down through the ceiling. The air was thick with the sour leftover smell of steamed vegetables. The girls watched Steven's and Sonia's every movement.

"Come on," Steven whispered, feeling Sonia stiffen beside him in the doorway.

The girls sucked in their breaths.

"*WE WANT OUR SNACKS!*" they screamed in unison, and collapsed together in a chorus of anxious laughter.

After Sonia had taken the girls upstairs with their snacks, Steven turned out the dining room and kitchen lights and stayed in the kitchen. Mercifully, the only light left was the dim red bulb in the square wire cage over the exit door. Ronnie's watch in his pocket seemed to be ticking loudly against his side; he had to take it out and hold it against his ear to make sure it really was broken. Then he was aware of a throbbing in his head. Hunger, no doubt.

He looked for something to eat in the steel lockers, and brought out some bread, a gallon jar of mayonnaise, and a long institution-size loaf of luncheon meat which he put down on a butcher-block counter. He found a cleaver in a drawer.

Peeling back the cellophane wrapper, he hacked the meat, trying to make a sandwich-sized slice. Instead he cut a wide hunk. Trying to slice it in two, he only made a wider one. He hacked it again. The heavy blade sliced through the meat, striking the table with a solid *whack!* that reverberated up his arm. He raised the cleaver. Again and again he hacked the soft meat, harder and harder. Low groans bubbled up his throat. *Whack!—whack!—whack!—*pieces of meat flew off into the darkness. *Whack!—*the handle of the cleaver slipped through his fingers, caromed off the table, skidded across the floor. It clanged loudly into the stove.

Silence. Steven stood motionless, his heart crashing in his chest.

He switched on the lights. Bits of pink-brown meat lay strewn all over the floor, the stove top, the counters. Moving fast, he picked up the carnage, flung it into a garbage can, fastened the lid down tight. Then he turned out the lights and, in the faint red glow of the caged bulb, stood staring out the window, his hands pressed to the sides of his head.

The darkness outside washed in toward him in a huge, heavy wave. When he half-closed his eyes, the wave swelled. Curling over, it took up the entire sky, hung poised in the air. Then, slowly, it receded along the parking lot and across the fields to lie in wait above the edge of the woods. The violence in his chest gradually faded; he could almost breathe normally again.

He walked out into the rec room. The music rehearsal was over; most of the girls were gone. After the dim light of the kitchen, the room seemed ablaze with incandescence. Who had those people been, dancing around in here? The white tubes of light on the ceiling gave off vibrations that made the walls jiggle faintly in his peripheral vision. The whole building seemed like an unwieldy ocean liner drifting across a vast empty sea—a refugee ship cut off from the mainland, forbidden to dock anywhere, and held together only by plaster and paint and willpower. In the ship's blazing ballroom he could visualize bizarre figures perpetually dancing and shouting. Around them the floors seemed to creak, the walls strained, cracks spread beneath the paint like skeletal fingers, and the whole shaky structure began to list. . . .

A teenage girl—a real one—with flame-colored hair moved across the room toward him: Inez, in beige slacks and blouse, smelling of sweat and loud perfume. When he sat down on the couch, she sat beside him.

"Sonia said to tell you the hospital called. Whale's all right," she said. "She will be coming back tonight."

"That's good." Steven's voice was whispery, flat.

Inez nodded. "Hey, Mr. Fox, you got any more pictures in the mail from your daughter?"

"I got one last week. It's at home."

"Aw."

"I'll bring it in for you to look at, if you want."

"Okay." Inez's plump cheeks dimpled. She reached down into her blouse and pulled out a folded piece of paper, which she smoothed onto her lap. It was a crayon drawing of a huge yellow sun; there was a black line for the ground and a tiny stick figure. "That's my daughter," she said, laughing. "She is a good artist, ain't she?"

Steven smiled. "Yes, she really is."

Inez took a last look at the paper and refolded it carefully. "Your daughter, she draws good. That picture in your office I seen, it's better than this."

"No, it's not. My daughter's a lot older. When she was your girl's age she couldn't draw anything."

"Yeah?"

"I'm telling you." Steven looked into Inez's face until he saw the smile come back. She didn't look at all bizarre. She was beautiful.

"Well, I am glad your daughter sent you another picture," she said, standing up to leave.

"Me, too." I love you, Inez, he thought. "Thanks for showing me your drawing," he said.

She gave him a wave as she headed for the stairs. Steven sat back, listening to the reverberations of footsteps spreading across the ceiling. Finally, he pushed himself up off the couch and climbed the stairs to the third floor.

The girls had brought their cookies, apples, and milk cartons into the TV lounge.

"I thought we have to scrape you off the basement floor with a spatula," Inez said to Sonia. "You're badder than you look."

"Badder than I look." Sonia wiped her forehead. "You better believe it."

When the girls spotted Steven, they whispered and pushed Peaches toward him. "Could we stay up and wait for Whale to come back?" she asked in a subdued, polite voice, her eyelashes in motion. "We'll even let you watch the late show on TV."

"Sonia can, too," Lucia chimed in. The girls laughed.

"No, square business—" Vonita wasn't laughing. "We worried about Whale."

"I understand," Steven said.

"Well, can we?" Peaches asked.

Steven rested his chin in his hand, pretending to think about it. "What's the late movie?"

Cheers went up. The girls fanned out, switching off lights and dragging chairs into position. Steven and Sonia shared the couch with Yvonne and Inez, a very tight fit, but the girls liked it that way. Mary and Pam curled up at either end of the couch with their behinds on the armrests, their upper bodies half-draped over the back cushions. Inez nudged Steven hard with her hip—"Come on, man," she grumbled, lifting his arm so that he had to rest it on the cushion behind her. She snuggled in against the inside of his shoulder. Yvonne lifted his other arm behind Sonia's neck.

"No grabbing titties in there!"

"Whose, Sonia's or Inez's or Yvonne's?"

"Shit, the man's only got two hands!"

"How you talk, girl!"

"Watch the movie!" Steven said.

The film was a comedy-Western that everyone had seen several times before. The girls talked in low voices, passed candy and gum and cigarettes back and forth, brushed or cornrowed each other's hair, dozed off for short stretches.

"Isn't this amazing—how long can it last?" Sonia whispered in Steven's ear.

He shook his head, smiling. He could feel the movement of Sonia's jaw as she chewed some gumdrops someone had dropped into her lap. The dark forms surrounding them murmured sleepily, their faces lit by the flicker of the screen. Inez snored, her breath smelling of licorice; her head made a damp, warm patch on Steven's chest. Radiators hissed softly. Clouds of cigarette smoke rolled up into the pungent darkness like steam from a pot of stew. Steven half-closed his eyes. . . .

Suddenly there was a quick movement in the back of the room. Vonita shoved open the door to the front stairwell. "Whale's here!" she screamed. "She's back!"

The girls scrambled out of their seats and rushed onto the landing.

"Hey, Whale!"

"Get it, Whale!"

In the dim light of the emergency lantern, Whale became visible, a bulky form trudging up the stairs, grunting with every footstep. The girls cheered, clapped, stomped their feet. Ronnie and Peaches ran down and pulled Whale up the last few stairs and into the lounge. Someone switched on a light.

Whale had a big butterfly bandage over one eye, and her hand was taped, with two fingers in splints. She leaned over so that the girls could study the bandage, and let Vonita, shoving into her backward, make a resting place for the taped hand with her shoulder. Everyone pushed in close to examine it.

"How many bones got busted?" Lucia asked.

"I ain't seen the X rays," Whale said, still out of breath. "Maybe a dozen. No big thing."

"Hey, Whale, you know you can't beat no door!"

"Seems to me I whupped it pretty good," Whale said. "Seems to me that sucker went flying when I hit it!"

"Whoo!"

"Get it, *Whale*!"

Whale held out the palm of her unbandaged hand for slaps all around. "You're lucky it wasn't you, Sonia," she said.

"So are you," Steven said.

"I know it." Whale glanced away. "You mad at me?" she asked Sonia.

"Give me five." Sonia raised her hand.

Whale rolled her eyes. "You people never learn to say it right!"

Sonia's hand whipped down, smacking Whale's palm so hard that Lucia, standing next to her, shouted "Ow!" and jumped back.

"You put a little something extra into that." Whale looked at her palm.

"Could be." Sonia smiled. "But I'm glad you're okay, Whale. Welcome back."

"I got to pay for that door, Mr. Fox?" Whale asked.

"Hell, yes," Steven said. "We'll take it out of your chore money."

"Hmph. Next time I'll off a staff. Be a whole lot cheaper."

Inez pushed her way through the crowd. "It's a good thing

Sonia don't give you your suitcase," she said. "We wouldn't
have saved you no snacks if you'd have AWOLed." She held
out a paper plate with cookies and an apple on it.

"We got them state raisin cookies again?" Whale took
the plate, grinning. "That's all right, I'll eat them. They
didn't give me nothing at the hospital but five doughnuts."
To answer the girls' questions about her excursion, Whale
took over the couch, propping her taped hand on her knee
like a trophy.

Sonia rubbed her eyes. Then she glanced around the room,
doing a head count. "We're one short," she said to Steven.
"I could have sworn they were all here."

"Katrina's missing." Steven headed up the corridor.

He slowed down when he saw her door ajar and her light
on. She was sitting sideways on the window shelf in her frayed
jeans and a flannel shirt. He knocked on the door.

"What do you want?" she asked.

"Whale's back." He saw her flinch. "Aren't you relieved?"

"Yeah. I mean—what do you mean?" She tried to stare
out the window, but her face was reflected back at her in the
black glass, and at Steven; she couldn't escape his gaze. "What's
Whale got to do with me?"

"I saw you talking with her, then the next thing I knew,
she was rampaging through the basement."

"It's not my fault she busted down the door."

Steven noted the ragged edge to her voice. "I don't think
it is either. You're not responsible for Whale's temper. But
I do think you set it off tonight."

Katrina frowned.

"I think you snuck into the staff office and read about
Whale in the log," he said. "Then you told her about what
her PO had written, before Sonia or Leah and I could do it
without upsetting her so much. I think you wanted to see
Whale explode. I know you've got a lot to be upset about
right now, but it was still a rotten thing to do."

Katrina pressed her chin against her raised knees. "I didn't
mean for her to get hurt."

"No. . . ." Steven leaned wearily against the doorframe. "You didn't realize you could have such an effect on people, did you?"

She lifted her face. "Not really."

Silence. Steven stared at a collage of photographs that Katrina had covered the wall over her bed with. The glare from the overhead bulb made highlights on their glossy surfaces. He'd been checking the collage's progress over the weeks as the faces of the third-floor girls had been added to an ever-widening circle around, at first, a photo of him. Last week the center of the collage had been blank. Now it was filled again: Katrina's own face, with her new glasses and a big lopsided grin.

"I'm glad you're discovering this ability to affect people, at least," he said. "I wonder what you're going to do with it."

"How the hell should *I* know?"

"If you don't, who does?" he asked.

"Not you, anyway." She jumped down from the window shelf and hurried past him into the corridor. "I'll let you know when I find out," she said over her shoulder, grinning for a brief moment like the girl in her collage.

21

Penned in by the last cold weeks of April, the girls had been watching through perpetually smudged windows as the drizzle ate away at the snowdrifts on the edge of the woods and left the hillsides the color of drowned dogs. Now, as May began, the sun stayed out for two, three, four days in a row. Windows were left open; fresh air could circulate all through the building for the first time in half a year. The place seemed to expand a little, no longer having to pull in its walls against the cold outside or the threat of exploding nervous systems inside. The girls started to go outdoors in their sweatshirts and shorts and bare feet. It was spring. Suddenly there was room to move around in. The girls explored the grounds, running across the lawn, around the pond, even into the fields and woods. As Leah wrote in the log, everyone's juices were flowing.

Mrs. Lert had strict instructions to lock up the log during her shift, but she usually forgot, and Katrina continued to read it late at night in the staff office. She liked indulging her curiosity, finding out things about girls that even they didn't know. For instance, Ronnie's mother was out of jail but was being investigated for welfare fraud; as a result, Ronnie's probation officer wouldn't let her go home until the fall, if then, and not the summer, as she'd been counting on. In a counseling session Ronnie had had with Leah, Katrina learned from the log, Ronnie had said she knew everybody was treating her cautiously, but she was more afraid that she would lose control of herself than the girls were. Knowing Ronnie was scared gave Katrina a feeling of having the upper hand; it also let her stop hating Ronnie so much, which had gotten exhausting.

Also in the log were copies of letters that girls had written to their probation officers, trying to set up summer visits to relatives. Katrina had no relatives she wanted to write to, but Steven had spoken to her about trying to arrange a visit to a group home. Katrina didn't admit that she liked the idea— it was hard to talk with Steven these days without losing her temper—but she was considering it.

She noticed that the warm weather was making Peaches especially restless these days. Even after returning from being with Ronnie or Yvonne, Peaches sometimes liked to stay up to talk with her across the darkness in their room. She talked to Katrina about her little sister Lurleen, about her home, which was no place for a sweet kid like Lurleen—it was just a leaky old trailer on a back road surrounded by rusty car bodies that her brother Bobby towed home for parts. She hadn't gotten along with Bobby any better than she had with her mother, but she sort of missed them now; she even missed her older sister, who'd killed herself when Peaches had been eight. In those days, Peaches' mother had always told her she was ugly and disgusting to be around—that was because her stepfather had liked her too much. But when she got to be eleven and started growing titties, all the guys at school wanted to grab her. She loved being popular all of a sudden, like the ugly duckling, but sometimes she wished she could be flat-chested—"like you," she told Katrina, laughing.

When she was fourteen, Peaches said, she met Harvey. Harvey was a biker, and his gang, the Falcons, was the baddest in the state. He'd given her her first tattoo: his initials on her upper arm. Sometimes she rode with him and his gang brothers. Once for a whole weekend they lay around this one dude's house doing reefer and bennies and uppers. Talk about wrecked! But then it got weird. Harvey passed out and his brothers started grabbing at her. They all made her have a turn with them. She didn't remember much except she threw up a lot from all the pills and come she'd swallowed. After that, she wouldn't go to any more biker parties.

She thought Harvey was through with her, but he wrote her at Fairbanks, and just last week, he asked her to marry him. Katrina was so sleepy that she didn't say much when she heard this. But the next night she found a letter in the staff office from Peaches' probation officer and, on impulse, had taken it. Now, as Peaches started talking about Harvey again, Katrina felt awful. Sometimes she wished she had better control over her curiosity.

"You really want to *marry* him?" Katrina asked, as they went out the front door into the parking lot together.

Peaches shrugged. "It'd be better than working in those fucking grape arbors. Harvey's got a job and everything. I know he really cares about me."

"You do?"

"He even paid for my abortion once."

Katrina wrinkled her nose. "Doesn't Ronnie get jealous?"

"Aah, she knows what I'm like!" Peaches tossed her hair, making it splash gold over her shoulders. Jumping the season, she was wearing her too-small cutoff jeans and a halter that showed most of her boisterous Hollywood breasts.

Near the bank of the pond, they sat down under some trees where the ground was soft with needles and the shade smelled like pine.

"I decided to check out that group home the Fox told me about," Katrina said, glancing at Peaches.

"I thought you called him Steven. You were the only one who did."

"I wised up." Katrina turned away before Peaches could get a look at her face. "Anyway, the home doesn't seem like a bad place."

Peaches lay back, staring up at the pine branches overhead. "He was talking to me about one, too. But I told him, No way. I got a real home, even if it ain't much."

Katrina pulled the letter out of her back pocket. "If it didn't, like, work out there, you could get your PO to let you try a group home."

"You sound like a fucking commercial." Peaches dug her heels into the ground. "I'm going home. The Fox is setting it up for the summer."

Katrina took a deep breath and let it out. "You know how you been after him to write your PO about that? Well, he got a letter back."

"He did?" Peaches sat up. "How'd you know?"

"I found it in the office last night. The Fox ain't even seen it yet." Katrina squeezed the paper in her fingers, trying to remember the way Steven talked to girls who had home problems. "It's not good news, Peaches," she said, her voice soft. "But you know, a lot of people here care about you and you're not alone."

"What the hell are you talking about?" Peaches frowned at the letter in Katrina's hands. "Stop talking like an asshole and give me that!"

Katrina sighed, unfolding the paper. "Lie down and I'll sort of read it with you, okay?" She knew that Peaches, who got Ronnie to do her homework, could hardly read.

She and Peaches lay on their stomachs, side by side, with the letter pressed lumpily on the pine needles in front of their faces.

"It says your mother's been busted, Peaches," Katrina said, squinting at the paper. "For 'contributing to the corruption of a minor.' Your sister Lurleen—she's the minor."

"Oh, shit...." Peaches' voice faded off. She stared off into the trees.

"Your sister complained to the Welfare. Like, your brother Bobby and"—Katrina crumpled the letter in her fist, remembering the pale-faced little girl who'd visited Peaches in February—"and Harvey's been doing stuff with Lurleen." She glanced at Peaches, who seemed to have gone into a state of paralysis. "Your mother was drinking in the living room while they were all in the bedroom," she went on quickly. "The Welfare's put Lurleen in a foster home 'cause she's pregnant. Harvey and Bobby got busted too. They're all out on bail."

Peaches started hitting the ground weakly.

"So the PO says," Katrina finished, "you can't go home

right now.'' She lay down to look at Peaches' face. ''I'm really sorry.''

''I *got* to go home!'' Peaches choked, her eyes filling with tears. ''If I don't get there right quick, they'll all be in jail!''

''You never knew none of this stuff was happening?'' Katrina asked her.

''Not Harvey. I knew fucking Bobby was no good,'' Peaches said into the ground.

''He was doing that with your sister before?''

''Yeah, my mother kicked him out of the house a whole bunch of times. Then he smacked her around and she gave up.'' Peaches narrowed her eyes. ''I hit Bobby with a radio once. I never let him with me, at least not since I knew Harvey....'' She shook her head, grinding her forehead back and forth against her fist. ''Fucking Harvey! I mean, Lurleen's only just *twelve*! *I can't believe this shit!*''

Katrina had to stop looking at Peaches' face.

''I got to talk to Ronnie!'' Peaches' voice was strange, whimpery. Holding her hand over her mouth as if to keep from throwing up, she scrambled to her feet. ''Ronnie'll help me!''

She took off toward the building. The planks of the bridge made a loud clattering sound as she ran across them. When Katrina reached the bridge, she could feel them still trembling beneath her feet.

While Katrina was outdoors with Peaches, Steven was in the director's office confronting Ronnie about the missing keys he suspected she had; he was hating every minute of it. Ronnie sat with her fists pressed against her stomach in the leather armchair beside the desk. As Steven spoke, tears ran down her cheeks, making shiny dark lines on her skin. He'd never expected to see her cry.

''... I can't allow any girl to have room keys,'' he said, going over it a second time. ''Keys get lost, or somebody could rip you off. Somebody could get into a room and use it for other things than what you were ... using the storage closet for.''

Ronnie turned her face away from him as far as possible.

''Before the New Program, some girls got into a classroom and beat up another girl so badly she had to go to the hospital for months. . . .'' Steven hated standing over her like a police inspector. He hated the fact that he was white and she was black, that he was wearing an expensive suit and she was in her usual faded sweatshirt and jeans. He wished he didn't suspect her so strongly of being the one who had attacked Katrina. Pulling the chair from behind the desk, he sat down beside her. ''I'm only concerned about getting the keys back,'' he said in a quieter voice. ''I'm not trying to hurt you and Peaches.''

''Leave Peaches the fuck out of this—'' Ronnie shut her eyes tight.

''The keys, Ronnie.''

From the expression on her face, it was obvious to Steven how she was interpreting his demand: she thought he was trying to destroy her relationship with Peaches. He explained all over again that he was not, but found himself resorting to social worker jargon that left a rancid taste in his mouth. In fact, he'd been trying to weaken Ronnie and Peaches' hold over the third-floor girls for a long time, and everybody knew it. He'd hoped that he could break up a political alliance without destroying a personal relationship. Now, as he looked at Ronnie, her face clenched to hold back tears, he began to suspect that this was impossible to do.

If it was, then there was no way he could encourage the girls to care about each other and then prevent them from loving each other. Nor could he demand that they feel responsible to a peer group and then keep them from feeling loyal to a made-up family that protected them from the crushing loneliness and sense of banishment that the institution imposed on them. The girls needed each other in this place more than they needed him or any program he could offer them.

The more the place denied them what they needed, the more willing they would be to destroy the place, and the more brutal he would have to become to preserve it. Perhaps, then, it was impossible to do anything but hurt people in an institution. This was a proposition too simple—and awful—for comprehension. Steven did not articulate it fully to himself; all he knew at the moment was that he was frustrated beyond endurance by this hurt, sullen girl, and by the sound of his own voice.

The last thing he'd wanted to do was shout at Ronnie, yet he began to shout. He stood up, shoving his chair back noisily, and paced to the window. "You know," he started again in a lowered voice, "you've been here long enough to be eligible for a discharge—"

"You threatening to keep me here now, huh?" she said, barely moving her lips.

"No." Steven sighed. "I just don't want to see you mess up your chances."

"It ain't me that's messed up."

"No one said you were."

Ronnie turned away. Eventually he had to let her go, promising further discussion of the matter in group session. This, he realized, was also a threat. And it would probably work. Even Ronnie wasn't tough enough to have her private life examined in front of all the girls. At least he hoped she wasn't. No matter how carefully he might speak about the necessity of recovering keys, everyone would know what he was really talking about. He would feel like a gynecologist demonstrating the use of a butcher knife in a medical theater.

After Ronnie had left the director's office, Steven did, too; though the office was quieter than the one on the third floor, he didn't feel comfortable talking with girls there. He'd seen Peaches through the window running toward the building, and asked Leah to bring her to the staff office upstairs right away, before Ronnie could speak to her.

Peaches was moving like a zombie when she appeared in the office door. Leah guided her toward the tattered armchair by the door and then left. In the corridor, she encountered Katrina, who demanded to get into the office and speak to Steven immediately. Leah told her she'd have to wait, and took her away.

Peaches stared at the poster on the opposite wall. The

woman in it had bare white arms; she suddenly wished her arms were clean like that, not tattooed. The woman was dancing on tiptoe in a white nightgownlike dress that was so pretty it hurt Peaches' eyes to look at it. Everything else in the picture was blurred colors, as if seen through smeared glass. The dancer began to look smeared, too. Then the whole room did.

Steven was asking her something about Ronnie and a supply closet and a key. She gazed up at him. "What?" she asked in a faraway voice.

He asked her the question again. Though she didn't understand the part about the keys, she did suddenly take in the fact that he knew that she and Ronnie had been making love in the basement. *He knew....* She stared at his face. His lips moved and his eyes grabbed at her brain through her eye sockets. He wanted to keep her and Ronnie from being together!

"Peaches, at this point I'm only asking you about the keys you and Ronnie might have...."

She began to tremble. A sick feeling started to rise up from her stomach again. "I got to see Ronnie!" she said, her voice hollow. "Ronnie's all I got!"

"That's not true, Peaches," Steven said. "As soon as I hear from your probation officer, you can start getting ready to go home for a visit...."

HOME! Peaches' mind did a sickening flip-flop.

The room was unnaturally quiet. A breeze that made the pine trees' top branches sway outside the window blew softly into the room, stirring some papers on the desk. Peaches' halter top had slipped sideways on her shoulder, leaving a raw pink line in the skin. Several pine needles were sticking out of her hair. Her face was deathly pale.

"You're not listening," Steven said. "Are you feeling okay?"

Peaches gazed back at him. Suddenly her teeth came unclenched. "I want to see my little sister!" she screamed. "You people can't stop me from going home! She's my fucking *sister!*"

Peaches shoved herself up out of her chair, but her legs buckled under her. She would have fallen on her face if Steven hadn't grabbed her arm. She pitched forward, propping herself up with her hands against the radiator, and raised her face to the window. "I want to die! *I just want to die-e-e-e-e-e ... !*"

The sound poured out in long moans that expanded until they became a full-throated shriek. Peaches' mouth was a bottomless well of shrieking—there was more rage and grief and terror and pain in her than it seemed possible any normal-sized, pretty sixteen-year-old girl could contain and still live.

Finally she gagged and went dead silent, her mouth collapsed at the corners. Only when she began to tilt toward the floor did Steven unfreeze, propping her up with her face resting against his chest. Leah and Katrina stood in the open doorway. Katrina still had her hands pressed over her ears.

As Peaches leaned sideways, one breast flopped out of its halter like an enormous soft-boiled egg, peeled and white. Steven turned her toward Leah, who, shielding her, took her into her arms. Katrina looked away, wincing.

Suddenly Ronnie rushed through the door, knocking Katrina sideways against the wall. She stopped in the middle of the room, her eyes narrowed, one arm raised in the air. She snapped it down. Keys bounced and skidded across the floor, striking the toe of Steven's boot.

There!" Ronnie shouted, drawing her shoulders back. "You *satisfied,* man? You gonna leave Peaches *alone now?"*

She turned and strode out of the office. The door slammed with a loud crack behind her.

Katrina pushed herself away from the wall. Behind her, the dance poster was torn off at the taped corners. It fluttered to the floor. The room was silent as a held breath.

In a second the doorway filled with girls all rushing in to ask what had caused Peaches' scream. Katrina tried to push through them to the desk, where she wanted to leave the letter she'd read to Peaches, but Yvonne, her fingers being pried loose from Peaches' arm by Leah, knocked it out of her hand. She saw it vanish among the shuffling feet and then reappear on the floor by the armchair. Steven and Leah herded the girls out of the office.

In a few minutes, Katrina saw Leah bring Peaches into her room and help her to lie down. Peaches looked as if all her bones had caved in. When Leah said she wanted to talk to her alone, Katrina was glad to leave. Once out in the hallway, though, she didn't know where to go. The girls were talking about Peaches in the lounge; she didn't want to face them. Their voices, ragged and panicky, ricocheted off the corridor walls like trapped birds.

Feeling queasy, she stood outside the office door, watching Steven through the small square window in it. The knuckles of one hand pressed against his lips, he stared down at the top of the desk where he'd dropped Ronnie's keys. His tie hung crooked, his face was sweaty, his eyes, narrowed in pain, were scary-looking. He hadn't seen the letter on the floor yet, but Katrina knew he would—in a few minutes or a few hours, it didn't matter. Then he'd feel even worse, and it would be her fault. He'd know that for the second time in a month she had caused an explosion with her curiosity.

She leaned against the door, her cheek touching the cool wood. The office was silent. She remembered the times he'd smiled to see her barging into his office for a talk. It seemed now that she would never be able to do that again. Her eyes burned with tears. She stepped back and shuffled away down the corridor, the reverberations of Peaches' scream striking a lonely chord in the pit of her stomach.

22 🦋

Steven and Matt Steiner had been keeping detailed records of all the staff problems, runaways, and fights among the girls on the second floor; after six months, they had enough evidence of Ben Paleno's incompetence to bring him up before a state review board—the only way a civil servant with as much seniority as Ben could be fired. A hearing was scheduled for June.

At first, Ben took the news hard. His smile sagged to one side; the pouch under his left eye was deeper than the one under his right. The way he combed his grown-out crew cut made him look as if he were wearing a cheap wig that was about to fall off.

He was past anxiety, past despair, he told Mrs. Evans, the other nurses, the maintenance men, and anyone else who would listen—the matter was out of his hands, and he could stop playing administrative politics around here. In the privacy of his own office, however, he was on the phone to Albany constantly, lining up support. In thirty-one years of state service, he had made some good friends in the Youth Service hierarchy. Now he invited them all to the musical show that would coincide with the June commencement ceremony. Many would come, he knew, for there was a family campground in the mountains nearby that was popular with the Head Office crowd.

Meanwhile, eleven of Ben's second-floor girls ran away and were brought back, poised to flee again. Steven was worried. So far, the New Program had operated only in weather so foul that few girls had tried to brave it. Most of those who had left had phoned begging to be taken back. They missed the school, they said with quavers in their voices, and Steven knew that some of them really did. They were terrified of living without their time being scheduled in twenty-four-hour blocks, their personal possessions chosen and provided for them, their every decision made for them by others. These were kids who would never again be able to function anywhere but in institutions. This was how Fairbanks, and the other places they'd been, had rehabilitated them.

But most of the girls weren't that frightened of freedom. One reason they'd stayed here all winter was that the idea of striking out to find an opening in the arctic fields and frozen dark woods surrounding the school was beyond the girls' imagination. Like passengers on an iced-in ship, they'd adapted themselves to life indoors. In their isolation, the building had become their whole world. Since they'd been relatively free in it, they'd begun to forget the freedoms they were missing outside the walls.

But now the sea had thawed; the mountains of ice had floated away; the shoreline, blooming into life, was visible and so close that this massive stranded vessel of a school seemed contiguous with the rest of the world, suddenly and vividly remembered. Perhaps, Steven thought, he would have to be more careful to limit the kids' movements lest they try to become part of the wider world. Perhaps a free program was possible only in a restricted environment.

The warmth of spring was coursing through the girls' veins; their hormones were jumping. They were chasing each other in ever-widening circles on the lawn. How long, Steven wondered, before his girls started running away? Only Katrina, so far, had tried, back in March. But Steven suspected, from the mud on her sneakers, that she'd recently been going off for long walks as far as the outlying fields. If he didn't do something soon about her restlessness, she might go a lot farther.

He missed Katrina. He missed the way she used to stroll around his office as they talked, inspecting his paperweights and ashtrays and the framed pictures of his daughter; she would hold his volcanic rock in her hand and glance at him as if trying to feel the connection between it and him. He missed the way her voice might swing into a screech of rage or a whoop of laughter, and the way she used to stick out her lower lip at him, a defiant expression that melted into a grin just before she covered it with her hand. Nowadays she looked at him sullenly, calculatedly. When she spoke she said what was required of her and not a syllable more.

Steven wanted to have a long talk with her, but there was rarely time to schedule individual conferences with girls. All indications from Albany were that he would take over as acting director sometime in June. His days were taken up learning about budgets, payrolls, community relations, physical-plant operations. Most of the problems he would be spending his time on had nothing directly to do with Katrina or any other girl.

In one of his meetings in the director's office, Matt Steiner brought this up. "You and Leah are getting like Mom and Pop on your floor," he said. "I think that's why your girls aren't going AWOL."

"Could be." Steven glanced at Matt's spectacles glinting in the sunlight, aimed at him.

"What do you think'll happen to all the warmth up there?"

"I don't know," Steven said.

"You look sad." Matt had a way of using words like "warmth" and "sad" with the accuracy of a sniper. "You don't have to take over the school," he said.

"I know. But I will."

"You'll probably have to let in a lot of new kids from maximum-security facilities."

"Then I'll get as many of my girls out of here as I can. Four of them are scheduled for discharge over the summer."

"And the others?"

Steven thought of Katrina. "They'll be all right," he said. "I'll make damn sure they are, one way or the other."

After the meeting, the first thing he did was to schedule an evening conference with Katrina. But, as had happened before, an emergency came up that forced him to postpone it. Some second-floor girls were threatening to fight, and the woman in charge there, alone on her shift, requested that a man walk through the unit to let the girls know that she had support if she needed it.

On his way to the lounge, Steven stopped to read a list of rules that was posted on every bulletin board along the corridor.

GROUP NORMS
UNIT TWO

1. Young ladies are responsible for taking care of their personal belongings. No tight clothing or extreme makeup. No tattooing, ear piercing, nostril piercing. No cutting sleeves off sweatshirts or bathrobes.

2. Unit staff will give out clothing, soap, toothpaste, shampoo, and personal supplies at specific times. Do not ask for them at other times. Exception: sanitary napkins. You must sign the Tampax log and bring back soiled napkins in bags provided. Stained sheets or clothing should not be washed with others.

3. Do not smoke or horseplay in the bathroom. One girl to a stall. No looking under or over stall doors.

4. Only *3* girls on a couch at one time, *1* to a chair, *1* to a bed. Bedroom doors are to be left open at *ALL* times.

5. During rec room chapel services, do not whisper, slouch, turn in your chair, or cross legs at knees. Legs may be crossed at ankles.

6. Only good-taste posters are allowed on bedroom walls. No nudes, drugs, etc.

7. Scissors may be borrowed from the staff office and used *with supervision* for sewing purposes in the lounge only. Scissors *must* be returned to staff office before evening snacks.

8. If you are in doubt about a group norm, ask permission.

Steven walked on down the corridor, shaking his head. What was the point of posting mostly unenforceable rules like that? They amounted to nothing more than a list of ways to defy authority.

Most of the girls were gathered around the television in the lounge in bathrobes and slippers, whispering, glancing around, whispering, glancing around. The air was blue with cigarette smoke and hissing profanities. From one of the rooms came the voices of several white girls singing the Beatles song "Rocky Raccoon" and yelling out "coon!" at the top of their lungs each time the word came around.

Mrs. Michaels, a chunky, middle-aged black woman in a beige pants suit, was trying to convince a tall white girl named Margo, aka Beep-Beep, to leave the lounge and return to her room, where she had been restricted after a recent runaway. When Margo saw Steven, she padded away down the corridor, but in a moment she was back. She sat on the floor against a wall in a pink bathrobe over panties and a T-shirt with a cartoon roadrunner bird on it. When Mrs. Michaels tried to pull the girl to her feet, the bathrobe came all the way open, revealing a large pair of sewing scissors in her hand.

"Fuck off, Rocky." The girl grinned at Mrs. Michaels. Her eyes were dilated and pale: one look at her and Steven could tell that she'd brought back some drugs from her runaway that were now churning recklessly through her brain. He told Mrs. Michaels to phone a weapons alert to the office downstairs, and cleared the lounge of spectators.

Margo got unsteadily to her feet, holding the scissors up, points aimed at Steven. "I'm telling you like I told that gold-toothed nigger, I'm tired of being shut in my freakin' room all the time! Gonna see my TV show!" She jabbed the scissors in the air. "Anybody touches me gonna get his dick cut off!"

A maintenance man and a nurse, both wearing heavy gloves, walked into the lounge. For half an hour, everyone talked quietly to Margo, trying to get her to let out her frustrations with words rather than with the scissors. She stood swaying in place, clutching the scissors to her chest. Eventually the staff had to do a by-the-books operation to get the scissors. Mrs. Michaels and the nurse pinned her arms behind her, the maintenance man grabbed her wrist, and Steven plucked the scissors from her hand. Margo shrieked, her face contorted as if a vital organ were being ripped out of her body. She thrashed until suddenly all her strength was gone and she lay gasping in the arms of her captors.

The nurse took her to the infirmary for a long rest to let the drugs wear off. When another staff member arrived from home to help out, Steven was finally able to leave. An hour and a half had gone by—Katrina's conference appointment. Steven kicked an empty soda can the length of the corridor.

Someone had torn down one of the typed list of "norms" from a bulletin board. Its cork surface and the wall all around it were scrawled with ornate calligraphy like the screeching graffiti of the New York City subways:

freedom

PACO
#1

sheri
sucks

JULIE H.

&

BEEP-BEEP

BORN
TO
~~LOSE~~
~~WIN~~
~~FUCK~~
DIE

SMOKE
&
M.B.   A*W*O*L

—FOREVER—

SATANS SLAVES 168th STREET

luv luv luv luv luv
luv luv luv
luv
V i n n i e Z.

a n g e l o

159th
STREET
DRAGON-S
dOWN TO KILL
LIKE A MF

* SHAWNITA ** & ** BATMAN *

i
love
you

sheri
sucks

F-I-N-G-E-R
P-O-P-P-E-R

```
- you play -
- you pay -
                          J.J + P.B.

FREE
  FREE
    FREE                          JORGE
      FREE
        FREE  FREE  FREE ----   sheri      -y-
          FREE                  sucks    BLANCA
            FREE
          FREE
        FREE
      FREE
                      fuck
                      staff       SUPREMES
R*E*E*F*E*R                       !!!!!!!!!!!!!!!
                        S
                    J E  U S
```

As Steven read, the jagged letters seemed to stab at his eyes like the points of scissors. Going down the back stairs, he could hear the white girls beginning to sing in the corridor behind him, ''Rocky Raccoon. . . . ''

The first thing next morning, Steven walked into the assistant director's office. Standing, he drummed his fingers on the edge of the desk until Ben Paleno finished talking on the phone.

''The musical show's got to be canceled, Ben,'' he said.

Ben gazed up at him. The skin under his eyes was pink with tiny veins. He shook his head, smiling faintly. ''Can't do it,'' he said.

''Why the hell not?''

''I've invited too many people—folks from Head Office, from the local communities.''

''They can be uninvited.'' Steven spoke slowly, through his teeth. ''Your girls are running wild. Things are too unsettled here.''

''I don't agree. The show'll be just the thing to pull us all together.'' Ben lit a cigar stub. ''We've got a 4-H club and a gospel group coming. There's a drum corps and a modern dance group, and a rock band from some little town in Ontario.''

Steven paced away from the desk, staring into a case full of shining trophies. The glass reflected his black corduroy jacket and open maroon shirt; he looked as dark as he felt. ''That's terrific, Ben.''

''It's an international event.''

''I see. Lots of press coverage?'' Steven tugged at the corner of his mustache.

''*Youth Service News,* of course. Plattsburgh and Boonsville papers, I expect. WRNY-TV might send a video team.''

''Goddammit, you are beyond belief!'' Steven leaned over Ben's desk. ''Have you ever thought what'll happen when all those marchers and singers and dancers start performing? Our girls are going to feel outclassed and miserable.'' He stared through the cigar smoke at Ben. ''Haven't you had enough excitement around here, after Margo last night?''

Ben tapped his cigar ash into a heavy ashtray on his desk. ''I know it's been hectic. My staff and girls have had some trouble adjusting to the New Program, but that's to be expected.''

''You've only partly started the program. You've been offering a little freedom, raising expectations, and then slamming kids down the minute they take what little you've given them. They're confused and panicky and furious.''

''That's the kind of girls we get here.'' Ben shook his head sadly.

''Cancel the show, Ben.'' Steven narrowed his eyes.

Ben sat forward, his hands folded on his desk. ''Matt already talked to Head Office about the possiblity of postponing the show, but they seem to feel that it's an important indicator of how well the New Program is working. If it didn't go on, Matt's promotion might get held up.''

''Ben, you're up before the Review Board in a couple weeks. A blowup here could finish you.''

''Not me.'' Ben sighted along his cigar at Steven.

Steven stepped closer to the desk. ''If things haven't calmed down here real soon, I'm going to personally call up every organization you've contacted and see that this show's called off.''

''Now I know you're bluffing.'' Ben's smile thickened his lips. ''But, then, I think you've been bluffing all along.''

''We'll see,'' Steven said. He turned and strode out of the office.

The rec room was empty, its armchairs and couches left against the walls by the girls who had mopped it. Steven wandered over to the piano, rehearsing explanations he wanted to make to Head Office and community organizations, and knowing that he would never utter any of them. He found himself sitting at the stool in front of the chipped keyboard.

His left hand pounded some blues chords he'd learned at college. With his right hand, he began to pick out some of the opera melodies that were always going through his head.

The chords and melodies didn't blend together, but the crashing dissonance sounded just right to him. Musical notes fell around him like a rain of falling bricks. Prickly heat broke out along his hairline. His fingers paused in the air over an incomplete melody and unresolved chord. Then he brought his hands down hard again, but not onto the keys. The wooden keyboard cover cracked into place, trapping most of the fractured music inside, freeing the escaped notes to ricochet around the room toward the open doors and windows.

23

By reading the log, Katrina learned about the plans to double the school population over the summer with felons from a maximum-security institution that was being shut down. If she needed any specific justification for a runaway, this was it. Sometimes she thought she should leave with Yvonne, who wanted to create a disturbance with their skit at the end-of-classes ceremonies and take off with Peaches and her while the staff was busy calming down the other girls.

Pam, too, was eager to leave, and urged Katrina to run away with her. She and Katrina could hitchhike across the country and live on a friend's farm and pick artichokes. Pick what? Katrina asked, laughing. I don't know, it's some kind of vegetable they got in California, Pam said. They found a picture of an artichoke in a library book and lay on Katrina's bed examining it. It looks awful weird to me, Katrina said; I'll have to think about it.

Pam never went anywhere without a camera strapped around her neck now. One night in the darkroom they started talking about personal things. Katrina told Pam a secret: she'd been gaining a little weight and discovered that she finally had breasts. Not big titties or anything, but definitely some fat bulging up underneath the nipples, enough so that she'd have to buy a bra soon. Pam congratulated her; when she asked to see, Katrina kicked her.

Pam began talking about how cozy life had been in the old days when her commune had really been together. She got weepy about it and for some reason, maybe the chemical fumes, Katrina did, too. Pretty soon they were holding each other and crying on each other's shoulders about some old family problems of Katrina's that she hadn't cried about when they'd happened.

With only the yellow safe-light glowing from the corner, the room was dim and shadowy and hot. They kept bumping into shelves and giggling in between sobs. Katrina was hardly aware of it starting, but suddenly she and Pam were kissing each other. They couldn't stop. Pam's mouth kept moving all over her face, wet and warm and slippery. When Pam's tongue wriggled around in her mouth, Katrina felt herself breaking out in a delicious hot sweat. Her new breasts tingled, something she had never felt before. Pam was stroking her under the unzipped front of her jeans; suddenly she couldn't stop pushing herself against Pam's fingers. Finally, exhausted, she leaned back against the counter, gasping for breath.

Pam begged for a turn, so Katrina finger-popped her until she grew hysterical and Katrina had to grab her mouth with her free hand to keep her quiet. Afterward, it was embarrassing how grateful Pam was. The air in the room was too hot to breathe. Katrina ran out and had to sit down suddenly on the floor. Pam followed her and sat beside her. They couldn't speak or look at each other.

Finally, Katrina got up and went into the bathroom to splash cold water on her face. Alone at the sink, she wasn't quite sure what she felt. She'd been thinking that there must be something wrong with her because she could never get turned on in this place like most of the other girls did. Now she knew she could. Okay, she knew that. Good.

Or was it? Maybe it meant that if she stayed around here much longer she'd get into more weeping and fumbling with Pam and other girls. After a while, maybe she'd start getting flaky like Peaches.

One thing was sure—if she started wondering about these things, it was time to get the hell out of this place.

On the night before the commencement ceremonies the rain came down hard, leaving puddles on the back parking lot which the girls had to sweep away the next morning with industrial-sized push brooms. In the bright sunlight, the sky was a blank, cloudless blue that made the outdoors look bigger than it had ever been before. Katrina took off her sneakers and walked through the grass beside the pond, shivering at the cool furry tickling between her toes. From the bridge, she watched the guests arrive: a teenage rock band, a gospel group in red robes, a drum corps in spangly uniforms. Men and women got out of black state cars, stretched, and smiled uneasily at the watching girls, who retreated back to the building. For the first time in many months, Katrina realized, the girls were outnumbered by adults, by males, by strangers. Even the staff, all dressed up, looked strange today. She watched Ben Paleno, in a plaid suit, pumping men's hands, patting children's heads, laughing with the wives of Youth Service bigshots. Steven, the only man the girls were used to seeing in fancy clothes, looked subdued in a beige corduroy jacket, dark shirt, and slacks. He was staying near the girls by the back door, talking quietly with Sonia.

She had on a long turquoise skirt and cream-colored blouse; with her yellow hair flowing over her shoulders, she looked so radiant that few girls dared approach her. The black girls wanted Leah to hand out the awards, but she wasn't here. They were reluctant to start without her, but when Ben Paleno spoke over the public-address system, everyone had to sit down. Katrina sat between Yvonne and Peaches in the girls' section—the back rows—of the audience. In a single row of chairs facing the guests and girls, the Youth Service officials, Steven, the director, and some photographers sat waiting for Ben Paleno to return to the podium.

Katrina slouched in her chair, smoking, her fingers drumming on her knee. She had blow-dried her hair so that it stood out from her head in tight curls, adding several inches to her height—her "Mr. Fox" getup for the skit. Peaches and Yvonne, however, hadn't dressed as Sonia and Leah, and Katrina doubted that they would. The skit had been fun to talk about; sometimes they'd laughed until their stomachs hurt thinking up deliciously filthy lines. But talking about something and acting it out in front of people were very different things. Katrina wasn't all that eager to do the skit, now, either.

But what were they going to do for a disturbance instead? How was she going to get out of here? When she thought of standing on a roadside with her thumb out, she couldn't wait to get moving, as if ants were running up and down the veins in her legs. But then all the ants crawled into her stomach and died there, soggy and heavy, and she thought about staying awhile. She wished this awards ceremony would at least try to convince her to believe in Fairbanks again, but nothing that was going on seemed connected to her.

Everyone had to stand up for the Pledge of Allegiance, led by a second-floor girl named Heatwave, who was dressed in a sexy yellow slacks outfit. Just yesterday, she'd been talking about how, in a gang fight last year, she'd walked up to a black girl and punched her in the face with a jeweler's screwdriver between her fingers. The girl's eye had squirted out, she'd bragged, like a bloody grape. And here was Heatwave, singsonging the pledge, giggling when she forgot the words and had to be prompted by Mr. Paleno.

He introduced the commencement speaker, a woman in a heavy skirt and loose white blouse that was supposed to hide how fat she was. Her hair was fluffed out around her ears like feathers; she looked like a pigeon caught in an updraft. Smiling at everyone, she read from a stack of papers about how she had changed direction in her own life, from an English major in college to a career in law enforcement, and so the girls, too, could change direction and leave antisocial behavior behind for productive behavior. To Katrina, this lady's rap wasn't any realer than the pledge. She might as well have been talking out of a TV screen advertising Cadillacs.

Finally it was time for the awards. A black staff member handed them out to the second-floor girls, but there was still no sign of Leah, so when the third floor's turn came, Sonia carried the stack of stiff papers up to Steven at the microphone. Katrina wanted Steven to be unreal like everybody else—he'd be so much easier to hate. At the same time, she was scared to see him being phony, because she'd have to hate everything she'd ever felt about him.

Whether real or unreal—it was hard to tell—he was certainly being successful at cheering up the girls. He wasn't just giving out awards and shaking hands, he was giving the girls little hugs and kissing them on the cheeks or foreheads and talking with everyone for a few moments before they returned, blushing at all the applause, to their seats. Sonia was doing the same. And damn!—the bitches were eating it up.

It was a party. For these few minutes, the girls were truly glamorous in their high-heeled shoes and stockings, their skirt- or slacks-and-blouse outfits they'd made in sewing classes. The makeup on their faces looked polished and buffed. Even Katrina, who'd planned to look slobby, hadn't been able to resist Yvonne's array of eyeliners and rouges and lipsticks. Then she'd had to borrow a bright orange blouse and blue skirt to go (sort of) with her cheeks and eyes. She'd even filled one of Pam's bras with toilet paper—not too much, only enough to give her a slight shape so that her blouse wouldn't look too big on her.

Ronnie, Whale, and Inez trooped up to the podium to get academic prizes. Pam got an award in photography. Katrina thought she was going to get a photography award, too, but when her name wasn't called out, she sank back in her chair, both relieved and hurt.

More prizes followed. Katrina tried hard not to listen, but when her name was called, she jumped up so quickly that the girls around her laughed. She wasn't used to wearing a skirt; the warm air against her bare legs made her feel suddenly breathless. Not wanting to blush when the photographers' flashbulbs went off, she kept her eyes downcast as she walked toward the podium.

She stood in front of Steven. He took hold of her hand and drew her close. She smelled the tobacco scent of him, felt the corduroy of his jacket against her cheek and the tickly brush of his mustache against her forehead. She had to shut her eyes tight to keep from screaming.

Then she was on her own again, blinking. There was daylight behind her and him. She reached out her hand to steady herself and discovered a piece of stiff paper in it.

Steven was smiling down at her. His gaze flicked over her face everywhere but her eyes. "Nice work, Katrina," he said.

"What—" She cleared her throat. "What for?"

He pointed at the paper.

She held it away from her face. LEADERSHIP AWARD, it said.

"You deserve it," he said.

Then she understood. She remembered standing on the bridge over the inlet with him months ago, and the way he'd smiled at her then—like now, but better then—and the way he'd put his arm around her. That had been private; this was public now. Somehow, everything that had happened between them that day was supposed to have led up to this . . . piece of paper.

"What good is this?" She squinted up at him.

Steven's smile was gone. Nothing was left in his face but a sudden sadness. She stepped back from him, biting her lip. If he had yelled at her or smacked her face, her heart couldn't have beat harder. Before he could answer, she turned away. The *Youth Service News* photographer was exploding flashbulbs in her face. She tried to glance once more at Steven, but his face was gone. It was a blank white afterimage of a flashbulb. As she turned to go back to her seat, the blank patch floated out before her like a windblown balloon wherever she looked.

"I want to tell you, I'm really proud of the third-floor girls." Katrina heard Steven's voice as she pushed her way down the row of knees toward her chair. Still flushing from the applause they'd received, the girls basked in the praise booming at them through loudspeakers for all the world to hear. Katrina tuned most of it out. She knew that the girls were aware that they hadn't been quite as good as Steven was telling them, but that didn't matter. When he told them their accomplishments were going to pay off in the future, the girls allowed themselves to believe that they truly did have futures.

But then Mr. Steiner, the director, stood up beside Steven, looking solemn in his slacks and white shirt. His black beard moved up and down slowly as he spoke—something about just getting the official news this morning. Katrina sat far back in her chair, trying not to listen but hearing anyway. The director was saying good-bye to everyone ... and welcoming Steven Fox as the new acting director.

Now? Today? Katrina gaped at Steven. She'd known this would happen sometime soon, and shouldn't have been shocked, but she was. The other girls, who had heard only rumors, now appeared to be learning the reality for first time.

As Mr. Steiner's amplified voice echoed off the side of the building, the mood changed visibly along the rows of third-floor girls. High heels scraped against the asphalt; noisy whispering broke out. Cheek rouge and green eye shadow and scarlet lipstick began to look like war paint. The girls' visions of their futures fizzled out as quickly as they'd come to life a few minutes ago. All their plans for trial visits home, for family and group-home placements—what would happen to them? Where was the payoff for all this good behavior Steven had been praising them for? There wasn't any!

Steven was going to turn into a director like Mr. Steiner—always in his office poring over papers and talking on the phone, or away on important trips to Albany. He'd never have time to come up to the third floor to see the girls again, except maybe on holidays to smile a director's smile and pat the staff on the back. Suddenly the girls were without anyone to help them unravel the red tape of the juvenile justice system that might lead them out into the world again, or which could keep them tied up in institutions for the rest of their lives.

They'd lost a father, a big brother, a friend. No longer would he sit in the lounge joking with them about the TV programs, or invite them into his office to talk over home problems, or listen to them trying to express their feelings in group sessions, or even—they would miss everything about him—yell at them for cutting classes or put them on restriction for shoplifting. It wasn't that they all liked him so much, but that he'd been *theirs*. He'd cared about them. That was what had been remarkable about him. They'd come to think of him as always having been in their lives. Suddenly he wasn't going to be there any longer.

"Meanwhile," Matt Steiner concluded, his voice sounding more choked up than anyone could recall, "I'm glad that I had a chance to run a unique institution that didn't behave like an institution, but like a group of human beings who trusted and helped and cared about one another. Thank you."

Katrina squirmed in her seat. The whole trouble, she thought, was that even though the place sometimes didn't behave like an institution, it always *was* one. If it had just warehoused girls, set rules, and gave out beatings when they weren't obeyed, then it would have been an easy place to deal with. You could simply hate it. (And hating was easy : it was familiar, definite, clear.) You could write nasty stuff on walls, curse at staff when they threatened to smack you, and after they had, you could dump their purses upside down into the kitchen garbage or slash their tires—and then feel fairly satisfied that you'd expressed your feelings appropriately. When you got treated like a piece of shit, it wasn't hard to retaliate by doing shitty things.

But when staff—or at least Leah, Sonia, Steven—gave you tantalizing glimpses of what it was to be treated like a human being, how were you supposed to react ? How were you supposed to feel when you realized all the more painfully that you were still trapped inside an institution for state kids whom nobody else wanted ? When you realized that the person there who'd seemed to care for you the most was now—as everybody else always had—abandoning you ?

You reacted like a human being—with rage. I'm only human, Katrina thought, lighting a cigarette and flicking the match down hard at the ground. She squinted at Steven standing at the podium in the direct glare of the sun. His face looked scorched ; his eyes were still that bright blue but with all the craziness, the humor, the intensity gone. His lips moved ; he was making sounds into the microphone like a director. His voice strained to sound right—deep, authoritative—but the words he spoke floated far above Katrina's head. He'd taken off his corduroy jacket—she remembered its tobacco smell—and now his dark blue shirt stuck to his chest with sweat. His collar was open—no fancy, swirly tie today. Without one, he looked terribly . . . unreal.

Katrina poked her finger under her glasses to wipe her eyes. The Leadership Award paper was still in her hand. She stared at it until it came into focus. Then slowly she tore it into strips and let them flutter down onto the black asphalt.

24 ✎

At the outdoor lunch after the awards ceremony, Katrina loaded her paper plate with ham, barbecued chicken, potato salad, and cake with blue icing. She sat alone at a picnic table, a piece of sticky cake in one hand, an unlit cigarette in the other. Every few minutes she squinted up at the parking lot, where Steven was talking with Mr. Steiner and some men in suits from Youth Service headquarters.

When he came down the grassy slope, she was sure that he'd spot her and come over to explain that Leadership Award, or try to. She couldn't wait to see his face when she told him she'd torn it up. When he'd ask her why, she'd refuse to speak; he'd lean forward, the worry wrinkles deepening in his forehead, and finally she'd turn back to him and really let him have it. . . .

She froze: he was walking toward her across the grass. A man with a cigar was walking with him, blocking his view of her. She edged sideways on the bench. The man took hold of Steven's arm and laughed about something, but Steven didn't even smile. Now he was no more than a couple of arm's lengths away from her. He saw her. His face relaxed a little. But then several other men stepped in front of him and soon all she could see of him was the back of his head as he walked slowly into a crowd of guests. The cake fell out of her fingers, landing on its side on the table.

Yvonne sat down across from her with a plate of food. ''What's happening?'' she said.

"Nothing." Katrina lit her cigarette. "You ain't dressed for our skit, are you?"

Yvonne picked up a roll, then put it down and licked the butter from her silver fingernails. "Naw. Don't look at me cross-eyed, girl. I don't see you getting ready."

Katrina shrugged.

"Peaches don't want to be in the skit either," Yvonne said. "There's too many people."

"We chickened out," Katrina said.

"Maybe. You still planning to take off?"

"Probably."

"With me?"

"I ain't decided yet." Katrina glanced away.

Yvonne wiped her mouth with a paper napkin. "That's a fine shirt. Where'd you get it?"

"Borrowed it off Peaches," Katrina said.

"Where'd you get the titties?"

"Hey, fuck you!"

"Just seeing how mad you were."

"Don't check me out, Yvonne."

Yvonne smiled and licked her fingernails again. "Peaches set to go this afternoon with me," she said. "Ronnie don't know nothing about it."

Katrina sat forward. "Peaches told you that? For sure?"

"Square business. I spotted some cars with keys in them, and I'm going to take me one. All we need is a distraction, like that skit would have been." Yvonne sat back. Her wine-colored blouse stretched tight over the sharp points of her breasts. "We got to think of something better."

"I know that."

"So you got any ideas?"

Katrina put out her cigarette in a glob of blue icing. "I'm thinking," she said.

After lunch, Steven stood by the back door where the secretary could find him quickly if Leah called; he'd expected her to arrive hours ago. She was in Albany, having been called again to testify at a hearing about abuses in the institution where she and Steven had worked before coming to Fairbanks, and had planned to start driving back early this morning. The sun beat down, baking him and the brick side of the building behind him. His hand felt clammy from shaking the hands of cigar-chomping, backslapping Head Office bureaucrats. Already he'd been invited to three meetings around the state during the next week, and didn't see how he could get out of them. The county building inspectors were coming tomorrow morning; tomorrow night he had to address the local Rotary Club—when was he going to have time to help the third-floor girls make a smooth transition from him to Leah? When was he going to be able to talk with Katrina about that award? He scanned the crowd for her, hoping to get a few moments with her now, but the second-floor girls were assembling on the asphalt staging area to start the show.

The girls looked good in matching blue T-shirts that Ben had got them, but their dance routine soon became sloppy, then chaotic—they'd rehearsed to a record, and weren't used to this local high-school rock band that tried to make up for their lack of talent with earsplitting volume. Dancers lost the beat, bumped into each other, and finally retreated to their seats before the music ended. The girls in the audience laughed into each other's shoulders; the adults clapped politely.

The next number was a display by a 4-H drum corps from one of the nearby towns. Steven groaned inwardly as the girls came marching in to the booming of bass drums and clatter of traps, their sequined uniforms sparkling red, white, and blue in the sunlight. Knees rising, elbows swinging, they strode back and forth; rows filtered through rows in perfect step while cymbals made the air crack and echo against the side of the building like artillery fire. Four majorettes began flinging their batons high in the air and catching them behind their backs. The faces of the crowd turned up and down, up and down. People ooh'd and aah'd. All the girls in the group had nearly identical pink faces and short yellow hair and white smiles. Even their final bows were synchronized.

The black girls, Steven knew, had never seen anything like these kids, and stared after them as if they expected them to jump into a flying saucer and soar away. The rural white Fairbanks girls, who were "greasers" to 4-H kids like these at high school, knew about them, though.

These kids were the ones who were always chosen for cheerleading squad and National Honor Society and were praised by the principal at assembly for their school spirit. They wore clean blue jeans and big varsity sweatshirts and new cowboy boots. They were perpetually cheerful and busy busy busy— memorizing speeches for VFW programs, cooking for Grange BBQ suppers, setting up county fair booths. Steven had often driven by the big farms or neat ranch houses where they lived, away from the grubby little towns and trailer camps where the Fairbanks girls lived. The 4-H kids were never hauled into the vice-principal's office for drinking on campus. They were never visited by Welfare workers. They never drove bashed-up cars with the mufflers dragging. They never got stoned, or pregnant, or busted. And they never, never had anything to do with "greasers."

The next group up was supposed to be another dance team from Unit Two, but the girls refused to go on. Steven didn't blame them—they weren't about to make fools of themselves as the first group from their unit had, especially when they had to follow the drum corps. A dispirited restlessness was moving through the girls' part of the audience. Ben Paleno hurried the next act on: a red-robed gospel group called the Heavenly Sunbeams.

Steven watched the black girls lean forward in their seats. The Heavenly Sunbeams were the only "outside" black people the girls had laid eyes on in months. Some of the young men were handsome, with long sideburns and processed hair. The women were fat and jolly-looking. They clapped their hands to get the beat going, and some members of the audience joined in. But when the group started to sing, the black girls looked at each other and sighed.

The music was the same high-pitched harmony they'd heard in wooden churches during visits to relatives in the South: old-timey stuff, spirituals. The women shook their hands and rolled their eyes heavenward; the men, as if following the women's orders—the women outnumbered and outweighed them—did likewise. It was the radio music you ironed to on hot Sunday afternoons when you had to stay in and do chores instead of hanging out with your friends drinking Ripple wine in the park. It was music that came wailing out of the spinster boarder's room when you were trying to watch "Soul Train" on TV. It was the music you wore starchy dresses for when an "uncle" you'd never seen before took you and your mother across town to his church and afterward ate up nearly all the ribs for dinner, smiling his fake gold-toothed smile at the silent children around the table. It was the music that promised you an Everlasting Glory that sounded as dreary as day-old collard greens in the sink drain. It was black music all right, but it was a shade of black that had driven the black Fairbanks girls right out into the streets looking for dashikis and Afro piks and clenched-fist pendants and the latest Motown sounds.

When the Heavenly Sunbeams had finished, Steven saw several girls leaving the audience to go behind a nearby clump of bushes for a smoke. Among them was Katrina, looking strangely fierce with her bright pink cheeks and frizzed hair, and older than usual in the too-large blouse. Steven waved to her, but when she turned her face away, he couldn't tell if she'd seen him or not. He started toward her.

"Mr. Fox?"

He stopped. Behind him in the doorway a secretary was beckoning to him.

"Mrs. Gomes is on the phone for you," the woman said. "Long distance."

Steven glanced in Katrina's direction, but she'd already gone behind the bushes. He hurried into the building, amplified rock music splashing through the doorway behind him.

When Katrina came out on the other side of the bushes, Steven was nowhere in sight. Fuck him, she thought, just fuck him. She had more important things to think about. If we want to get something going, Yvonne had told her, we can get Ronnie in an uproar about Peaches. Katrina looked around for Ronnie. Spotting her with Whale and Vonita, she walked over to her.

"I want to talk to you," she said.

Ronnie scowled. "What about?"

"Private."

"We got nothing to talk about private."

"It's important." Katrina walked several paces away and waited.

Ronnie glared at her, then followed. "All right," she said. "What's your problem?"

"Not *my* problem."

"Yeah, whose?"

"Maybe yours."

"I don't need you to tell me my problems. This ain't no damn group session." Ronnie folded her arms over the front of her spangled T-shirt.

Katrina forced herself to look up into Ronnie's face. She hadn't been alone with Ronnie since the night in the bathroom; she realized she was trembling. "I'm only telling you because of Peaches," she said.

"Damn, will you out with it, girl!" Ronnie's voice had an anxious edge to it.

Katrina took a step backward, but felt the trembling sensation leave her body. Ronnie's eyes were even darker and more brooding than usual: they suddenly had a familiar look in them, as if she were wretchedly lonely for someone who was about to leave her. For a moment, Katrina couldn't speak. "Yvonne's going to take Peaches to New York to be a hooker," she said finally.

Ronnie's fingers dug into her forearms. "I already heard that rumor. It's shit."

"No, it's not, Ronnie. They're going to take off this afternoon."

"Who told you that?"

"Yvonne."

"Come on. How they going to get out of here?"

"Yvonne's finding a car with keys in it. Listen, I'm telling you this because I don't want Peaches to get hurt." Suddenly Katrina meant it; she wasn't trying to get Ronnie upset. "Peaches ain't got no mind of her own these days. I hope she listens to you. She's got to!"

"Yeah, okay ... thanks." Ronnie glanced at Katrina, then away again. Wiping sweat from her forehead, she turned toward the audience, where Yvonne and Peaches sat in the back row, their heads leaning toward each other as they talked. "I'll get on Peaches' case," Ronnie said.

"Good." Katrina watched her stride off, and then looked at the back door again. Steven was still gone.

"Are you okay, Leah?" Steven sat on the edge of the desk in the director's office, pressing the phone receiver hard against his ear to bring her voice closer.

"I'm still in Albany. They called me back to the stand this morning," Leah said.

"How's it going?"

"The Youth Service is doing such a cover-up, Steven. They tried to make me look like a liar, make those poor kids look like scum." She sighed. "I think I'm finished with this organization very soon."

Steven paced to the end of the phone cord and stopped by the window. "I'm sorry to hear that."

"We can talk about it. I'll be there tonight, is a promise. Have you got enough staff?"

"Mrs. Lert's off till tomorrow. Mrs. Healey's off at four, but Sonia's on. We're okay for the time being." Steven reached out to touch a windowpane; the glass vibrated faintly against his fingers from the music outside, a sensation that was both pleasant and unsettling. "I'm acting director now, Leah. Those Head Office people brought the news this morning. Matt's already taken off."

"How are you feeling?"

Steven turned away from the window. "Strange. Like I'm suddenly on the other side of a huge ocean from the girls and I can't get to them."

"Perhaps they will find a way to get to you," Leah said. "How did they take the news?"

"Sort of stunned. I thought we'd at least get a chance to tell them in group session before it happened." Steven leaned against the window frame, lighting a cigarette. "You know, while I was giving my speech, I could feel them getting upset, and I suddenly remembered how panicky I used to feel those weeks I was in jail when I was their age. One time all the kids were running to get into a brawl that'd broken out. I usually stayed away from fights, but that day I'd just heard that my father wasn't going to come get me—nobody could find him—and for the first time in my life, I really wanted to kick ass. I just wanted to *hurt* somebody. So I was running toward the brawl with everybody else when this guard stepped out in front of me and yelled, ''No you don't!'' I stopped. I don't know why, but I did, and I went out through a side door and stayed in the yard till the fighting was over. I never went near another fight again.'' Steven wiped his forehead with his sleeve. ''Anyway, I kept wishing I could say something like that to the girls today, something that would keep them from—I don't know what, rushing off to bash people and get bashed back. But the words coming out of my mouth— I could hear them echoing over the public-address system— they had nothing to do with what I wanted to say. . . . ''

''Perhaps you'll get a chance to say it sometime,'' Leah said.

''Perhaps.''

''Are the girls having any fun at the show?''

''Not much. All the guest performers are outclassing them. Katrina, Yvonne, and Peaches canceled their skit. Ben's girls are getting antsy as hell.''

''Matt should have taken him off the second floor months ago.''

''We couldn't hire anybody else to replace him. Anyway, the theory's always been, if we give Ben enough rope he'll hang himself. I think the plan's going to work, but I've got a feeling he's not the only one who's going to get hurt.'' Steven paced back to the desk with the receiver. ''I want to find some way to get our girls the hell out of here before it all hits the fan, Leah. Can you stay around long enough to help me?''

He heard her take a deep breath. ''A month or two, yes. Then we'll see.''

''Good. I just hope that's enough time.''

''I wish I were there with you right now.''

"You will be." Steven leaned against the desk. "You must be tired. Drive carefully, will you?"

"You take care, too."

He put down the phone and looked around the big, empty office—his now, officially, and not his. The noisy music outside rattled the windows urgently in their frames. The girls weren't the only ones on the other side of the ocean; a part of him was still there, too. He knew that he would have to walk out into the noise if he were ever going to find it again. He had only been in here about five minutes, but already he felt he had been gone too long.

Katrina had heard Ronnie rehearsing the "R-E-S-P-E-C-T" song for weeks, singing the melody alone by having one of the stereo tracks switched down when Aretha Franklin's voice came on. Today, with a series of extension cords that snaked across the asphalt, Ronnie had rigged a record player to the band's speaker system. Smoke, a stocky, black, second-floor girl in a striped T-shirt, was posted by the console, ready to turn the left speaker up and down, giving Ronnie trumpets and rhythm accompaniment between phrases.

Katrina watched Ronnie walk into the middle of the staging area. Yvonne, who'd been sitting beside her, got up to go inside to the bathroom—she said. Katrina didn't see her work her way through the audience to stand beside Smoke near the folding chair that the record player rested on. When Ronnie gave the signal, Smoke put the needle on the record. Behind Ronnie, Whale and Vonita began to dance.

Ronnie's voice came out of the loudspeakers with a resonance that, to Katrina, belonged to someone she had never really seen or heard before. Suddenly fascinated, Katrina watched Ronnie sway in place, holding the microphone close to her lips, her eyes half-closed. The voice had some of the startling urgency of Peaches' scream in it, yet that pain had somehow been turned inside out and made gentle. Ronnie was displaying her own vulnerability for all to see, sharing it, daring to insist on her right to ask RESPECT for it—and getting it, not only for herself but for everyone who listened. Sometimes the voice was rough and angry, and Katrina felt her own rage being lifted from her. Sometimes it faded, high and lonely, to a delicate thin ribbon of sound, and Katrina felt her loneliness fading away. Katrina couldn't fear or hate this Ronnie—or anyone else. She wanted the voice never to stop.

But it did, abruptly. Yvonne, hidden from view, had been dancing in place, bumping hips with Smoke harder and harder. As Ronnie did a turnaround, Yvonne clapped her hands over her head and, swinging her hip sharply, knocked Smoke off balance. Smoke grabbed the chair beside her for support. The needle skidded across the record. The turntable slid off the chair and crashed to the asphalt.

"You fucking bitch!" Ronnie screamed into the micro-phone at Smoke, the words exploding out of the amplifiers. Ronnie strode toward the stereo, where Smoke was standing. Guests scattered. The girls were on their feet, drawn after Ronnie. Katrina, suddenly feeling deprived like someone woken roughly out of a beautiful dream, ran alongside the girls. Ronnie had grabbed Smoke around the neck; Sonia had hold of Ronnie's arm. Girls were shoving each other and screaming insults. Several second-floor girls had hold of Yvonne, shout-ing that the fallen record player had been her fault. Katrina lunged at one of them blindly, wanting to feel her fist strike flesh, but she was shoved sideways by somebody rushing Yvonne. She ran around the crowd and jumped up onto a folding chair on the grass to watch.

Mr. Paleno was dragging Smoke backward. Sonia, trying to tug Ronnie away, was sent sprawling face-first onto the asphalt. Then Steven was wading into the girls, grabbing Ronnie from behind to put her in a full nelson. Someone backed into the chair Katrina was standing on: she toppled onto the grass, landing on her arm and rolling over several times. Her forearm burned. Skin had been scraped away; through the yellow-green grass stain, red beads of blood were appearing.

"Steven?" Katrina called out.

He couldn't hear her though, still struggling as he was with Ronnie. Ronnie kicked the air, tried to hit him by swinging her fists blindly behind her. He bent her almost double, and gradually her body went limp, her arms dangling down. Steven eased her onto her stomach on the grass. Katrina caught a glimpse of her face: eyes closed, lips stretched in a grimace.

Steven knelt beside her. "Don't—move—" he said, trying to catch his breath. He signaled for Mrs. Michaels to come over.

"Leah?" Ronnie raised her head. Then, seeing who it was, she dropped her face to the grass again. Tears rolled down her cheeks.

Katrina sat up, holding her elbow. Again she called out to Steven, but there was too much shouting and thudding of running feet for him to hear her. He stood up, his back still to her, and rushed off toward a clearing in the crowd where someone was helping Sonia to stand up. She had a blood-streaked scrape in her forehead. As Steven reached her, she lost her footing, and he had to pick her up, his arms under her legs and shoulders, to carry her off toward the building.

Katrina stood up in a daze and looked around. The second-floor girls, still shouting threats at the third-floor girls, were being herded around the side of the building by their staff. Mr. Paleno's voice came over the public-address system, urging the guests to be seated again, but most of them had scattered toward the cars. Katrina shuffled toward the back door.

In the dining room, Mrs. Healey sat all the girls down, telling them over and over again to keep quiet, calm down, just stay put until Mr. Fox came in. The girls took out their cigarettes, grumbling and cursing. When Mrs. Healey told them not to light up—"No smoking in the dining room, you know that!"—they looked her straight in the eye and blew smoke out of their mouths. Everyone was talking at once, voices dropping to low murmurs and rising again. Still feeling a little dizzy, Katrina added her own voice, her face thrusting foward like someone spitting mouthfuls of gasoline onto a fire.

Suddenly the back door to the dining room was filled by

Mr. Paleno. "Now what the hell are you girls doing in here?"
he bellowed.

For a moment, the girls glared back in silence. Katrina
was first to speak. "We're having a war council," she said.

"Oh, you are, are you?"

"Yeah."

Mr. Paleno peered around the roomful of angry faces. The
girls tipped back in their chairs, flicked ashes onto the floor,
watched him out of the sides of their eyes. "You're a wiseass,
aren't you?" Mr. Paleno turned his dark red face back to
Katrina. "I wouldn't be surprised if you weren't behind this
whole thing."

Katrina grinned for a second, liking the sound of that.
Then she narrowed her eyes. "It wasn't us that knocked over
the stereo," she said. "Ask those bitches upstairs."

"Right on!" Yvonne shouted. She got some cheers and
nervous laughter in response.

"I get the picture." Mr. Paleno began to pace back and
forth. His voice projected like a cannon in the big room. "You
girls think that if somebody lets you down, you've got to lash
out like Ronnie did."

"Goddamn right!" Katrina said, almost shouting. Her
words sounded slurred to her, as if she were drunk. She grinned
again.

Mr. Paleno glared at her. "That's the attitude that got
you in here in the first place! That's what's going to keep
you all in institutions your whole lives!" He wiped his face
with his hand and slouched against a table. "It's sad, is what
it is, you know that?"

Several girls turned their chairs away from him.

"You blew it today," he continued. "You made the place
look like a zoo!"

"They're rattling the cages upstairs, man," Katrina said,
staring up at the ceiling.

"That's right!" Vonita screamed, squirming in her seat.
"They're the ones! We were putting on a good show and those
motherfucking bitches fucked everything up for us!"

Mr. Paleno began to pace again. "I'm not giving up on

you girls, even if you do act like losers. I'm going to make goddamn sure that not a single one of you gets out of here until you've learned something.''

''We already learned plenty,'' Katrina said.

''A lot of good it's done you.'' Mr. Paleno shook his head sadly. ''You're not getting any trial visits or discharges this summer—don't think you are! Your Mister Fox isn't the boss of the Youth Service. It takes other people—people I *know*''— he poked his chest with his forefinger—''to approve his decisions.''

The girls were suddenly silent.

''We'll make our own decisions,'' Katrina said finally.

''Don't count on it.'' Mr. Paleno turned abruptly away from her. ''Mrs. Healey, I think we've heard enough of this. Would you take these losers back up to their unit now?''

''Mr. Fox told me to keep them here,'' Mrs. Healey said, half-rising from her chair. ''But we do have to let the kitchen staff start to get ready.''

''I'll straighten it out with Mr. Fox,'' he said. ''Now let's everybody get the hell out of here.'' Taking a step forward, he reached down and grabbed Katrina by the arm.

She gasped in pain as he yanked her to her feet. Jerking her arm free, she saw him stare at his hand; the fingers were smeared with her blood.

''You bastard!'' she muttered, her voice quavery, almost a sob. The skin of her arms felt about to burst into flames. ''You phony fucking bastard!'' she screamed at him. Then she broke into a run, bumping into several girls in her dash for the door.

No one was behind the desk at the Nurses' Station, so she tiptoed up to the door and peered into the examination room at the far end of the hall. There she saw Steven sitting with his back to her beside the table where Sonia lay, her forehead being taped by the nurse. Her hair, bright yellow beside Steven's dark shirt, seemed to be cascading off the edge of the table into his lap. Katrina couldn't hear what he was saying; she just heard the soothing murmur of his voice.

She stepped back from the doorway. Rubbing her fingers

along her scraped arm, feeling the damp skin sting until her eyes teared over, she shuffled off toward the back stairs.

At dinner, Katrina picked at her food and said nothing to anyone. Afterward, Sonia, who was now wearing a white bandage across her forehead, insisted on washing the dried blood and stained grass from her arm. The scrape, when cleaned, was rather small, Katrina was sorry to see; two gauze bandages covered it. Now the pain passed just under her skin in waves that made her feel like crying out and, when she gritted her teeth to keep silent, left her feeling trembly.

Steven and Sonia held an emergency group session that lasted two hours. No one spoke unless spoken to. Katrina turned away from Steven in her chair, trying to tune out his voice. She wanted to demand to know if Mr. Paleno's threats were true—that nobody would be leaving over the summer— but she figured asking was futile: he'd just deny what Mr. Paleno had said, and then do as he damn well pleased. When he put the group on indefinite building restriction, her suspicions seemed to be confirmed. She looked round the circle of girls; everyone was sitting with lips pressed together, glares focused on the floor. For the first time, she felt a solidarity with all these girls against the staff.

They were forbidden to leave the floor, but the girls found excuses to go downstairs anyway and shout taunts at the second-floor door on their way past. They had to get a soda from the machine, to look for a book they'd left in the rec room, to go to the Nurses' Station for some aspirin. The second-floor girls were doing the same, and there were several scuffles that kept Steven and Sonia racing up and down the stairs. Any excuse for a brawl would have worked, the way tempers were flying.

Yvonne's story was what started things. She returned to the lounge gasping that some second-floor girls had shoved her around in the downstairs bathroom; when she'd gone in, she'd been carrying her sweater, but after the girls had run out, she couldn't find it. "First they mess up our show, then they rip off our stuff!" she said, narrowing her eyes.

"I bet that sweater's on the second floor," Katrina said.

''Where else it going to be?'' Yvonne glanced at the girls who had gathered around her. ''We ought to check it out.''

"Check it out!" Katrina shouted, and the girls started chanting.

"Check it out!"

"Check it out!"

"Check it out!"

25 ❧

On his way up the front stairs, Steven heard the girls chanting, and managed to head them off as they reached the second-floor landing. Sonia joined him in pushing them back up the steps, but not before they'd seen the second-floor girls, also restrained by their staff, shaking fists and mouthing taunts behind the thick glass of their lounge windows.

Once back in the third-floor lounge, Steven, yelling until his voice went hoarse, quieted the girls down. "Get your chairs," he shouted. "Let's all sit down—"

"Not another group session!" Katrina groaned, and a chorus of groans went up.

"Yes, group session!" Steven walked around pulling folded chairs from against the wall and handing them to girls, but everyone just milled around. Either Katrina or Ronnie had always gotten them to sit down for group sessions, but tonight Katrina looked dazed and Ronnie was sullen and silent. Steven realized how successful he'd been at getting the girls to take responsibility for their own group sessions—now, when they wouldn't start one themselves, one wouldn't start.

"Where's Leah at?" Ronnie demanded, her voice cutting through the others. "If she ain't here, it ain't fair."

"We'll start without her," Steven said. Whale, Vonita, and Lucia stood beside Ronnie, their eyes burning at him. He ran his fingers under the back of his collar. "Leah'll be here soon."

Ronnie leaned sideways against the television set, and a

book that had been lying on top of it dropped to the floor. ''I think you jiving us again!''

For a moment the room was quiet. Steven glanced around. Everyone was grinning or glaring; it had been a long time since he'd been the center of so much hostility. The girls started talking and shouting.

''Jive!''

''Why don't you go be in the director's office?''

''That's where you belong now, not with us peasants!''

Steven walked over to Sonia, who was standing in the hall doorway looking pale and alarmed. Even with his girls yelling he could hear the second-floor girls thumping around downstairs. He'd never locked the third-floor girls in before, but there seemed no other way of keeping all this rage from spilling onto the second-floor—if the second-floor girls didn't find a way up here first. He glanced at Katrina; as nasty as she looked, with her eyes narrowed and a cigarette poking out of her mouth, he could picture her defiant expression knocked sideways into terror as soon as Heatwave or Smoke came thundering into the lounge at her. ''Go get the keys to the lounge door,'' he said to Sonia. ''Go around and lock it from the outside.''

As soon as she left, Steven tried again to calm the girls for a group session, but they continued to pace around muttering and whispering. The book that had fallen onto the floor was being kicked back and forth by the girls as they shifted their feet pretending not to see it. Steven's heart sank, watching it getting trampled and torn. Vonita was bouncing up and down, darting around the room like an electric toy short-circuiting. The girls cheered her on.

''Gonna raise some hell up in Fairbanks!'' she screamed, grinning maniacally. ''Check it *out*!''

''No, you're not,'' Steven said, keeping his voice as calm as possible. He felt his control over the girls slipping away second by second. The best he could do now was to stay among them, keeping his own temper, keeping them from bolting off the floor. He lit a cigarette, cupping his hands around it as if in a storm. Most of the girls, he noticed, were still looking to Ronnie. He took a step toward her.

"Aw, don't *even* talk to me, man!" Ronnie kicked the book, sending it spinning across the linoleum into the wall. Its cover skidded away. The sight of it seemed to make Ronnie suddenly jump inside her skin, as if her own cover were coming unglued. "We being blamed for shit that ain't our fault!" she screamed at Steven. "Being locked in here because of it! Not me—I'm getting my ass the hell out of here!"

"Right on!" Katrina pushed several girls aside to face Steven across the circle. "Better than staying here, getting killed by all those new girls while you sit in your director's office!"

Steven took a fast drag on his cigarette. He remembered the Lakewood riot, the boy lying in the closet with his head smashed, his lifeless eyes staring at the floor. *"No!"* he said. Several girls backed off quickly. "Nobody's getting killed!"

"Only one way out of this place!" Lucia yelled from the back of the room. "That's burn, baby, burn!"

Several girls laughed raucously. The last unit in their American history class had been about the uprisings in Watts and Newark, and the slogan had caught on.

"Burn, baby, *burn!*" Yvonne snapped her hips from side to side, getting appluase.

"We going to raise so much hell you going to *have* to let us out now!" Ronnie said. "You can't keep us in here if we violent, unruly, *ungovernable,* can you? Have to ship our asses then, won't you?"

"Fairbanks is only for girls who want to be here!" Katrina shouted. "That's what you told me when I came in! So I'm *un*-volunteering!"

Steven looked from Katrina to Ronnie and back again. All the excitement today had made them sudden allies. "You can do better than getting yourself shipped to another institution," he said, keeping his voice low.

"Better? How?" Ronnie leaned toward him, her nostrils flared. "I done *did* better! What it got me? I can't go home this summer, can I?"

"If I could, I'd release you," he said. "It's not my fault about your mother—"

"Whose fault is it? *Hers?*" Ronnie shouted in his face. "Ain't it that fucking probation officer say she unfit? Don't he work for the state? Don't *you*? Ain't you and him *brothers*?"

"No."

Ronnie snorted and turned away.

Steven saw Sonia approaching the window in the lounge door. Her key made a scraping noise in the lock.

Lucia whirled around. "They're locking us in here!" she shouted.

"It's only till you all calm down and get into a group session," Steven said, and tried to get between the girls and the door. But they rushed past him and tried to turn the doorknob. Vonita pounded against the glass. Katrina was the first girl to push her way out of the mob toward Steven.

"You told us you'd never lock us in. I always believed you. Shit!" She paced away from him again. The girls' eyes followed her now.

"I'm doing what I have to do to keep people from getting hurt, Katrina." He rubbed the back of his neck, his hand coming away sweaty.

Katrina turned back to him, her eyes narrowed. "What good's anything been? I tried to take responsibility in this place, be a fucking *leader* like you said to—what for?"

"What *for*?" several girls chorused. They continued to kick the book, ragged and coverless, across the floor.

"You know what I did with that leadership award?" Katrina demanded, her cheeks aflame, her hair frizzed around her face as if by electricity. "I ripped the motherfucker *up*!"

"Awright!" Several girls cheered. Vonita, doing a little dance, staggered into the stand-up ashtray, making it totter on its narrow cylinder. Katrina snatched it up and began swinging it back and forth.

"Katrina, don't—" Steven made a grab for it, but she darted away, her loose blouse flying out behind her.

Pivoting on her heel, she swung the ashtray around in both hands and heaved it toward the picture window. Steven shielded his face. Glass exploded; fragments rained onto the floor. The curtain rod came crashing down. The girls danced out of the way, cheering wildly. The ashtray, broken loose from its stand, rolled across the linoleum and clanged against the wall.

It seemed to be a signal. The girls all took off after Katrina, dashing into the corridor.

Steven walked quickly after them. A crash echoed from the other end of the hallway, causing most of the girls to come to a skidding halt. Sonia had slammed the door to the back stairs; he saw her stand in front of it, her hands on her hips. Only Vonita was so out of control that she bumped blindly into her. Sonia sidestepped, letting the door absorb most of Vonita's onrush. The girls started to retreat toward the lounge, but Steven blocked their way up the corridor. They ducked into various rooms, buzzing, shouting, laughing.

"Hell up in Fairbanks!"

"Burn, baby, burn!"

"Whoo!"

One by one the doors slammed shut. Steven heard scraping and thumping sounds behind them—the girls were dragging furniture into place to barricade themselves in. He walked the length of the hall, slowing as he passed each door to make a mental note of who was inside each room. Sonia was leaning against the wall at the end of the hall when he reached her. The smudged white bandage on her forehead had slipped down over her eyebrows.

"Are you all right?" he asked her.

"I think so."

"Good."

She touched the bandage, then pushed it up. "The cut doesn't really hurt, but I can feel my pulse beating in it." She stared at him. "What are we going to do, Steven?"

He took a deep breath. "We're going to keep our girls from getting into a rumble with the second-floor girls." His voice sounded calmer than he felt. "Let's see if we can lock this door."

None of the keys worked. The lock was jammed. Standing beside the door, Steven stared through its window up the corridor, breathing through his teeth. The glass reflected a partial image of him: his face shiny with sweat, his shirt unbuttoned, his mustache ragged-looking. Then a girl's silhouetted figure ran across the reflection of his chest.

It was Ronnie. Steven saw her shouldering open the door to Yvonne's room. He dropped the keys into Sonia's hand and took off up the corridor. Ronnie was trying to pin Yvonne to the wall while Peaches sat on the floor whimpering. When he grabbed Ronnie, Yvonne slipped away from her and ran out the door.

Then he heard a shout from the corridor—*"Fire!"*

"Fire!" Inez screamed at him as he stepped out into the hall. He saw clouds of smoke pouring out of Lucia's room. Several girls had poked their heads out of their doorways to look.

"Burn, baby, burn!" Lucia shouted happily, backing out into the corridor and tossing lit matches into the room.

As Steven rushed up to her, she ducked away, dropping a bent half of a soda can behind her. He saw what she'd done with it: her mattress was ripped open, the cotton stuffing spilled out of the wound all over the floor. Flames rose from it. Foul-smelling brown smoke floated up toward the ceiling.

"Bring the fire extinguisher!" Steven shouted at Sonia.

Inez was closer to it. She pulled it from the wall beside the office and ran with it to him.

''Get back!'' he yelled at the girls, who'd started to gather around. They hushed but didn't move away. For a moment the flames continued to lap up the wall beside the bed. Then, as Steven tilted the copper cylinder, a blast of foam shot out and buried the fire with a hissing sound and an acrid stink that had the girls backing off and coughing. The wall was dark with smoke smudges, the pictures on it were charred black. White slush covered the bed and the floor. Girls crowding in to see the mess tracked it into the corridor.

Out of breath, Steven put down the fire extinguisher and began trying to herd the spectators toward the lounge. He saw Katrina beside him one moment, the next moment she was dashing headlong through the girls, carrying the big

cylinder in her arms. Steven lunged after her. Foam squirted
everywhere. Skidding to a halt in front of the office door, she
kicked it open.

"Get it, Katrina!" Ronnie yelled, and a chorus of cheers
echoed up the hall.

Foam shot out into the air, sweeping papers off the desk,
splattering the window like artificial Christmas snow. As Steven stepped into the doorway, Katrina pointed the hose at
him. He saw the grin on her face, her blue eyes bright and
almost playful behind her streaked round glasses.

Then the foam sprayed the wall beside him, covering Sonia's Degas dance poster and finally turning to a trickle.
Katrina's smile was gone, she looked drained. With a swing
of her arm, she tossed the empty canister toward the open
window. It struck the sill and flipped out into the night; a
second later, Steven heard it clatter onto the asphalt below.

Another cheer went up. Katrina whirled round, foam flying
from her heels, and rushed out the door. The girls ran slipping
and sliding after her down the corridor. The sounds of doors
slamming rang out like pistol shots.

Once the girls had barricaded their doors again, the corridor
grew oddly quiet. Steven stood in the office doorway keeping
watch. It seemed as if years had passed since the last time
the girls had been quiet in their rooms, doing homework and
discussing the afternoon soap operas. He had a sudden intense
longing for those evenings when he'd checked upstairs before
going home and had heard the muffled voices and music along
the hallway, smelled the sweet soapiness in the air, watched
the last kids go to bed looking like Halloween in their curlers
and face cream. He wanted to think of tonight's rebellion as
a kind of trick or treat; remembering the brief playful expression on Katrina's face, he almost could. But he also remembered Lucia and her matches, and knew how deadly the girls'
game could suddenly become. At the far end of the hall, the
red EXIT sign glowed like coals, tinted puddles of foam a
dark, shadowy red. A breeze blew in from the broken window
in the lounge, but it did not clear the air.

"Do you think they've wound themselves down?" Sonia

asked, walking in from the lounge with a wastebasket full of glass she'd swept up. Her blouse and long skirt were damp with foam; strands of hair hung limp over the corners of her bandage.

"I'm not taking any bets on it yet," Steven said.

She kicked a wad of soggy mattress stuffing and almost lost her footing. "I'm sorry," she said, her voice quavery. "This is my first riot."

Steven took her arm and led her into the office. "A riot's when the girls get into brawls setting old scores and attacking the staff," she said. "They don't just trash the place."

"Oh." Sonia managed a weary smile. "That's good."

Steven guided her toward the armchair. "In a minute, we're going to try talking to some girls one at a time."

"Isolate the leaders," Sonia said, sitting down.

"Right. You see if you can get Lucia's matches. I'll talk to Katrina or Ronnie."

"Steven, do you think we can keep this thing from getting worse?" She stared at him.

"Yes," he said, facing the corridor. "One way or the other, we're damn well going to have to."

Katrina lay facedown on her bed, kicking the mattress with her toe in a steady, thudding rhythm. Her cheek was pressed against the sheet, her eyes shut. Every so often she made a noise that seemed as involuntary as the motion of her foot. Sometimes it was a chuckly sound, but sometimes it was a short groan, as if she'd suddenly swallowed something foul and was trying to force the taste up her throat. The taste was really the smell of her sheet where she'd wiped her fingers—smoke and chemical foam: nauseating. She felt as if she'd already thrown up from one end of the corridor to the other, and might be about to again. So she ought to lie still. At the same time, lying still was impossible. She kicked the mattress harder.

Suddenly she froze, her heart slamming the inside of her chest. Someone was knocking on the door.

"Katrina?"

It was Steven. She opened her mouth to answer, but then

pushed her face into the sheet. If she said anything to him, it would come out ugly.

"Katrina, we need to talk." His voice sounded faint through the door.

She stuffed a wad of sheet into her mouth and bit down hard on it. The cloth was sickeningly bitter, but she didn't dare let go of it. The bureau she'd wedged between her bed and the door gave a jump as Steven tried to push the door against it.

"Katrina . . . goddammit!"

He was mad. The chuckly sound bubbled up her throat, then, acidically, back down again. She sat sideways on the bed, spitting out the sheet. He was very mad at her. Well, wasn't that what she'd been wanting—how the hell else was she going to get his attention, to let him know how awful she was feeling? She stood up and gripped the bureau with both hands—too late. His footsteps faded down the hall. Ronnie must have come out of her room—she heard Ronnie arguing with him.

By the time she got her door open, Steven was headed for the office with Ronnie walking backward in front of him, trying to dodge around him. Her spangled T-shirt was soaked, her short hair flecked with foam, her eyes red-rimmed. She backed into the office; he, too, disappeared inside.

If I'd been Ronnie, Katrina thought . . . she pictured herself ducking one way, then the other, making a dive past him, being grabbed around the waist, his arm hard and tight against her stomach. . . .

Lucia's door opened suddenly. Sonia and Inez were shouting at Lucia to give up her matches. Lucia was laughing and yelling back at them in English and Spanish. Whale's stereo started blasting up the hall. Katrina bounced on the balls of her feet, loving the rumbling sensations in the walls and floors that egged her on like before. But not quite like before. She began wishing she could calm down now; a kind of dread rushed through her along with the excitement. She remembered the way Steven revved up his car engine until it almost exploded under the hood—she felt like that: stuck in neutral but with more energy than she could contain.

Then she saw Yvonne rushing down the corridor with Peaches toward the back exit. Whale, Vonita, Pam, and Mary were running along with them, everyone splashing bits of foam onto the walls and each other's legs. Katrina covered her ears as the panicky voices flew up the corridor like pieces of bright glass in a kaleidoscope tunnel refusing to settle.

"Come on, Katrina!" For a moment, Katrina saw Yvonne's face poke out at her, the strange green eyes sharp and determined. "Now's the time—let's get out of here!"

But Vonita was trying to hold Peaches back. "Ronnie!" Vonita screamed. "Yvonne's got her, Ronnie!" Her sneakers skidded along the floor as she held onto Peaches' arm.

"Will you help me, Katrina—damn!" Yvonne shouted.

Katrina caught sight of Peaches' stricken face under the red EXIT sign on the landing. She pulled back from Yvonne. "No," she said.

"Double-crossing bitch!" Yvonne screamed at Katrina. Then she yanked Peaches toward the top of the stairs.

"Stop *grabbing* me!" Peaches shook her head hard, her hair flying, and began flailing her arms. Vonita, hugging Peaches' other arm, was shaken like a puppy. She lost her grip. As she lunged after Peaches, Yvonne hit her on the shoulder. Vonita stumbled sideways, off balance, and bounced off the wall at the top of the stairs.

For an instant, she seemed poised at a crazy angle above the steps. Katrina caught sight of her mouth opening wide, her pink tongue showing. Her eyes rolled back. Then she fell. Her skinny arms flew in the air; her legs rolled over her. Bumping backward down the stairs, she turned over twice before landing with a thud at the bottom.

Katrina stared down into the dimly lit stairwell. Vonita lay crumpled in a heap, one arm twisted under her, her bare legs splayed out. No one spoke or moved. Katrina looked around for Peaches, expecting to see Yvonne with her, but Yvonne had disappeared. Peaches, looking pale and dizzy, wandered down the steps toward Vonita.

Then Katrina was knocked sideways as Ronnie, then Steven, rushed past her. She slid slowly down the wall and sat on the top step. Confused voices echoed up at her from the landing below. She hunched forward, covering her face with her hands. "Steven," she groaned into her fingers, "I didn't mean for this to happen!"

Ben Paleno heard the shouts on the stairwell and was on his way up the steps two at a time when Peaches, rushing blindly through the dim light, collided with him. Her feet went out from under her.

"Where do you think you're going?" Ben panted at her, pulling her up by the arm.

Peaches squirmed free and scrambled on down the stairs. He pursued her to the bottom and out into the dining room.

She ran skidding across the linoleum into the kitchen, with Ben close behind. Her eyes were blurred with tears. She collapsed into a serving table and pushed herself along it, groping blindly ahead of her. She grabbed the first thing her hand found.

Ben stopped in his tracks. "No!" he gasped, covering his groin. "I'm not afraid of that!"

Peaches looked down at her hand. She was holding a long carving knife. Her vision cleared a little. She saw a red face leaning toward her, and lifted the knife, pointing it at the face even though she did not want to be holding a knife and pointing it at anyone. She wished she could drop it but her fingers were locked around its handle.

"Give it to me now," Ben said, stepping forward. He held out his hand.

Though Peaches could hear his breath coming out roughly, his voice was clear, resonant, almost happy. She looked at his hand and saw that it was trembling, but it did not drop; its fingers spread wide, demanding the knife.

She took a step back, then another, until the edge of the serving table dug into her back. The heat of the kitchen drenched her; her vision blurred again from the glare of the light reflecting off the shiny metal surfaces. She saw the hand rising before her. It was slowly coming closer. She waved the knife at it—not a slash but a light movement of her arm as if it were trying to clear the air in front of her.

Suddenly the hand had hold of her wrist. It yanked her

arm back. The knife dropped with a clatter against the table. Peaches relaxed, grateful to be rid of it. Then she cried out— two arms were wrapping around her. She was being carried out of the kitchen. The arms were crushing her. She thrashed against them, but the hold on her just got tighter and tighter. She was turned sideways and fitted through a doorway into a smaller room and then an even smaller room. She shut her eyes tight, going limp.

Ben carried her through the Nurses' Station into an infirmary room. He dropped her onto a bed and stood back, panting. "No more knives, Peaches," he said. He turned and left, slamming the door behind him. It locked automatically.

He felt dizzy walking out of the Nurses' Station, and had to slide his hand along the wall to steady himself. As he approached a chair in the dining room, he realized he was soaked with sweat. He pulled off his coat and, like someone half-asleep, dropped it onto a table. He sat down hard. His heart slammed in his chest, his pulse racing.

The air around him seemed changed, lighter, less dense, as if a terrible weight had been lifted from him. A warm glow radiated through his groin. He could feel his pulse beating there as the heat grew more intense, rose toward the surface . . . and throbbed deliciously from him. He gazed down, bemused, and saw a tiny damp spot in the plaid material of his fly. Tilting his head back, he shut his eyes slowly. He was smiling.

Sitting at the top of the stairs, Katrina followed the beam of Steven's flashlight as it passed over Vonita's sprawled body. For a few minutes, Katrina thought she'd never stop trembling—she thought Vonita was dead. Then she saw Vonita's back rising and falling as she breathed. The nurse who examined Vonita said that her wrist had been rebroken and her collarbone possibly fractured. After the nurse went away to call an ambulance, Steven and Sonia continued to kneel beside Vonita, talking to her in their quiet voices.

Yvonne, who'd left when Vonita had fallen, was back. Katrina stiffened as Yvonne stood over her. "Where's she at?" Yvonne demanded.

"Who?"

"Peaches. Bitch—don't play no games with me!"

Katrina glanced down the stairs where Peaches had gone. "I think she's hiding out in one of the third-floor classrooms, Yvonne," she said.

"You better not be lying." Yvonne turned and disappeared down the back corridor that led to the classroom area.

Katrina sat very still, trying to hear what Steven was saying and watching Vonita breathe. The minutes went by very slowly. Occasionally sounds of thumping and yelling rose up the stairs from the second floor. Then there were long periods when Katrina could hear nothing but the rhythmic whine from Vonita's lips. If only she'd come out with one of her foul-mouthed curses, then Katrina would know she was all right. The other girls sat watching, waiting, too, but Vonita said nothing at all. Katrina's stomach began to churn; every breath of Vonita's seemed to send waves sloshing through it. That awful taste was in her mouth again. It crept down her throat. Suddenly she grabbed her mouth and leaned sideways.

"Mr. Fox, Katrina's sick!" Pam, sitting beside her, called down the stairs. "Can I take her to the bathroom?"

Steven's flashlight beam lit up Katrina's face. Vomit was streaming through her fingers.

"She can take herself to the bathroom," he said. "You stay where you are."

Katrina stood up dazedly and shuffled away. Kneeling on the bathroom floor, she rested her forehead against the icy back rim of the toilet bowl. When her stomach was empty, she flushed the toilet over and over again, but the stench still hung in the air around her.

It's me that stinks, isn't it? she said to herself, watching the water swirl uselessly down the hole.

He hates me, her mind told her, as if in some weirdly logical answer to her question.

After a long time, she took hold of the sink and pulled herself up. Not daring to look in the mirror, she splashed water onto her face and wiped herself with handfuls of toilet paper. Her blouse, hanging almost as low as her skirt, was soaked. Her sneakers made squishing noises as she walked slowly back into the corridor.

On the landing, Pam was standing with Mary, clicking her camera down the stairs. Steven and Sonia were standing back as two men with stretchers knelt beside Vonita. Katrina stared at Steven. His dark shirt was out, his slacks were smudged with dirt, and his hair was a wild, uneven shape as if someone had been trying to yank it out. Katrina touched her own hair, feeling tight, damp curls looping onto her forehead. As Steven started helping the ambulance men, Katrina wanted to rush down the steps and help, too. But then he and Sonia and the men went around the corner of the staircase with the stretcher. The girls on the top steps began to move around again.

"You coming?" Katrina heard Pam whisper to her. Pam rested her hand on her arm. "Me and Mary are taking off."

The ambulance men and Vonita—what better distraction could there be? By the time Steven came upstairs again, she could be out on the road with her thumb out, maybe even riding in a car already.

"How're you getting out of the building?" Katrina asked Pam.

"Mr. Fox's office window downstairs. It's never locked," Pam whispered.

Katrina gazed down the steps. She remembered sitting in the chair beside Steven's desk in that office. She'd run her fingers along the smooth leather frame of his daughter's picture. Sarah, the little girl's name was: pretty dark eyes and lips just starting a smile, Katrina would tilt back in her chair staring at the photo and listen to the murmur of Steven's voice coming across the desk at her.

"I don't want to go in that office," she said, swallowing hard.

"Why not?"

"I just don't." Katrina turned her face away. When she finally looked back again, there was just an empty space on the landing where Pam and Mary had been.

She walked slowly into Pam's room and leaned out the window above the side parking lot. In a moment, she saw a figure climbing from a ground-floor window. The spotlight shining from the corner of the building gave her a long darting shadow as she ran across the asphalt. Suddenly she ducked behind a car. The air began flashing with long red streaks of light. A silent ambulance rolled by, its beacon sweeping over the pond and bridge and trees. When the night beyond the parking lot was dark again, the girl ran into it, down the dusty road toward the highway. Katrina rested her forehead against the window. Good luck, she thought.

On his way up the back stairs with Sonia, Steven passed by the door to the second floor. The girls were running in and out of rooms while a woman staff member stood guard at the end of the hall. When the girls spotted Steven, several of them made fishfaces at him through the door's window. ''Better lock up your girls, man!'' one of them shouted. ''We gonna fuck them up good!'' Cheers came out of the rooms nearby.

Some rooms on the third floor had been trashed: ripped-open pillows, plastic bottles, stuffed animals, and clothes were strewn about the corridor along with the damp mattress stuffing. Music thudded softly behind several doors; the air smelled sour.

''I feel like we're about to walk through a minefield,'' Sonia whispered beside him.

Steven nodded. He cocked his head. ''It's too quiet in here.''

''Head-count time.'' Sighing, Sonia walked slowly back down the hall. In a few minutes, she was back in the office, where Steven was trying to reach Mrs. Healey on the phone.

''Pam, Mary, and Yvonne—all gone,'' she said, shaking her head slowly. ''Vonita in the hospital, Peaches in the infirmary....''

Steven sat down hard in the desk chair. An empty feeling passed through him like a slow-motion shiver. ''Listen,'' he said, ''they could still be in the building somewhere.''

''Maybe.''

''If they're gone, the police will be looking for them—*if* I call them.'' Steven looked at the phone, black and shiny, on the desk.

"Are you going to call them?" Sonia asked.

He stood up and walked to the doorway. "If I were a good acting director, I'd tell them to look out for our girls and bring them back. I'd also ask for cops to come here and help us out. Head Office would like that—I'd probably get a commendation. If I don't call them pretty soon, I'll get fired."

Sonia watched his face. "What would happen if they come?"

"They'd bash a lot of heads and drag a lot of girls away— for good." Steven took a deep breath, inhaling the smoke and chemical stink, and somthing nastier, as well: fear sweat. It seeped out from beneath the doors on the corridor, and it came from him, too. He remembered the smell from juvenile jail, where the very air he breathed vibrated with threats of violence. Hot or cold, his world had perpetually stunk of fear sweat, even at meals, where the food tasted as if it had been fried in it. If he called in the police, his girls would be locked up in dungeons like that one, charged with assault, resisting arrest, rioting. Steven thought of Ronnie trying to fight off two-hundred-pound matrons, Peaches being molested by inmates, Pam freaking out, Mary lapsing into catatonia, Vonita getting stabbed. He thought about Katrina sitting in a cold corner of her cell at night, as far removed from him as his daughter was. He pictured her staring at her locked steel door hour after hour, month after month, remembering him, cursing him.

"Steven?" Sonia stood beside him in the corridor. "Are you going to call the police?"

He leaned back against the wall, his whole body aching. A police sweep could end all this trouble; afterward he could start his career as acting director with new girls. He tried to think like an acting director, but all he could see in his mind were uniformed men swinging nightsticks as they shoved their way down the hall, as they had done at Lakewood, grabbing kids, cracking skulls. He saw Katrina retreating in panic, her face bloody, falling as a stick whipped down through the air. "No," he said, and cleared his throat. "I'm not calling the cops in here. I don't want them picking up our girls on the road tonight, either, if they're out there."

"Good," Sonia said. "But what if the girls get away?"

"Then they do." Steven took a deep breath. "Yvonne won't. No black city girl would ever try hitchhiking up here in the boondocks. Pam and Mary'll know how to survive, though."

Sonia smoothed a strand of hair away from her eyes. Her face looked a little less drawn and tense—she'd become a survivor herself. "It'll be a vacation for them."

"Eventually the cops will pick them up—tomorrow or next week, when all this is over. But I don't want them back here."

"Never?"

Steven shook his head. "No. They've gotten as much rehabilitation out of this place as they'll ever get. I'll write that in my reports. Now that I'm in charge, I can pull some strings and get them into group homes." He stared through the office out the window. "It looks warm and peaceful out there," he said. "Not a bad night for a walk on a country road. I hope they have a little while to enjoy it."

26 ✍

Yvonne ran down the back stairs, her blouse and face dirt-streaked from rummaging in the back of classroom supply closets. She had uncovered half of a pair of two-foot-long garden shears with a sharpened blade that Smoke had stolen weeks ago from the maintenance shop and hidden. At the bottom of the steps, Yvonne pulled up short. She heard voices behind the nearest door and opened it a crack. One voice was the nurse's, the other was ... Peaches'. She caught sight of Peaches walking down the hall from the bathroom and into an infirmary room; a nurse locked her in. Yvonne shut the door silently and paced away, swinging the long blade at her side, cursing under her breath. When she came to the dining-room door, she lashed out with her foot, kicking it open so hard that it cracked against the wall inside.

The room was empty; most of the tables were bare, their Formica tops reflecting the glare from the buzzing fluorescent tubes overhead. On one table, Yvonne spotted a crumpled plaid jacket. Instinctively, she went through the pockets. No wallet, a half-chewed cigar butt, yucch ... this was Mr. Paleno's jacket. She was about to drop it when her fingers touched something thin and metal—car keys. She dangled them in front of her face. "Thank-you-Lord!" she said aloud, startled by the sound of her voice in the big room. For a brief second, she remembered being a little girl in her mother's church, hearing women with quivering eyelids make spontaneous exclamations of thanks in the pews around her, words she'd never understood the reason for until now. Something caught in her throat; this memory was the closest she would ever come to her mother and the church. The life she'd chosen with Sugar was the only one she had left. Slipping the keys into her blouse, she ran out of the room, still holding the long blade by its wooden handle.

On the landing again, she stopped. If she were to continue down into the basement, she could get out of the building through the poolroom window. Sugar wouldn't be mad at her, would he, if she delivered a brand-new cream-colored sedan with a landau roof? A pimpmobile, the girls called it. She tried to smile.

Instead, she broke out in a cold sweat. Her eyes stung with tears. She could picture Sugar's face when she showed up: his lips would curl back from his teeth, his eyes would grow hard as bullets. A girl for his stable was what she'd promised him in return for all his help. Without one, she'd feel all his hatred turn on her. Without one, she'd be cold meat on the street.

Rubbing her eyes, Yvonne walked silently up the stairs.

Katrina stared out her window into the darkness, pretending not to hear the bumping behind her, trying not to think about what she would say to Steven when he finished battering his way into the room. The bed jiggled along the floor a half-inch at a time as the bureau, struck repeatedly by the door, banged into it. The noise stopped. Then she heard rapid footsteps; an instant too late, she realized that they were not Steven's.

A sharp jab in the middle of the back sent her sprawling face-first into the wall beside the window. Her glasses were gone. She fell to her knees, the impact of the floor knocking the breath out of her. A hand on her shoulder twisted her around. She stared up at the blurred figure of Yvonne leaning over her.

"You *crossed* me, bitch!" Yvonne screamed, her lipstick-stained teeth showing between her lips. In her hand she swung some kind of stick—no, a strange-looking sword with a long blade that shone dully in the overhead light. ''You sent me looking for Peaches in the wrong place! You knew she wasn't in the classrooms, didn't you?''

Katrina opened her mouth, but the only sound that came out was a gasping for breath. The blade flicked past her. She lifted her arm in front of her face and stared wide-eyed over it.

''You give me any shit now, I'm going to cut your fucking throat with this!'' She jabbed the point of the blade into Katrina's shoulder, making her recoil in pain.

Still kneeling, Katrina clutched her shoulder. She could feel her heart banging fast as if it were just under her fingers.

''Now—you're coming to New York with me. Get up!''

Katrina's limbs refused to move. Yvonne's hand shot out, yanking Katrina up by the hair. Katrina lunged forward, her legs rubbery beneath her. The blade jabbed in the air just in front of her face.

''Don't you make a damn sound when we walk out of this room, or you've had it,'' Yvonne snarled, her voice quieter but seeming like a scream because it came from so close to Katrina's face. Yvonne's eyes shone like green stones; her hair, usually so smooth, was bristly around her forehead as if an electric current were zapping through her. ''Don't be yelling for Mr. Fox when we get outside!''

Mr. Fox. His name seemed to wake Katrina up. She took a step back from Yvonne. ''No!'' she said. ''I'm not going with you!'' As Yvonne jabbed the blade at her, she ducked sideways and bumped into a chair. With strength she didn't know she had, she picked it up by the back and swung it at Yvonne. It flew out of her hands and crashed against the wall, falling onto Peaches' bed. ''Steven!'' she screamed suddenly. ''Steven! *Steven!*''

A face appeared in the doorway—not him, but Ronnie. Katrina groaned. But then Ronnie was gone up the corridor shouting, ''*Mr. Fox!*''

Yvonne grabbed Katrina around the neck, tugging her backward toward the door. Katrina sank to her knees. The point of the blade jabbed into her side, making her cry out.

Then she saw Steven, blurry and big, standing in the doorway, one hand reaching out toward her. Yvonne's arm around her neck yanked her back. Then the blade was in front of her, tucked under her chin; it touched her skin, sending a cold shiver through her. "Steven—" she gasped, and froze.

"Get out of the way!" Yvonne screamed at him. "Get the fuck out of my way!"

Steven didn't move. He seemed to take up even more of the doorway than before. "No, Yvonne." His voice was deep with that determined, teeth-gritted sureness with which Katrina had heard him calm down so many hysterical girls in the past. "Put down that blade," he said very slowly. "I'm not going to let you take her anywhere."

"I'll kill her!" Yvonne said, her voice ragged.

"No, you won't." He took a step forward, and Katrina could see his face more clearly. His eyes were that bright, fiercely focused blue; he stared at Yvonne. "No way are you going to hurt Katrina," he said.

"I ain't talking with you! Just stand back!"

Steven shook his head slowly. "We're going to talk, Yvonne, and you're going to let her go," he said. "Now tell me, what are you doing this for?" Every time he spoke, his hard, calm voice seemed to make Yvonne loosen her hold on the blade. She tried to get a tighter grip on it; her fingers were suddenly red with blood, she was squeezing the sharp metal so hard. Katrina could smell Yvonne's sweat, rancid with fear.

"Come on, Yvonne," Steven said. "Relax and let her go. Nobody's going to hurt you."

"I ain't letting her go! I'm taking her to New York!" Yvonne shouted as if she were about to burst out crying.

Katrina, feeling stronger, raised her hands and grabbed Yvonne's wrists, pushing the blade farther away from her neck. "She was going to take Peaches—" Katrina grasped. "She was going to turn her out for a whore. Now she wants to take me—"

"Shut *up*!" Yvonne tried to pull the blade closer, but she seemed to have less strength in her arms than before. A thin trickle of blood crept along her thumb toward the underside of her wrist.

"Well, that plan's not going to work out now, Yvonne,"
Steven said.

"It's got to work!" Yvonne cried out. "He'll kill me if
I don't go—" Her voice choked off.

Steven took a step closer, sliding his foot along the floor
slowly. "Who will?" he asked.

Yvonne sucked in her breath. "There's no place I can hide
from him. I *seen* what he does to girls who try to get away
from him." Yvonne allowed Katrina to push the blade another inch down as if it were too heavy for her. "He brought
back this one bitch all the way from Maryland and he fucked
her up for good—he cut off her titties with a straight razor
right in front of us!"

"I don't blame you for being scared. But I can find a
place for you where nobody can get at you."

"Naw!" Yvonne sucked in her breath hard again.

Katrina held Yvonne's wrists tighter. "Listen, Yvonne,
this ain't going to work," she said. "I mean, what are you
going to do, walk to New York with this blade around my
neck?"

"Shut up!" Katrina felt herself being rocked back and
forth as Yvonne shook her head hard. "You crossed me! You
messed everything up!" Yvonne screamed, yanking the blade
closer to Katrina's throat.

"Yvonne!" Steven shouted suddenly, his face so near to
Katrina's that she could feel his breath and see the bloodshot
rims of his eyes. *"Stop it, Yvonne!"*

Startled, she staggered backward, pulling Katrina with
her. Katrina pushed against Yvonne's wrists as hard as she
could, but the blade came closer and closer. Blood was streaming down Yvonne's hand onto Katrina's fingers.

"Don't you hurt her!" Steven screamed, his hand rising
in the air. *"Drop that knife! DROP IT!"*

Katrina had never known he could lose his temper like
this—his voice filled the room like a hurricane blasting open
a door. She felt the strength leave Yvonne's arms; she shoved
with all her might, and the blade fell away from her. Whirling
around, she punched Yvonne hard in the stomach, then stumbled forward and had to grab the windowsill to keep from

falling. Yvonne doubled over. But she still had a grip on the blade's wooden handle, and as Steven lunged toward her, she swung the blade at Katrina.

Then everything happened in a blur. Katrina felt Steven grab her arm and fling her sideways onto the bed. His whole body fell on her; his hand covered her face as the blade swung by her cheek. Then Steven was gone. She heard shouts and running footsteps in the hall.

She lay still, gasping into the blanket, her heart crashing in her chest. Slowly she found the floor first with one foot and then with the other. Walking unsteadily, she kicked something—her glasses. She put them on. In the hall, she saw Steven talking with Sonia. Yvonne's blade was in his hand, but she was nowhere in sight. Everything seemed unbearably bright and sharply focused—the walls, the bulbs in the ceiling, the mounds of mattress stuffing and clothing on the floor. Katrina shielded her eyes, listening to Steven's voice, low and quiet now, its rage gone.

"Yvonne's not dangerous without a weapon," he was saying. "We can't afford to go chasing her all over the building now. Let's take care of the girls who're left." He turned around and saw Katrina. "Are you all right?"

Katrina nodded. She shuffled back into her room and sat down hard on her bed. She was trembling all over. Her blouse stank of puke; she'd never felt so ugly in her life. She bent her head; her fists rested on her knees. When Steven walked in, she expected his voice to slam into her, but all she heard was the silence swelling between him and her.

"That was a close call, wasn't it?" he said finally.

"Yeah." She looked up. He wasn't smiling at her but he wasn't scowling either. His hair was still wild and his eyes bright. She realized, as if in a delayed reaction, that if he hadn't fallen on top of her as the blade swung by, she might have been killed. Her eyes flooded with tears and she turned her face away. "Thank you," she said, her voice very small.

"That's okay." He leaned forward and wiped his forehead.

Katrina stared at him. "How'd you get Yvonne's blade?" she asked.

"She dropped it when she took off." He stared past her at the wall, where bits of tape still clung here and there. The collage of girls' faces was gone—she'd torn it down earlier in the evening. A few photos were still scattered on the bed; the rest were on the floor.

"I miss them," he said, pointing to the empty place on the wall.

Katrina leaned over and picked up some pictures. Holding them against her chest, she rocked in place, her breath catching in her throat. "You must have hated me," she said finally.

"I hated what you did."

"It wasn't *all* my fault, Steven."

"I know."

"The place was getting ready to blow up weeks ago." She sniffled hard. There were damp, foamy footprints on the floor, a chaos of them turning every which way between the radiator and the sink and the bed. "It seemed like you didn't care anymore, you stayed away so much. I couldn't stand it."

"I cared a lot," he said. "I still do."

Katrina wiped her eyes with her knuckles and pushed her glasses back against the bridge of her nose. "Maybe that was the trouble," she said.

"What, that I cared?"

"Yeah, we got spoiled. It didn't go with this place." She stared down at the floor. "Like it reminded us of the way we always wished things would have been at home. It made us feel like we *were* home. For the first time. But then something bad would happen, and we'd wake up and remember we were really in an institution. Everybody got real upset when they woke up. We felt like we had to bust out. Then when you pulled away from us, there was nothing to stop us. You know what I'm saying?"

"Yes." He sighed. "But you keep saying 'we.' What about you?"

She hugged her arms tight across her chest, squashing the photos. "I hated you," she said. "I hated that award. I felt like you'd been using me."

"I wanted you to get an award for something. I wanted you to feel good about all the work you did."

She gripped the photos tighter. The silence swelled in the room again, but this time she didn't feel as if she had to be the one to fill it.

"I can see how you'd feel that I used you." His voice was very quiet. "I did. I maneuvered you into taking more charge of yourself, and getting the girls to listen to you more. It wasn't just to break up Ronnie and Peaches' power. I wanted you to help everybody feel as strong as you."

"It sort of worked." Katrina gave a little laugh, pointing toward the mess in the corridor. When she felt Steven's gaze on her, she dropped her hand fast.

He stood up. "This thing's not over, Katrina. Yvonne's still around somewhere, and they're raising hell on the second floor. I'm going down there, but first I'm going to check on Peaches in the infirmary."

"What's the matter with her?" Katrina stood up, too.

"Nothing. Mr. Paleno locked her up," he said. "Do you want to come with me?"

"Well . . ." Katrina rocked on her heels. "Well, okay."

"Let's put those pictures in a safe place."

He helped her pick up the rest of them, and she stuffed them under her pillow.

In the Nurses' Station, they took turns looking through the little square window in the door. Peaches was lying on her side on the white bed, her knees drawn up, her thumb in her mouth. She was asleep.

"She's probably better off in there," Katrina said. "She was getting flaky, with everybody after her."

Steven took one more look, then turned to her. "You'd be a lot better off, too, if you'd spend the rest of the night in the other room."

"I don't know." She took a step backward. This was where she'd lain on the bed with her leg cut, her mind unraveling.

"It could get nasty upstairs."

"I don't care."

Steven rested his hand on her shoulder, turning her toward the empty infirmary room. "Go on, Katrina."

His hand weighed hundreds of pounds. "No," she said, but took a step forward. As long as he held her shoulder, she walked in the direction he pointed her. The room was brightly lit and smelled like clean white sheets.

"Not too bad," he said. "Anyway, it's just temporary."

"You're not going to lock me in here, are you?" With his hand gone, she felt trembly. He was backing away now. "Don't leave me here!" she shouted, rushing toward the open doorway.

He stepped sideways, blocking her way. "Katrina—"

She plowed into him. When he didn't move, she banged her head against his chest until suddenly her legs nearly went out from beneath her. His arms went around her. Pressing her cheek against his chest, she felt herself enfolded in warm darkness. Then his arms gradually loosened. She stepped unsteadily away from him, blinking hard.

Was he headed toward the door? *"No!"* she screamed. "You're not locking me in here!"

"All right!" he shouted back, startling her. "You helped make the mess out there—you want to see if you can survive in it?"

"What's going to happen to me?"

"I don't know."

"You don't?"

"If you leave now, I can't do anything about what happens to you," he said. "You can go upstairs and take your chances with Yvonne and the second-floor girls. Or you can find a way out of here and go catch rides to all those places you were bouncing around to before you got here."

"I can survive," she said. "I done it before."

"Go ahead."

But I'm spoiled now, she thought. She shifted her weight from one foot to the other.

"Listen." He walked slowly toward her. "This door will lock automatically when it's closed. You can do whatever you want. It's up to you."

"You don't care what I do?" she asked, her voice very small.

"Yes, I care." He reached out and rested his hand on the side of her neck. "If I didn't, I wouldn't be leaving this door open." He leaned over to give her a long look, his eyes bright blue again and not as scary as his voice. Then he walked away down the hall.

Katrina tiptoed out of the room. She could hear the thumping of rapid footsteps above the ceiling; the air still reverberated with chaos. Not long ago, the screaming and excitement had gotten under her skin like swarms of bees and she'd swooped and swarmed with them all, feeling more alive and free than she had in years. But now what she mostly felt was tired and half-sick and trembly; the only thing that felt good was the warm sensation of Steven's hand remembered in the skin of her neck.

She stepped back inside the room, putting her hand on the doorknob. Very slowly, she swung the door toward her. As soon as she heard the lock click, she tried the knob. It wouldn't turn. Pressing her forehead against the window in the door, she saw Steven standing under the white fluorescent light at the end of the hall, watching her.

"Don't leave me!" she screamed.

"I'll let you out in the morning," he called to her. His voice sounded faint. "I promise, Katrina."

She kept her face pressed against the glass after he had gone. The room was silent, as if it had just sunk into a basement far, far under the building. She pounded against the door until her arms ached. Then she began to kick it.

27

Ben Paleno had completely lost control of the second floor. Seven black girls had barricaded themselves into the lounge with a pile of furniture and were holding four white girls hostage. Two of the white girls were the lovers of their captors and seemed rather thrilled by their predicament. The other two were clearly terrified. All the lounge windows had been broken and the curtain had been ripped into heavy dark capes that several girls wore over their shoulders. On the floor amid glass fragments and smoking cigarette butts the television blared out a rerun of "Love Boat." Every time Ben stood on a chair to peer over the barricade, the "guerrillas," as they called themselves, put their hostages on view. One girl held a stolen kitchen knife against her captive's chest. The girls were demanding state cars to drive them to New York City. It was impossible to tell how serious the girls were, but it was also impossible to get past the barricade.

On the other side of it, the bulbs along the ceiling had been lopped off with a broom; the corridor was illuminated only by light from bedroom doorways, creating wide stripes of brightness and shadow. The floor was a junkyard of destroyed possessions; six girls calling themselves the "White Power Army" had filled it with black girls' smashed mirrors, pictures, stuffed animals, and torn clothing. They roamed up and down the corridor calling the two middle-aged black staff women "nigger" and "coon" and threatening to storm the barricade if the hostages were not released by midnight. Ben divided his time between chasing the white girls away from the barricade and trying to talk to the "guerrillas."

Mrs. Evans, whom Ben had called in, consulted with him at 11:15 in the office. In bulging khaki slacks and a flannel shirt, she looked relatively fresh, like a substitute about to enter a football game in the last quarter, but her face, like Ben's, was red and sweaty, and she could hardly speak from shouting at the girls.

"What do you think, Ben? Can we handle them alone?" she asked in a scratchy whisper. "I don't think we can," she answered.

Ben leaned back against the wall and shook his head slowly. His shirt was dirt-streaked; his eyes were watery and his hair stuck in a damp fringe along his forehead. "I just don't know."

"We could have an awful mess in here," Mrs. Evans said. "I think we have to call in the police."

Ben wiped his face with a handkerchief. "If the cops get in here, somebody could get hurt. It wouldn't look good at all."

"Wouldn't look good for *him*." Mrs. Evans glanced up at the ceiling: Steven's unit. "How's it going to seem to Head Office if the police have to be called in on the first night he's in charge? He won't last a week."

"I know, but the bastard will never call them."

Mrs. Evans glared at him. "You do it," she said.

"I'm not authorized. I could get in real trouble."

"You can call your friends in Head Office. They'll give you an emergency executive order. They always have before when you needed it."

He sighed and shuffled to the window. Then he leaned forward to stare outside. A car's engine was starting up in the parking lot. "What the hell—?"

The car backed up and crunched into the front of a van, then rolled forward into an area lit by the spotlight. It was a big cream-colored sedan.

"Christ, they've got my car!"

Mrs. Evans strode to the window. The car's tires squealed; it shot out of the parking lot and down the dirt road, taillights blazing in the darkness. "Who was driving?" Mrs. Evans asked. "It must have been one of Fox's kids."

"It looked like Yvonne." Ben paced away from the window, slamming his fist into his palm. "Oh, Jesus Christ!"

"You know what that is?" Mrs. Evans' voice was hushed, serious. "That's grand auto theft. That's a felony!"

Ben slammed his fist into his palm again.

"Ask Head Office to tell the police to come in with their lights off." Mrs. Evans pushed the telephone across the desktop toward him. "We can let them in the back."

Ben picked up the receiver, hi eyes narrowed, and started dialing.

Steven was on his way to the second floor when he heard the front door buzzer echoing up the stairwell. He continued down to the foyer and unlocked the door. Leah stood outside on the step, looking up at the building.

"Steven, what is going on?" she asked, hurrying forward. "Is noisy like hell up there, all the windows lit up." She wrinkled her nose as she stepped inside, her arm around Steven's waist. "And that smell!"

"We had a fire," Steven said, walking with her into the rec room. "It's bad, Leah."

She stopped and stared at him, the lines around her mouth tightening. Her eyes were puffy from lack of sleep. She wore the respectable blouse and gray suit she must have put on for the hearing that morning. "I should have been here," she said.

"You didn't have a choice about it. I'm just glad to see you now." Steven pointed to a couch by the fireplace. "Let's sit down."

He told her about Vonita and Yvonne and Katrina, about the girls who had run away, about the fire and fights. He could hear the weariness in his voice; sometimes it sounded choked, but he didn't have to hide his feelings from Leah.

As he spoke, her face aged; her dark eyes glowed with sadness.

"What about the second floor?" she asked.

"More of the same but worse. They're still spoiling for a fight with our girls, and vice versa, as far as I can tell. We've got to do something soon or we'll have a full-scale riot."

Leah rested her hand on Steven's arm. "Damn, Steven."

They walked through the Nurses' Station on their way to the back stairs. Katrina was fast asleep now, but Peaches was up, asking to be let out so she could find Ronnie. The last thing we need, Steven thought, is Ronnie and Yvonne fighting over you. "I'll come get you as soon as things calm down," he told Peaches.

They continued upstairs. When Leah saw Sonia, she put her arms around her, leaning back from her bandaged forehead. "What happened to you?" she asked, brushing a strand of hair away from Sonia's eyes. "Who hurt you?"

"It's just a scrape. I got pushed." Sonia shrugged. "It seems like such a long time ago that it happened. Such a long night."

"You both look like you've been marooned up here for weeks," Leah said.

Sonia nodded slowly. "Listen, we got a phone call from the second floor while you were downstairs."

Steven frowned. "What now?"

"Yvonne's gone."

Steven let out all his breath. The twinge of loneliness passed through him as it had when he'd learned the other girls had gone, but it didn't last very long this time. "How'd the second floor know before we did?" he asked.

"Well..." A faint smile appeared on Sonia's lips. "Ben Paleno looked out the window and saw Yvonne driving off in his new car."

"No shit!" Steven stared at her. Then he leaned against the wall, his forehead touching the plaster. "There is some justice in the world after all," he said softly. "Very little— just enough to keep us laughing."

Sonia covered her mouth. "How can we laugh at a time like this?"

"We must be terrible people," Leah said. She was smiling too.

Steven could picture Yvonne driving down the highway, the radio blaring. He felt as if he were suspended above the building, watching the car through thick clouds that were gradually clearing. But when he looked at Sonia, her face drawn and serious again, he stopped smiling. "We're going to have to call the cops about Yvonne eventually," he said.

"They're on their way here," Sonia said. "Ben got Head Office in Albany to call them."

Leah groaned.

"Oh, Christ!" Steven said. "Damn...."

"Is it that bad?" Sonia asked.

"You've never seen the police hit an institution," Leah said. "Is a very ugly business."

Steven turned back to Sonia. "How long ago did he call them?"

"About twenty minutes."

"We can't stop them. It's too late," Steven said. "They've got their orders from Albany. If they see a riot going on, they'll break down the doors no matter what I say to them."

Ronnie, who had been listening, stepped out of her room and stood in the middle of the hall, her feet planted apart. "I ain't going to let no cops put no handcuffs on me!" she shouted at Steven. "I'll *kill* me a cop before I let anybody put me in a squad car!"

Whale came out of the room behind her. "She means it, man. Me, too!" She was carrying a wooden chair with her. She smashed it suddenly into the doorframe—once, twice, three times. The wood shattered; splinters flew. Ronnie grabbed up a weapon-sized piece of chairback.

Lucia stepped out into the corridor. Whale lumbered toward her. "Cops coming!" she shouted. "U.S. Cavalry! Get you a weapon!"

"Cops? Whoo!" Lucia's eyes narrowed. *"Coño.* Going to get my bed apart, take one of them slats!"

"Hey!" Steven shouted at the top of his lungs. The girls froze. "No cops are going to come on this floor," he said. "There's not going to be any fight. Nobody's going to get hurt."

"How you know?" Ronnie asked, rapping her chair back against the wall. "You going to be able to keep them out of here? You going to guarantee it?"

Steven's mouth opened, but for a fatal second no sound came out. By the time he said, "Yes," the girls were in motion again. Their doors slammed behind them. Steven heard the sound of bed barricades being scraped into place. Suddenly he felt detached from the building again, not very high above it now. There were no clouds. He saw the lights blazing in the windows and, inside, four terrified girls trying to sharpen pieces of wood against the floor, cracking their windows to pull out pieces of glass for weapons and wrapping them in cloth to hold in their hands. Then he heard Ronnie's window shatter, followed by the tinkling of glass against the floor.

"That's it!" Steven narrowed his eyes. "It's all over."

Sonia was staring at him. "What is?"

He continued to stare down the hall at Ronnie's door. His hands ached—he'd been making fists at his side as the girls' noises echoed in the corridor. Now he slowly relaxed his fingers. "If there's nobody around to fight the cops—or the second-floor girls—then there won't be any riot here," Steven said slowly. "It's time to get our kids the hell out of this place."

"Now?" Sonia asked, her voice shaky. "Isn't there some other way?"

"We tried other ways, and look!" He pointed to the rubble all the way down the corridor.

Leah looked at him, her eyes wide. She smiled. Then she touched Sonia's shoulder. "To the lifeboats," she said.

While Sonia filled out state travel vouchers in the office, Leah talked to Inez and Lucia. Steven tried Ronnie's door, then reared back and lunged into it, opening it far enough for him to squeeze into the room. Ronnie and Whale crouched with their sticks held in the air. Blankets and sheets lay tangled around them on the floor. Bits of glass caught the light like sharp mica pebbles.

"Drop the sticks!" he shouted. *"Listen up!"*

"Ain't listening to you no more," Ronnie said, but she lowered her stick.

"Yeah, you are. You want out of here? You want to leave tonight? You can."

The girls stared at him out of the sides of their eyes.

"Don't be fucking with my mind," Whale said. She shifted her weight from one foot to another; the fat under her chin shook.

"You do have a choice." Steven dropped his voice. "Stay or leave. If you stay, you have to be locked in your rooms when the cops get here."

"Ain't staying in *my* goddam room," Ronnie said. She had put on her red sweatshirt—for protection, it seemed now. Her face was mostly hidden inside the hood.

"If you leave, you get the bus home tonight," Steven said. "You've only got about twenty minutes to pack and leave, so make up your mind."

"I ain't leaving without Peaches."

"Peaches is going, too. If she wants to."

"What'll happen to us?" Ronnie rested the end of her stick on the mattress. "You having me put in jail?"

"No. You'll go home tonight. I'll call your probation officer and he'll get you a court date," Steven said. "I'm going to send the judge a letter recommending probation for you, either at home or a group home. You'll have to take your chances in court."

"I'll take my chances." The stick fell from her hand and clattered to the floor.

"What about me?" Whale asked, thrusting her lower lip out. "Same for me?"

Steven pointed at her stick, not speaking until she lowered it and then laid it on the bed. "Same for you, Whale," he said finally.

"Damn!" she said. "Let me at my suitcase!"

▲   ▲   ▲

On his way past Inez's door, Lucia called to Steven from inside. Most of her possessions having been burned or ruined by fire-extinguisher foam, she'd finished packing first and was frantic with nothing to do.

"I don't know if I ought to stay here or go, Mr. Fox," she said, rubbing her eyes.

He went in and sat down on the bed near Inez, who was still packing. "You don't have such a great choice now, Lucia," he said. "If you stay, I'll have to transfer you to maximum-security place. If you leave, I'll have to charge you with arson, but at least you'd get your day in court."

"Maybe I get probation," Lucia said.

"Credit for time served is probably the best you can expect."

"It depend on the judge. Some are too busy—they just throw you out in the street."

"Anything's possible. The wheels of the juvenile justice system move in mysterious ways." Steven looked at his watch. Fifteen minutes.

Lucia shrugged. "Probably I spend my whole life in places like this. Maybe they better for me. I had friends here." She glanced at Inez. "In the street, you can't trust nobody. They kill you fast, man. Here, we are all in the thing together. We can help each other a little."

"That was the idea," Steven said.

"I be okay in a max joint," Lucia went on, scuffing her sneakers along the floor. "I been in them. We make wine, smoke herb, do family business, get on the staff's case. It is where I belong. Only hard part is leaving friends here...." She turned toward Inez, her eyes damp.

The girls' clothes told of their different destinations. Lucia had on faded brown slacks and a blue T-shirt—they could have been a prison uniform. Inez had put on a dark skirt and white blouse with ruffles down the front, as if she were ready for a job interview, even in the middle of the night. Her round face was scrubbed, her hair brushed, her eyes alert though exhausted.

"Hey, Inez," Lucia said, "you come and visit me sometimes?"

Inez was sitting on her suitcase on the floor now, trying to fasten the clasp. "Sure, baby," she said.

"No, you won't, but that's okay. You going to be with your daughter, your Sofi."

"You think I can go home, Mr. Fox?" Inez asked. "You think I can get probation?"

"I'm almost certain. I'll recommend it," Steven told her. "I won't forget how you helped tonight with the fire extinguisher. You've done well here."

Inez clicked her suitcase closed. "You know, if they didn't send me to this place last year, I would still be strung out on drugs. I would have stayed with my boyfriend, maybe gone to jail helping him do a robbery, or got shot."

"Are you going back to him?" Steven asked.

"Hell, no. He don't care about Sofi. He don't even send her money on her birthday." Inez stood up when Steven did and lifted the suitcase onto the bed. "A lot of girls here, they don't know what they would have been on the outside," she said. "This place could have saved their lives."

"Save some, lose some," Steven said. "The nature of the beast."

"You try to help me, Mr. Fox. Nobody ever done that before—" Inez's eyes, too, were wet. She wiped them with her hand.

Steven put his arm around her shoulder. Her face pressed against his chest. "I'll miss you," he said into the top of her hair.

"You going to miss *me*, Mr. Fox?" Lucia demanded, pushing her way into Inez so that Steven had to let go.

"I'll miss you all," he said.

"Can I get a hug, too?"

"You try to burn the place down, then you expect a hug." Steven let out all his breath. "Listen, Lucia, are you going to forget all that shit about belonging in institutions?"

"You really think it's shit?"

"Of course I do."

"All right," she said. "I forget it."

"All right." Smiling, Steven hugged her.

▲   ▲   ▲

Ronnie, Whale, Lucia, and Inez waited with Steven on the back parking lot while Sonia and Leah got the state car out of the garage. The air outside was clear; in the warm darkness they could smell the damp grass and bushes again, strong and sweet after the stench of the corridor inside. The girls took long deep breaths.

"It smells like freedom," Ronnie said.

Chairs from the afternoon show, scattered at odd angles on the asphalt, shone in the bright silver light of the moon. Its glow outlined the bandstand and bushes and rocks starkly. The tree branches, lacey against the gliding moon-streaked clouds, cast exaggerated shadows across the asphalt.

"When I get to the city, I'm going to write about this place, Mr. Fox," Whale said to Steven. She pressed her notebook against her side. "Make it a war story."

"I feel like I been in a war," Ronnie said. "Like that one they had in Africa, with the Mau Mau."

"Hey, we revolutionaries!" Whale slapped Ronnie's palm.

"'Cept the building still standing," Ronnie said. "Oh, well, we tried."

Steven nodded. "No one'll ever accuse you of not trying, Ronnie."

"Square business, Mr. Fox," Ronnie said, her voice suddenly serious. "I needed this place in a way. But after a while it fucked me up. I had to stay too long."

"That's true," Whale said.

Everyone watched the garage, where the car was being started up. Steven thought of telling Ronnie that she hadn't been a revolutionary—people who made revolutions were idealists, they sacrificed and worked for a cause. But it occurred to him that this wasn't necessarily true. If *he* were a revolutionary, he'd be that kind. But Ronnie—she and Whale and Katrina and the others *were* the cause. They had discovered this the only way people ever really find out anything: on their own, spontaneously. They might never again have the experience of changing their world by taking charge of themselves, but perhaps once would be enough to carry them through their lives.

"I'm tired of raising hell," Ronnie said. "I hope I don't have to anymore."

"They don't let you be doing none of this stuff on the outside," Whale said. "They just off you, and walk away blowing the smoke from the ends of their guns."

"I know that, girl!" She turned toward Steven. "You must have wanted to murder me tonight."

"The thought crossed my mind at times." Steven smiled. "But not really."

"How come?"

"I guess I cared more about you than I did this place."

"You going to put all the stuff I did on your report?"

"I'll have to. But I don't have to stress it. There's a lot of good stuff to write, too. Even tonight, you called me when Yvonne had Katrina with that blade."

Ronnie sighed. "My mama's going to whup me when she sees that report, though."

"She'll be glad to see you," Steven said. "I'll bet she'll keep you in line, too."

"If I can keep her ass out of jail."

"Keep your own ass out of jail," Whale said.

Ronnie bumped her with her hip. "I can take care of it pretty good," she said.

Peaches walked slowly out the back door carrying the shopping bag Ronnie had packed for her—she had no suitcase. There wasn't much of a spring to her step, Steven noticed; she hadn't been particularly eager to leave, once given the choice, but she hadn't wanted to be left behind. Steven had decided to let Katrina sleep all night in the infirmary, not wanting to test the limits of her alliance with Ronnie, now that the revolution appeared to be over.

Peaches dropped her shopping bag on the asphalt and stood with her chin an inch from Ronnie's shoulder. Her hair was very pale in the moonlight, her face covered in shadow. She started to speak.

"We'll talk at the bus station." Ronnie cut her off. She took hold of Peaches' arm. "We going to have a wait about five hours, Mr. Fox says."

Peaches nodded and turned toward Steven. "Is Vonita all right?" she asked.

"I called the hospital," Steven said. "She's got some broken bones, but she'll recover."

"I'm sorry about what happened to her," Peaches hung her head.

Steven walked over to stand beside her and Ronnie and Whale. "It wasn't your fault."

"She was trying to help me," Ronnie said. "It was my fault."

"No, it wasn't," Peaches said.

"Whose fault was it?" Ronnie asked.

Steven stared past her at the building's massive silhouette looming up, blocking out part of the sky. This place's fault, he thought. Then he shook his head. "Vonita is everybody's fault," he said.

No one spoke for a while. Finally Peaches lifted her face. "I'm going back to family court, huh?" she said to Steven. "You think they'll let me go home?"

"I expect they'll let you visit your mother sometimes," he said. "But you'll probably get a place in a group home. I'm going to recommend that you live in the one where your sister is."

"Yeah? I'm going to live with Lurleen?"

"I'll do my best," Steven said, and looked at his watch again.

"Thanks, Mr. Fox." She turned and punched Ronnie lightly in the shoulder. "You can come visit me," she said. "I'll sneak you in and we'll get high."

Ronnie, who'd been staring down at the ground, looked slowly up into Peaches' face. "We'll find a way," she murmured, and wiped her eyes.

"I can't wait to see my sister." Peaches bounced on the balls of her feet. "Hey, Mr. Fox, I was thinking—it's a good thing I wasn't living home when all that shit happened with Harvey and my brother. I probably would have killed somebody, and I wouldn't be getting to see Lurleen now."

"The way you was carrying on, you *would* have killed somebody, too," Whale said.

"You did some freaking out yourself," Peaches said.

"I didn't kill nothing but a door." Whale's cheeks puffed out in a smile.

"I remember that," Ronnie said. She wrapped her arm around Peaches' neck. "That was *bad*! Whoo!"

"We sure had us some times in this place," Whale said. "Didn't we, Mr. Fox?"

Steven gazed at the girls. All three of them were smiling. "Yeah," he said finally, his mouth turning up at the corners. "We had us some times."

Leah drove the state station wagon up to the back door and the girls got in, Whale in front, Ronnie and Peaches behind her, Inez and Lucia squeezed into the far-back seat beside Sonia. Steven leaned over to look at them through the driver's window.

"You don't have to say nothing." Ronnie sat forward. "We going to behave ourselves."

"Speak for your own self," Lucia said from the back. "I'm going to hijack this car, fly it to Puerto Rico."

"No, you ain't." Inez rapped Lucia on top of the head with her knuckles. Then she waved at Steven as the car moved forward. "Good-bye, Mr. Fox!"

"Good-bye girls." Steven stepped back, waving. "Good-bye...."

"Good-bye, Mr. Fox!"

"Good-bye, Mr. Fox!"

"Good-bye, Mr. Fox!"

The car glided beside the pond, across the parking lot, and onto the dirt road that led into the woods. The red tail-lights flickered through the trees and were gone. Steven stood still, listening to the engine sound fade. Then, leaning against the building, he let out all his breath. The air was damp against his face and very, very quiet. The dark shape of the woods became a tree-high wave of vast sadness churning in on him out of the night, gathering momentum so fast that he could almost hear it ... and then stopping at its highest peak— still there, but hanging over him, suspended.

Another sound grew louder. Two cars, headlights off, rolling slowly like tanks into the parking lot from the road. Under the spotlight, they turned blue and white with glass bumps on top. Steven could make out the faces of policemen inside, plastic shields cocked over their eyes.

He turned and walked quickly back into the building.

28 ❧

Ben Paleno had seen the police cars roll into the parking lot, too, and had unlocked the back door to his unit. Steven met him on the stairwell and pushed past him before Ben had a chance to speak. He felt a strong tug on his arm and turned quickly sideways, smashing Ben's fingers against the wall. He yanked his arm free.

"Stay on your own floor!" Ben shouted, rubbing the back of his hand. "Stay off mine!"

"It's not your floor now. You've left it to the cops."

Ben glared up at him. Then his shoulders moved, a barely perceptible droop, and Steven knew that he could continue up the stairs without being tackled. Ben turned, headed toward the back door to let in the police.

Steven walked into a mob of white girls on the second floor. They tried to block him but he walked into their midst. "You want to take on the cops with their nightsticks and guns? Get your heads cracked open?" He drowned out their protests. "If you get in your rooms, you'll be safe! I mean it! *Move!*" he shouted, walking up the corridor.

He paused for a moment before the barricade, then put his shoulder to it and pushed hard. A table slid off a desk and crashed to the floor; a rolled-up carpet flopped into the lounge. He swung his legs over the desk.

"Police are coming! Get in your rooms!"

A girl with a sharp-edged ashtray stepped in front of him. Without a break in his stride, he grabbed her wrist and wrenched it back in both hands. The ashtray clattered to the floor and he stomped on it. The girl was bent backward and sideways; he yanked her down so that she fell on her side. Then he pulled her to her feet and shoved her as hard as he could toward the desk. She scrambled over it and into the corridor. Two other girls fled behind her. Screams echoed from the far end of the hall—not all the white girls had taken Steven's advice. He heard running footsteps, slamming doors, then fast-walking heavy boot-steps. A blond girl, her cheek bleeding, was shoved face-first into a wall by a uniformed man.

"Get behind the chairs! Lie on the floor!" Steven yelled at the remaining black girls in the lounge, and most of them scattered. A girl with a kitchen knife stepped forward. She was holding a small white girl around the neck from behind.

"You really want to kill her, Claudia?" Steven said, lowering his voice, his breath coming out fast.

"Don't fuck with me!" The girl's face had a desperate, enraged look on it, but she lowered the knife. The girl she was holding whimpered. Steven was suddenly surrounded by uniformed men with plastic shields covering their faces.

"If you don't drop it now, it'll be too late," Steven told the girl. He turned to the nearest policeman. "Give me a minute to talk to her."

"Sure. Take as much time as you need—"

Another policeman's arm flicked out. With what seemed like one motion, his club knocked the knife out of the girl's hand and cracked her in the side of the face. The knife flew into the window. The girl toppled backward.

Out of the corner of his eyes, Steven saw a girl going to her friend's aid; he reached out, grabbed her face in his hand, and shoved her backward.

"Gonna kill these motherfuckers!" the girl screamed, and tried to bite his hand. He swung her arm up behind her back and gripped her shoulder. Crying out in pain, she stumbled foward where he pushed her. At the barricade, he lifted her arm higher so that she had to flop forward onto the desk. Once she was on top, he gave her a shove that sent her toppling into the arms of a staff woman, who half-carried her down the corridor.

Two policemen were kneeling at the feet and head of the girl who'd had the knife. One had her pinned to the floor with his club pressed down on her neck; the other had her shins pinned with his club. The remaining girls cowered behind chairs.

"They won't give you any more trouble," Steven gasped, glaring at the men.

The oldest-looking of the men stood beside him, his shield flipped up. "We got our orders. Anybody tries anything, we know what to do."

No one doubted him. When Ben stepped over the desk, several men, whom he seemed to know by their first names, consulted with him. Steven sat down on the desk, feeling dizzy. He heard Ben telling the men which girls he wanted taken to the county jail in handcuffs, to be transferred to maximum-security facilities in the morning. Steven could have intervened, but he knew that the only way to keep the girls out of trouble now was to stand guard over them all night, and the next night, and the next. He had no intention of doing that. Some girls had to go.

A black staff member stood behind him, complaining under her breath about what Ben had just said. Steven realized that all the girls Ben had named were black. The "White Power Army" had come out of their rooms and were beginning to shout catcalls at the staff. One of them was swinging a bottle in her hand.

"Wait a minute." Steven pushed himself off the desk to face Ben. "You're not leaving *those* girls!"

"We can handle them," Ben said.

"No. No way." Steven turned to the man who seemed to be in charge of the operation. "I'm the acting director here. I'm authorizing you to put all five of those girls"—he pointed at the yelling girls—"under protective custody. I'm discharging them."

Several girls fled toward the back entrance as the police began moving down the corridor. Mrs. Evans yanked one into the staff office. Then, Ben tried to block a girl's way. Steven, walking quickly behind the police, saw Ben suddenly double over, and ran toward him as he slid down the wall into a sitting position.

Mrs. Evans reached him first. She knelt beside him and carefully pulled up the front of his shirt. A red gash ran diagonally along a roll of fat. "Was it that kitchen knife?" Mrs. Evans asked him.

"A bottle." Ben rolled his eyes toward the back door, where several girls were trying to get away from the police. "A broken bottle."

"It doesn't look too deep," Mrs. Evans said, "but there might be some glass in there."

Ben's shirt was stained bright red, and his pants were darkened all along his waistband. He touched the wound, then stared at his hand and shut his eyes tight. The sight of him bleeding on the floor seemed to have subdued most of the girls, at least the ones who were being taken down the hall by the police.

Steven knelt beside Ben. "Sorry," he said through his teeth, "but that's it for you tonight."

"I'm all right now," he said, breathing hard. "I'll just get this taped—"

"I'm suspending you until the Review Board meets. Starting right now." Steven turned to the nurse. "You'd better get him to the hospital, Mrs. Evans. Let me know if you want some help."

She ignored him, examining Ben's gash. "Don't argue, Ben. You're going to need some stitches."

Ben stared around wildly. "My girls—" He started to stand up, then slumped down again, covering his face with his hands.

Steven walked down the back stairs among the police and girls. A van had pulled into the back parking lot behind the squad cars, and a woman officer was there to help load the girls. The police went through the third floor, knocking open doors. Finding no one there, they came back downstairs without, to Steven's relief, asking where the girls were. He gave them the names of the girls they were taking. Finally, the two cars, the van, and Mrs. Evans's station wagon rolled away out the dirt road toward the highway.

Steven crossed the dining room heading for the back door, his legs beginning to feel unsteady. He had to press his whole weight against the door to get it open. The fresh air revived him somewhat, and he walked quickly toward his car as if it would shelter him, but as he leaned over its hood, he knew that there was no shelter for him. The realization of all he had lost swept over him—the enormous black wave he had sensed before hanging in wait for him now crashed down out of the darkness. Shuddering, he shut his eyes tight.

Finally he lifted his head. He looked around, dazed. The first thing he saw in the moonlight was the monstrous shadow of the building like a dark stain on the asphalt. Then he looked up at the building itself. He felt his heartbeat slowing back to normal. He stood up straight, regaining his balance.

The windows blazed from all the rooms, almost gaily. On an ordinary night, his mind would have started racing—anticipating what new misery or old remembered one might be keeping his girls up so late, what form their rage and despair would take when he walked into the waiting storm, absorbing it.

Now there was nothing to anticipate. The third floor was empty.

Gazing up at the bright windows, he felt as if the wave had washed through him and left him with a glorious emptiness inside. The sorrow he felt was real enough, but it was only his own now. The wave had rolled on into the night and out of sight forever. He would miss all the girls terribly, but he would never again feel the need to carry the weight of all their sadness. They had taken it away with them.

And the night, warm and clear and vast, really did smell like freedom.

When Leah returned several hours later, those second-floor girls who had not been taken away by the police were in their rooms asleep, or faking sleep. The only sound in the building was the clatter of Steven's typewriter from high up in the third-floor staff office. He had cleared the desk, but the rest of the room was still strewn with damp pieces of paper:

memos, reports, official letters. Steven sat on the desk, study-
ing one of the girl's file folders from the stack beside the
typewriter. He looked up when Leah walked in.

"Hello," she said, resting her hand on his shoulder.

He stood up and held her tight, pressing his face into the
soft mat of her hair. "I'm glad you came back," he said
finally.

"Of course I came back," she said. "Sonia wanted to as
well, but I sent her home."

"Is she all right?"

"She'll need a few days off."

"She's earned it." Steven sat down again. "What happened with the girls?"

"They are waiting at the bus station. I bought them enough
candy bars to last them until morning. They were happy and
sad at the same time."

"Me, too," Steven said. The overhead light caught the
tiny white corkscrews in the deep black of Leah's hair; her
eyes were tired and sad and warm.

"You must be a wreck, my friend," Leah said.

"I was before. I seem to be all right now." He leaned
back in his chair. "I learned something tonight, while you
were driving the girls. I learned how to run an institution."

Leah cocked her head.

"When I was on the second floor, I had to get rough—it
was the only way to deal with the girls. The thing is, I didn't
mind doing it. If I'd been alone, without the cops, I probably
would have smacked a couple of kids damn hard."

"And that's how to run an institution?"

"Mm-hm. First, you have to not know the girls very well.
I could do what I did because they weren't my girls. And it
worked. It was a language they understood. Violence." Steven
shook his head. "I could be a good director now."

"Do you want to be?"

"No," he said quietly. "I don't want to be any kind of
director. I don't feel anymore as if I need to be."

Leah smiled, and sat down in the armchair near him. "You
almost had me worried."

"I had myself worried." He closed his eyes for a moment.

"I let them go, Leah. It was the best I could do for them."

"The best anyone could do." She rested her hand on his arm.

He stared at her. "I feel like I freed myself, too. Of something I've been carrying around all my life. Does that sound crazy?"

"Not very," she said. "Not for a crazy night like this one."

Leah went off to the bathroom to fill the electric pot with water for tea. When she returned, Steven was typing again. She took a girl's typewriter from one of the rooms and set it up on her lap in the armchair. Together they filled the office with rapid clacking. The reports were finished in two hours.

Still restless, they cleaned the office, mopping the floors, scrubbing down the walls and windows. The glass, cleaner than it had been in months, reflected starbursts of light from the overhead bulb. The walls looked freshly painted. Except for the stained dance poster, the office looked normal—more ready for business than ever. But there was no business left to do.

Even so, Steven didn't want to leave. He sat down at the desk with his feet up. Leah sat in the armchair, her tea mug resting on her knee. The office was silent. Outside the door, a torn stuffed animal, lying on its side on a pile of mattress stuffing, seemed to be looking into the doorway.

"I thought of something," Steven said, turning away from it. "Just a story I heard years ago."

"We haven't told stories in a long time." Leah rested her head back.

"When I was in Belize," Steven said, "in Central America, some people told me about an eccentric white man, a wildlife conservationist, who wanted to photograph a jaguar. He got the villagers to build him an elaborate tree house in the jungle. They charged him fifty dollars a day to bring him peanut butter sandwiches." Steven smiled faintly. "He sat up there week after week in his expensive safari suit, with all his lights and cameras and equipment."

"Did he get his jaguar?" Leah asked.

"No. One day he climbed out of his tree and went away."

"Why didn't he see the animal?"

"Well, because there was no jaguar. There'd never been one spotted in that part of the country, ever."

"And the villagers, they knew this?"

"Of course. They all knew. But they saw no reason to tell him. He seemed happy up there in his tree. They were happy bringing him what he wanted. It was a perfectly fine arrangement for everyone, as far as they were concerned."

"While it lasted."

"Right." Steven shrugged. "Perfectly dumb story. I don't know why I thought of it."

Leah smiled at him over the top of her tea mug. "You don't?"

"Yes, I do. I'm trying to cheer myself up." He gazed out into the corridor again. The stuffed animal was a lamb, he noticed, with dirty fleece and a pink tongue hanging out and no tail. "But there's my jaguar," he said. "And it's dead."

Leah looked. "It was alive once, Steven."

"That's true." Steven's voice caught in his throat. "It was more alive than the man's jaguar. It kept some kid warm in the night. It kept the terror away."

"Yes." Leah's fingers gripped Steven's arm.

"You know, I didn't want to come up here, after the girls had gone," he said. "I was going to set up the typewriter in my old office downstairs. But when I went in there, I found my daughter's picture gone from the desk. One of the girls had stolen it."

"Somebody must have wanted to be your daughter," Leah said.

"Maybe they all did."

"We wanted them to be our children." Leah sighed. Her eyes were damp. "Was that wrong?"

"I don't think so now," Steven said. "It's just hard when they leave the nest."

"Some nest. Brick and steel and broken glass." Leah rubbed her eyes and smiled. "But we were good to them while they were in it, weren't we?"

"Yes," he said. "Yes, we were."

They finished their tea, making it last as long as possible.

Then they walked down the corridor together. When Steven reached the switch box on the back landing, he clicked off the lights in the rooms until finally the corridor behind him was dark. He leaned forward to peer out the window. In the pale blue-gray sky, the moon floated motionlessly like an old lightbulb tossed overboard, and along the horizon the faint glow of dawn was turning the tops of nearby trees to silhouettes of water spouts. The air was warm and smelled of the pond and the wet grass below. Leah leaned out beside him. Then, their arms around each other's waists, they walked slowly down the stairs.

29 ❧

When Steven arrived at work the next day, the afternoon was heavy with pollen and heat. Willow branches sweated their leaves onto the wooden bridge across the inlet. From the outside, the school looked eerily the same as always: an incongruous brick-and-stone structure in the midst of green lawns and fields, still shiplike, still formidable. He had half-expected it to be gone, floated away or sunk beneath the surface of the pond.

He walked through the foyer and stood in the empty rec room, looking around. Someone had brought in the broken stereo and left it on the floor in the corner: turntable, console, speakers lined up as if ready to make music. The dining room had been cleaned by the kitchen women; chairs were pushed in at the tables, silverware and plastic glasses set out for a lunch practically no one would eat. The building was hushed; the few ordinary noises it made—the clatter of typewriters, the jangle of phones—sounded like ghostly echoes of its former self. Like the Flying Dutchman, the building sailed on. But soon, without its captain, Steven thought.

He went into the Nurses' Station, glad not to encounter Mrs. Evans there. Katrina had been up for hours and had been asking continually to be let out of the infirmary. Steven opened her door. As soon as she heard the lock click, she swung her legs down from the bed and stood up with a bounce. Her face was washed and her hair brushed back into shape, reddish-yellow and springy. She didn't look scrawny anymore, just slim. A pretty girl, Steven thought.

"Good morning," he said. His voice sounded normal to him, but it made Katrina's cheerful expression vanish.

"It's afternoon," she said.

"You seem to be okay."

"Me? Yeah. They let me sleep till ten." She raised her eyes to the level of his open collar. "Is it—is it all over upstairs?"

"It's all over."

"You don't look so good." She squinted at him. "I mean, your face is all messed up around the eyes."

"There's a reason for that."

"Are the girls okay?"

"They're all gone, Katrina," he said.

"*All* of them? How?"

"They either ran away, or went to the hospital, or got driven to the bus station. They won't be coming back."

"*Nobody's left?*" Katrina looked about to cry.

"You're left," he said, smiling, and turned toward the end of the hall. "Let's go figure out what to do with you."

Katrina followed him across the rec room, her sneakers scuffing against the linoleum. In his office, he pulled his chair beside the desk so as not to have to talk to her over it.

"What's that?" Katrina asked, pointing to some film canisters on Steven's desk.

"Some girls went out the window last night. They left these—probably Pam." Steven pushed the canisters into a tighter circle on his blotter. They reminded him of a group session. "Action photos of the riot, I expect. Pam took one of the cameras with her."

"She always said she wanted to be a photographer when she got out," Katrina said. "She wanted to take pictures of rock stars and murderers."

"I wish her luck." Steven turned to the window, which was still open. Then he heard footsteps from the office doorway.

A secretary stood in the hall. Beside her was a middle-aged man in an old felt hat, clean khaki shirt and pants, and worn work boots. His face was heavily lined and somber; his eyes above his high cheeks were very dark.

"This is Mr. Dogflower, Mary's father," the secretary said, glancing uneasily at the man. "Do you want me to have him wait?"

"No, that's okay." Steven stood up. "Thanks."

The man watched Steven's face intently, as if reading it. When Steven reached out his hand and introduced himself and Katrina, Mr. Dogflower shook hands without a smile. He did not look angry, just pensive, and when he spoke, his voice was calm and powerful, as if his body were a great deal larger. "I've come for my daughter," he said.

"I'm afraid she's not here," Steven said. "Some of the girls ran away last night, and she went with them."

The man shook his head slowly. "No," he said.

"Excuse me?"

"No." The man's gaze was still fixed on Steven's face. "She called me on the telephone last night from an office. She said she would be here today. My daughter don't lie."

Steven pulled a chair from the corner and set it near his desk. "Would you like to sit down?"

The man shook his head again. "I've come for my daughter."

Katrina leaned closer to Steven. "Maybe she's hiding in the building."

"She told me she would wait in the building." the man said, focusing on Katrina, then on Steven. "You could find her."

Steven wiped his forehead. "It's possible, I guess."

"I told you," the man said.

"All right, let's look." Steven stood up, aware of how loudly his chair scraped against the floor. "Come on, Katrina."

They searched in the empty rooms off the secretaries' office, then went down into the basement. The vocational classrooms had been opened for cleaning; Steven and Katrina went into each one, calling Mary's name. When they walked into the rec room, Mary was standing in the middle of the floor.

Her dress was dusty; wisps of hair hung beside her dark, round face. She stared at Steven.

"Where were you, Mary?" Steven asked, staring back less calmly.

"Behind that." She turned her head toward a couch that had been pulled away from the wall. "Is my father here?"

"He's upstairs."

Mary started across the floor. Katrina glanced up at Steven and shrugged. "Well, she always said he'd come."

Steven let out all his breath. "That's what she always said."

In the doorway to Steven's office, Mary embraced her father. He stood with both arms around her, his eyes closed. When he heard Steven and Katrina approaching, he dropped his arms and stood away from his daughter.

"We'll go now," he said in his deep voice.

Steven walked back into his office and sat down behind his desk. "Mr. Dogflower, I'm afraid it's not that simple. If you'll sit down, I'll explain."

"Mary has been here many months. She says she's ready to leave now." The man didn't move.

Steven drummed his fingers on the blotter. "Mary's a ward of the Family Court of Makonic County. She's under the temporary jurisdiction of the Youth Service. In order to discharge her, I'll need a court order. . . ." Steven could tell that Mary's father was not listening. The man was simply waiting for him to finish.

"We have a long way to drive," Mr. Dogflower said. "Mary's mother is waiting in the truck."

"I understand but . . ." Steven's voice seemed to get swallowed up in the silence that the man left hanging in the air like a vacuum whenever he stopped speaking. It was an almost restful silence. Steven looked at the man, then at Mary, then at the file folders on his desk. "Never mind," he said. "Have you got your things packed?" he asked Mary.

"They're in my room," she said.

She did not move quickly, but it took her almost no time to come back downstairs with a full cardboard carton in her arms. Her father took it from her and turned to Steven.

"Mary will be all right," he said, and for the first time the lines in his face moved: he was faintly smiling. He shook hands with Steven, his grip calloused and hard. Then he turned toward the door.

Steven and Katrina followed him and Mary out to a battered pickup truck. Its left fender was rusted away completely, exposing a big bald tire. In the truck bed, duffel bags, crates, and suitcases were stacked up to the height of the cab roof. In the space remaining, four children sat with their knees up. They watched their sister in unison.

"Hello," Mary said. "These are my brothers and sisters," she told Steven.

"Hello," Steven said to them.

They looked at him silently.

Mary got into the passenger side of the cab. A woman in bib overalls and a flannel shirt got out to make room for her in the middle. She was holding a baby against her shoulder.

"This is my mother," Mary said, sitting down.

"Hello," Steven said.

The woman nodded.

"This is Mr. Fox," Mary said. "He was my counselor. He helped me."

The woman glanced at Steven as she sat down, then looked away quickly. The engine sputtered and caught, discharging black smoke out the tailpipe. Mary's mother pulled the door shut with a crash of metal. Then Mary reached her hand out toward Steven. He took it and held it. "How far are you going?" he asked.

"Georgia. My mother's people are there."

He smiled at Mary. "Good luck," he said.

"Thank you, Mr. Fox," she said. "So long, Katrina."

"Take it easy." Katrina, standing beside Steven, tried to wave but had to wipe her eyes. "Good luck, Mary."

The truck shifted noisily into gear and rolled out into the parking lot.

"Good-bye," Steven called.

Mary, leaning over her mother's lap, looked out the window and waved at him and Katrina. It was the first time that Steven had ever seen her smile.

He watched the truck move slowly across the parking lot and out into the driveway. The children in the back waved, staring up at the building. Then the truck was gone, leaving a cloud of dust in the air that floated off into the trees. The engine sound faded.

Steven sat down on the step where he was. Katrina sat beside him. They didn't speak, but continued to stare down the driveway. A haze of pollen remained under the canopy of tree branches. Typewriters clacked inside, but from behind the heavy front door, the sound seemed very far away. In some weeds beside the steps, bees were buzzing in the hot, still air.

"I used to dream about leaving like that," Katrina said finally. "Not dream. Daydream, sort of."

Steven rested his elbows on his knees. "What was it like?"

"Well, you know those Old Spice commercials, where the sailor comes on shore and walks through the town? And all these beautiful women lean out of windows and he tosses them presents—bottles of that stuff, cologne or whatever it is?"

Steven hadn't seen this, but he nodded, smiling at her.

"So this dude comes walking through town tossing bottles and he gets to this jail—which is like the one I was in in Troy, near the river. The Hudson River...." Katrina smiled. "Anyhow, he just walks into the place and I'm the one he's come for. We walk through the front door and down the steps and away from the jail. All the women are looking out the windows hoping he's going to throw them a bottle, but he's forgotten about all that now, 'cause he's with me...."

"That's nice," Steven said.

Katrina shrugged.

"Your grandfather was a sailor, wasn't he?"

"Yeah. Sometimes it's him that comes and takes me away from that building."

"Do you go back to his ship?"

Katrina shook her head. "We go out into the country, like. This hillside, where there's a whole bunch of white trees behind us. He *talks* about his ship sometimes. But mostly we just look at the clouds."

"That's nice, too."

"Yeah...."

Steven smiled. He sometimes thought of adopting Katrina and taking her to the islands with Leah, the three of them sailing out of New York Harbor past the Statue of Liberty ... but what would Katrina do in Trinidad or wherever he would end up? Better just to enjoy Katrina's daydreams with her now. He felt the heat of the afternoon against his face. There seemed to be birds chirping nearby. He couldn't remember the last time he'd heard the sound of birds. Fairbanks was finally as peaceful as he'd always hoped it could be.

30 ɞ

Steven found Katrina a place in a group home in a farming community several hours to the south, where she and five other girls from around the state would live with a young couple who were trained as houseparents. She would go to the local high school, earn extra spending money working on a farm on weekends, go out on dates, and in general live like an ordinary teenager.

On the Saturday morning she was to leave, she had her suitcase packed in fifteen minutes and was waiting for Steven outside on the front steps. Sonia and Leah came out to say good-bye. She hugged them both, and then ran off to Steven's car, where she settled into the big front seat.

"Aah," she said, smiling, as he got in. "Free at last!" She had on a clean blue blouse that matched her eyes and a new pair of jeans which, she had to admit, looked sensational on her. She rested her feet on the dashboard.

As Steven started the engine, the tape he had been playing earlier blasted out of the speakers. He switched it off.

"What was *that*?" Katrina stared at the tape deck.

"An opera," he said, "called *Fidelio*. It's about a woman who rescues a man from prison."

"If you say so." Katrina poked around in his box of tapes. "You got anything by the Stones?"

"It's all classical."

Katrina wrinkled her nose. Then she glanced back at the building, and kept staring at it as Steven put the car into

reverse. "I never thought I'd get out of this damn place,"
she said.

"That bad, huh?"

"I don't know. I grew up, I guess." Katrina faced forward
and hugged her arms across her chest. "Hurry up, will you,
before I chicken out."

"What's the matter?"

"Nothing." The car stalled, and she flung herself back
against the seat, sighing loudly. "I don't think this heap's
going to make it."

"Careful how you talk about my vehicle."

"Yeah, yeah." She pulled out a cigarette and stuck it in
her mouth. "Listen, maybe this ain't a good day to go."

"No?" Steven smiled.

"I mean, maybe the car needs a checkup or something."
She leaned forward to look into Steven's face. "I could stay
around here till next week. Lucia's wall's all messed up from
the smoke. I could help you clean it."

Steven started the engine again. "It's hard to leave, I
know." he said. "A lot of kids feel like that on their last
day."

Katrina slid down in the seat. "If you don't want my
help, okay, fuck it."

"Wait till you see this place you're going."

"I don't want to go to a new place."

"It's a big old house in the middle of town, with a front
porch and a yard out back." He pulled the car slowly out of
the parking lot. "You'll have your own room, and there's a
dog that's just had puppies."

Katrina took the cigarette out of her mouth. "Ain't this
car even got a lighter?"

Steven pushed the dashboard lighter in for her.

She drummed her fingers on her knee, watching for it to
pop out. "What're they going to do with the puppies, drown
them?"

"Yeah."

"What?"

"No, I spoke to the housemother and she said they were
keeping some for the girls."

"One for each girl, or just one for all the girls?"

"I don't know." Steven glanced at her. "We'll find out when we get there."

"Better be one for each," she said.

Steven drove onto the dirt road under the tree branches and out toward the highway. Katrina never looked back.

Some of the fields beside the road were green with new hay coming up, others had been combed into long brown furrows that, when seen from a rise, made geometric patterns across the landscape. The farther south they drove, the fewer trailers and junk cars they passed. Farmhouses were big and solid, surrounded by ancient trees. Once Steven had to stop as a teenage boy in overalls and a baseball cap herded a dozen trotting sheep along the road toward the car. Katrina leaned forward to peer through the windshield, leaving off playing with the radio dial. The first sheep stopped short to stare at the car; the others did, too, bumping into each other.

"Man, it's a traffic jam. Look at that." Katrina laughed. "Is that really wool they got all over them?"

"It's not polyester," Steven said.

"Hey, you see the expression on that first one's face? He looks so embarrassed!"

"Sheepish."

"Ba-a-a-a," Katrina said out her window. The sheep didn't move.

Steven draped his arm over the back of the seat. "Well, we're in no hurry."

"I know."

The boy in the baseball cap, visible over the animals' woolly backs from his waist up, pushed the sheep forward. Keeping their distance from the car, they passed on both sides. Each one turned to stare curiously into the windows.

"So long!" Katrina called out. "Bye!"

The boy turned and waved.

"I was yelling at *them*, not him," Katrina said. "But he was kind of cute, too."

"Lots more where he came from," Steven said.

She shrugged. "Aren't you going to go?"

"Yeah. . . ." Steven took his arm off the back of the seat and reached for the ignition. At the top of the hill far ahead, the road seemed to meet the sky, pale blue and full of sheeplike clouds. He glanced at Katrina as he started the engine. "I'll always remember this spot, you know?"

"Yeah," she said, smiling. Then she started turning the radio knobs again.

The valleys grew deeper and the hillsides longer, and in the distance, Steven and Katrina began to see the mountains. The closer ones rose up rounded and green like enormous moss-covered boulders outlined against the purplish higher skyline behind them. The sun was directly overhead now, making the asphalt shimmer on the road. Steven looked at Katrina, slouched down in the seat with her ankles crossed on the top of the dashboard; he wanted this drive to go on forever.

The car passed through more towns now. Katrina forgot about the radio and stared out her window, asking repeatedly if each town was like the one where she was going to live. Eventually Steven began to look for a place to stop for lunch.

"There!" Katrina pointed to a strangely shaped structure surrounded by white gravel and evenly spaced bushes. Its bright yellow roof was rounded off at each corner and the windows were huge glass ovals in the blue cinder-block walls. After a landscape of old farms and firehouses, the building looked very alien, like a breeder station left behind by a flying saucer, but Steven knew it to be one of a chain of fast-food restaurants that had been springing up around the countryside over the past few years. A truck-stop loyalist, he'd never even considered eating in one of these places. They seemed to be primarily for children, with comic-book lettering on the signs, and playgrounds supervised by huge painted steel clowns and pop-eyed hamburgers wearing sneakers and derbies. Steven swung the car off the road into the parking lot.

Katrina got out and, stretching, gazed at the building. It seemed to gaze back out of bulging oval eyes. "Wow," she said.

"Did you ever eat at one of these?" Steven asked.

"They didn't have them where I lived. They probably do

now, though. I feel like I was just a little kid when I left home.'' She rushed up the gravel path ahead of him and pushed open the big glass doors.

Grinning, Steven followed. Inside, she was standing by the wall, waiting. She'd seen a great many television commercials for this chain of restaurants and seemed to have planned far in advance what she wanted. All the food items had their own names. Standing slightly behind Steven, she dictated them to him in a low voice. He repeated the order to the counter-girl: a Double Hujie Burger, a Zesty Shake— strawberry—a Big Bucket o' Fries, which turned out not to be very big, and a Golden Flaky, which was an apple turnover. He thought he sounded silly ordering, but the counter-girl, a teenager in a yellow uniform, repeated what he said expressionlessly, as if she'd been speaking this new language all her life. When she noticed Katrina staring at her, she smiled, and Katrina dropped her eyes to the floor fast. Steven carried the tray of food to a booth.

''Man, I can't wait to eat this! It's the first meal I've had in the real world in months and months,'' Katrina said, sliding into a plastic seat. ''It seems like years.'' She took as big a bite as possible out of her hamburger and sat back, sighing.

To Steven, the hamburger tasted like salted Styrofoam and the milk shake like a chalky, candy-flavored laxative. But the French fries were good. And the place was immaculate, with its blue walls and rows of yellow booths and potted plants hanging from the stucco ceiling. Like Katrina, he looked around at the people. Most of the men wore colored T-shirts and work pants; the women had on slacks outfits or shorts and sleeveless blouses. Steven felt a little strange in his dark suit and open blue shirt; he would have taken off his jacket except that the air-conditioning gave the room the feel of perpetual early spring. Katrina had goose bumps on her arms.

''It's amazing, all these people,'' she whispered to Steven, and turned to watch some teenagers playing a pinball machine in one corner of the room.

They were dressed more or less like her, Steven noted, but they looked different from Fairbanks kids. All of them were white. They seemed bigger, healthier, more relaxed, and their eyes were innocent of that bruised look that Steven was used to seeing. In fact, to him, their faces looked vacuous, as if they'd never been through anything more emotionally devastating than watching the home team lose a football game. They all walked out in a group, talking in what seemed like abnormally quiet voices.

Through the window, Katrina watched them get into two cars and pull out onto the road. Then she concentrated on scraping the yellowish sauce off her hamburger bun with a napkin. Eventually she left part of the meat uneaten.

"None of these people in here know I just got out of reform school," she said leaning forward again. "If they did, they'd probably think I was going to rob them or something."

"I doubt it," Steven said.

"I bet people in this town I'm going to, they'll think the girls in the group home are a bunch of delinquents." She looked down at her plate. "Probably at school, too. Shit."

"You might get hasseled for a while, but nothing compared to what you've been through," he said. "People will get used to you."

"I guess I got to watch my language, huh?"

"I wouldn't worry about it." Steven watched her face. "Listen, you've got as much right to be in that town as anybody else."

"Damn right. Fuck 'em if they don't like me." Katrina clapped her hand over her mouth, glancing away. Then she began to lick her fingers. "Those French fries were really good. They were the best I ever ate."

"Have some more."

"Can I have another Big Bucket?"

"Sure." Steven took out his wallet and pushed a dollar across the table toward her. "But you can get it."

"*You* get it." She sat back suddenly, her face flushed.

Steven pressed the bill into her clenched fingers. "Go on, Katrina," he said, as she bit her lip and squinted across the room. Her hand, small and warm, relaxed in his. Gradually he loosened his grip. Her fingers slipped away.

She stood up and walked stiffly down the aisle of booths. At the counter, she gave him a brief wave, grinning.

Once settled into the place, she didn't want to leave, and went back several more times for cups of coffee and for a Fudgie, which was chocolate cake too sweet even for her. Then she spent a long time in the bathroom. Steven sat back in his seat, looking around at the people again. They probably thought he was just a father having lunch with his daugher. He got up and played a game of pinball. When Katrina returned, she wanted to play, too, as he'd hoped she would. She knew how to nudge the machine with her arms and thighs to get the ball to bounce hard off the cushions for a high score. Steven glanced from her face to the ball and back. She tried to show him how to bump the machine, but all its lights suddenly switched off except for the word TILT. Thereafter, when either of them tried to nudge it even slightly, the TILT sign came on, as if the machine were on to them.

In the playground, two children ran around among the three-dimensional metal cartoon characters. To reach the top of the slide, they had to climb into what appeared to be the anus of an enormous smiling clown, and then emerge again from a hole in its chest. Moving closer, Steven was relieved to see that the clown actually had no backside; the slide was just a half-shell of a clown. The children ran into the parking lot.

"Do we have time?" Katrina gestured toward the playground.

"If you want," Steven said.

"I'm just curious." She walked through the opening in the barred black fence, past the giant toadlike metal hamburgers, and stood looking up at the slide. Then she disappeared around the back of it. For the second or two that she was out of sight, the playground seemed empty, bleak. There were no children. There were only the dumb metal creatures crouched on the white gravel, the barred fence, and, presiding over it all, the tall steel figure with the bulging yellow eyes and painted grimace.

Then Katrina's face appeared out of the thing's rib cage. She swung her legs around, positioning herself, and Steven could see that what he'd taken for ribs were just the crossbars of the ladder behind the opening. Katrina pushed herself off.

Steven held his breath. Down she plummeted on the curved slide, giving out a little squeak.

At the bottom, she lay on her back with her legs bent, sneakers dug into the pebbled ground. Steven stepped forward to help her up but she scrambled to her feet before he reached her. She was smiling.

"How was it?" she asked.

"All right." Out of breath, she gazed at the playground and the restaurant. "I guess it's time to go," she said.

"I guess so." Steven put his arm around her shoulder as they walked toward the car.

A little way down the road, they passed a sign that said their destination was seven miles away. Katrina sat up straight and began to chain-smoke. She became quiet and unresponsive as she had sometimes been at Fairbanks, but without the sullenness. Steven filled the silence by telling her about his plans to go to Japan and then, he hoped, to the West Indian islands where Leah would be living. She glanced at him when his eyes were on the road and said nothing.

"Would you like me to come visit you this summer, before I go?" he asked.

"Okay."

"Good. And then I'll write you from wherever I am."

"You got my address, at this place?"

"Yes."

"You better write." Katrina switched on the radio and turned the volume up loud.

The town was at the end of a long valley. They drove down into the flatland, passing fields that smelled of fertilizer. At the edge of town, the road went through a college campus, a collection of bunkerlike buildings sparsely landscaped with small new trees. The main street had the feel of a much older town, with brick and wooden storefronts, uneven sidewalks, dusty shop windows, and a flag hanging over the red garage door of the one-vehicle firehouse.

In fact, the town seemed an anachronism, nothing like the outside world Katrina would have to deal with one day. Steven drove as slowly as possible. Was he crazy to leave her here? Well, it was too late to change plans now. She'll be safe here for a while, he told himself, and if she can just hold on for nine or ten months, a year . . .

"Is this the only street?" Katrina asked.

"I think so."

"Where do kids, like, hang out?"

"Beats me," Steven said, looking around. "But listen, you'll have lots of things to do with your house sisters, and school." He heard his voice get louder. Please keep her busy, he thought. "And you'll work on the farm," he added.

"Oh yeah, the farm." Katrina said. "I hope they got lots of animals. You think they got a tractor?"

"I bet they do."

"I hope they let me drive it."

"Me, too," Steven said. For a moment, he shuddered to imagine Katrina behind the wheel of a tractor, a cloud of dust rising behind her, chickens and ducks scattering on all sides, but then he smiled.

Driving up a side street, he felt the warm air against his face from the open window. Most of the houses were old and large, with wide porches and gables and painted shutters on the windows. Some were boarded up, with broken glass on the walks and shaggy, littered lawns, but most were well kept. The sunlight streaming through the leafy branches overhead made bright patches on the asphalt street. Two women pushing baby carriages stopped to talk; an old man smoked a cigar on a front step; a boy loaded a basket of laundry into the trunk of a car. From far across town came the honk of a train. The air smelled of newly mown grass.

"I never been in a place like this," Katrina said, staring out of the windshield. The air from the window had blown her hair almost over her eyes.

"I have." Steven coasted into another block. "When I was a kid, I used to go on the road with my father sometimes, and we'd pass through towns just like this. I always wished we could stop and live in one."

Katrina nodded, watching the houses along the street. They went by more and more slowly. Finally the car stopped in front of a big white house with a front porch and an oak tree beside the flagstone walk.

"That's it?" Katrina asked, sitting back.

"That's it," Steven said.

"It looks like all the other houses. I thought it'd be sort of different, like Fairbanks, only smaller."

"It's just another house." Steven leaned sideways to look out Katrina's window. In the deep shade of the porch, a swing seat was swaying slowly as if someone had just left it to go inside. All the windows were open, their curtains billowing in the breeze.

"It's a pretty house, don't you think?" Steven said.

"I guess."

Steven turned off the engine. Katrina stubbed out her cigarette in the ashtray and took a deep breath.

"It's sure quiet around here," she said, cocking her head to look down the street. "Man, nothing's moving."

He glanced at her. "It will be."

She turned away, grinning. "Aren't you going to come in with me?"

"Sure. I want to meet your houseparents and see your room and everything."

"I'm really going to have my own room? No shit?"

"No shit, Katrina," he said. "There's lots of space in the house, from the look of it."

"I hope so."

Katrina rested her chin on the bottom of the window, squinting across the lawn. The sunlight shone through her curls onto the pale skin of her cheek. Watching her, Steven gripped the steering wheel tight.

She lifted her head and then yanked down the door handle. Stepping out onto the sidewalk, she opened the back door to pull her suitcase off the seat.

"Come on," she said. "I ain't going into that house by myself."

But before Steven had opened his door, she was on her way up the front walk.

EPILOGUE

The Girls 🐚

MARY moved with her parents to a reservation in Georgia and worked in the general store her father opened there. For several months she was married to one of her father's drinking buddies, but he was sent to prison for killing a man in a brawl. She now lives in a cabin within walking distance of the store where she works, and has two small children.

PAM was picked up by the police in Iowa and returned to Fairbanks. Steven found her a place in a group home downstate, where she lived for sixteen months, attending high school and, toward the end of her stay, a drug rehabilitation program. After moving to a ranch operated by a born-again Christian sect, she married a man chosen for her by her pastor. She sings in the sect's traveling gospel choir.

WHALE lived in a group home in Brooklyn for a year, finished high school, and moved to South Carolina, where she found her child living with relatives. She enrolled part time at the state university, and after six years graduated with a degree in social work. She is now working for the state's Department of Family Services, but has had to take several leaves of absence because of hypertension-related ailments. For the first time in her life, she is on a diet.

LUCIA served a year at a maximum-security girls' training school. Released on probation, she was arrested for setting

fire to her mother's boyfriend's car and, while out on bail
awaiting trial, for dealing in narcotics. She was treated for
heroin addiction in prison, where she is serving a five-year
sentence.

INEZ returned to live with her mother and daughter in New
York, where she found work as a university custodian and
took secretarial courses at night. She eventually left her job
to have another child, whom she had trouble supporting on
welfare payments. Arrested for stealing a carton of frozen
chickens from a delivery truck, she was given a sentence of
probation. She is married now, with a third child, and works
as a clerk in the city's Bureau of Motor Vehicles.

VONITA was released from the hospital after a month and
placed in a series of foster homes, where she was unable to
adjust. Once, locked in her room at night, she broke all the
windows and was found the next day walking the streets in
her bathrobe, shouting and cursing. The courts transferred
her to a state mental hospital, where she was often locked up
for antagonizing other patients. After she had complained to
the staff about a patient who threatened to stab her with a
knitting needle, several patients attacked her on a loading
ramp outside the kitchen. She was taken to the medical unit
with her face smashed in beyond recognition, and pronounced
dead on arrival. When no relatives could be located, she was
buried on the hospital grounds.

YVONNE drove Ben Paleno's car to New York and delivered
it to her pimp, Sugar, who sold it and kept her out of sight
for several months. She then began working the streets, and
earned Sugar considerable extra money as a courier in the
cocaine trade, delivering shipments from members of the dip-
lomatic community to dealers in Harlem. When Sugar was
killed by a rival pimp, she worked on her own as a dealer,
call girl, and model. She was arrested five times on various
charges and served a total of seventy-two hours in jail. She
was also treated for cocaine addiction. She eventually became
the mistress of a Venezuelan diplomat. He has given her a

light blue Alfa Romeo convertible and installed her in an apartment in Fort Lee, New Jersey. To keep from getting bored, she frequently drives into Manhattan on shopping sprees.

PEACHES appeared before a Family Court judge who, unable to find her a place in a local group home, allowed her to live with her mother. To avoid standing trial for the neglect of her other daughter, Lurleen, Peaches' mother left the state and never returned. Peaches stayed in her mother's trailer in the woods for three years, living on money earned working in the grape arbors and given to her by boyfriends. For most of this time she cared for Cindy, Lurleen's baby girl, who had originally been given to an aunt whose husband had started to molest the child. Peaches knew nothing about raising a baby, but took courses in parenting at the high school, and Cindy grew up skinny, ragged, boisterous, but healthy. One day, a local church group complained to the police that Peaches, with so many male friends, was not a suitable guardian for the little girl, and that her trailer, an "eyesore" surrounded by rusted car parts, was not a suitable home. Cindy was placed in a foster home pending a Welfare investigation. Distraught over losing her, Peaches got roaring drunk at a party given by a local motorcycle gang. When two men got into a fight over her, she began hitting them both hysterically. One of them hit her with a closed fist. Her head struck the cinder-block wall as she fell. The party went on around her for hours; everyone assumed that she had merely passed out. Peaches never recovered consciousness.

Lurleen's daughter has been adopted by a farm family. Lurleen is serving time for robbery and prostitution at the Fairbanks School.

RONNIE moved back with her mother and three sisters under a strict sentence of probation. Unhappy about not being able to go see Peaches, she was often suspended from high school for fighting, and eventually dropped out to work and study on her own for the high school equivalency examination. When she passed it with the highest score in the city, the local armed forces recruiter sent her a letter of congratulations. She was inducted into the army on her nineteenth birthday. After basic training, she was stationed in Houston, Texas, where she became a member of a women's basketball squad that toured bases all over the country for several years. On a pass in upstate New York, she drove to Peaches' hometown and discovered what had happened to her. She sat drinking all afternoon in the local bikers' bar, staring into the men's faces. The gang members had never seen a black woman in the place before, much less one in uniform; thinking she might be some kind of cop, they gave her a wide berth, even when she went outside and shoved over five motorcycles parked at the curb. Back in Houston, Ronnie graduated from communications school as a radar specialist, and was promoted to sergeant. After reenlisting, she and her lover started an organization called the Black Women's Military Caucus, which investigated cases of discrimination on Texas army bases. She was quickly transferred out of Texas, and is now stationed in Germany.

KATRINA remained at the group home, attending high school and working on a local farm on weekends. She was expelled from the home once for smoking marijuana with several other girls, and, on Steven's orders, spent a week at Fairbanks helping the maintenance men clean out the pond. Promising perfect behavior evermore, she was allowed to return to the group home. A year later, after having herself legally declared an emancipated minor, she bought a secondhand car, drove it through the Midwest, and finally crashed it into a utility pole in Pierre, South Dakota.

Katrina caught a ride out of town with a tall, long-haired man in his early fifties who was on his way to a lake in Montana where he, two of his sons, and their families were opening a fishing resort. She went with him, joining the venture as a waitress, and within a year she had married him. Learning carpentry, she helped him build a new house with its own dock. She often tends bar where she can keep an eye on the customers who try to flirt with her husband. The extended family owns a number of horses, powerboats, and recreational vehicles. When life gets too crowded, Katrina loads her pickup truck with camping equipment and a dog or two and, sitting on extra pillows to squint over the dashboard, drives off into the mountains to Canada for weeks at a time. Her family has stopped asking her where she goes.

The Staff 🌿

MATT STEINER became regional director of facilities in the Albany District. He has served on the Governor's Task Force on Rehabilitation Services.

BEN PALENO survived a Review Board's investigation into his problems at Fairbanks, and has stayed on in the position of assistant director, now an office job that keeps him removed from direct contact with the girls.

ALICE EVANS left Fairbanks during the month it was closed down, and took a position as a staff nurse in a large downstate psychiatric hospital.

SALLY LERT did not return to Fairbanks when it reopened. She had been secretly battling stomach cancer for years, and died on her farm.

JEAN HEALEY has continued to work at Fairbanks through several changes in administration. She has recently started a 4-H club at the school, attracting six girls who are raising goats in a converted toolshed behind the back parking lot.

SONIA PORTER stayed on at Fairbanks for several months and then left with her husband for California. They settled in a town near San Francisco where an alternative school hired her as an art instructor. Her works have been shown in local galleries.

LEAH GOMES left for Trinidad a month after the riot. Steven arrived in the fall, and together they took over a small, private day school that attracted Third World embassy children and Trinidadian scholarship students. She adopted two sons of a relative who could not afford to raise them. Two years later, when the school was well established, she resigned her post as headmistress and completed her dissertation, which has been published in Canada under the title *Disposable Children: Capitalism, Poverty, and Delinquency.* She now teaches in the Sociology Department at the University of the West Indies.

STEVEN FOX remained at Fairbanks over the summer. He received stacks of reports on girls that the Youth Service wanted to send to the school, but he delayed their arrivals by asking for more legal data, and kept the third floor virtually empty. He was also able to find placements for most of the remaining second-floor girls. After Katrina returned to her group home, he visited her twice, and for years continued to correspond with her.

In September, the Youth Service closed Fairbanks. Steven was called before a Review Board in Albany. At the board's request, he wrote a full report on the riot; in contradiction of civil service regulations, he gave a copy of the report to the newspapers. That day he resigned from the Youth Service. He then went on a three-day binge and spent a night in a county jail for disturbing the peace. Before leaving New York State, he wrote another newspaper report advocating small community-based group homes for adolescents as alternatives to large reform schools.

He spent a month in Japan visiting his daughter, and then joined Leah in Trinidad, where he became business manager and eventually headmaster of the school they decided to run together. He and Leah bought a house in the hills overlooking the capital city. In the past several years, he has expanded the school to accommodate secondary-level students, has had a science lab and five new buildings erected with contributions from foreign companies, and has doubled the number of scholarships available to local students. His daughter, Sarah, whose family has been transferred to Washington, D.C., visits him every summer.

The School 🍂

FAIRBANKS reopened in early October under a new administration and immediately filled with girls transferred from
two maximum-security institutions that were closing. The staff
were told that the new residents were dangerous felons; Mrs.
Healey, however, found that, aside from being more scared
and streetwise, they were very similar to the old girls. The
new director had locks installed on all the doors and ordered
a chain link fence built around the grounds. Girls were seldom
permitted outdoors; they were routinely confined to isolation
rooms for fighting. A year after the school's reopening, there
was a riot in which a dozen girls set fire to their mattresses.
Seven girls and two staff members received injuries that required hospitalization.

A new director was appointed. He kept the staff posted
at the ends of all the school corridors on a twenty-four-hour-
a-day basis, monitoring the girls' every movement. Coils of
razor wire have been installed along the top of the fence.
Reality Therapy, the institution's new treatment philosophy,
has been written up favorably in the *Youth Service News*.